The Arc o:
Book

A Novel by Peter Thomas Kirk

This book is for my mum, Christine, and my dad, Tom... without whom quite simply, my imagination and dreams would never have been shaped and realised...

Also, for my dear brother Tom, an inspiration of unfathomable magnitude, my own personal hero and often, the reason I don't give up...

And finally, Cheryl, Annabel and Thomas, my brother's wonderful wife and children.

In Loving Memory of Anne Worthington.

"You should have stayed with the captain, for she is a far better dancer than the devil shall ever be".

— *Tristan, First Mate*

To my darling Rachel, may you always Illuminate the pages of my tales, both written & unwritten

Love. PK x

The Devil in the Darkness

My skin crawled with bugs. Cockroaches scuttled up and down my arms and across my chest. Spiders everywhere, enormous legs. They towered over scuttling aphids, pedipalps clapping, fighting among themselves for room on my shins and thighs. My spine rattled with the nattering of their detestable limbs and pincers as I brushed them feverishly from me.

"Oh God, get them off me". All manner of creature fell to the ground by the handful, scurrying away into the darkness. A shrieking burst like an acidic bubble behind me and echoed throughout the cold tunnel, piercing my ears drums and jilting my frame with fright.

He has come for me again, I thought, turning back to see only darkness. The shrieking ceased, leaving the sound of water droplets pattering against stone. Before long, a chilling roar rang out that shook the ground. But closer than before. Much closer.

Tristan, run, you fool, the words ran through my mind as I began to take cautious steps over the insects. The roaring grew louder, as though incensed by my flight, becoming interlaced with pig-like snorting and the clanging of metal on stone. I couldn't help but look back into the darkness as my legs took larger strides. My arms reached out to the walls for balance and hampered my attempts to negotiate the quickening pace my heart longed for. A pinprick of light shone minutely in the dark ahead of me... an end to the tunnel I wished, pleaded and prayed for.

"Please let there be light, let this be the way out, please", I gasped, striding towards the tiny dot. Something inside wouldn't let me run flat-out, a sense of danger, of preservation. There could be anything hanging from these walls, creatures like the ones crawling around on the floor, maybe even bigger ones... hooks, knives, a noose that would scoop me up and hang me until dead. Anything.

No, in this darkness, who knew what horrors lurked? The terrible sounds grew louder and louder, creeping into my loins like worms. Goosebumps covered my skin and that disturbing

1

feeling, that sense when there is someone looming behind you, threatened to disengage my legs. Butterflies in my stomach nattered insanely across my guts and chewed at my nerves. I turned and saw a figure steal from the darkness before sinking back into the desolate black.

My legs spun faster and my inhibited plight became one of all-out haste, dashing as fast I possibly could. Something was pursuing me and it was moving faster than I. The metallic clanging recaptured my fear, and a screeching that could only be that of a pig being butchered, belted at my eardrums without mercy. The wailing was terrifically loud and all but upon me, but this time I dared not look. I ran and ran as fast as my feet would carry me, betraying speeds I had not imagined possible in such grim darkness.

Grunts and squeals bit away at my heels and a boiling breath billowed down the back of my neck as I went. The pinprick of light grew larger and became a manhole-sized ring of neon white. The light spurred me to burst further ahead and the adrenaline must have been bubbling beneath my skin as I felt not a whisper of fatigue. The ever-growing light at the end of the passage grew luminous and pulsated brightly. Enough to blind me, perhaps, and yet I did not stop. I looked back once more, just as the light enveloped me and spread out to consume my world, all except for something more terrible than darkness—something that transcended the grimy neutrality of darkness.

The towering suit of armor shadowed over me in flight. A helmet of spikes and horns, thorns and bloodied shards. The sharp visor reached out to stab me and huge arms hung in the air clutching an ever-lengthening broadsword poised to strike. My ever-present nemesis, the perseverance of evil, of whom haunted my life. The giant shrieked and squealed in pursuit, as together we fell into a world of perpetual light.

The House that was Built on Love

I sprang up, clawing the air and crying out, "No". My eyes opened to my own reflection, one of terror, eyes wide and fingers crookedly frozen before my face. Beads of sweat rolling down my temple and my heaving chest belting out stunted breaths. I looked around and found myself in bed, bare chested and trembling, my sheets clinging to me, akin with the perspiration of desperation. The net curtains blew in from the veranda and ghosted up across my face, bringing with them the sounds of early morning. Braying melodies bleated the airwaves from the world outside, stifled only by an Arabic chuntering from the market stalls below. I climbed to the edge of the four-posted bed and planted my head in my hands and rubbed my eyes tightly. My arms stretched themselves above my temple until I heard the familiar cracking from my joints, somewhat akin to a host of glowsticks being snapped and toppled like dominoes one after the other. A ceremonious, and collective snapping of my achy bones each morning, I did suffer. I stood gingerly and retrieved my Saint Jude from around the post at the foot of the bed, gently placing the chain around my neck and watching it sway back and forth.

"Can you help my cause today, Jude?" I asked, walking to the veranda, "because it sure is a lost one".

Sweeping aside the curtain, my arms pressed against the hot iron rail as I looked out over Jerusalem in the morning. The ancient Jaffa gate stood across the street milling with people of all creeds—orthodox Jews, Arabic Muslims and Christians crossing paths, coming and going through the stone archway. Cars chugged by and donkeys clopped along, laden with goods while the sun beat down and begged a hot shine from the stone of the walls and the baked tar on the ground. Cursed nightmares had cast a dark shadow over my mind and stopped my cheerfulness from breaking through on such a beautiful morning.

Each morning was the same, such a word as cheerfulness had become a rare gem, the like of which I hadn't cradled for the longest time. The dreams had worsened, almost as though they had become my reality, and this place was now nothing to me but my place of depressing slumber. The visions had undergone a metamorphosis from frighteningly vivid to as real as the fruit being traded below my balcony, as tangible as the wrought-iron bar my fingers now ground tightly against. I loosened my grip on the veranda rail and rubbed my palm. A man's voice boomed up from below.

"Good morning, Tristan", it said. "More bad dreams, my friend?" The man tossed up a large orange I captured in both hands.

"Thank you, Samuel", I said. "Just dreams, nothing more".

Samuel stepped back, brushing his beard. "You know, Tristan, what you must do", waving a finger in the air, "you must face your fear. After this..." he opened his arms as though for mercy, "no more bad dreams".

"What if I don't know my fear?" I called down, "or where it is?"

"Then you must find it, my friend, and learn it", he replied, unpacking the saddle bags of a mule. Samuel looked up again. "Find *it*. Before *it* finds you".

"I might just do that, Samuel", I said, flicking a shekel into the air. He caught the coin in one hand, nodded to me and then turned to tend to an old woman sizing up a melon. "I might just do that", I repeated in little more than a mutter.

Trouble was, I knew my fears... all too well. My fears knew me... all too well. I showered and dressed into a white linen tunic and cargo trousers and swept my satchel over my shoulder. The time had come again to check the gates, 'twas time to see if they would let me leave this place. The Sun lashed across my face immediately and the heat prickled at my skin, drawing a shimmer of moisture from my pores. The heat from the sun was intense, but I suspected the ball of anxiety in my stomach accelerated the process greatly. A fresh bead had already stolen the distance from my temple to my jawline, and my breathing grew heavier walking only a hundred yards.

4

"They will still be there", I whispered under my breath, looking around sheepishly while trying to look completely natural in doing so. Did not a lick of good because I could feel my hands shaking. I raised them up and watched my fingers tremble. "Jesus", my hands clasped together uneasily.

The gates of the old city stood before me like a portal to the free world. Walking through a stone archway. What could be so difficult in accomplishing such a feat? After all, I'd entered the city the same way... well, at least I assumed I had, for the particulars of my arrival here still remained very hazy. Nonetheless, I approached the gate and stopped, placed my hand on the stone wall and leaned over the threshold. The wall was too thick to see beyond, so I shuffled my feet along the gravely floor until my toe tips perched rigidly on the line between the old city and the rest of Jerusalem. My fingers dug into the stone as I strained to glimpse what lay beyond the blind spot. The sky turned pale, putrid grey polluted the air, and with it the warm light drained away like water down a plug hole. The distant sound of thunder resonated high above, clapping like perched gods watching their earthly soap opera. They were still here, waiting for me.

A scorched hand wrapped around my neck and squeezed. My own hands attempted to wrestle the fingers away, but they were clamped fast. Pieces of skin slid from the hand as I frantically grappled, stripping chunks of tissue away like a barbecued chicken leg. A pungent smell of smoke, of burning flesh, stung my nostrils. Arching from beyond the threshold appeared a crazed and haunted face, a terrible gape perched upon an elongated neck that pulsed with rampant veins and bubbling sinew. Eyes white and glowing like neon, staring into mine, locking themselves to me through squalid pupils. The grimace was charred and melting, molten red veins of plasma bubbled beneath its porous features to portray a quite horrific yet silent scream. The thing widened its mouth further to display a serrated set of sharp, filthy teeth dripping with yellow goop. And a corroded tongue lay slouched like a slug, festering in the ashes of its own breath.

"You cannot leave this place. Master has not yet graced you with his presence", the fiend said, its features contorting with every word. "The stage is almost set for the reaping of souls... you must not leave". No sooner than the last word spoken from its lips, the hand released me. The figure vanished from whence it came and the warm, sunny air flooded back into the world. I slid down to the ground, clutching my throat. My body convulsed and my eyes felt as though they would burst, stinging with a prickly heat born of the creature's rancid wheezing. I rolled myself back into the safety of the old city and crawled against the base of a palm, where I remained for some time, breathing as though I had just run a marathon. My fingers wrapped themselves around my St. Jude and with mighty trembling, I squeezed with both hands.

'Please, God, help me'. My eyes closed over and I sat for a while longer, too afraid to move.

I awoke to see the long features of a donkey bleating into my face. A string of drool was dripping from its frothy and famished mouth. I jettisoned myself backwards along the ground like a frightened spider as a pair of legs rounded the animal and stepped closer.

A man and his shadow stood over me.

His eyes... his eyes were missing, and long, sinewy streaks of blood trickled from void ovals. "What is the matter, my friend? You look as though you have seen a ghost". The man raised his hand towards me.

"No, don't", I gasped, recoiling into myself. "Don't touch me". I stumbled backwards, holding my hands in the air. The man's motives and emotions so patently absent from the black holes where his eyes should have betrayed them. I turned and ran through the crowds, bumping into people and rounding others in flight, never stopping until it became too crowded to continue. The light of day had dimmed considerably and the sun was nose diving headlong into a bottomless horizon.

There in this frightening land was a carnival atmosphere finally breaking out and hundreds of orthodox Jews, broken by groups of tourists, skipped about singing and shouting. I slowed myself and attempted to gather my senses, but before long, my

6

steps joined the flow of their surroundings and I forced out a smile to some passers-bye as the crowd carried me away. The stream of revelry leading straight for an archway, one that crossed a threshold between the old and the new... I sheared the fear from my mind for the moments it would require and let myself be coerced by the people, by the momentum of hope. I thought I felt the grumbles of the grey skies returning, the growling of the creatures that guard the walls, but those elements seemed to recede with the onslaught of the happiness around me. We carried the procession up through the valley until I saw much larger groups had congregated around a great stage set in the town square. Rock music pounded out through enormous amps and the speakers were dressed and festooned with jovial-sounding youths. The closer I got to the stage, the more crowded it became as cup carrying youths milled around like grazing cattle. I halted myself outside a doorway and looked at my hands, still, they trembled uncontrollably. I folded my arms and looked up. The doorway was the entrance to a drinking establishment. I entered and took a stool at the bar. The barman was large, with a long pony tail and a bushy beard.

"What'll it be?" he asked.

"Double whisky, neat", I replied, reaching into my satchel and removing a handful of shekels. The coins shook wildly in my hand and the barman paused as we both watched the shekels ricochet against each other like Mexican jumping beans.

He pinched two of them. "Jeez, you really need that drink, don't ya, kid?" I closed my eyes and lifted the glass to my lips. My gag reflex threatened the butterflies in my stomach as I gulped the liquor down as fast as I could.

"Easy fella", said the barman.

"Just dreams". I pointed the glass at him, "they're just dreams".

"Whatever you say, kid", holding his hands up. "Another?"

I nodded and looked around the bar feverishly. The barman poured again, but paused as the bell on the entrance door rang out.

"Could ya leave the door open, friend? My buddy's band are about to play", the barman said. I looked at the door and saw a tall man. He wore a long black coat, dark sunglasses and a straight-rimmed Stetson. The stranger approached and leaned against the bar. I looked back at my drink and fixed my eyes on the yellow liquid.

"What can I get ya?" the barman asked him. I waited for the stranger's voice, watching him from the corner of my eye.

"Tell me, Mr. Barman, what is our friend here drinking?" My eyes widened, but I didn't move. His voice was low and his words ground cryptically against one another.

"Whiskey, double... neat. You want?"

"I do", he said, removing his sunglasses and placing them on the bar. The man looked across at me, but I pretended he hadn't. "Are you okay, friend? You look as though somebody stepped on your grave". And then he sat down and sipped slowly from his glass, staring at me all the while.

"I'm fine". I picked up my drink, wanting to gulp it down in one and leave, but my stomach wouldn't have allowed that. I'd chuck it up all over the bar, so I settled on sipping about half forcefully. My throat winced and my gag reflex rose swiftly. I pushed myself off the stool and made for the door. A hand gripped my arm. Our eyes met.

"Your drink—you haven't finished it. Shame to waste good whiskey", he said. His eyes were strange, one of them blue, the other brown. I looked down at his hand, rested on my forearm and then back to his eyes. He smiled faintly and released me.

"I have somewhere I need to be"

"Still friend, what's the hurry? You can be where you need to be when you finish your drink... surely you must have heard".

"Heard?" I replied

"What they do to men in Hades who waste fine whiskey".

Curse my cowardly wilt. I relented and sat back down on my stool, wondering why the devil I wasn't walking out that door. Part of me was afraid of where I would go. Darkness had almost fallen again and those things would be lurking about the walls, maybe even searching for me on this side of the wall. But staying here struck me just as dangerous. The barman observed the situation with uneasy eyes.

"What do they do to them?"

"Barman, get our friend here another, and pour one for yourself", the man said, holding out a note between his fingers. "Every man deserves a last drink before..." he paused and raised the glass to his lips.

"Before?" I asked, "before what?"

He gulped down his drink. A rotten-toothed smile crept across his face and he nodded towards the barman. The barman shrugged and with that lift of his shoulders he spontaneously combusted in a bright flash. His arms flailed with flames and he wailed terrifically, backing into the bottles on the shelves behind and smashing them to the ground as he swooned in agony. I kicked against the bar and fell backwards off my stool, only narrowly escaping the immense heat lashing out from the poor soul. I closed my eyelids tightly and cried as the barman moaned.

Silence washed over me and the screaming stopped. I opened my eyes to see the stranger glaring down. The barman leaned over the bar, a bemused look on his face. "Are you okay?" he asked.

"No, I'm not okay", I said picking myself up. "In fact, I'm far from it. I need to get out of here", starting for the door.

"Boy". The stranger's tone caused me to freeze. "Did you see him burn?"

"Yes, I saw".

"If you walk out that door, he will burn again, only this time there won't be no pretending", the stranger said. "You hold his life in your hands, boy".

"Why are you doing this to me?"

The barman frowned. "Doing what? What did I do?"

"Not you, him..."

"Who?"

"Can you not see the man sitting at the bar?" I pointed. The barman scanned the entirety of the bar, twice looking directly at the stranger. "I don't see anyone else here, there's only you".

"He's sitting right there. You spoke to him when he came in". I advanced towards the barman. "You asked him to leave the door open so you could hear the band. You served him a drink". I picked up the stranger's glass and thrust it towards the barman, "see?"

9

He stepped back and raised his hands. "Whoa, there". I looked at my fist and saw a knife where the glass had been. The stranger began to laugh.

"Who are you?" I turned and thrust the knife against the stranger's chin. "What do you want with me?"

The stranger released a low chuckle that tapered off into a growl. His eyes turned black and his rotten teeth became visible through his thin lips. A rat now squirmed in my palm where the knife had been. I recoiled and tossed the rodent against the wall, stumbling backwards in the process.

"Tell me, Tristan, do you know what is real and what is not?" The stranger advanced and grabbed me around the collar. "Do you ever get the feeling someone is watching you?" he asked, breaking into sly laughter.

"Let go of me". I struggled to loosen his grasp. My fingers dug into his grip, but he had vanished and it was now my hands around the barman's neck. His disgruntled face suddenly flashed before me as he protested angrily and shoved me back across the bar and into the wall.

"What the hell is wrong with you?" he cried, "are you crazy?"

"I..." my fingers trembled before my eyes again. "I'm not sure what is real", watching my hands. "What is happening to me?"

"You've lost your mind", he shouted. "Get outta here before I call the cops, ya crazy fool".

I scrambled out into the crowds, colliding with a group of young people who scowled and scolded. One of them threw a cup at me but I didn't stick around to give them reason to further their discontent. I fought through the crowds of revelers, crowds of revelers that seemed to be growing increasingly agitated by my presence.

A charred face appeared between a couple holding hands, grimacing and poking its snout over their shoulders like a nosy badger. I backed away, stepping on people's toes and spilling their drinks. Each group chastised my actions with snarls and shouts, some yelped in protest, others tugging at their partner's sleeves... but *they* didn't scare me. More and more of those terrible faces began popping up wherever my eyes did lay, each

10

crazed and devilish, glaring through neon eyes. I fought even further through the crowd, changing direction whenever I would see one, but they were incessant and innumerable, a tapestry of hellish décor drawing evermore towards me.

A narrow street opened up behind a fence of people, so I stole my way into an empty channel with a covert shove between two men with guitars. I ran down the cobbled street, away from the crowds, until there was not a soul around. The silence was surreal, unnatural. Could it really be this quiet? I hadn't run that far from the people. Was this real or another trick?

The creepy laughter broke out all around me and a gust of wind carried it into my ears with a sting.

"Is it real?" a whisper mocked on the air. I spun around to search for the source but there was nobody in sight. I turned again and caught a glimpse, a suggestion of a figure in a dark corner. A growl resonated from the shadows. My body shuddered and chills ran down my spine and into my toes.

"Who's there? What do you want from me?" *Nothing.* "Enough of your trickery", I braved. The growl came again, but deeper, curdling with violent rage. I froze and hoped it wasn't what I thought it was. "This isn't real, it's not really happening", I whispered. "This is your imagination", I told myself. A beastly shadow swayed from the darkness and howled into the night air. The thing moved on four legs, sweeping across the street and growling with a hungry intensity. "This is not real, this is not real, this is not real", I said over and over. The beast bolted for me with ferocious guile, scraping its claws against the cobbled stone. My stomach turned over and my feet broke in the opposite direction, carrying me back towards the crowd.

"This is real, this is real, this is real", I chanted, listening to the gargle of the creature salivating. The famished growls bleating at my heels served to persuade me of a very real danger.

The outer layer of the crowd appeared, as did the thumping sound of rock music. I looked back to see the wolf bearing down on me. Serrated teeth dripping and mouth agape, the animal pounced through the air just as I breached the wall of people, crashing through a herd of them and rolling to the floor. Landing atop of me, the jaws of the beast pressed around my skull. My

11

fingers searched out the wet teeth and wedged themselves between sharp crevices near the gum line, but the heat of its breath suffocated my consciousness. The monster turned to dust quite literally, leaving me flailing, kicking and punching thin air. A circle of people formed around me, pointing and staring. And then a cruel wave of laughter broke out and swept through the ranks like wildfire. I froze my floundering and saw the many eyes and shiny white teeth all around me, like stars in the sky, their fingers prodding and feet dancing with giggles.

I stood up and burrowed through them, disappearing into a sea of monsters. The people turned on me in swarms, kicking and screaming like banshees. A woman ran towards me, brandishing her finger nails like knives and yet another pointed at me and shrieked nothing but insanity. I darted through a group of laughing children who were intent on chasing me.

"There he is", one of them cried. "He's here", another screamed.

A hand grabbed at my arm and a face leered into mine. "Don't you know what is real, boy?" the old woman garbled. Her nails dug into my arm and pierced the skin. I cried out and shoved the woman over onto her back. Everyone froze and looked at the hag squirming on the floor. A collective of glowing eyes set upon me like those of roving wolves in a dark wood.

"I'm sorry, but she…" I began, but the horde cried their vengeance and drowned my speech. I knocked over three of them, intent on grappling me to the ground. They failed by little more than a whisker, but there were more of them closing in on both sides. The road opened up ahead, so I took it with nimble strides that led me away from the crowds once more, until I could see the old city walls again. Clusters of eateries and restaurant appeared at the top of the hill, indented by brightly lit stores. I looked back down the dark road to check for my pursuers and saw a pack of figures congregated not far behind. The moon was out in the royal blue sky and nightfall was all but complete.

The darkness was coming for me.

I skipped up the steps, climbing higher and higher and rounded the city walls, mounting the citadel of eateries and shops. I leaned over the fortifications to peer down the trail on which

I'd tread. The same pack of figures hovered slowly over my footsteps like rabid sniffer hounds on the bloody scent. *Wretched dogs,* I thought, squeezing a piece of the wall so hard it broke off in my hand.

"Sir, would you..." a voice began in my ear. A hand touched on my shoulder and the fright in my loins caused me to jump like a jackal. I turned and was met by a woman holding a menu. "I am sorry, sir. I didn't mean to frighten you", said the young lady. "Would you like to dine at my restaurant?"

I looked back down over the wall and saw the figures had disappeared.

"I'm sorry, but I just lost my appetite", I said, pushing past her and scurrying in among the social gatherings. People sat around eating and drinking in ambient lighting and conversing on the pleasant evening, gulping wine from their fancy flutes and fingering plates of pretention. I wandered among them, wondering if I was safe.

The stranger had asked me, *'Do you ever get the feeling someone is watching you?'* Well, right now I had that precise feeling. Where would I go now? Where would I be safe? I felt myself revolving, slowly, staring inquisitively at random patrons, until I let myself slump into a wicker chair on a decked platform.

A waiter approached and stood over me. "Welcome, sir. Would you like something to drink or something to eat, perhaps?"

"Water", looking up. "Do you have water?" I asked, stealing another series of glances around the people.

"Of course, sir. We have sparkling..." he began to list.

"Tap water will do if you have it?"

"Tap, sir?"

"Yes, that's what I said. Tap water".

"Very well". He scribbled into a notepad before waltzing back into the establishment. The waiter returned with a tall glass of water and placed it down on the table beside a bowl of olives. My eyes were set firmly on the walls as I reached and took an olive from the bowl. I bit into the olive, scanning the people around me. My mouth was dry and there sat a strange irony taste on my tongue. I picked up the glass and raised it to my lips.

My blood ran cold.

An eyeball staring at me from the bottom of the glass, a large eyeball with bloodied tentacles reaching all the way back to the sinewy tendons it was trailing. I drew the glass away from me in fright, splashing the table and floor. In my other hand, there was no olive, but another eyeball—partially eaten. My loins quivered and my gag reflex hankered to explode. The glass dropped from my hand and I tossed the eye away in the same way I'd dispose of an imminently exploding grenade. My disgust carried my frame over the back of the chair and pushed me along the floor by my heels, away from the table.

Heads turned at the sound of smashing glass and the waiter came running. "What is the matter, sir?"

"You know what the matter is", I cried. "An eyeball in my glass is what the matter is. Eyeballs that look like olives is what the matter is". I scrambled around the floor. "Don't pretend you don't know what the matter is". My hands foraged through the broken glass and found an olive. "Look", I said, thrusting the olive up towards the waiter from a kneeling position.

He held out his hands before him. "Sir, it is just an olive".

I focused on the little round fruit. "Precisely, it's an olive…" I became painfully aware of the fifty or so patrons staring and whispering. "It's an olive, but it wasn't an olive before... was it?" Chuckles and sneers broke from the diners. The olive dropped from my fingers and rolled along the ground among the shards of glass. I looked around the faces and then back at the waiter. "Are you one of them?" I asked, pointing at him.

"One of whom?" he asked, attempting to help me up.

"Don't touch me", I snapped, now bordering on frenetic. I backed slowly away, still crouching but gradually rising to my feet. "You'd better not follow me, any of you". Not one of them spoke, but instead watched in awe and bewilderment as I stalked away, almost on tiptoes. I rounded a corner and pressed my back tightly up against the wall and took deep breaths looking up into the star lit sky.

Was I losing my mind? Would I know if I had? If one were to lose his mind, then how would you know? How can one who has lost his mind determine it so? My mind raced with nonsense. *Good God, Tristan, stop this and pull yourself together,* I told

14

myself, with some ferocity. I wandered again, into a square of quaint, brightly lit rug-and-ornament stores, where colorful wares spewed out from their entrances like inviting tongues of mystery and wonder. Narrow souk trails cut into the stone, leading into alleys and tunnels of stores and shops, vendors and tradesmen dressed in all the shades of the Near East. My feet carried me down such a trail.

A shiny man wearing a black-and-white shemagh wrapped around his face, broke into manic laughter and touched my arm. "Where do you think you are? Tell me, boy?" he asked through rouge, spittle covered lips.

"I know where I am—I'm in Jerusalem".

"A word of advice, brother. The next time someone asks you that question, you tell them Palestine". He patted my cheek. "Look around you, we are Palestinians, do not mistake it". And then he smiled and squeezed my shoulder.

"You don't... you don't suppose I'm losing my mind, do you?"

"Losing your mind?" he boomed in laughter. "No brother, your mind is present". The man stared at me. "I see it as plainly as I see the rubies in my rugs, though you will lose something else entirely if you wander into the dark corners of this place".

A place sprung to my mind: a place of light in a world of dark corners, a place that would surely be safe. "The Sepulcher. The church of the Holy Sepulcher", I said, hanging tightly to my senses. "Where is it from here?"

"A Christian?" he smiled. "Go safely into the night, my brother. Follow this path to the end and climb the cobbled valley that splits the two houses, this will bring you to the 7th station of the cross. From there, you will find your way".

"Thank you, brother".

"Stop for no demon nor entity of darkness, but trust thyself". He placed his fingers to his lips and offered them to the sky. "I shall pray to Allah you have safe passage, my brother".

I bowed my head reverently and waved before turning and taking the path that would lead me to the church of the Holy Sepulcher. I strode meticulously through the most colorful, vibrant souks I had ever imagined, followed by the howls and cries of vendors biting at my heels as arms and fingers brushed and swept over me for every yard calling for my attention. My blood was cold and a fear gripped me, for I could not know who was friend or foe. I tread on towards the seventh station.

A passage led me to an ornate red-and-black door with a plaque above which read VII.ST—the 7th station. The place it is said Jesus had fallen for the second time. A man in crude and tattered robes was stood beside the door.

"My son, I am of the Franciscan chapel of St Christopher. You must hurry, there are things that follow you. They stalk the Via Dolorosa, seeking you out". He pointed left down a narrow passage I followed in blind faith.

There was no time to stop or contemplate. My eyes scanned the walls for clues, street signs broken up by peering faces and wavering banners. Souk Khan al-Zeit—the words sprung out from an ancient stone wall. A busy market street opened up and I knew the 8th station was across the square and down the steps. I wriggled across the way, between the vendors and bodies, stumbling down the steps and halting against a wall bearing the plaque - VIII.ST.

Short of breath and heaving, was I, but it would not be far now. My fingers brushed upon the plaque as I continued on. A scream burst into the night air behind me on the Via Dolorosa, somewhere on the trail, something was getting closer. My nimble feet carried me along the passage for some yards, until I ghosted through an archway and saw, beaming into the night sky, the cross and dome of the Church of the Holy Sepulcher. I entered the monasteries and ran through their halls, disturbed by the searing echo my soles made against the tranquility of the place.

A courtyard spread out before me, but a feeling inside told me to stop, chills ran within my ribs and my feet teetered on the edge of the steps. The butterflies sprang to life in my stomach, fluttering with no small tickle. *Trust the butterflies.*

There was something here with me.

A chiming bell rang out and a flock of birds burst from a chapel roof with frenzied wings. Another scream belted through the dark passage behind me, revolting against the cold stone walls and zapping into my ears. The hairs on the back of my neck stood up and pointed like rose thorns. I leapt from the step and sprinted across the courtyard as a shadow moved beside me on the wall. My left foot took flight as I landed on my right, but something quickly chewed my momentum. I looked down to see my foot snap beneath the stone tiles and a gooey substance clinging to my ankle. *'What on earth'*, my left foot faltered and pressed against a brittle surface that crumbled and enveloped the top half of my toes.

My shoulders arched and my hands planted down against a manhole-shaped mosaic in the center of the courtyard. The face of a saint, cut from tiny pieces of stone, met my eyes and its halo shone into my pupils. *Thank God the mosaic did not give way.*

My hands did not breach the saint but instead flattened against the surface, offering me precious leverage. I looked down to see my legs up to my thighs had vanished beneath the courtyard tiles. An unforgiving force began to pull me downwards, pressing tightly around my legs and creeping up to my abdomen. A low snarling crept from the door behind me and filtered into the courtyard, clinging to the dark walls among the ghosts and shadows.

The sounds of teeth gnashing and rancid tongues rasping the night air danced like devils around me. Pieces of the courtyard began to fall away, crumbling and plummeting into the black abyss my legs now dangled precariously into. I dug my fingers so hard into the mosaic, their tips turned white and stung, but my resolution was not to let go, not for anyone... or anything.

I kicked and strained my legs until I lost my breath, yet I continued to squeeze the stone under my fingers, somehow managing to press hard enough to angle my elbow up onto the edge and grapple the stone circle. From there, I pressed and wrestled until my body was elevated by the sheer might of my effort. This precious circle was just wide enough for me to sit on without falling off, as the ground around me was ever faltering and chunks of masonry had completely diminished and disappeared into the darkness below.

I had to move forward before it was all gone, otherwise this is where I would stay. The snarls snatched out from the darkness surrounding me, anticipating my attempts, or at least intentions of escape. They were readying to pounce the moment I made my dash. Whatever was out there wanted me for supper. Another mosaic circle lay a few yards away. A leap away, it seemed.

I felt around my neck for St Jude.

"Patron Saint of lost causes don't fail me now", I whispered and kissed the small pendant. "Here goes nothing". I took a deep breath and jumped out with everything I had. My toes slapped against the stone but quickly slid off, cracking my shin and knee against the edge. My chest thumped down onto the surface and my arms clutched around the rim of the circle as my cheek, too, crashed against the tiles, causing my desperate exhalations to blow away the dust from the artistry.

I rested, wheezing for a few moments with the cold stone against my bleeding jaw. The crazed shadows broke into a manic shuffling of grumbles and snapping. Still, they remained invisible, hiding in the shadows of this holiest of places. I breathed deeply and heaved myself up onto the circle.

And there before me was the archway that led to the church entrance, a saviour of sorts reaching out to me from the darkness. My eyes closed over and I braced myself for whatever was waiting for me on the other side. Another jump away, it seemed. I set a foot on the edge of the circle and sprang out. The feeling of floating through the air engulfed me ever so briefly, until the crash landing against the rock stunned me into painful shock. My momentum rolled me over and over before striking the wall and continuing down some steps, on and on, tossing and turning, desperately trying to hold onto something. My temple struck the floor and brokered a quite savage halt.

The flames from a torch attached to the wall gathered my dizzied attention. I shook my head and saw the great wooden doors to the church on the other side of a courtyard. "Not another courtyard".

A snarl lingered behind me and a piercing scream frightened me to my feet, echoing around the yard like a rocket. I seized the torch down from the wall and waved it around wildly as the flames roared and drooled small fireballs across the dark expanse. I attempted to compose myself and began backing away towards the great oak doors, carefully brandishing the flame before me. A horrible face appeared from the blackness and charged headfirst into the torch. The burning tip melted against the creature's mug—melding its eyes to its mouth—the nose and cheeks fusing and bubbling like some awful pizza topping. The screams from the figure were horrific and churned my very insides, drawing out my own yells as I pushed against the monster. Another entity ran across the torch light and grimaced at me with such anger and apparent disdain before disappearing again.

My arms trembled and sent the torch fire rippling in all directions, just at the moment my shoulder blades impacted with the sturdy doors. This served only in frightening me into a crazed, swiping frenzy. The torch head bounced off the wall, sending sparks flying and left me open to attack, yet I continuously swung the torch in revolutions and wide-eyed terror, attempting to repel anything that came near. More screams polluted the silence and growls from every corner of my world reached out and jabbed at my guts. A disfigured face glared into the light and bellowed furiously against the fire. The licks of the flames danced in the ghoul's black eyes like mirrors of despair—windows into Hell itself. With a howl, the thing buried its features into the torch tip and quickly recoiled backwards in terrific agony.

I can't take much more of this, I thought, watching the horrors come out from every dark corner of this place. My trembling shoulder blades pressed up against the doors again with a thump and I thundered the sole of my foot against the wood over and over.

"Hey, let me in, let me in", I cried up to the heavens. "I want to come in", calling so hard and desperately my lips dribbled, and boiled tears from the heat of the flames welled in my eyes. "Do you hear me? Let me in, let me in, please", I bellowed for my life. My throat strings twanged and snapped, finally, against my despairing cries. Three faces attached to gangling, naked bodies sprung from the dark and raised their long arms above my head. Razor tipped fingers dripping with scum primed themselves to lacerate my face beyond recognition... I had to act.

The flames illuminated further their terrible features, and their distorted forms became monsters of unimaginable horror. I

19

cried out and lanced the middle ghoul sharply with the torch. The figure shrieked and combusted with diabolic squeals. The monstrosity beside it clutched the torch and buried its own face into the fire and began chewing up the torch head. I attempted to withdraw my only defence by force, but the thing would not relent and proceeded to consume the fire entirely.

"Let me in, let me in, please", I cried, on the verge of losing my grasp of the torch handle. All around me now, these figures leered menacingly, and as the flame dimmed and the creature chewed the last orange embers of light, I slumped down against the doors and watched their awful faces unite over me in a cruel collage of Hell's most-wanted mugs.

My shoulders slid sharply backwards as the doors swayed open and my head bumped against the cold floor. A great light shone from within the church and emblazoned its brilliance across the horde of creatures, and with it a mercurial agony, one that sent their flailing, gaunt limbs and bleeding torsos retreating into the darkness.

"What are you?" I mumbled, my mind consumed by the light, my temple ringing with the deafening wails... my consciousness faded to black.

A glowing light shone through my eyelids and warmth spread over my face. My eyes opened reluctantly, like two ancient oysters from the bottom of the sea. Soft and snowy, a face peered over me with cascading locks hanging like curtains from a flawless temple. Their silken tips brushed over my cheeks and onto my face, each as beautifully scented as a breeze that blows through an orchard. Her bright eyes widened as she observed mine opening. The girl immediately drew herself away. My own eyes strayed upwards to follow such a wonder, but this only succeeded in causing me pain and my sight to blur further.

Upon inspection, I found myself lying flat on my back upon a table or alter with a small window, allowing golden spears of sunlight to flood in through a grill near the ceiling. Those creatures invaded my mind suddenly and I twisted onto my side and back again, expecting to see their awful faces converging over me.

My eyes darted around the room like dizzy bluebottles looking for some clue as to where I was. A wooden door closed over slowly where someone had just left.

I rolled off the altar and lowered my feet to the ground. The floorboards creaked. The little room was peaceful and quiet, veiled by velvet curtains and constructed from fine wood panels. I pushed my hand against the door. The hinges groaned. A spiral staircase of stone appeared to be the only way in or out of this peculiar little room, so I descended the steps to find myself at the bottom of an arch-shaped tunnel lined with stained-glass windows. The strong sunshine outside was stifled by the deep colours of the glass creating sparkling edges that shone through in tangible rays across my path. At the end of the hall, I entered a hot, green garden of towering flowers and twisting footpaths.

"Hello", I called out, brushing aside a sunflower that reached over me like an impending guardian. There was no reply, but a shadow moved away quietly, beside a small bench, where the reddest of roses grew in huge clusters. I edged forward and caught a glimpse of two bare feet beneath the tail of a white gown, skipping away through the tall grass to leave the green blades swaying. I followed along the gravely maze and ventured between the grass, pushing them aside with inverted palms. A sturdy gate indenting a sandstone wall slammed shut and bounced against its frame several times before standing still. I could see crowds of people milling about through the grooves and gaps between the panels of the wood. The voices were so welcome to my quarried mind—humans walking and talking, laughing to one another in the light.

I closed an eye and peeped through a small knot hole in one of the panels, and there I spied crowds of people in coarse animation. Market tradesmen thrust their wares from all sides as tourists marched along unblinking and open-mouthed. I was just about to open the gate when an eye appeared on the other side of the knot hole. Blinking and sparkling, the long eyelashes fluttered and the sweet laughter of a girl funneled under the gate and up to my ears like music. I stumbled backwards and fell onto my back.

21

"Who was that?" I asked myself. When I stood, she was gone, but her chuckles still echoed in my mind. I opened the gate and left the beautiful confines of the garden behind. The gate swung to a close, clipping my shoulders and nudging me sharply into the path of a donkey. "Sorry", I backed out of the way, only to bump into a man holding a lamp.

"You like lamp? You buy lamp from me, you will like this lamp", he squawked from a bushy beard that covered his lips entirely.

"No, thank you, sir".

"You no like lamp? This lamp is good", he persevered, elongating the word '*good*' to go on for a very long time. His right eye widened and zoned in on me as a fly landed on his beard.

"I am in no doubt of the quality, sir, but I have no use for a lamp". I crossed the street.

"Tristan", a voice called out. I turned. There stood a pretty girl. Barefooted in a flowing white gown dress. Her dark locks shone and gleamed in the warmth in such a way it appeared there were sun beams resting on her shoulders. Her face, dainty and bright eyed, climbed out from her curling tresses like an angel's might, and a haphazard row of freckles had been sprinkled across the bridge of her nose and cheeks in a delightfully unkempt fashion. Her smile almost waltzed, dancing and stretching out for what felt like forever. Eyes so adorably large they festooned themselves around my beat-skipping heart like ovals of pure light. Everything else seemed to become invisible for those moments. I couldn't even manage to answer. Had she asked me a question? My mind would neither confirm nor deny it.

"Tristan", she said again, her lips curling at their edges.

"Yes, that's my name", I said cautiously. "How did you know… have we met?"

"I don't know", she replied. "Have we?"

"How do you know my name?"

"I saw you... and thought you look like someone who might go by the name of Tristan. And I was right, wasn't I?"

"Yes". I smiled.

"Are you alone, Tristan?"

"Everyday", I said, trying to put a jolly spin on it and doing quite well. "I'm looking for something".

She skipped closer. "What are you looking for, Tristan?"

"I..." my mind wandered among all the possibilities—last night's events, my nightmares and fears. I settled for none. "I don't really know yet", I said. "You think that strange?"

"Oh, I don't know. Do any of us really know what it is we truly seek until we find it?" she asked.

"I suppose not".

"Sometimes along the way, others remind us of what it is we seek because we can forget Tristan, we can forget what we once knew... would you like me to remind you?"

"How would you do that?"

"Walk with me", she said, breezing by with a close stare. Stopping at the corner of a wall, she turned and offered out her hand.

I joined her without a scrap of apprehension. I was a loner, but something put me at such ease beside her. We walked through the bustling alleyways, cooled by the looming canopies but cajoled by street sellers and merchants. The girl skipped around them, reaching out to take my hand, stopping to show me trinkets and jewels, before dancing to the next display with joyful smiles and requests to catch up. Who was this strange, angelic creature? How had she grazed into my trust so easily and how could she know my name? All of these thoughts ran through my spinning head as she stood on her tip toes to hold a giant sea shell to my ear. The sound of rushing air and the crashing of waves seeped into my mind and I felt my eyes widen.

"Can you hear it?" she asked.

"I can". She drew herself closer to listen and her locks brushed my face. I inhaled and closed my eyes in a puff of jasmine and sweetness. "Who are you?"

"Remember those sounds, Tristan, for one day you will listen through one of these again and you will not be far away from me". She left her tip toes and stepped back to place the shell down again. "Will you remember them?"

"Who are you?"

"Will you remember them?" she asked again.

23

"I will remember".

"Promise me?"

"Promise", I replied instantly. "Will you tell me your name?"

"I am, Eleanor". She smiled.

"Eleanor?", I said. "Pleased to meet you, Eleanor".

She took my hand in hers and curtsied, pinching up her dress. Then she drew herself closer and whispered, "Tell me Tristan, has anyone ever asked you about your hopes and fears?" She looked into my eyes expectantly. Her close proximity and the sweet tickle of her breath left me a little dumbstruck. I frowned and looked at the sky. A foray of children's faces peered down from the windows above, staring upon us as though awaiting my answer.

I looked back at Eleanor, "I don't remember".

"Why don't you tell me, Tristan?" She spoke softly and gave my hand a squeeze before releasing me and wandering off without a care in the world. I followed her, wondering where such carelessness led. We meandered through the city streets, where two women emerged from a flower shop and offered Eleanor a small, colorful flower arrangement. She received them graciously and thanked the women. They curtsied and whispered curiously to one another, while watching us continue along.

Eleanor dipped her dainty nose into the petals, then pressed them to my nose and giggled. "Tell me, Tristan, what do you see when you go to sleep at night?"

I bowed my head and felt the butterflies in my stomach rise and wander, the chalk and dust of the stone masonry from the courtyard on my shoes reminded me of last night. "I fear it's not just my dreams to be afraid of anymore". I looked upon her beauty while feeling a dark dread in my loins. "I…" my words began with difficulty, but she seemed to anticipate this and placed a finger to my lips.

Her own lips whispered to me like a slow wind. "Let me take you to a place I know". She lowered her hand to my side and entwined her fingers around mine. "Will you come with me?"

Nodding and under her spell, she led me away.

We walked further through the streets and the squares, ascending the steep inclines of cobbled stone, finally mounting the beaten steps upon the city walls, where a castle plateau opened up, encompassed by views of the old city and her surroundings. The people below were small, distant figures and the sounds of the town were all but drowned by the solitude. The golden dome of the rock gleamed brilliantly in the aged but still hardy sun, and the swarms of worshippers buzzed about the Western wall like ants around a nest. Looking out, I could see Mount Moriah reaching towards the heavens, sweeping high above the roving valleys of graveyards and gardens.

"Beautiful, isn't it?" A light breeze brushed Eleanor's locks back to reveal a face that exuded such fairness upon my eyes, one comparable only to her aura that sauntered around this warm plateau. She turned to me with a demure expression.

"Yes, it is".

"They say a fearful man can look upon beauty, and yet never see past his own unending terror. He can never truly behold the part he must play in the world among the many wonders that surround him. A fearful man will carry the heart of the shrinking violet without shame, and watch the world and all its mystery slip into the shadows and perish without regret. The fearful man will do this until he himself slips the way of the place he called home, without ever having truly resided there".

I closed my eyes and saw visions of the ghouls that surrounded the city walls, jumping and cajoling me from the crowds. My cheeks burned with a prickling heat and the grim squeal of the dark figure who wears the armor rang in my head. I opened my eyes and spoke:

"Some men have plenty to fear. You say I am a fearful man, but there is much to fear and little to fight, little to fight *for*". My fingers tightened on the wall and I focused on the furthest reaches of mount Moriah. "Devils and demons, nightmares and visions". My voice deepened and rose. "Magic and chicanery, you cannot touch, that chases you through the darkness. Who, I ask you, is really afraid of who?" turning around and pointing. "Tell me who is the real coward, me or them?" I cursed, stepping forward. "Do you know what is in my head, what haunts my mind, those creatures last night? Who are you and what do you know of such things?"

Eleanor watched me with soft eyes. "Calm yourself, Tristan. I do not call you the fearful man through spite or ill meaning. I do not call you fearful for wish to stir those butterflies you feel so in here". She pressed gently on my stomach.

"How can you know?" I whispered, but she placed a hand on my cheek and said:

"Do not be ashamed of your fear, fear is useful, your fear means you are alive. For as long as you feel it, you will live".

"I'm sorry, forgive me". I drew her into me and hugged her. "I should not have spoken to you so". She relented and looked up at me. The sun was setting behind her in a wondrously fiery glow on an amber horizon. "It was you who saved me last night?" I relinquishing her and looked out over the wall. "Those things follow me everywhere I go. They are not of this world, they cannot be".

She stood beside me. "No, Tristan, they are not". The fear crept inside my chest and into my throat. I was riddled with the unquenchable fear of the world, its enormity. Of being alone in such a world. The cursed feeling halted the questions on my lips that roared in my shrinking violet cage of a heart. For I so feared the answers.

"Would you like to take some tea with me", I asked her instead.

"I would like that very much".

Samuel greeted us at the hostel by tossing me an orange and a smile. "Welcome back, Tristan. You have returned to the finest hostel in all of Jerusalem, finest oranges too", he said, stepping down from a cart. "It is sundown, my friend, will you take your tea?"

I returned his greeting and we shook arms. "I always return, Samuel. I've brought a guest for tea, if you'll permit".

"Of course, of course, Tristan. Everyone is welcome here", he said, opening his arms.

"Samuel, this is Eleanor. She is my friend".

"I am pleased to meet you, Eleanor". Samuel offered a polite hand, to which she obliged.

"Go inside, my friends, I will join you shortly", Samuel said, before turning to a young boy carrying a box of fruit. Samuel spoke Arabic to him and patted the back of a mule sharply.

The boy smiled and rushed away with the box. I offered my hand towards the door and Eleanor walked inside. Before I could follow, Samuel took my arm and said:

"Sometimes Tristan, when we go looking for nightmares, we find dreams", he winked and smiled. I smiled back, though, fighting a feeling the impending darkness always brought forth... cagey, malignant trepidation. Curse the night.

I ventured back into the safe house as I had come to know it. The reception smelled warm and culinary, with spices whipping the air. I led Eleanor through the hanging beads into a mystical tea room that really was a sight to behold. The room never failed to scintillate me each time I entered. More than once, I had retreated down to this very room, in the middle of the night, to be around people, to study, perhaps or, quite simply, to lose myself in the charming décor and ambience.

Grandiose silken cushions lay scattered along benches and couches bearing golden tassels that hung down to the mosaic floor tiles. Colorful, vivid paintings and murals adorned the walls, climbing out into the shadows of a dimly lit period chandelier hanging from the ceiling. Just like today, there were always traditionally dressed Arabic men and women taking tea and smoking hookah pipes that bubbled away with rocks that smelled of aniseed, jasmine and fruit scented tobacco. Smoke plumes caressed the walls and crept up to the ceiling, wandering the cracks and picture frames like a mist on a moor.

Eleanor sat in the corner, away from the people. She hitched up her knees, locking them together and wrapped her arms around them. I poured some tea into two glasses and took a chair opposite her. We sipped the steaming fruit tea and watched one another in the shadowy light. She looked deeply into my eyes and I felt a powerful sense of familiarity. Her gaze stirred clouded memories, forgotten times. A well of nostalgia formed in my stomach and warmed me into a comforting daze.

"Do you ever get the feeling you have met someone before? Almost as if you…"

"Yes, Tristan", she said quietly, and we both leaned in closer to each other, searchingly and without a blink. A world of wonder swirled around her pupils, reaching out, soothsaying eyes, whispering my lost memories back to me.

"Ahh, I see you have tea, my friends. Here, we have the best tea in Jerusalem", a voice boomed beside me. Our connection broke and we snapped from the moment. I shook my head and sat back. Samuel took to the counter and poured himself a glass of tea, then sat on a stool and lit a cigarette.

"Your tea is why I return each day, Samuel". I raised my glass.

He chuckled, "Ah, you are too kind, Tristan. You know, my father ran this inn, and before him, his father. For many, many generations, my family has welcomed travelers just like you. The people I have watched come and go over the years. Pilgrims, tourists, the lost, the found, and everyone in between. I could tell you a tale or two, my friends". He mused, smiling to himself. "Of course, they all have their own tales to tell".

"I should think they do", I said, sipping my tea.

"Would you tell us some of your tales, Samuel?" Eleanor asked, crossing her legs and placing her tea on the table beside her.

The kindly inn keeper glanced between us and stubbed out his cigarette. "As you wish".

Samuel lamented stories of the people who had passed through, tales of long ago and childhood memories of his father and grandfather. He had us rolling with laughter at times and at others, fixated, awaiting the next breath of raving, mad lunatics, holy preachers and dark strangers, some of whom had sometimes vanished in the night, never to be seen again. Of the friendships and bonds, too, made over the years between those who sit and had sat in this magical tea room.

"One thing I promise my guests, you will always be safe while you are under my roof", he gestured with his hands around the room. "This is a house that was built on love. Evil has no business here". Samuel looked down and took out a packet of cigarettes from his shirt pocket, lit one and shook the match.

"When I found Tristan, he was sleeping beneath a tree near to Jaffa gate, and when I managed to rouse him, he lashed out at me with eyes of madness. Some might have left him there, afraid to go near such a tormented soul. But it is my belief I was meant to find him. It was divine fate that sent me to bring him back here, to the house that was built on love".

Eleanor gave me a wounded look. Samuel took a long drag on his cigarette and stubbed it out. "You see, that night, a storm swept across the land, a violent electrical storm struck Jerusalem, causing trees to fall and cars and animals to collide. Some of the people even attested to seeing strange animals, animals unlike any we had seen before—strange creatures roaming the streets, ferocious and unafraid of the chaos. But the strangest of all things that night was the scream". Samuel pondered his tea.

"The scream?" Eleanor asked.

"Yes, an almighty scream that rose above all other sounds, a scream so piercing the windows of many of the buildings were blown out, shattered into pieces. Evermore curious a thing was that it led me to Tristan. Whoever was responsible for such a scream must have been with Tristan, or very close to him. Though when I found my way to him, he was quite alone. I carried him back here and every step of the way I felt as though we were being followed, followed by someone or something evil". Samuel's tone lowered and he glanced toward the entrance before resting his stare once more. "When we arrived back, Tristan broke into a violent panic. His eyes opened only once to look into mine and he said: 'He'll find me, don't let him in'. Then his eyes closed over and his struggles died away. He slept for three days and three nights without sound nor stir".

"I wish I could have found you", Eleanor whispered.

"You did", I whispered back.

"Forgive me, Tristan", Samuel continued. "But there is something I did not tell you. A man came here that same night asking to see you. Were it not for those last-spoken words, I may well have let him in. But Tristan, this man, I did not trust. He was a dark soul, his face shrouded by a hat..."

"A Stetson".

"Yes", Samuel nodded. "You know him?"

"I don't remember much before waking up in this house, just bits and pieces, flashes of those awful creatures, but the man you speak of, Samuel, he has visited me since... out there in Jerusalem".

"I did not know this, Tristan".

"No matter. I managed to lose him, but there are things out there and they are not afraid of the light of day. I fear I'm starting to lose sight of what is real and what I may be imagining".

"You are safe here, Tristan, let that be the only thing you imagine right now. Remember, this place was built on love, evil takes a strong aversion to such a place. I have seen this many times".

"I should like to stay in a place that was built on love", said Eleanor, spending a long stare upon me. "Do you have a room for me, Samuel?"

"My dear, you are in luck, as the room beside our friend Tristan has just been vacated. You will find it very much to your liking". Samuel led us to the room and unlocked it with the turn of a large key. The door drifted open and he offered out his arm. "Sleep well, Eleanor, friend of Tristan". Samuel turned to me and placed his hand on my shoulder. "Tristan, try to get some sleep, though I fear you cannot. Just remember my promise. You are safe in this house. Evil shall never breach these walls".

"Thank you Samuel, you are the best of men".

He nodded. "Until the morning, my friends", bowing theatrically, he descended the stairs. I stared at the floor, wondering what horrors awaited me this night.

Eleanor popped her head from behind the door. She was smiling. "Tristan, go to your balcony", she said and vanished.

Her enchanting smile extinguished the dread in my loins and I unlocked the room. Pushing open the veranda doors, the night air flooded in with the sounds of the world. There she was, stood on her balcony.

"I like it here". Leaning over the rail and breathing in, she asked, "how long have you been here, Tristan?"

"Almost three months".

"You've been here that long and I've only just found you?"

"You were looking for me?"

"Didn't I say we are all looking for something?"

"I think I said that".

"You did". She bowed her head. "Sometimes we forget what it is". She looked at me coyly, "but it remains always deep inside".

"Have you ever forgotten?"

"No, never". She neared the edge of my balcony. I stepped closer to the edge of hers.

"Eleanor, what have I forgotten?" I whispered almost. Her face was within touching distance of my own. Our lips would have met, but she spoke.

"You should sleep now, my Tristan". She stepped back. "Tomorrow is a new day".

I nodded. "It's not tomorrow I'm afraid of... goodnight, Eleanor".

"Goodnight, Tristan", she said, taking slow steps backwards. Her silhouette disappeared behind the glass doors as they drew to a close. I looked up to the full moon in the sky, closed my eyes and opened them again. "I'm still here... alive".

My eyelids creaked to a close almost the moment my head touched the pillow.

Oh Brother, Where Art Thou?

My mother called out to me in the dark. "Tristan, Tristan, it's time to come in". I hid behind a tree and watched her look about the gardens. My chuckles almost gave me away as I pretended to be a lion—stealthy, invisible to its prey, crawling along behind the foliage lining the apartment. Mum paced around the wall near the bushes. "Tristan, Tristan, where have you gone?"

I sprang out with a roar, shaping my fingers into claws. Mother yelped and stumbled backwards, but a veiled relief set about her face and she almost smiled, not a moment later.

"That's not funny, Tristan. When I call out your name, you come to me at once. Do you hear me?" she said, taking my arm and leading me into the apartment.

"Sorry, mum".

"Don't be sorry, just come running next time". Mum stooped down. "I suppose it was a little funny". She kissed a tissue in her hand and wiped the apparent muck from my face that always seemed to accumulate each time I stepped outdoors. Sometimes I wondered if this muck actually existed or if it was just something mothers did to their sons when they were too short to reach the mirror on the wall.

Father was standing at a breakfast counter, pouring red wine from a bottle into two glasses. "Scaring your mother again, Tristan?" he asked, looking up from the drinks.

"Dad, you really shouldn't have", cheekily reaching for one of the wine glasses. Mother pinched the hood attached to my jacket and made me walk on the spot.

My father chuckled and took the glasses out of reach. "Not for a long time, boyo. I catch you with wine and it'll be your last drink in this world". He smiled and handed my mother a glass. They stood shoulder to shoulder near the door that lay ajar, gazing out to the Hellenic coastline.

A fist plowed into my arm, causing me sharp pain. My brother stood grinning widely, his rose-red cheeks and wood-chip freckles reaching out to me, gleaming, almost. And my blood simply exploded. I lunged for him, but he somehow yanked my hood up and over my head so it engulfed my face. His giggles danced around me as I swung my fists blindly through the air. The hood loosened when I drew it back to find him burrowing between my father's legs on his hands and knees. I chased behind him, but our parents had already intervened.

"Will you two stop fighting—we are on holiday to relax. We didn't come here to watch you boys fight", my mother said, taking the scruff of my jacket. Dad seized my brother's arm and pulled him up from the ground.

"He punched me in the arm", I seared, pointing at my brother. He grinned and arched his body so that he peered from beside our father's knee, fingers grasped around his shin and smiling like a Cheshire cat.

"No, that's not true Tristan". He looked up to my mother with angelic innocence. The petty injustice in my loins broke forth and

I cried and laughed at the same time. "Oh, I'm gonna get you for this".

We left the apartment and crossed the gardens beside the tepid hotel pool, where the towel-strewn sun loungers were scattered. My mind danced with the fun my brother and I had competing who could do the most flips in the air before hitting the water. He'd won, of course, but only because I'd let him... I think. He was trundling along, holding my father's hand and he noticed me watching him. He screwed his face up and pulled a tongue. I pulled one back and we laughed. I wasn't really going to get him, he was my brother. I loved him and besides that, he was great company. The best actually.

'Spyros' - the neon sign, appeared through the overhanging trees in the street at the bottom of the hill. The cool warmth of the restaurants lining the street crept out with the smells of seafood and tapered laughter. The four of us sat and ate and laughed the way we always had. And after dinner, my brother and I—as always in time immemorial—darted from the table and ventured beyond the clay walls to watch the adults drink and stumble around the quaint town.

"Tristan, here's a good one", my brother grinned. He approached a wandering couple and stood in front of them. I chuckled and skipped beside him. He produced our camera and clutched it behind his back. "Could I interest you in..." he began, as bold as brass. The couple halted and giggled. "Aww", the pretty girl said, arching into her companion's ear.

"...Shock and awe, suckers", my brother shrieked, thrusting the camera into their bemused faces. The flash exploded as he pushed the button. The couple for a moment lit up in an astonished grimace that sent the two of us into sustained laughter. We scrambled away behind a white villa and down into a mass of forest we used as a haven from our victims.

I picked up a branch and threw it down into the ravine. "Oh brother, their faces were priceless", twisting around. My brother was gone. "Hey, that's not funny, are you there?" I froze and listened quietly. "Where have you gone?" I whispered. A snap and a crack emerged behind me and my foot gave way. I slid over the edge of the ravine, grasping and clawing at the mossy ground as I went. My fingers caught a vine and entwined themselves, but it soon began to tear slowly away from the rock. My eyes darted around me in terror, desperately trying to find something else to cling to. "Oh no", I gasped as the shaft of the vine reached snapping point. Looking down, I saw a sheer drop into a green mist of plants and rocks, with little else to break such a fall. I attempted to snatch at a thorny bush sitting precariously on the edge of the ravine, but the moment I moved, the vine severed. My body hung in the air for a surreal moment, as if time had stopped. The pit of my stomach ignited with a feeling of indescribable fear and the realization of what was happening screeched beneath my chest like fingernails down a chalkboard.

Time resumed. The one thing other than this fall, nothing could halt. Though simultaneously, a hand flashed over the edge, grabbing mine not a moment too soon. My descent faltered and became a gradual slipping, skin grinding against skin. Another hand reached out and my brother's face loomed over the edge, bearing an almighty grimace. "There's something not right, Tris. I think there is someone here with us", he said, straining with all his might.

"Who is here with us? What do you mean?" I struggled my words out.

"Where did you go, Tristan?"

"I could ask you the same thing".

"Tristan, I can't hold you. What are we gonna do?"

"I don't know, I'm scared". My voice broke and I felt my brittle legs dangle into the nothingness. I gasped, "it's too far down to fall, I won't make it".

My brother saw the tears welling in my eyes and heaved with all the might in his bones. His own eyes, in contrast, burned with fire and the veins in his neck and temple pulsated. With gritted teeth, he heaved against the ravine edge. He had always been stronger than me, strong as an Ox, but his effort now was Herculean. My body gradually rose as he pulled, lifting my entire weight, and my wrists now scraped the edge of the ravine. "Almost there", I said, pinching my fingers against the soggy moss. "I don't know how you're doing this, but don't..."

34

My lips froze when a dark figure leered over his shoulder and snatched him away. Bare hands were mine, no longer attached to my brother's. He was gone and the descent began with breathtaking momentum. I don't remember making a sound, because the fear and dread in my stomach chewed up any murmur my chest may have held. The wind whipped past my ears quickly and the world became a green blur.

I awoke in motion. The ground was moving beneath me, branches and leaves whizzed over me, slapping and prodding me in the face and arms. My head continuously bobbed over bumps in the ground and dragged up my spine, jaggedly tearing at my clothes. My eyes widened when a rock ran under me and struck the back of my skull with such force, causing my eyes to wince acutely as my skull rang like a church bell. A hooded figure was pulling me by the leg through the forest. Sharp, spindly fingers were gripped around my ankle, yanking me through the undergrowth.

"Tristan", a voice shot up in the distance. My brother's voice. Unmistakable.

The figure halted on hearing the voice and squeezed my ligaments tightly. I looked up to the surrounding layers of forest, snatching hurried glances in an attempt to spot his face. My brother called my name again, only this time closer. The figure sniffed at the air like a bedraggled hound and mumbled something inaudible.

"Down here", I cried through cupped hands. The claws latched to my ankle squeezed tighter, causing me to cry something other than for my brother, for I thought my skin would break and the bones shatter, such was the searing force. The figure continued on, dragging me out onto the beach and along the sand, to the entrance of a cave, where a dim light crept along its inner walls like a dancing jester.

"Let go of me, you old…" I struggled against the stone blocks leading into the cave. A full moon was the last thing I glimpsed before being swallowed up by the cavernous hole in the rock. Deeper still, the cloaked figure dragged me down a tunnel with fire torches and bones hanging from the walls and ceiling. We stopped beside a cage and the stranger excitedly jangled a set of keys about before thrusting one into the rusty lock. The cage opened with a creak and I was bowled in like a rag doll.

I seized the bars and pushed my face between them. "Let me out of here. You can't just go around locking children up in cages". The figure turned slowly and disrobed before advancing towards me.

"Silence", the unsightly crone shrieked. Her green fingers wrapped around mine and squeezed them tightly. A large and crooked nose, with a blackened wart on the end protruded through the cage bars, almost poking me in the face had I not ducked. And her thick, greasy tresses cascaded down a grotesque boil and sore-laced frame. Black beady eyes locked to mine and a corroded tongue coiled out from her lips and licked them, as though appetized by my very presence.

"You... will... be... silent... boy", she hissed slowly. "Such fear", she cackled, "how delicious". Her tongue receded back into her rancid mouth with a chuckle. "You know, oh yes, you know why you are here, boy. Pure of heart as you are, you will restore it". She forced her decrepit features against the bars so her skin almost perforated. "You will restore it, boy. Twill be mine".

I backed away to the rear of the cage and cringed at the detestable face. "I don't know what you're talking about, but my brother will find me. You heard him calling for me. My father will be with him and when they do... you'll be sorry".

The crone broke the smoky air with a long and lingering cackle. "No one is coming for you, my sweet boy. Even if they do, they won't find you", her laughter simmered. "Your bones? Perhaps, but long after today, when they are old and dank, like my own". She stood stark-naked and her skeletal body crept away, down a dark passage. My skin crawled and a tear ran from my eye.

A face peered silently through the bars of a cage beside mine. I blinked rapidly and wiped away my tears. The face climbed the shadows of the flames of a torch on the dripping cave wall, pale and pretty. Freckles dotted her face and her eyes glistened in the firelight. Strands of jet hair clung to her cheeks and her lips shaped to move. "Tristan".

"How do you know my name?"

"You look like a Tristan. I'm right, aren't I? Your name is, Tristan".

"You can't look like a Tristan. People don't look like their names... do they?"

"Maybe not". Her eyes looked up at the ceiling and she smiled. "But I still knew yours, didn't I?"

"I suppose you did".

"She hasn't hurt you, has she, Tristan? You tell me if she has and..."

"No, I'm okay, I guess. But I can't say I care too much for being locked in a cage". I lowered my voice and leaned through the bars. "What is she going to do with us?"

"What do you do, Tristan?" she asked, studying me.

"What do I do? I don't do anything. I'm a kid like you. I go to school".

"I am a kid like you, aren't I?" She grinned broadly. "I bet we are the same age", she said. "I knew we would meet".

"How did you know we would meet?" I asked. "How could you?"

She bowed her head and smiled. "Oh, nothing, ignore me... I think I have been locked up in this cage far too long". She reached for a strip of her matted hair and stretched it out, "look", her face screwed up amusingly. "Stiff as a board".

I stared at her and couldn't help but smile. "Who are you?"

Her face softened and she peered closely between the bars. "Your friend, if you'll let me be". Her large eyes glistened in the firelight and she smiled.

"Friends". Our hands met and we shook on it.

The smile was replaced by an open mouth and two incredibly wide eyes. "Tristan, how will you remember me if we lose one another?" She squeezed my hand.

"I won't forget you, how could I?"

"No, Tristan, you will forget me in time".

"Not if I write your name down in my books, on my walls, on my desk, too. That way, I could never forget your name".

"Write it down?" she asked curiously.

"Sure".

"Do you like to write names?"

"Names, stories, anything really".

"You are a writer?"

"Maybe one day, when I grow up", I sighed.

She smiled and shook my hand again. "Then promise me you will write my name down so that you won't forget it. Promise me you will write about me in your books".

"I promise. There's just one problem".

"What's that?"

"You haven't told me your name".

"My name is... Eleanor".

The crone returned, scrambling along the walls and clawing at the stone as she went. She carried a glass jar speckled with dust and dirt. I curled myself into the corner of the cage tightly and closed my eyes, but the cage door began to rattle wildly. I clung to the bars and prayed.

"Boy, open your eyes or I'll pluck them out like pickles", her voice rasped, spittle raining over me. I opened my eyes for fear of the threat and saw her horrible features pressed against the gate. "Come closer, my sweet".

"No, I won't".

She reached into the cage with a skinny, decomposing arm and elongated her fingers to within an inch of me. Her forefinger appeared to stretch and dislocate from the joint, allowing it to bridge the gap. The serrated nail scraped my leg. "Come closer to me, boy", gargling croaks and sputum escaped her flaking lips, "come closer". I slapped her hand away from me and crawled to the opposite corner of the cage. The hag cried out with blusterous rage and withdrew her arm. She shook the cage gate ruefully and rounded the bars like a scorpion. Her joints snapped in and out of their sockets and her grey hair wound around the rusty bars like jellied eels.

"Leave me alone".

"Do not be afraid, child", she hissed, "there is something you must do for me". Her features calmed, eyes narrowing. "If you want to leave here alive, you will do as I ask". Her eyes suddenly widened into milk-white ovals, veins of black and blue pulsated across her forehead and her voice rose again, sharply. "If you do not, your family will never see you again, not in one piece. They will find your eyes in the trees". She gestured with a claw skywards, "your arms festering in the lapping tides there yonder, and your legs buried, toes poking like blackbirds from beneath the salty sands". She pointed at me through the cage. "Your insides will be spread out across the beach for the gulls to feast on". She licked her lips. "And your heart... I shall eat your heart from within", she crowed, running her tongue along a set of sharp teeth. "Oh, yes, I will keep the heart just for me. The tastiest part of a little boy is the heart, everybody knows that".

"I haven't done anything", I cried. "Please let us go". My eyes darted around in desperation. "I won't tell anyone, I promise".

She held the jar against the bars. "Give me your hand, boy". Inside the jar was a withered and blackened stem of a flower bearing a single white petal. "Give it to me", she wailed, her fingers clapping impatiently. But a glimpse of the girl in the cage, she was picking at the lock on the gate. She looked at me and pressed her finger to her lips.

I slowly offered my hand towards the crone, drawing from her a rotten smile. "Yes, that's right, child", her fingers twitched excitedly. "That's it, come to me... closer... closer". My fingers gravitated towards the jar and the petal began to glow through the dark, speckled glass. "A little closer, just a little closer", the hag whispered. My fingers touched the glass and the petal ignited into white flames, and before long, I watched more petals begin to form from dormant black buds along the stem.

"What's happening?" I whimpered.

The crone drooled and cackled excitedly. Her eyes gleamed in the face of the petals and she stared maniacally at the flower. "It's happening", she crowed in awe. Suddenly, her features contorted and her eyes widened and flicked to her left. Eleanor had escaped and was standing over the witch, holding a fire torch raised above her head. Before the crone could muster, the girl rapped the blunt torch over her skull, igniting her locks into roaring flames. The crone screamed and dropped the jar to the ground. She began leaping backwards, and while she held her face in cupped hands, the rest of her body combusted into a roaring inferno.

"Burn, you mean old witch", Eleanor cried.

"No, no, no", she screamed, her cries echoing throughout the cavern.

The girl continued battering the torch furiously across the witch, swatting and prodding her away from my cage. The crone rushed around blindly on the spot and bolted, crashing headlong into the cave wall with a terrible crack. She dropped to the floor in a glowing fetal shape, trembling against the sand and mumbling as she burned. Eleanor dropped the torch and looked at the flower on the ground, just lying there, exposed, surrounded by the broken shards of the glass container. The petals had multiplied and were glowing brightly and the stem pulsated with green life. I was drawn to the wonder and found myself reaching to touch it.

"Don't touch it, Tristan", Eleanor snapped, approaching the cage. She knelt before the wonder. "You must not restore it, or he will come".

I quickly drew my hand back. "Who will come?"

Eleanor unlocked my cage with the keys and opened the gate slowly. "You cannot touch it", she took my hand, "come out carefully. Be sure not to touch anything", guiding me from my prison. "We must destroy what remains before it can be restored".

"But it's just a flower?"

"No, Tristan", she surged closer still. "It is not *just* a flower". A scream shot around the cave and we twirled to see the crone's body had vanished. "Oh, no", Eleanor gasped, rushing to the wall and plucking down another torch. "Tristan, we must burn it now and bury the ashes".

Out from the darkness, a skeletal figure rushed into Eleanor and knocked her down. The charred remains of the crone had re-animated, the whites of her eyes emanating from her crispy, smoldering features. "No", the hag screamed, grappling me to the ground beside the blossoming flower. We rolled over and over along the sandy floor of the cave. I managed to pin her down, but out from her rancid mouth rushed a geyser of black sludge and vomit that crashed into my face. Gasping for breath, I rubbed my eyes, but she had already dragged me away before I could see again. My eyes opened and saw the crone clutching the flower and screaming with delighted and detestable squeals.

"No", Eleanor screamed—she was running towards us—she was too late. The crone forced my trembling fingers against the stem of the flower and squeezed them closed over the petals. A bright light enveloped the cave and the ground shuddered and rumbled. The crone snatched the flower back again and raised her fingers into the air, and with burning rage she thrust her claws into my stomach. The witch wailed triumphantly. Staring deep into my eyes, she said cruelly: "Sleep now, my child. Go to sleep".

Liquid spewed out from my throat and over my lips and I spluttered violently, choking on my own pulsing retches. The bitterness rasped upon my mind; cold iron was the taste on my tongue.... it couldn't be blood, could it? Touching my lips with numb fingertips, my sight faded into a crimson and misty vision. My hands were bloodied and my eyes welled with painful tears. I couldn't understand what was happening. What had I done? My stomach hurt so bad and an awful coldness set about my skin and bones.

The crone showed me her crimson claws, face glowing, and her rotten, burnt teeth chattering – eyes alive with my own harrowing reflection. I watched the blood drip down onto my chest in large droplets that splashed about a growing pool. The flower held aloft, bright and wondrous, against the cave ceiling, 'twas beautiful and the rays from the petals numbed my pain. The crone's head detached from her sloping shoulders with a swipe, unleashing a jet-spray of yellow slime across the cave walls. It rolled along the ground and came to rest on its ear. The eyes remained wide and shocked, but they did not blink. Dead eyes.

"Tristan", Eleanor pushed the crone's body away. "Tristan", she cried, looking into my eyes.

"Eleanor, what's happening to me... Eleanor?" I spluttered, as the sound of hooves thudding against stone bleated at my mind and thundered into the cavern around us. The neighing of a horse echoed in my ears and stung at them like a swarm of invading bees.

"Tristan, I'm so sorry, you're... you're bleeding", she touched my face. Her eyes had welled, and a tear drop escaped the corner of one of them, running down her face and landing in my blood. "You are dying, Tristan". She scrambled across the sand and retrieved the flower from the crone's body. "He has come to collect". Eleanor fired agitated glances around the cave, as if expecting something. Something imminent. Something terrible.

"Eleanor, I don't want to die down here. Please don't let me die down here".

She lowered over me and kissed my lips. And her own lips shimmered with my blood. "You don't have to die, Tristan. I won't let you", she whispered.

"Help me, Eleanor", I whispered back, feeling the big sleep beginning to creep slowly upon me.

The sound of clopping hooves drilled the cave floor from the passage I'd entered and the whole place erupted with the squeals of what sounded like a pig being butchered. Eleanor plucked a petal from the flower and put it on my lips. "Consume this petal, Tristan", she said, and placed the flower over my chest. "Septumerus hernokshai, velesuman", she spoke the strange words before placing a petal into her own mouth.

The Horseman burst through the cavern entrance and loomed over us. His arm drew forth a long blade that darkened the cave walls with its shadow.

Eleanor threw herself down over me and squeezed tightly against my chest and the flower. "Find me", she whispered in my ear. His arm came down over us and she cried out, "Eloptrimus, Nellium". White light engulfed our world and the furor fell to a silence.

I awoke with a start, "No". My eyes opened. There was a figure sitting on the edge of the bed, facing the veranda. Eleanor. My arm was reaching and rested upon her shoulder, her two hands were clasped over my hand, holding it against her soft skin. She was still and silent, her head bowed. The veranda doors were wide open and the curtains ghosted around the room in the night air. The moon sat in the black sky, huge and luminous.

42

"I remember", I whispered. "But it was a dream, a nightmare".

"No, Tristan… it was not", she said without turning to me. "I'm sorry".

"The years I spent believing that night was just a dream. So many times I wished and prayed you be real. You are the girl who haunted my dreams for years afterwards. It broke my heart I would never find you".

"I am sorry, Tristan", she whispered.

"Why do you say that? Please don't be sorry, not for anything".

"Because it was I who burdened you with this curse. Tristan, you were never meant to touch that rotten flower. I was supposed to change your fate, our fate... it was all supposed to end that night… but I lost you". She bowed her head deeper.

I arched myself up and put my hand on her opposite shoulder. "You have nothing to be sorry for, Eleanor. It was you who saved me from that witch and brought me back".

"No, Tristan, you don't understand. You were never to touch the flower. We were supposed to destroy it. We were supposed to run. Just you and I. Together. Instead, I allowed her to mortally wound you. It is because of me they stalk you".

"No, Eleanor. Whatever we were supposed to do that night no longer matters. I understand one thing and that is, I am alive today because of you… nothing else matters anymore, just that we are alive. Don't you see? Nothing matters except we both live and breathe right at this moment, in this moment, you are real and I am alive. Tis far greater a thing than I could have ever hoped for".

Her hands tightened over mine and she turned her head to look at me. "I have searched for you since that night".

"And I, you". She tilted her head and kissed my hands, "I just didn't know it". There was a long silence as she lay her cheek on my arm and closed her eyes. I watched her and wondered... "What happened that night, Eleanor, when we were children?"

"We found each other again", she whispered back, leaning against me and lifting her legs onto the bed. I held her around the stomach and we lay down beside one another. Our fingers entwined.

43

"Again?"

"Tristan", she whispered.

"Yes?"

"Can I tell you something?"

"Anything", I whispered back.

"I was not always this way… I am from another place, not like this one or any you would have seen. From this place, I escaped long ago to find something, just like you, Tristan. I found something I had wanted for the longest time".

"What did you find?" I exhaled, less than a whisper.

"Life…" she stopped short, and a short silence ensued. "I saw you, always from afar. Maybe you can see me?" And with this whisper, she turned to face me and held my hands. "Tristan, can you see me?" Her eyes grew dark and her pupils glinted sharply, like mirrors, "can you see me?" she whispered against my lips.

The world turned black and spiraling shapes of red and blue whirled in an abyss of shooting stars. I emerged from the blackness and into the sparkling snow fall of the sky. A window to a hospital where a baby cried grew closer. My fingers pressed against the glass, toes floating on the ledge beneath.

Whispers ghosted into my ear from the snowfall all around me. *Eleanor, Eleanor,* they said. The parents seemed to nod in agreement, and they smiled at their creation. The window melted away and I fell from the ledge down and down with the cold flakes. The road below me was layered with snow and my feet touched softly down. Yet another window lay beyond a garden. I stepped through the gate and pressed my fingers against the windowpane, where a warm, lovely atmosphere soaked through the glass from the other side.

The whispering returned, *"Eleanor"*. A little girl ran through the room and was snatched up by a doting mother. Father sat in the chair by the fire with a mug. *Eleanor,* the name came once more, but this time from the cold… outside with me in the darkness. The voice that spoke it was screechy and searing. The evil whispers from the cold world outside the house began rasping her name repeatedly.

Two figures, ghostly in essence, materialized from the snow. White gowns that crawled about their hidden feet reached out to me with each step, their faces staring and piercing from behind flowing locks, pale and cold. *Eleanor, Eleanor,* they hissed. The two girls levitated towards me and I froze as they passed within me and beyond the glass into the house. Fear and dread saturated my being and I turned to look through the window. But before I could, a force took me away again, raising me up into the air among the icicles that were so large and ornate, magnified many times to become wonderful intricacies.

Screams tore from the house, screams that ripped into me with terror. Screams that shattered the wonderful snowflakes dancing about my face. I was powerless to intervene, but left to float there above the house just as the snowfall did. Licks of fire smashed through the windows from the inside and leapt out onto the snow, only to be followed by others wilder and hotter. The two figures emerged from the home, dragging the little girl with them. They tore at her arms and drew her down the garden path, but she broke free and escaped back into the growing inferno. Their murderous shrieks reached up to me in the heavens as they pursued the little girl with grasping claws.

I rose up, higher, up and up and up, until the snowflakes became one and the little house and its flames I could no longer see. The cold and snow dissipated around me and my toes lowered to the wet sand with whipping waves and a lapping tide. I was ghosted into the dark cave I felt I knew somehow. The young girl from the house, a little older now. She was slumped in a cage and a hunched figure shrouded by a hood stood over her.

"Eleanor, you should never have let yourself become like them. You do not belong here", the figure moaned.

The girl seized bravely at the bars of her cage, "I am one of them. I am like them in every way", she challenged. "I have parents, a family… I am a child, just look at me", she cried. "I am human".

The hag reached for the gate. "Your parents are dead. Wiped out by your sisters. Your family is gone", she squealed. "You are no more human than the rocks of this place, you will never live as one of them. They will not accept you. The boy will never see you as you want him to".

"Yes, he will", Eleanor cried with an ancient pain in her young voice.

"No, false child. He is a mortal, a human, a weak being without courage. He will reject you", the hag cackled. "You gave up immortality, the promise of the eternal, powers they can only dream of... and for what? To be born into a frail shell of an existence that crumbles evermore with each moon, each sunrise".

"I..." Eleanor began.

The witch raised a disgusting finger and began sniffing the air rabidly. "The boy is close", she crowed.

Eleanor reached through the bars, "Don't you..."

"Quiet". The witch turned and dawdled out excitedly.

I touched down beside Eleanor's cage and watched her. She rested her forehead against the bars and sighed, despairingly it seemed. She could not see me. I tried to touch her face but the world dissolved around us and the blackness reigned once more. Cold, dark and desolate.

My eyes opened to bright sunlight and an airy breeze. Her sweet scent still hung in the air. But she was gone, the room was empty. I was alone again.

"Tristan, are you there, Tristan?" a voice came from below my balcony. It wasn't Samuel's. I rubbed my eyes and stumbled outside into the intense sunshine. There, below was her angelic face looking up at me. I smiled and did well to contain the wondrous feeling running up from my stomach and into my chest cavity, a sensation that would have forced even the hardiest to smile, surely. "I thought you had left me".

"Me? Never", she smiled back. "Samuel told me to give you this". She threw up an orange.

I captured it in both hands. "Thank you", a smile ever widening on my face.

"Are you ready to leave this place?"

"Where will we go?"

"Cairo", she replied, drawing a waterfall of locks from her eyes.

"What's in Cairo?"

"The first steps of a journey we must take. Gather your things, Tristan, we leave at sundown".

I placed my belongings into my backpack, swung it over my shoulder and stood at the door. Looking back, I watched the curtains twirl in the breeze, the impressions on the bed from our bodies, and the mirror I thought would be my eternal waking moment, forever watching my fears and nightmares. "So long".

Samuel greeted me at his fruit stall. "Today is the day you leave, Tristan", he said warmly.

"I guess it is, Samuel", nearing him. "Samuel, I want to thank you…"

"Tristan, my dear friend, it is not necessary, for you are always welcome here. Though you could do me one service in return.

"Anything".

"Tell all you meet that my house is a good place to stay. Tell them it is a house that was built on love, and that it is a sanctuary from evil. This is all I ask... for then we will have both fulfilled our debt of gratitude".

I nodded. "Of course, Samuel. It would be nothing short of the truth". We embraced in a hug. Eleanor approached and watched us.

"Ah, your beautiful companion awaits you", Samuel chuckled. She smiled and it made me smile. We began our journey into the street. "Tristan…" I spun around. "One for the road, my friend". He tossed an orange to me. "Stay safe, and remember, my brother", he winked, "never stop fighting your fears".

I held up the orange and nodded with a smile. "Always", I said... for that fight may never end.

"Eleanor, is it okay if we make a stop?"

"Yes, what is it?"

"Just something I need to do".

She nodded, "Okay".

I led Eleanor to the bar I'd encountered the man in the Stetson. The door was open and music coming from inside.

"Hello", I knocked on the door. Eleanor stood behind me and looked over my shoulder.

The barman's face appeared from beneath the bar. He stood and tossed aside a towel. "You're not welcome here, ya crazy".

"Sorry". We both twisted away back into the street as though some invisible force propelled us.

Eleanor skipped behind me and took my arm. "Who was that?" she asked.

"Nobody, El. Just a fella who doesn't want any trouble, that's all". I felt relief that the man in the Stetson hadn't killed him. I would surely have blamed myself.

"You called me, El", she replied with a glint in her eye.

"I did. You don't like it?"

Her eyes scouted the sky and once more locked to mine. "I do", she smiled.

"El..." I hesitated, "last night you were in my dreams. I saw what happened to you".

"I know you did, Tristan. I wanted to show you". She stepped closer. "You and I, just as it will always be".

Watching the universe swirl in her eyes, boundless, endless. "You and I".

We returned to the church of the Holy Sepulcher, to the little room I had awoken. Eleanor removed a wooden panel in the corner of the room and retrieved a small rucksack from a hidden compartment.

"Now, neither of us will be alone". Her smile radiated my insides, hastening the butterflies to a daze. She led me out into the garden and unlocked a large oak door veiled by ivy. Inside was a library with stained glass windows that lent spears of light across the endless walls of books. The shelves climbed so high; the patrons had employed several of those wheeled ladders in order to climb the upper tiers. A large wooden table dominated the center of the room and all manner of objects lay upon the red felt surface.

"El, whatever is that thing?" I asked, pointing at a brass-colored canister with canvas straps attached to either end.

She picked up the straps and wrapped them over her shoulders. "This, Tristan, is for your protection". She reached down for a hose with a nozzle that fed from the canisters and squeezed, sending a stream of water tearing from the end. "Holy water", she grinned. I stepped back and covered my face. "Do not be afraid, Tristan, tis not harmful to you or I". "What about this?" I picked up what looked like a torch. "Is this just a torch?"

"Not just any torch", she smiled and took it from me. "This torch has a lens forged from crystallized shards of the rock of Skelendor".

"The rock of where?"

"Shine light through this lens, and there are things out there that will find it quite upsetting". She angled it towards me and flicked the switch. "Not lethal to you either, Tristan".

I turned and walked towards the books on the shelves behind me. "Those things that follow me", I muttered, running a finger down the golden spine of a book, the woven letters read: The Sacred Female by R.W. Moonstruck...

"Tristan", she neared me from behind and touched my shoulder. "Where we must go, you may never return from. But if you do not want to go, then I want you to know that you do not have to. I will stay with you. We can run together. Where you are, I will be. We would never be safe and your nightmares would follow you forever. But we would be together".

I turned to look upon her face, her eyes held a sadness that plucked at my deepest sorrow. "Eleanor, tell me there is a chance we could live without this fear, that we could go home together and live... just live".

"We could never do that if we run". The sorrow in her eyes deepened among the swirling nebula.

"Then I don't want to run anymore. I've been running all my life. I want to know what follows me. I want to know what I must do".

"I will show you, Tristan. Together, we shall seek your destiny".

"Thank you, Eleanor". I sat down and looked up at the wonderful colors reflecting through the stained glass. Shafts of light reached down to me and drew out my curiosities. "Eleanor, what did the witch mean when she said you should not have let yourself become like them?" Eleanor looked away as though

49

ashamed, her eyes met the ground and she stood silent. "It's okay, I didn't mean…" I started, but she looked at me again with those eyes.

Leaning forward, her expression held a yearning, "Tristan, I am human now, you must believe me, as human as you are. But do I belong here?" Her eyes lowered once more and she continued quietly, "I don't know".

I reached across and held her hand in mine. "I don't understand, El. Why wouldn't you belong here?"

Her eyes lifted once more and met my own. "A long, long time ago, before I came here, before I found my way to you, there was a place called Delphi. A place where destinies could be read. Delphi was home to three oracles whose beauty and wisdom was said to be so potent that no man, woman or immortal, could resist visiting them. One day my sisters and I fell upon this place where all at once the oracles seized upon us in an attempt to spoil our futures. They knew who we were and so attempted to turn us against one another by whispering lies… lies laced with truths among my sisters and I. Two of my sisters fought them off and fled, refusing to listen any longer and pleading with the rest of us to follow. But I could not leave and chose to stay beside my two remaining sisters. Darkness had been cast over our spirits and we craved to know, to seek out what lay ahead…" Eleanor closed her eyes and then opened them slowly. "When it was revealed, what we saw divided us forever".

"What did you see?" I whispered.

"My sisters recoiled in horror at the monsters they were to become, their very spirits blackened, vengeful, fury driven by the descension of their divination into deplorable evil".

"You are no monster, nor are you evil", I edged towards her in an attempt to coax her spirit to brighten.

"My sisters and I were so divided… because we did not all share the same fate".

"Then what did you see?"

"You. I saw you, Tristan".

I didn't know what to say, searching her eyes for reason, for truth. "Why me?"

"I don't know, Tristan, but after our revelations, I left my sisters and cast them from my mind. All I knew since that day was that I had to find you".

"Delphi and the oracles, your sisters, how long ago did all this happen?"

"A very long time ago, Tristan. So long ago, you will not find it in any book", she looked about the countless titles surrounding us.

"Eleanor, if not human. Then what were you?"

"Does it matter?" She squeezed my hand and arched closer to me so that I could feel her breath against my face. "Do you really need to know someone other than who I am today, the little girl you found when you were a little boy, she's still here.... I'm still here". She pressed my palm against her heart. "Tristan, my heart beats like yours. My soul loves like yours... my blood runs through my veins so I can help you find what you are looking for... this is who I am now. I am a mortal asking you to look upon her as only this".

I Nodded and smiled, "You and I, just as it will always be".

"You and I, Tristan". Her request commanded me seamlessly and my heart ran warm. She touched upon my face. "There is something I want to give you, Tristan. Can you wait for me?" We stood together and she extended herself onto her tip toes and kissed my lips softly. My eyes closed, the kiss lingered for a sweet moment and then she left. I opened my eyes to the empty room.

For the first time in my life, I felt good butterflies in my stomach, light creatures that tickled. I wondered if they were a sign. Do people get this feeling when they find that person who...

A loud crash from the stained-glass window shattered the peaceful silence. The euphoria collapsed around me like a house of cards in a storm, and a creepy laughter syphoned in through the broken window. The door Eleanor left through creaked jaggedly and swung open.

"Eleanor", I called through trembling lips. Another *first* struck me. The first time my own safety, my own well-being was not what I cared most for. A figure stumbled from the shadows clutching the door frame. "Eleanor". My lips trembled again. Her face appeared in the light and she looked at me with those sorrowful eyes. She stumbled towards me as though blind. I was frozen with dread, and grief tore at my insides like a jackal would upon a fresh carcass.

"Tristan", she called out weakly, exhalations riveted to a whisper, her fingers clutching a book to her chest. "Tristan... I..." her other hand was rested over her stomach where a crimson tide was climbing slowly outwards.

"No, please, no", I gasped, running to meet her faltering steps. She collapsed into me, pressing her face against my chest. "Eleanor", but her legs broke and I lowered her body to the floor. Her face was never paler but her eyes were open.

"Tristan... Tristan", her fingers tugged pathetically on my sleeve, "this is what I wanted to give you", spluttering through broken words. "I made it for you when we were children... for your stories, for names... I knew someday I'd find you again". She wheezed and lifted the book from her chest. "It's for you, Tristan".

Tears broke from my eyes and sprinkled upon the book. "Thank you, Eleanor", I whimpered. "I'm so sorry that I forgot to write your name. I forgot about you, just like you said I would".

She shook her head slowly and touched my temple with her blood-soaked forefinger. "Oh, but you didn't, Tristan, don't you see?" Her finger pressed against me gently. "It was written up here all along", she whispered, before her hand slipped away. "Tristan... Tristan, close the door before they... don't let them in, do not allow them in or..." gesturing towards the door she had fallen through. I couldn't leave her side.

"I can't, Eleanor, you have to stay with me".

"You must", she whispered, her hand pressing weakly against my arm. I looked at the door and felt a coldness rush in like spirits. I approached the door and a chuckle broke from the darkness on the other side. Two faces appeared at the doorway, soft female faces with eyes like snakes and hair wavering as though it were submerged beneath water.

"Let us in", one of them sneered, as the other leered forward hissing. "Won't you invite us in? We can help her". I slammed the door shut and pressed my back against the panels. A beating began on the door that shook the wood and reverberated into my bones.

"No, you can't come in. Leave us alone, just leave us alone". I rushed back to Eleanor who reached out to me with harrowing desperation.

"Listen to me, Tristan... there's not much time. You must go to Cairo. There is a man there you can trust, a friend, he can help you". She recoiled again in pain and grasped my hand. "Find him, Tristan. His name is Doctor Rambo, he has a Bazaar in the old city... you must find him. He'll tell you the things you wish to know". Her words became whispers. "He knows who you are". Eleanor's face contorted with pain, her breath growing evermore labored. "I wish I could go with you". She had stained her face with blood from her wandering fingers and they came to rest on my jawline. "Tristan, that night in the cave when we were children, the Lotus flower... he had come. It was the only way to save you. The flower healed your wounds, gave you life again... the flower kept a link between us, but it is a curse to carry the one thing evil will never stop chasing. You had your life to live..." she wept softly and her hand caressed my cheek. "We had our lives to live if I could only find you again..." her words took great effort and summoned yet more blood from her lips.

"And you did, El. You found me". Utterly bursting inside with despair, I smiled.

She smiled. "Yes. I found you, didn't I?" Her eyes dimmed. "To live for a moment beside you, was to never live eternally without you... goodbye, my Tristan", she whispered. Her breath trailed off and her eyes left mine as her head tilted gently to the side.

She was gone.

I was alone again. Deep inside my soul, my good butterflies perished forever under a storm of agony.

"El", clasping her face in my hands. "El, please speak to me again, say something". I was dribbling now, pathetically, and tears streamed from my eyes like rainfall across her bloodied face. "Come back to me, please come back. Say everything will be okay, that it will be just you and I", bowing my face to hers.

"Please say that to me". But nothing stirred and her pretty eyes would never again lock to mine, however I held her. She was no longer behind them. I hugged her into my chest, wrapping my arms tightly around her, wanting to be close to her physically, wanting to hold her so tightly her soul would have nowhere else to go except to climb into my own.

She was cold, so cold. My fingers pressed into the arch of her shoulders and felt little resistance. Her dainty frame began to break into pieces. I opened my eyes to see her mortal body dissolving into countless atoms, thousands of sparkling particles that spiraled and whisked around my head and shoulders. The twisting whirlwind of her spirit danced high above me and rode along the ray of a moon beam that had funneled in through the broken window. I watched the last of her atoms meander and escape through the cracks, into the celestial world descending outside. But something remained, suspended, glowing. Something that did not escape. That something began to flutter back down towards me erratically, like a butterfly. The object came to rest on the book and shone against the leather-bound cover. The petal she'd consumed in the cave that night, our connection for all this time. I picked it up and cupped it in my hands and wished upon wish. I prayed she would reappear through this petal, digging my knuckles against my temple, brutally pressing into my skin. Nothing stirred. No white light. No voice. No Eleanor.

I ran my hand over the rough cover of the book. There was a rising sun carved into the leather at the top and below was an indentation of a long boat with no oars or sails, and, as though commanding the vessel, a long-haired figure sitting at one end, below a blue ribbon. The figure appeared to be looking out for someone or something. I turned the cover over and found an inscription:

The chronicles of Tristan begin here. Some stories need to be written before they are forgotten. Be brave and follow your heart right to the end. I am proud of you, for the courage you will show in the face of what is yet to pass. Thank you for looking for me... thank you for finding me,
Yours always, Eleanor xxx

The words wracked my heart and a volcanic whimper burst from my chest. I cried loudly and freely. The feeling inside was one of dejection, debilitating and ruthless. I lay on the ground and heaved my heavy breath against the cold stone and drifted away.

There were no dreams, no nightmares, nor visions of ghouls or nasty, lamenting witches. Just darkness, sorrowful, all-consuming darkness, for this stood coldest and strongest against the chilling loss of the heart of another. Far and infinitely gloomier a foe is this than myths and monsters.

I awoke to those cold tiles with a depressing shudder. Twas colder for her departure, the world darker, far bleaker in her absence. My breath seared the icy air in plumes, running up to the moonbeam she had left by. The petal was crumpled in my palm, the book beside me. I placed the petal in between the pages and closed them over.

My eyes stung and my lips tasted of iron and salt. My joints were all wrong and my heart was beating so heavily I could hear it, but so slowly, it frightened me. I looked around this place, but my mind was blundering with fear and sorrow. I clutched at the table and pulled myself up to my feet, knocking things to the floor. The objects clattered against the stone and sent me spinning around in fright. Whispers began to flutter around the room, tearing my attention to and fro, window-to-window, door to bookshelf.

"*Tristan, Tristan*", they jangled cruelly. I backed myself against the table and felt around the surface until my fingers brushed something metallic and cold.

The water canisters. I dragged them from the table and drew them over my shoulders. The torch lay beside them. I plucked it from the velvet, aimed at the wall and flicked the switch. A powerful light illuminated the book shelves, sending neon rays shooting across the pages of manuscripts and scrolls high above. Despite this great, the darkness in my heart crept up on me again and brought with it a terrible loneliness to blanket such a thing.

I swung my backpack over my shoulder against the canisters with a clink and made for the door we had both entered together. On the other side, the beautiful garden swayed in the breeze and the moon shone down like a spotlight. There was no smiling face, no bare feet tapering through the grass... the tall gate stood still, as still as her prettiness had been when her eyes closed for the last time. My heart sank further as I took the path I'd chased her not so long ago. I peeped through the knot hole in the wood. There would be no bright eye peering back, no fluttering eyelashes. No sweet laughter. My stomach tightened and I felt like smashing this lonely gate to pieces.

Instead, I drew it open and walked out into the street and ran through the alleys and passages until halting at the archway to the outside world. The world beyond the old Jerusalem sparkled with the illumination of countless homes and the lingering headlights of the city. The world lay out there if only I could just reach out.

Closing my eyes and taking a deep breath. "Thank you, Eleanor... I will find you again", I whispered into the night air. And just like that, I stepped out and through to the other side.

The night was cool, but the atmosphere buzzed with the hot sense of freedom. Danger was all around me, but she had given me purpose, the courage to chase such a delicacy. My palm ground on the handle of the torch and my fingers felt sticky and pained. A howling shot up into the night sky like a rocket. Before me a road, busy with cars and people. There had to be a way to get to the airport from here. I ventured forward but a figure raced out from behind a car and blocked my way. Two more stalked out from behind a wall. *Maybe they were just people, regular people.*

Three pairs of yellow beady eyes immediately ignited and an intense growling simmered on the darkness. I lit up the torch, causing a spread of blinding white beams across all of creation. Their black silhouettes yelped and scattered back into the shadows. I kept the light shining and edged quickly on, but I didn't get far before a sharp pain struck me in the shoulder and pinched my skin tightly. The claws of a jaggedly strong hand scraped beneath my shirt and dragged me to my knees. I swung the torch over my shoulder, but it slipped from my hand and rolled away.

The figure clouted me in the head and knocked me onto my side. A beastly face drooling from gaping jaws leered over me. The hose nozzle was still wound around my arm, so I whipped it up and unleashed a burst of water into the creature's face, causing a painful revolt of hissing and screaming. Wild steam shoots sprayed from its eyes and ears as the figure tore away. Another figure emerged, running at me from my right side just as I rolled and squeezed the nozzle, sending a stream splashing across its torso. Shrieks of horror abound the air as more steam began to rise and fizzle.

I scrambled to my feet and spun around while thrusting the hose nozzle at anything and everything. I grabbed the torch from the floor and bolted for the bright lights. My over-exuberance for flight took me floundering into the road, where oncoming traffic screeched and veered around me. Tires squealed and people screamed. A truck slalomed through the halted cars and headed straight for me.

Frozen in terrified animation, and in the face of bright headlights, listening to the hissing of brakes condensed with the straining hydraulics, I stood watching tons of steel slide along the tarmac towards me. Just when I thought my number was up, a misshapen body flashed into the juggernaut's path... the figure smashed against the grill and was dragged under the wheels. The truck halted against my rigid palms, but its momentum bundled me to the ground, causing me little more than grazed knuckles. The beaming lights of the vehicle blurred and I could see two of the truck still growling and hissing. The driver shot his head from the window and began screaming at me. His door opened and he started to climb down from the cabin, but, as he descended the steps, a smoking arm clawed at his ankles from beneath the wheels.

The driver slipped and stumbled to the ground, crying out as he went. A pair of yellow eyes lit up the dark and two arms emerged and clawed at the ground. Something mangled, something gnarled and steaming, dragged itself from underneath the blood-spattered grill of the truck's cab. The creature that emerged screamed bile across the road, spewing sludge upon the glass-strewn way as it struggled to stand. It soon became clear that its legs had been torn off and the sinewy tendons were all that remained, smearing the tar with bloody trails.

I floundered around for the hose and directed it towards the snarling monstrosity. "Stop", I warned him, but he wasn't listening. "Do you know what this is? It's holy water", I screamed. "You saw what it did to the others. You'll get the same if you don't stop". The contorted face of the monster snarled through concentrated rage, eyes bulging, nostrils flaring, rotten teeth snapping together and chattering. This thing would hear no mercy call. Who knew if it even understood me? Salivating and licking its filthy lips, the creature made for me with evil intent.

"You asked for it", I cried, squeezing the nozzle. Nothing happened. I squeezed again and again, but not so much as a drop dampened the ground. The creature grasped my ankle and dragged itself up my thighs, digging its claws into my skin as it went. I could feel the bloody entrails hanging from the creature's waist as it hoisted itself ever further towards my face. My fingers closed around its throat in a bid to keep its snaking tongue from touching me, rasping out in all directions as drool and slime festered down in strings onto my cheeks.

The torch, 'twas my only chance. I took away one of my hands from the throat of the beast and felt around beside me. My fingers wrapped around the shaft of the torch and I smashed the torch butt twice against its head, spun it around in my palm and pushed the button. The light exploded into the creature's face, illuminating its features with fire. Flames engulfed the squirming entity and created a fireball as roasting flame tips licked and whipped around my chest and face. I forced the creature away, feeling pieces of burning flesh come apart in my hands. Those beady eyeballs popped violently, fizzing oily liquid across the street like party streamers. I rolled to my side, struggling to hold my breath and evade the spattering of stench that fizzed from the skull of the wretched fiend.

This time I wouldn't hang about. I took off and followed the trail at a quickening pace, running with the torch and hose in either hand. They won't get me now. I ran and ran for my life, following the signs for the airport. Never looking back.

The feelings I may once have expected to enjoy at this moment did not surface, each car that went by in the opposite direction, I wanted to flag down and return, return to find Eleanor. I wanted to go back to the place where we had met and sit down and watch the people who might have been there, who might have seen us together. They could all still breathe and enjoy the world, enjoy each other. Why was it Eleanor had to die? *You and I no more.* I wept again. While I ran, so too did my tears.

Exodus

I'd resigned myself to walking a long way back, my feet were sore and angry blisters had formed on my heels and toes. Sweat had dried on my face and was canvassed by fresh sweat that stung at my pores. I was surely lost, surrounded by bright lights that never seemed to get any closer. The world outside the old city walls was bigger than I had remembered. I'd walked by countless sign posts bearing the white shape of a plane, but how many could there have been? Each one caused me to trundle on a little quicker, only to drag on for miles until my feet scraped the ground again. My hope was fading of ever leaving this place.

A coach roared past me and hissed to a halt a little further up. A melee of passengers stepped off, huddled around a man who was hunched over. The man fought through them and made for the edge of the road, where he doubled over and threw up his guts into the undergrowth. Two women rushed behind and stooped over him. Another man in a blue shirt stepped off the bus and lit a cigarette. Some passengers approached the man in the blue shirt and seemed to be acting irately towards him. I approached the scene cautiously and hid near the brake lights of the coach to listen.

"Excuse me, sir, but our flight leaves in…" the voice began, but was cut short by the sound of the man's strained vomiting. The airport, of course. This coach must have been bound for the airport. Some foreign words were exchanged and I peeped around the edge of the bus. The man in the blue shirt was walking towards the near side of the coach. He grasped the handle of the baggage hold and tugged it open. The other passengers followed behind him, nattering away into his ear about flight times.

His voice rose suddenly and he spun around with his hands in the air, cigarette hanging limply from his lips.

"Please, my friends, you will not be late for your flight. Could you all get back on the coach", he pleaded, as the cigarette bobbed with each word and breath.

The poorly man groaned loudly and keeled over onto the floor. This caught everyone's attention and they all took a closer look. The man in the blue shirt flicked his cigarette to the floor, sighed and threw his hands up into the air. The baggage hold was still open. He stared at the floor and placed his hands on his hips. *Come on, man, go and take a look at the chap being sick, everyone else is,* I thought. He sighed again and walked into the crowd, shoving people aside as he went.

Go, Tristan, go now.

I rounded the bus slowly and put my back against the side, edging closer and closer to the hold. A painful groan came from the man and everyone burst into cries and squabbling.

That's my cue. I climbed in and rolled to the back, pressing myself through a gap behind some bulky suitcases. Once hidden, I collapsed onto my back and did my best to stifle my heaving, exhausted relief. My eyes immediately closed, but I forced them open.

Must stay focused until I reach the airport, must stay awake.

Visions of the passengers dragging me out into the road ran through my mind, though thankfully after a few minutes, the hold slammed shut and the engine roared into life. My eyes would not stay open, even with the juddering, 'twas the heat, the air rippling hot like a sauna. My eyes closed over several times, my body demanded sleep, nay, begged, and my eyelids obliged over and over until I had to practically hold them open with my fingers. I fiddled around for the hose and checked the nozzle in the dark – the blasted thing was hanging off. That had to be why it hadn't worked earlier. The fall must have dislodged it. I forced the nozzle back on and sprayed a blast of water into my eyes and doused my face, rubbing the dirt and sweat away.

Can't be far now. Stay awake, Tristan.

The coach ground to a rumbling halt, hissing, and the sound of feet thundered the ceiling above me.

Muffled voices and car horns erupted on the other side of the hold hatch. I pressed my back against the wall of the coach and aimed the nozzle of the hose and the torch towards the hatch. I wasn't taking any chances. Suddenly, warm air rushed onto the back of my head and I rolled backwards as the wall of the hold behind me disappeared. I fell to the ground and landed at the feet of the man with the blue shirt. He had opened the luggage hold from the opposite side I had climbed in. His mirrored sunglasses reflected my floundered form, and a cigarette once more, hung from his lips.

"Hi", I said. He pulled me up from the floor and looked at me curiously; the sight must have been a quite peculiar one. Some of the passengers gathered around behind him, mouths agape. The man who had been so ill was stood swooning, tightly wrapped in a blanket and being mollycoddled by two women.

"What is this you have on you, boy?" He prodded the hose and inspected the canister on my back.

"You wouldn't believe me if I told you".

He poked me in the shoulder. "What is it, eh, a bomb?"

"What?" I protested. "Certainly not". But the eyes on the faces surrounding him widened and they began muttering to each other with energetic disdain. The poorly man wearing the blanket balked at the very mention of the word '*bomb*', and kindly vomited down the back of the driver's legs.

"What the…" he stumbled away in disgust, dropping his cigarette to the ground.

"Get well soon, mister". I cried, slipping away and darting down the avenue of parked coaches. Running through the crowds, I could hear the driver's admonished cries for me to return.

I looked back to see him waving his fist in the air and pinching at his sodden trousers like he was dancing to a jig. The crowds closed around me and he disappeared. I slowed to a brisk walk and stepped into a quiet area and swung my backpack down from my shoulder. I reached in and took out a black windbreaker and wrapped it around the canister. The holy water dispenser had to go or I'd be arrested on entering the airport. I carried my backpack beside me to conceal the wrapped-up canisters against my leg. Wandering out of the airport grounds, I found a ditch beside the road, waited for a gap in the traffic and slung them into a pit.

"One way ticket to Cairo, please", I said, resting my hands on the counter. The fair-haired girl behind the desk looked at my grubby appendages, black with dirt and speckled with blood. She perused me suspiciously.

"Please take a step back, sir", she said finally.

"Oh, sorry, of course. I didn't mean to…"

The girl picked up a phone and spoke her native tongue while staring at me, almost as if she were talking about me. *Great,* I thought and turned away. I spat into my palms and attempted to scrape away the red blotches before anyone else could see them. Dirt was easy to explain away. Blood, however, was less so.

"Sir, excuse me, sir", said the girl.

I turned to her and swung my arms behind my back. "Yes", I replied. "I wonder if I could buy that ticket…" but the sight of two large men wearing military style fatigues, nestling automatic rifles in their arms, well, this gave me cause for pause.

"Would you mind coming with us, Sir?" one of them said, stepping forward imposingly.

"Whatever for? I haven't done anything wrong", my bloodstained hands were raised before me, without my considering the implication. They both looked at my filthy palms and then at one another. The one who remained silent raised a hand to his ear and spoke into a microphone resting on his bottom lip. I couldn't understand what he said, but I imagined it to be something along the lines of: W*e're bringing the suspect in.*

"Do I have a choice?"

"No, sir, you do not".

"Then why ask if I mind?" I said crossing my wrists, "lead the way". I was exhausted, scared and my insolence escaped me somewhat blatantly. They led me to a holding room and sat me down in a plastic chair. Covering the wall opposite was a mirror, and above, two closed-circuit video cameras stared down at me from either corner. The two security personnel stood flanking me and stared silently into the mirrored wall. I heard the latch on the door behind me click and a dark-skinned man entered, wearing a white shirt and a black tie, he was clutching a clip board against his chest. I watched in the mirror as he passed me and sat down in a chair opposite. He dropped the clip board upon the desk so that it slapped loudly against the surface.

"What is your name?" he asked, stooping and pulling his chair forward.

"Tristan".

"Do you have a passport, Tristan?"

"Of course".

"Please remove your passport and place it on the desk".

I dug into my satchel and removed my passport from a buttoned pouch and slid it along the table. He picked it up and flicked over the cover and winced into the pages, stopping on a particular page. I assumed it was my picture he was glaring at. He looked up at me for a few seconds and then back down again, doing this several times before a whisker of contentment dressed his face. He then proceeded to finger through some more of the pages before placing it back down and sitting back in his chair.

"So, Tristan, what was the purpose of your visit here in Israel?"

"I came to see Jerusalem".

"Jerusalem?" he said, as if pondering, "and how did you find the city? Pleasant I hope".

"Very".

"The old city?"

"The whole time".

"An interesting place, no?"

"Very".

He eyed the security personnel briefly and then spoke again. "Tell me something, Mr. Tristan. There was a disturbance near the old city walls earlier tonight, a road traffic accident", he said. "Were you aware of this?"

"A traffic accident? No, I wasn't aware of any such accident", I lied, feeling my temperature rise slightly, and also sensing a bead of sweat stealing down my brow. "I came in on a coach with a group of tourists. We didn't see anything like that". This was not strictly a lie but it felt like one all the same.

The man tilted his head upwards so his chin protruded and his mouth opened a little. "Oh, I see. These *tourists* you arrived with, where are they now?"

"I really couldn't say. We all went our separate ways when we arrived".

"Ah, how convenient", he said snidely. "And where exactly are you going next, Tristan?"

"Cairo, I'm going to Cairo. I was trying to buy my ticket when..."

"Some of the reports we have received tell a strange story, talk of creatures or animals chasing a man into the streets. From what we can gather, this was the cause of the accident. Another individual, a truck driver, has been hospitalized with lacerations to his legs and torso". He leaned forward. "This man is currently in a critical condition... but you wouldn't know anything about that would you?"

"I really have no idea about any accident, as I said before, I'm..."

The man interceded once more. "Going to Cairo... as you have said".

"Yes".

"Then you wouldn't mind me conducting the remainder of this interview using a polygraph?"

"A polygraph?" My stomach turned as he frowned expectantly. "You mean like a lie detector?" I stumbled through my words, feeling my brow grow with perspiration.

"Well, Tristan, we don't like to employ the word *lie* when interviewing visitors. But it is like I always tell people, Tristan. If you have nothing to hide, you have nothing to fear".

"Something tells me I don't have a choice".

"By all means, you may refuse, but you won't be leaving this room any time soon. You did say you wanted to leave Israel, did you not?"

"I must", the words sprung out without warning. "I mean... I do, yes".

The interrogator raised his glare and spoke his native tongue in an apparent command. A machine was wheeled in on what I would have described as a tea trolley, creaking and swaying from side to side. Another man entered wearing a white coat, the type a doctor would wear... though this failed to put me at ease, as I'd seen slaughter house workers wear that very same attire. He proceeded to roll the trolley beside my chair and reached across and lifted up my right arm. The *'doctor'* cast a glance at his colleague, accompanied by a raised eyebrow, evidently remarking on my grubby state. He then proceeded to connect my limbs to his machine, wrapping wires and Velcro straps about my chest and wrists, and finally pressing two sticky nubs to my forehead.

"Is all this really necessary?" I asked, wincing from some suspect electrical vibration flowing into my temple.

"Perfectly..." the creepy doctor looked at me, and I noticed one of his eyes was blue and the other brown, "perfectly necessary". He finished with a curt smile as he bound my right arm to the chair with the slip of his wrist. Before I had even realised. Before, too, my weary mind had even processed his eyes.

The man in the white shirt frowned. "Do not be alarmed, Mr. Tristan, this is all simply procedure. We just want to ask you a few further questions".

"I don't know what else I can tell you". My finger started to twitch and my brow wince. The pin on the machine wavered and scraped across the graph paper wildly. The doctor stood beside the security official, who flipped a page over on his clip board and handed it over. The doctor studied the page as though his sight was poor and then spied me with his strange eyes. Nonchalantly, he sniffed and appeared to read from the clip board.

"You were not alone in Jerusalem, correct?"

"That isn't..."

"Yes or no answers please, before you elaborate", he peered closely at me and winked, "for the machine".

"No".

"No?" he asked agitatedly.

"Is that a question, too?"

"Is what a question?" the doctor snapped.

"You said no as though it were a question. Am I to answer this with a yes or no answer? Hold on, that was a question, too. Aren't you the one who is supposed to be asking the questions? Whoops, there's another".

The doctor's brow dug deep into his eye line and he stole a glance towards the security detail. The doctor spoke again. "For the benefit of the test, I shall repeat the questions from the top.

Yes or no will be quite sufficient this time". I nodded. "You were not alone in Jerusalem..." he drilled me a stare. "Correct?"

"No", I answered and the machine went wild, scribbling like a child with a freshly sharpened pencil crayon.

"Your name is, Tristan?"

"Correct", I replied. His eyes shot up and burned like blue fire.

"Yes", I followed up quickly. The machine did not waver.

"You are a British citizen?"

"Yes". Still the line did not flinch.

"You left the city of your own free will?"

"Yes".

"You remained within the city walls of your own free will?"

"Yes". The machine pin went berserk.

"You arrived in Jerusalem alone?"

"Yes". The pin leveled out.

"You left the city alone?"

"Yes".

"You have friends in Jerusalem?"

"No". The pin defected, furiously running from left to right. My eyes shot between the doctor and the machine.

"Yes", the doctor yelled.

"No", I cried back.

"Yes", he cried louder still. "Tell us where she is". The doctor dropped the clip board, lunged forward and clenched his hands around my arms. He shook me violently. "What did she tell you? Tell us what we want to know. How did you get out? You must tell me".

"No", I cried into his face, our noses almost touching.

"Yes, yes, yes". His breath stank and his eyes burned into blood red ovals.

"She's dead", I bellowed. "Do you hear me? She's dead". The machine began to smoke and electrical sparks flew from the interface. "They killed her, and I couldn't..." my voice cracked and a tear rolled from my eye. "I couldn't save her", voice trailing off to a whisper. "She saved me, but I couldn't save her".

The doctor's face softened and his eyes returned to something closer to human. "It must be her". He stood upright and

67

approached the mirror, "the one who became a mortal, it has to be... he speaks the truth. She is dead".

My increasingly blurred vision made out my satchel on the table... if I could just get to the torch. I wiggled my wrists and found the restraints to be surprisingly loose. Enough is enough. I ripped my arms into the air, severing the straps and tearing the Velcro apart. I lunged forth, knocking the doctor aside and slipped my hand deep into the satchel. The security personnel broke into startled action, swinging their weapons across themselves in preparation to spray the deadly ammunition that sat idle within those curled magazines. Before that could happen, a great and deafening roar shook the room... the polygraph machine, the table, and the chairs all at once gravitated towards the mirror as though it was a black hole. A rattling of gunfire went off like firecrackers and zipped up across the ceiling, shattering the lights.

Bingo.

I lit up the torch and summoned the combined light of Eleanor's creation. Immediately, the abominably skeletal figure of the doctor and his cronies, and their monstrous contrast against the light, went into crazed dancing, sizzling and retching about the room like raging infernals.

"I know what you are", I cried, thrusting the torch across them as though a roaring flamethrower. The glass of the mirror began to shudder violently, and the light found its way through. The silhouette of the dark figure in the Stetson appeared, absorbing the light but trembling against it ever more so. A growling echoed throughout the room and my body was pulled in, crashing me against the mirror. But I managed to wrestle my fingers tighter around the torch handle and pushed the lens against the glass. My face and shoulders were pressed against the glass so tightly, my lips would only allow mutterings. "I know what you are".

The stranger's features materialized, sizzling and burning, and yet he showed little sign of distress. "You know nothing", he snarled. Smoke began to rise from the rim of his hat and his nostrils and lips discharged streams of black sludge.

"The light... you're dying". I struggled my words against the sheer force that pinned me.

His eyes glowed red and he smiled. "See you soon... boy". And with that he removed his hat and swung his billowing forehead into the glass, sending cracks running like lightning bolts across the length of the mirror.

I felt the glass shatter just as I snapped my eyes firmly shut. A few seconds passed by not of fury, nor violent bloodshed or anger, but ones of complete silence.

I opened my eyes. My heart skipped a beat as I found myself sitting down in the chair at the table I had been led to earlier. The room was empty and the lights shone down from the ceiling. The glass of the mirror was serene and intact. I was the only soul in the room. My satchel was securely looped over my chest, the contents all accounted for. I delved within and wrapped my hands around the torch, running my finger over the switch. *So strange*, I thought, looking around the room. My thought process, which must have been momentarily removed quickly resumed and I seized for the exit the way a mouse runs a skirting board. I turned back to watch the holding room door slam shut.

There was no door.

There only stood a desk, occupied by a smartly dressed lady sitting at a computer, and behind her, the wall was emblazoned with the words: Bureau de Change. She smiled at me. *Did any of that really happen...* I shuddered and walked away.

I found small comfort in the rings and huddles of travelers and tourists. The ticket desk was crowded and a couple beside me clung to one another in a loving embrace. *She* was pointing up at the destination board and *he* was whispering something into her ear. She smiled cutely. My heart palpitated and a bleakness rose in my stomach, bringing with it a tear and the willingness to clench my fists until they bled... she really was gone and I really was leaving her behind... I pushed through to the desk. "Could I please have a one-way ticket to Cairo".

The girl looked at her monitor and frowned. "There doesn't seem to be..." her eyes darted around the screen quickly. "Ah, yes, the flight just appeared on screen. There must have been a reschedule". She began typing furiously. "One... way... ticket..."

she strung her words out in apparent concentration, "…no return to…" she reeled off and stared closer at the screen.

"Cairo", I said, letting slip a whisper of the miserable rage coagulating inside me right now. "Egypt"

I walked away with my ticket and passport clutched in my hand. The happy couple brushed by and almost knocked me to the ground.

"Hey, thanks a bunch", I called after them, but they were so acutely enamored with one another that nothing else mattered. My scowl became a stare and my stare turned into a begrudging smile. I was about to make my way for the gate when the couple cried out in disdain, pointing up at the flight boards. More and more groans shot up from the crowds as faces turned and fixated on the digital schedule that stood high on the airport wall.

Cancelled, cancelled, cancelled, the words tumbled down the scheduler like dominoes.

Athens, Rome, Madrid, Antwerp, Lisbon. They all fell to the gasps of berating would-be passengers. Just one row remained.

One row of large, orange letters: Cairo – as scheduled.

I couldn't quite believe it. Somebody up there was smiling down on me, besides the kind soul who controlled the digital scheduling board, of course. I made my way to the gate and turned to look at the twilight wonders of Jerusalem, mere dots and streams of light from here, but each a life, each a livelihood, somewhere out there. The heavy sorrow fell upon me when faced with the countless mysteries.

Eleanor's face resonated in my mind... she wanders in just like the day we met, though just a beautiful ghost now. I had left her. I was leaving her behind. I couldn't save her, not once for the times she had saved me. I couldn't save any soul. I'm no hero. I closed my eyes and saw her face fade away, into the annals of my forgotten memory. Cowardly place. She was no more.

I handed my boarding pass to the check-in steward. She flicked through my passport and perused the photo. "Proceed, sir, and have a nice flight". The immaculately dressed woman waved me into an oval shaped tunnel.

There wasn't another soul around. "Excuse me, miss, is it normal for there to be no other passengers?"

"Please proceed onto the airplane, sir, and take your seat", she said with a gleaming smile. I nodded and walked towards the hatch of the plane; it was ajar but there were no flight attendants standing by. I stepped in and saw rows of empty seats, and a low humming resonated beneath the soles of my feet.

I looked at my ticket and found seat number fifty-seven, several rows down on the left side of the plane. Number fifty-seven was a window seat, although by the looks of it right now, I could have chosen any window seat on the plane. I opened the overhead compartment and saw not a single piece of luggage stowed. Nevertheless, I placed my backpack in and sat down.

A 'ding' chime startled me, and an oxygen mask dropped down from above and swung before me on a wire, swaying back and forth like a pendulum. "Okay", I recoiled and looked about. "What's going on?"

A hissing began and the compression door slammed shut with a firm finality, followed by a series of hydraulic clicking, and then the engines began rumbling throughout the fuselage, making the headrests tremble. *That was strange. Where were everybody else?*

The plane began to move off from the gantry and another 'ding' came from the speakers above me. Orange lights began to flash above every other seat. I stood up and edged out into the aisle, grappling the headrests as I went. "Hello, is there anybody there?" Nothing... yet the plane continued to taxi along onto the runway. I looked out of the window and watched the airport moving away. Motorized baggage carriers heaped full of suitcases snaked along the jet-way. I thumped on the window with my fist. "Hey, I'd like to get off, can't you hear me? I said I want to get off".

My calls bounced around the empty cabin, for they were sealed in with me and this stale air. My hands slid over the headrests until they caught and latched onto an armrest, bringing me to a halt. The inside of the fuselage shook violently, armrests bounced up and down, overhead compartments swung open and flapped about like clackers. The plane roared faster and faster, sending furious butterflies into my loins and causing my legs to wobble. The pit of my stomach was first to sense a backward tilt from the nose as we left the ground in flight. The front of the fuselage rose steadily upwards, climbing to an unnatural angle. I slipped further towards the back of the plane as it jolted upwards steeply, reaching what felt like forty-five degrees at least.

I clambered up desperately and wrapped my arms around a headrest, hugging it tightly like a baby does its mother. The force was unquenchable against my body and the air seemed to press against me with a thousand hands, and the frame of the seat creaked and bent as though it was about to give way. I clawed myself along to the window seat, feeling my cheeks stretch back across my face. My throat tightened, too, and words became almost impossible. The pressure grew and grew. I forced my rigid hands to my sides and dragged my seat belt together. My fingers dug in and squeezed the armrests until my knuckles turned white as the plane climbed higher and steeper.

My line of sight now pointed to the stars. I was facing directly into the sky, and my breath was whipped away from my lips each time I tried to exhale. Meager gasps poorly fed my straining lungs of what oxygen the cabin still held... there was no air to scream with. No breath to squander in futility.

The turbulence continued to an unbearable degree, everything was rattling so wildly, objects became blurs and squiggles and screws and bolts began to fall from the front of the plane like rain. I heard them rattle down for an age to the tail of the plane, pinging about in the furor of the impending oblivion I was heading into. My hand reached out and was met with such resistance, I could only move it a few millimeters, a few more still, but the unforgiving nature of my environment held total control over any further movement. A few more inches and the oxygen mask would be within my grasp. I used the last stunted breaths I could muster to push with everything I had. These would be my last breaths. My fingers turned purple, stricken to breaking point, and the veins on the backs of my hands pulsated with streams of blood fighting to break through the bubbling skin. I grasped the mask and snatched it back against my nose and mouth. Crazed and desperate, those sorts of breaths now sauntered down my trachea like flash floods, filling the starving reservoirs of my lungs. I couldn't get enough of them; such was my need. My eyes bulged and pulsed with the rampant blood flow that zapped beneath the skin of my temple, filling my cheeks to bursting point. My eyes were the only part of my body functioning and they shot around the disintegrating fuselage interior, watching the atmosphere being torn away at the seams. I was powerless but to sit and watch steel bend and plastic warp from the walls and seats, and the carpets, too, uprooting with violent frolic, burning up and shriveling into cinders. A sharp crack shot into my ear and my eyes searched out the window beside me. The glass had cracked diagonally in the shape of a thunderbolt and frosted icicles had formed on the outside. The clouds passed me by like free-flowing gas as the plane climbed further into the great beyond.

I was space-bound at this rate.

The light above flashed orange and the speakers crackled, the frequency was scrambled and strange sounds began to emit from them. Wailing and screaming emerged, intermittently beneath an inaudible moaning that ghosted around the cabin.

"You should have taken that drink with me, Tristan", a creepy voice escaped out above the interference, before trailing off to a curdle and finally rasping into chattering laughter. "Do you ever get the feeling that someone is watching you?" the voice mocked. My stomach churned and the revolting pressure drew me into queasy breaths that threatened to regurgitate my insides. "Tell me, boy, did you think the girl could save you?" the voice rapped. A deep sniggering climbed out from the speaker, cankering my ears with pain. I felt warm trickles drip down my ear lobes and onto the sides of my neck. The pores in the speakers began to bleed, too, and crimson droplets started running back into long streaks across the ceiling of the cabin.

My eyes caught the blurred vision of red speckles splashed across the inside of my oxygen mask. I choked for breath, squeezing the mask tighter, retching blood up from my chest in stumbling coughs. The pungent, sickening taste of iron writhing on my tongue served only to pepper my mind with fear.

"Are you ready to meet your creator?" the voice boomed. "Is your faith still so strong knowing you are about to die?" he bawled. "Why doesn't she come to help you. Why doesn't she help you now in your final hour?" the voice cried even louder, sizzling on the airwaves. "Where is this angel when you pray for her?" he chuckled. "Is it because you failed her? When she needed you most, you let her die, you did nothing". The voice croaked so disturbingly, so frenetically that the blood dripping from the speaker pores splattered across my face. "Just say the words, say it out loud. You let her die".

The blood in my eyes cast a glassy shell to the world and my eye lids opened and closed over the haze, spreading it like grease on a window pane. I pulled the mask from my face and choked on a mouthful of blood that overflowed down to the back of my skull and shoulders. I fought doggedly, gasping in droves, and for a long and labored breath filled with sputum, I cried out: "I let her die", for as long and as loud as my insides would hold. My sight faltered and my temple burned with a raging fire. Blackness enveloped my being and I slipped into delirium, neither awake nor sleeping but bundling mindlessly into an abyss.

My eyes opened gingerly; my sight was still blurred, but I could make out something swinging gently in front of me. The blood-smeared oxygen mask. I lifted my arm and realised I could move my body without restraint. The cabin was calm and the plane had leveled out, but the interior was almost completely destroyed. Most of the seats had been uprooted and lay scattered around in piles of twisted metal. The windows lining the fuselage had all cracked, but none, thankfully, had shattered. Through the window, a blue expanse stretched out for as far as the eye could see and we were sailing above the tips of mountainous clouds. I pushed myself up and climbed past the battered seats into the aisle. My satchel strap caught on a warped armrest. I unhooked it and looked inside. My book and the torch lay at the bottom.

I still possessed the things most precious to me. And my life, my life, was teetering in the balance aboard this wrecked airliner. High above civilization, high above the world.

The lights flickered as a rumble of turbulence shook the cabin before subsiding again. I steadied myself and walked slowly towards the front of the plane. The floor was an uneven waste ground of shrapnel and smoldering carpet, one that my feet fought for space to step carefully. Another shudder ran through the cabin and jostled free pieces of metal and plastic from the ceiling. My backpack rolled out from the overhead compartment and caught on the broken latch. The bag swung suspended in the air. I grappled it onto my back and took out the torch from my satchel and placed my finger over the button.

The lights began to falter again and jolts of turbulence ripped the creaky floor under my feet. The juddering frame of the plane made sounds as though it was hanging together by loose threads, and the joints and grooves moved apart to betray the spaces between them. A draft swept down the aisle. I walked cautiously to the front of the plane and saw the door to the cockpit. It was closed, but the frame rattled against its hinges and the latch was bouncing up and down. I stepped closer and listened in through the gap, too narrow to see anything, but there was an intermittent ringing coming from inside that sounded like an alarm clock.

What if there was no one flying the plane? I hadn't actually seen anyone aboard. I hammered on the door and stepped back quickly, training the torch lens upon the latch.

"Is there anybody in there?" I called out. "Hey, is there anybody in there? Come out and show yourself". The door jolted open and there stood the man in the Stetson, looming in the frame like the grim reaper himself.

"The fearful man", he hissed, stepping out of the cockpit. "Did you think you could escape him?"

"Escape who? Who is coming for me?" I demanded, training the torch on him. My finger hovered over the button.

He chuckled and stepped into the aisle. "How far do you think you can run before he finds you?" His eyes glinted and he licked his rancid lips. "He will follow you wherever you go. There is nowhere to hide now, my child. You are the one chosen to find that which he seeks".

He stalked closer.

"That's close enough". I brandished the torch as if it was a sword. He growled through his rotten teeth, considering, I'd wager the awful light bound within.

"Your weapons will be futile when he comes to collect what is owed to him".

"Who are you? What do you want with me?"

"I am Baal, purger of souls. You were not supposed to leave the city of David before his arrival. My master awaits you in the desert. He is most displeased".

"Who is flying the plane?" I asked, attempting to look beyond his massive frame.

"You have been delivered. The time has come for me to leave you". He turned towards the hatch door.

"No", I cried, "don't you touch that door, I'm warning you". I thrust the torch before me with both hands. "You have to land this plane".

He sniggered and grasped the hatch handlebar. "Too late". Baal began to apply pressure against the hatch door. I pressed down on the torch button and released the light. His body combusted into flames with a shrieking that pierced the compressed atmosphere, and his skin began melting and dripping from his face. But his hands remained rooted to the handles, turning them slowly and steadily. I tried to get closer to him, but the flames lashed out as far as my own face and hands.

There was only one thing for it. I ran for the cockpit and slammed the door behind me. My fingers trembled wildly as they scraped around looking for the lock. A whistling tore through the seams of the door just as I drew the latch handle down. The body of the door crumpled outwards like a tin can being crushed. The passenger section of the fuselage immediately lost cabin pressure and the thumping, lacerating sound of its contents being sucked out roared against my ears. The cockpit shook, throwing me against the instruments as I clambered around, trying to steady myself. I reached for the wheel and hauled myself into the pilot's seat. More and more alarms began to buzz, shrilling my ears and confusing my senses, and all across the dash and walls, the lights flashed red and orange. I took hold of the wheel and did the only thing I had ever seen pilots do when a plane was going down. I pulled up.

A cement-like resistance bound the wheel. No matter how hard I pulled, it would not budge, for it seemed the harder I pulled, the greater the wheel shuddered away from my burning palms. The nose plundered steeper still and that awful wailing from the engines roared from beneath my loins. I dragged the wheel back towards me again with everything I had, causing the land-sky horizon to shift a little in my favor, but the nose remained on course for whatever was down there.

I released the pressure again and shook my hands, flapping them about and blowing on them. The skin was bloody and peeling away, such was the friction from the frayed leather. My heart wasn't simply beating now, 'twas screaming through my chest plate and my ribs felt like they were beginning to separate with the vibrations running up my spine. I began flicking switches and pressing buttons, nothing here made any sense, numbers and dials, clocks and equations. I lay my hand on a large throttle handle that rested midway between a track-runner. '*Reverse Thrust?*' I squeezed tightly and yanked the handle back down the runner until it jammed.

What harm could it... The plane seemed to slip out of the sky like a brick and veered sharply to the left, dipping into a breathtaking descent. I pushed the handle back up the runner all the way to the top, summoning roars and squeals from beneath, and a sudden, powerful whining tore across the dash in a wave of electrical explosions. The plane rocketed forward with terrific thrust and pinned me back against the seat. The clouds cleared as we dropped beneath them like a spear nearing the end of its flight. A vast desert land stretched out beneath the horizon. Sweeping mountains of sand for as far as my lofty eye could see, growing in detail and clarity as the ripples on the dunes neared our impending and irrefutable collision. This was the end. Nothing could live through this. Nothing.

I took out Eleanor's book from my satchel and opened it. I ran my fingers over the passage she had written and read the words aloud. "*Follow my heart right to the end*". The nose dipped further with a jolt. "*Maybe this is the end*", I whispered.

The desert was getting closer and closer, the rattling of the cockpit and the plane's riotous screams intensified, growing evermore into a deafening, mechanical squeal. The final crescendo of my demise would not be an understated one. The zenith of chaos was seconds away.

I looked down at the petal to see it glowing. "Follow my heart right to the end", I said, defiantly holding the petal up towards the windshield. Brighter it grew, quivering against the force of our descent. I jammed my feet against the instrument panel and with my free hand I tore back the wheel with the last grit I could muster. My eyes closed to see her face bathing in neon rays of light. Her smile shone peacefully within me for a moment. Eyes gleaming like pearls, silencing the furor around me. My lips formed a smile and with that, my own light was extinguished.

The endless blue ran on forever. An everlasting river of blue without bed nor banks, a sea of purity free of rupture and speckle. This was heaven, it could only be. How instantly my transition had come, how painless and merciful it had been. Such horror and fear, snuffed out, extinguished, before it could lash me with its sufferance of mortal pain and agony. Was this how it would be for everyone? The blue turned black for a moment and then revealed itself once more. Again, the blue vanished beneath a veil before reappearing as before. A dark, rigid shade appeared beside the blue. Then, three slender forms invaded the heavenly expanse. Birds in the sky, earthly birds... they cawed and soared effortlessly through one single fluffy cloud. My eyes closed over and the blue ceased. I opened them once more to reveal the sky and the cloud and the birds.

I was alive...

The black shape beside the blue scuttled closer into my peripheral consciousness. My temple drooped to the side and my eyes met with a scorpion. My eyelids drew up over my eyeballs as far as they could go and fright snagged at my loins. I rolled away from the creature and felt myself slide down a layer of hot, prickly sand. My fingers dug beneath its grainy texture and burrowed deeply without resistance. The scorpion rallied away in the opposite direction and disappeared behind a dune tip.

Sunbeams struck the back of my neck like a Cat o'- nine-tails, but a pain in my chest dug deeper, far deeper than the hot rays lancing me from the endless blue.

I sat up and looked down at my chest to see that my shirt was lacerated, torn to ribbons, and beyond the ribbons, pieces of glass were lodged beneath my flesh. Most of them ran only skin-deep but lower down there was something else... something that provided amply, the lucidity to my most diresome predicament... another glinting shard had been pushed further in beneath my ribs. I lost my breath when I saw the blood seeping out over the shiny tip.

My pain elevated in tandem with my breathing. I looked around and saw thousands of glass pieces scattered over the sand like, glistening diamonds, dressing the pyramid dunes almost as innumerably as the grains of sand themselves. A cloud of black smoke billowed high up into the air, the source hidden behind a mountainous peak of shrapnel-strewn desert. I looked down again and cringed at the foreign body piercing my gut. I dared not pull it out, only more blood would follow. Probably every bit I had left. Instead, I dug my heels into the sand and struggled up while carefully cradling my stomach. Thick blood droplets cascaded to the dry sand and formed dark blobs. The blood was so dark, almost black. Black blood. Gut blood. I had read somewhere once that when you bled gut blood, well... you didn't have long left.

I made my way towards the smoke, feeling my feet sink and slide beneath the sand, and each time losing my balance caused stinging sensations to run riot across my torso. Breathing was painful and though the air was rippling hot, my body was still pleading the sweet stuff. Just enough for me to keep stepping forward. The journey of only a few hundred feet must have taken me an hour, but I finally toppled clumsily over the tip of the dune and saw the crash site.

The plane was barely recognizable, parts of the fuselage and tail stood crumpled from beneath the sea of sand. It appeared as though large sections of the nose and wings had already been swallowed up by the desert. I could only imagine I'd been thrown out through the windshield. But even so, how on earth could one survive this? The petal. The petal must have played a part, protected me in some way. My mind would only allow me to consider the irrationality of such a premise, simply because there was breath still running into my lungs. I didn't care to conclude anything further. How could I? Besides, I had gut blood pouring from my stomach and that wasn't exactly a sign of a miraculous survival by any stretch of the imagination.

I stumbled along, tending to the protruding shard in my stomach like a cradled baby. Small fires jostled out from some of the windows and a black cable was jumping around like an angry viper spitting out electrical charges. My legs begged to bend and forced me down onto my back. I lay my head to the sand.

The blue expanse I had believed to be heaven remained, infinite and ever watchful. Maybe it was heaven, maybe my body was simply delaying the inevitable, hanging on to the enduring biology of the human makeup. The brain sending its final energetic signals to the few receptors still functioning. The heart pumping the last of the blood and oxygen it could before surrendering, before flat lining. People could hang on for hours like this, even days. I wondered where the body ended and the soul began. When did the spirit refuse to make further contributions to the continuation of its existence in this flimsy, mortal frame? Maybe that part kicked in after the body had shut down entirely. Either way, I knew if I closed my eyes, mine would probably leave my body here and now.

I took my hands away from my stomach, lay them out either side of me and mingled my fingers beneath the sand, picking up handfuls and slowly letting the grains cascade out through small slits in my fists. I wondered how long I could do this before my time expired. My eyes closed and a calming peace washed over me. How many times could a man believe he was about to die before he actually did? Depends on the man, but I guessed it would probably be many, many times during his life.

Sharp, searing pain nipped at my knuckles, igniting my eyelids once more against the hot rays of the sun. A scorpion had attached to my hand and was lancing me with its tail. Another ran across my stomach, resolving to clap about in the blood pooled from my wounds, dancing ceremoniously in preparation to strike. Several more surrounded me like an army, assuming battle formations. An arachnid phalanx if you will. I lifted my shoulders sharply, receiving a burst of agonizing pain in my belly. But the fear of being overrun by the little blighters removed me from the floor with bubbling fluidity.

A small cavern opened in the sand, where hundreds of them emerged, scurrying across their natural territory. "What?" I cried, "I have nowhere else to go", retreating backwards with the feeblest of steps. A wave of maddening humor veiled my logic and I burst into a laughter that quickly turned to wails of despair. "Keep it, keep your little patch. I'll go somewhere else and die. So sorry to interrupt your morning stroll", I screamed. An angry red bump, crowned by a yellow tip, had risen on the back of my hand where the scorpion had stung me. I touched upon it and the thing burst. The pain was akin to a hot needle being stuffed down behind my finger nail, or so I'd imagine. My eyes winced and wept like lemons being squeezed and my gasps crept through the air above me.

"What a wretched place to leave me", I cried into the sky. "What am I doing here? Can anybody hear me?" I listened for a reply that would never come. Chuckles escaped my chapped lips and I prodded the piece of glass in my stomach, dabbing my finger in the blood. "What are you waiting for? That's gut blood, why am I still here?"

In the depressing distance, sitting atop of an enormous animal was a dark figure. Were my eyes now playing dastardly tricks on me? I squinted, narrowing my eyes to mere slits, allowing me to make out what appeared to be a horned helmet with a peaked visor resting above the broad shoulders of a horseman. My eyes widened against their drowsiness. A mirage, oh, let it be a mirage... it had to be. My mind was colluding with my eyes to play tricks on me once more. We both stood watching each other for a few moments until the great horse snorted violently and began dragging its front hooves against the sand. The rider reached down to his side and the slithering of metal seared the air as he drew out a long sword. He pointed the tip towards the sky and jolted his spurs against the belly of his mount. I backed away slowly, watching the horse approach.

This was the horseman from my nightmares, the demon who inhabited my slumber... but I wasn't asleep. He had always been in dreams, never reality. I turned with groans as the glass jostled for room in my stomach, the sharp tip scratching at my insides like a fingernail upon a chalk board. My feet dragged across the sand and my knees threatened to clatter each other, such was my crippled posture. I scrambled over another dune tip and looked back. The horse was scraping its way up behind me, with the rider lashing cruelly on the reigns. My feet gave way and I tumbled backwards down the steep dune, rolling and tossing in uncontrollable revolutions. My head thumped against a mound of sand beside a set of toes jutting awkwardly from a pair of leather sandals. The world was still spinning and my eyes wouldn't focus, but I could just make out a cluster of heads looking down at me. I raised my arm and tried to shield my eyes from the glaring sun. Someone pushed aside the floating heads and stood squarely over me. I couldn't make out any features, but the outline of a suit dressed his figure and the tip of a fedora overlapped part of the sun, as an impending eclipse might. The figure stared down, faceless and silent.

'Another mirage', I muttered, as my eyes closed over, and the whistles of vultures chaperoned away my thoughts.

The Darkness Within

My eyelids drifted open and a slow, methodical beeping ghosted into my ears. A harsh light greeted my eyes before vanishing again as my eyelids closed over again. My consciousness seeped back with no real intent, but I knew I was still alive this time. I forced my eyes open and winced at the neon bar of light hanging from the ceiling by small interlinked chains.

The beeping continued.

I wiggled my fingers and toes, rousing them from a tingling paralysis. My eyes darted about the bright room.

I was quite alone.

A solitary chair sat in the corner of the room, beside a window with horizontal lines of daylight squeezing through the slats of a drawn Venetian blind. I moved my head towards the source of the beeping, but my neck was stiff and my temple pounded with a mighty throb. There was a machine with an assortment of flashing lights and what looked like a heart monitor. A tall pole stood beside, with two transparent bags of fluid suspended on a hook, and a connecting cylinder with a tube feeding from the bottom of the bags ran down to the edge of the bed. My eyes followed the length of the tubing until it disappeared beneath the blankets covering my body.

I tried to raise my arms, but they were both bound by restraints of some kind. I forced against them, but my wrists ground on the rough material, to no avail. My feet were bound in the same manner. *Hospitals didn't normally tie patients down, did they? Why would they do this to me?*

I raised my head and watched my toes wiggle out from beneath the blanket, kicking my feet wildly and tugging my arms back and forth to rattle the bed frame, 'twas no good. I was rooted.

My insides teetered on the precipice of all-out panic and a strange tingle ran up my arm. Looking up, I noticed the edge of the blankets previously covering my right side had been swept away. The tubes from the bags of fluid were connected to my arm. My inner forearm had white strips of plasters running horizontally over two thin tubes that ran into my skin. Below the tubes, two small valves sat against my pulsating veins. The left one, to my horror, had a hypodermic needle adjoined. I shook my arm in an attempt to wiggle the apparatus from my skin, but the plasters clung tightly and the needle did nothing more that swing about like a rabid dog unwilling to release its favorite chew toy. My skin crawled with the unknown. *What was in those bags? What had they injected me with?* I began kicking and pulling again, furiously screaming at the top of my lungs.

"Hey, let me out of these things, let me go", I cried, feeling my headache cloud angrily into a migraine of brilliant pain. I kept it up until I could kick and shout no more, finally heaving onto my back in complete exhaustion. The light around me pulsed purple and red, thumping on my brain like a woodpecker. Slowly, the pressure subsided. But if I wasn't careful, I would lose consciousness again and I had to be awake to stop them administering any more of their poison.

A door opened in the corner of the room and a white suit and matching fedora entered, carrying an old man. He led himself with a cane. Two tall and burly, Arabic-looking men followed behind him.

"Ah, the patient lives", said the old man.

"Where am I? What have you done to me?"

"There, there, my boy. Never a gotten gain by needless struggle". He approached the bed. "You are still quite weak from your ordeal".

"I want to know where I am and why I'm shackled to this bed". I pulled at the restraints. "Take these things off me".

"Let me take a closer look at you, dear boy". He tottered forward, leaned on his cane and frowned. "My, oh my. You really have been in the wars, haven't you?"

"Who are you?" I asked, inspecting his ancient face. Dark, penetrating eyes pondered over me, fiercely unbetraying of his thoughts. And teeth, yellow and protruding like an aged jackal. "Why am I chained to this bed?"

"My name is Blackband, Charles Walter Blackband. Pleased to make your acquaintance. Of course, I'd shake your hand, but I notice yours are otherwise engaged". His eyes searched out my restraints and quickly found me again. "Fear not, for I shan't take offence to this ungentlemanly insistence", he concluded with a wry shrug of his shoulders.

"Ungentlemanly insistence? You have locked me to this bed against my will and hooked me up to these machines, and god only knows what else". I dragged at my arm bearing the tubes. "What are these damned tubes in my arm? I want them taken out immediately".

"My dear boy, it is generally considered customary to regard oneself and title to another, after one has done such". His face bore a mocking amusement.

"It is generally considered customary to not have one locked up like an animal without good reason. I demand you release me now and let me leave here".

He chuckled and moved towards me, his eyes narrowed and a vacant look crossed his face. "Let you go? And just where might I ask, would you go? Do you even know where *here* is?"

I paused for a moment and tried to piece together in my mind where I'd been last: the desert, the plane crash. "I don't care where here is, only that I am. It's none of your business where I plan to go, so release me right now. I'm warning you".

Blackband's features caved into a grimace and he glanced at his two henchmen before setting his dark ovals on me again. "I seldom care for your tone, for you would still be languishing in the desert, bleeding out and spilling your guts across the sand. The vultures feasting on your flesh like so many of the poor and unfortunate, if it were not for I. You would be wise to show a degree of gratitude towards me, young sir". The old man glowered.

I struggled forward as far as the restraints would allow and prepared to speak when an intense jab of pain struck me in the stomach. My teeth gritted and a crushing exhalation blew from within my lungs.

"Ah, you are curtly reminded of your wounds my men were so kind to attend, the very wounds you wish to temper now in foolish flight". His face harbored shadows and cracks riddled with an ancient wisdom. A dark, unsettling wisdom. The old man came closer still and leered over me. "That's right, boy, I saved your life and in return, you are going to do something for me".

"Please, Mr. Blackband, I don't know what you want from me. I thank you for the care you have given my wounds. I am grateful, really I am, but I need to leave now... if you'd just let me go, I won't tell a soul".

He chuckled, "Oh, I know you wouldn't, dear boy. But I have far too greater use for you to simply let you run off into that cruel world out there". He nodded towards the window. "Not until I've taken out some insurance, a little protection of my own". Blackband pushed on his cane and turned to the men behind him. "Show him". The brutish pair broke their statuesque poses and rounded the bed, either side of me.

"Show me what?" I asked, feeling a rush of panic. One of the men took away the sheets covering me to reveal my body, dressed in white scrubs. The other man restrained my shoulders and pulled up my clothing from my torso to my chin. I wriggled around trying to break free, but futile it was.

"Look", Blackband lurched forward and pointed the head of his cane at my stomach. "See for yourself, boy. I have sewn you", he crowed. My chest was covered with bandages and plasters. But just below my ribs, where the glass had pierced my stomach so deeply, ran a series of thick, black stitches. Vulgar and ugly woven laces ran across the most irritable of skin. My throat tightened and a trembling fright reached around in my stomach. Dr. Frankenstein sprang to mind, the morbidity bit hard... I felt like Frankenstein's monster.

"Dear God", I heard myself gasp. "What have you done?"

"God had nothing to do with it, boy. We simply stitched you back together again. You're alive, are you not? Do you see blood coming from those stitches, any major organs climbing out from your gut?" He watched me for a few moments. "We may not be surgeons, but you will live, of this I'm sure".

"You have to let me go, you must. I need to get to a hospital immediately".

"Nonsense, poppycock", the old man waved his finger at me. "I mustn't do anything except that which I choose. We have provided ample care". He prodded his cane towards the drip beside me, "observe the apparatus, you have been anesthetized and received, intravenously, the necessary hydration levels. The procedure should pass without complication".

"Procedure? What procedure?"

"Why the one we are about to carry out, dear boy. It's rather a simple operation and will cause you no pain", he tapped the edge of the bed with his cane three times and smiled, "at least not in most cases".

My blood froze and my breath was caught for a brief moment, wrestled away by his hideous words. "Listen to me, Mr. Blackband, don't do this. Whatever it is you are planning to do, it's not too late to stop. Just release me now and we can put all this behind us, no hard feelings, water under the bridge, whatever you'd like to call it". I took a deep breath and closed my eyes. The darkness scared me. I opened them again. "It's not too late", I gibbered almost.

"You're quite right, it's not too late. That is precisely why we must proceed immediately as planned", he squeezed my arm gently. "There is much you do not know, my child. Soon the veil shall be drawn and your destiny revealed".

"Please stop this". Blackband ignored me and turned to one of his men. He spoke to him in Arabic and the man left the room. "Mr. Blackband, please listen to me, you don't have to…" the jangling of metallic instruments stole my attention as a trolley was pushed through the door. My butterflies fluttered throughout me at the sight of what appeared to be an array of scalpels and cutting instruments laid out across the top tier of the trolley. "No, you cannot do this to me", I almost wept. Blackband rested his cane against the wall and tore a pair of surgical gloves from a box. He stretched them across his decrepit hands and let them snap against his wrist.

"Tristan, please listen to me very carefully. This procedure is going to happen. If you choose not to struggle, then it will pass quickly and with minimal pain. I don't want to hurt you, Tristan, but should you decide to resist…" he paused and neared me. "Well, things could get very messy indeed".

I gulped and nodded. "What are you going to do?"

"Are you familiar with a curse known as Coward's Debt?"

"Curse?"

"Yes".

"I don't know what you mean".

"Coward's Debt", he said again. "The consumption of the soul by execration of the flesh. You know the one".

"No, I really don't know the one".

The old man waved his finger in the air and rolled his eyes, as though attempting to recall a memory. "He shall walk through the valley of darkness, never once opening his eyes, never once feeling the warmth of the human spirit, nor his fellow-man, for he shall venture forth bound to regret and anchored solemnly to his fear. He is the one you shall not go tither, for he is the one who greets his fear with an all-too-mighty cheer. Go tither from he instead, this awful creature and look back not once as he wanders into the darkness". Blackband concluded, poetically, the cryptic consequences of the curse.

"I don't understand", I said pathetically.

"Your soul will be consumed by a spirit that is empowered by your very own fear. Your body will be decimated piece by piece, until you are no more. Every part of you, every atom of character, everything that makes you who you are, will turn in on itself and die. Finally, your soul will be spat out, regurgitated, into the darkness, into the underworld, where it will wander, spewing impurities and spreading hatred and fear among the lost souls of the wicked".

"But I'm not wicked, I've never hurt anyone", I said with vivid earnest.

"Curiously, most people believe such curses are administered using spells and voodoo clap trap".

"But why, Mr. Blackband? Why are you doing this to me?"

"When in actual fact", his eyes glazed and he stared into me. "Coward's Debt must be bestowed..." darkness filled his eyes entirely, "surgically".

"Why, please tell me why?"

"Why?" he replied. "Because when you find what you truly seek, you shall bring it back to me in exchange for your life. This is my guarantee, my assurance of your obedience".

"I will bring it to you. Whatever it is, I'll bring it back. You don't need to do this", I gibbered, feeling a numbness rise up my feet and thighs. Blackband spoke in Arabic again and gestured with a gloved hand. The man who wheeled the trolley rolled it closer to the edge of the bed and he, too, pulled on a pair of surgical gloves.

"Seti, give me 1% lidocaine via syringe, vial number four", Blackband said. Seti picked up a glass bottle and drew out some of its contents with a needle. He passed the syringe to Blackband, who squeezed a short stream from the tip. "Keep quite still, Tristan". The needle tip pierced my arm and the transparent liquid entered my vein. My body felt numb and my mind fought against itself, warring over my submission, but I could not break from these shackles and feared that any attempt to resist would, indeed only draw my own blood... just as I'd been warned.

"Seti, retract the curved J-tip wire into the plastic loop sheath. Direct it, carefully, into the introducer needle". Blackband placed on a surgical mask. "Have you done as I asked, Seti?" he said, placing a bud of cotton wool over the puncture spot.

"Yes", Seti replied.

"Splendid, now uncap the distal lumen, that's the brown one".

"It is done".

"Soak the gauze in betadine solution. We shall take the subclavian approach based on our recent failed external jugular. Hand me the introducer needle and apply the solution to the entire neck area", Blackband's words escaped from behind the mask. The man with the trolley made stay beside Blackband and proceeded to douse my neck and upper shoulders with a strong-smelling oil.

"What is that?" I asked.

"Iodine. You don't want to catch an infection here".

"But a curse, I do?"

"Too many questions. Don't you know it's fool's folly to converse with the surgeon during an operation?"

"I thought you were not a surgeon".

"I'm not", he replied, leaning in with a needle primed for my neck. I couldn't feel anything, but I knew the tip must have punctured my skin because he was pressing down on the plunger.

"Scalpel". His eyes darted to the side and he raised his palm upwards.

"Mr. Blackband", I spoke quietly, and my insides wept and threatened to tear my spirit down. "Please don't cut me". My eyes, half-filled with tears, met his own. The mask he wore distorted for a moment, as if pushed by a smile. His eyes left mine and set themselves on my neck. He pushed down with the scalpel. I closed my eyes tightly and gripped the bars of the bed, wishing I was in another place, one far away from here.

A strange, dream-like feeling washed over me and the bodies moving around the bed became blurred shapes. Blackband's arms moved from my neck to the trolley several times in slow motion, and others at high speed. The fingers of his surgical gloves were smeared with blood as he handled pieces of tubing and wires, each disappearing beneath my jawline. I couldn't make out what was being done, but I could feel a great pressure on my collar bone, and my neck and shoulders felt a great coldness, almost as though they were in the grip of a mountain of ice. Each time I blinked, the darkness lasted longer, my eyelids becoming harder to reopen until it was so difficult, I was content to only attempt to open them without any real conviction. Whatever anesthetic Blackband had administered had trapped me inside my body, frozen all feeling. Perhaps it was for the best.

Voices returned to my world and the darkness became light again. My eyelids had lost their previous weight and I opened them up to see a blurred image of a face. The old man Blackband, staring at me closely, his fedora tip almost touching my temple.

"Welcome back to the land of the living. I thought we'd lost you there for a while".

"Lost me?" I muttered.

"Yes, my boy, you were clinically dead for precisely twenty-one minutes and..." he looked at his watch and squinted, "twenty-two seconds".

I noticed two devices that looked suspiciously like defibrillator pads sitting on my stomach. "What have you done to me?"

"You have a central venous line. It's a thin tube inserted into the neck via a subclavian port implanted beneath the skin. The line feeds down into your right atrium, essentially acting as a pump for the administering of medicine directly to the heart".

"You're going to give me medicine?"

"Not exactly, my dear boy", he clicked his fingers. "Bring her". The burly assistant removed his surgical gloves and left through the door.

"What is happening?" I asked, still dazed and confused and struggling to look beyond Blackband. The stiffness in my joints put a stop to that. The feeling had not yet returned to all of my limbs. My toes were present but held no sensation, my thighs jostled with a trillion knots, and wretched pins and needles scraped at my fingers and wrists in equal measure. My journey was sinking deeper into Hell. My fate growing bleaker, nothing more than an ever-darkening tunnel with no signs of light or life, and, perhaps most morbid of all, the looming feeling I may have already crossed beyond the point of no return.

Blackband and his ogre stared at me without speaking. The old man had a splash of blood across his lapels and the ogre wore a finger-shaped blood streak down his cheek. The door opened and the man entered, holding an ornate purple bottle. A vial of a kind, but larger, with a gold stopper and tattered label.

"What is that?" I asked, pulling gently at my shackles.

"That, Tristan, is my insurance policy", Blackband replied, his eyes rooted to the bottle. He took possession of the bottle ceremoniously and held it up above his jaded temple. The liquid inside was dark and thick. "I give you life once more", he said reverently. Blackband lowered the bottle and removed the lid, releasing an odor that spoilt the room instantly. A most foul stench, rotten, demoralizing, a decaying filth that made me retch. Blackband's men covered their noses and mouths with handkerchiefs and their eyes squinted almost to a close.

My eyes searched the bed and watched my hands struggle against the wire shackles searing deeper into the bloodied, swollen skin of my wrists. Blackband picked up a tube with a lumen on the end and rested it against the lips of the bottle. My eyes searched along the tube and saw that it disappeared beneath my skin near the collar bone.

"No, no, no", I cried, dragging my wrists wildly against the shackles. "You can't put that poison inside me". My eyes filled and I pleaded, but the look in the old man's eyes confirmed to me that my pleas, my protests, would fall on deaf ears. This old man, Charles Walter Blackband, was evil. His eyes told me that much. My despair turned to anger and the thought of going out so pathetically propelled me into a rage I knew would only serve to bury me deeper. But what choice did I have? None, but to salvage my dignity... if nothing else, I could still keep that.

"Go ahead, Blackband, do what you will". My teeth gritted and my eyes seared into him, "but before you do, know this". His preoccupation with the liquid in the jar broke and his eyes found me. "Whatever your poison does to me. Whatever foulness you infect me with, I am the keeper of my own heart and I shall remain so long after you're dead and buried. Nothing you do to me will ever change that".

His eyes narrowed and he smiled. "That's the spirit", he sniped, and thrust the lumen into the bottle neck all the way to the bottom. The lights in the room flickered several times, and the lumen began shaking about in the bottle like the tail end of a rattle snake. The tube darkened and pulsed with the climbing liquid.

I watched as the dark stream invaded the port and breached my veins, causing them to bulge and rise to the surface of the skin. My limbs ran tight and rigid, stricken with an overwhelming strain. My fingers straightened to snapping point and my mouth gaped so widely my jaw felt as though it would split in two as trickles of saliva and blood ran over the edges of my lips and down onto my chest. Something was trying to inhabit me completely. My eyes shot around the room, wildly zipping from one end of the room to the other. They stopped on Blackband.

"It's working, it's happening", he said in wonder.

A soft voice spoke into my ear. Calmly and sweetly above the fury of my pain, it said: "Search for the sunlight, Tristan. You must be ablaze of her earthbound rays to halt this darkness".

The invading force now running through my body harbored a rage. A detestable, powerful hub of anger that infiltrated every fiber of my being. Whatever this thing was, I could feel its blatant sentiment being woven into my soul, slowly becoming my own. Such insatiable anger was not without strength, for the energy coursing through my limbs shook me erratically against the bed rails. A scream shot from my own mouth, long and shrilling. My arms tore away from the bed, snapping the restraints like wet tissue. Blackband stumbled backwards, his features turning from delight to horror. I leaped from the bed and watched my grasping arms seize one of Blackband's goons, an astonished face clasped between my hands, my own blackened fingernails pressing into his skin.

His features caved into a moan of terror. My fingers closed around his throat and I drove his head against the interface of the heart monitor. Sparks flew from the machine as his temple was buried deep beneath the wires and broken shards of plastic. His legs went limp and he collapsed to the floor with blood and smoke pouring from a large gash across his face. Before I could turn around, a shocking pain rattled my brain. I drove my face into the mattress of the bed and clawed at my skull in desperate agony.

The soft voice returned to my ears once more, calming and pure. "Sunlight, Tristan, you must". The soothing words afforded me a lifeline, a moment of clarity where my functions became my own again. I raised my head and stumbled around the bed, clinging to the rails. The light from the ceiling, paining my eyes with a severity afforded by my own rage. Whatever held me now harboured a strong aversion to light.

Blackband's other assistant seized towards me, but the old man intervened. "Leave them be", he cried. "They will come back, they must return".

I broke through the door into a dimmed hallway lined with framed pictures and brass lamp fittings. The texture of the carpet ground against the soles of my feet, the pattern causing my eyes to cross and blur. My hands reached out to the walls and guided me along the corridor until a set of sliding doors greeted me. I wavered over what looked like a handle and dragged the door towards the wall. The thumping in my head began to bleed into my eye sockets and my limbs rattled with every step.

A wooden counter lay ahead, with a cash register and some jewels strewn about. The rest of the space around me was obscured, to say the least, my sight tunneled for only a few more feet ahead. Stepping closer, I saw my satchel hanging over the edge of the counter. The sense of relief was dulled but evident when I grasped its rough buckle in my hands and dragged the strap over my head.

"Sunlight, sunlight", I gasped, stumbling and floundering against a pillar, knocking over something that smashed into pieces on the floor. Hinder me, it did, but I danced on in a stupor, towards a glowing roller blind that was drawn over what appeared to be a door. My fingers landed on the handle, which was all that stopped me from crashing through the glass behind the roller.

Turning the handle, the door fell away and the brass left my palm. Sunlight struck my soul, complete, unforgiving and wonderful. The heat of the sun and her rays dragged me into a blazing world of fiery relief, and revolution exploded inside my head. But only just before my face met the pavement, where many shoes and feet clopped by my grounded line of sight.

I smiled. I could only smile because the force sent to my heart had relented for a time. I smiled because it was still mine.

As for the cruel world out there, as Blackband had referred to it, well, 'twas just that. A world of passing people, so many were they, there was barely enough room for me to lay on the pavement, at least not without being trampled to death. Their feet, some donning shiny shoes, open-toed sandals, others bare, like mine, jostling between and around my limbs. I climbed from the floor and looked up into the sky. Clear and blue was she with a rapier of a sun, lording it over all creation.

The traffic squirmed like screeching eels, twisting and turning yet violently overlapping, and neon lights were visible through the fresh green leaves of trees lining the pavement. The din of a thousand car horns rang out above the chatter and the admonishing cries of drivers and passengers and pedestrians. I looked down to see my hospital garments crumpled and creased, bloodied and dirty. The crowds carried me away without my realising, and my feet were taking steps on the hot stone, and my shoulders were pinged back and forth by the multitudes that surrounded me. Yet I allowed myself to be swept along. And there I found myself, walking, down a street with no name, in a city I did not know. Not a stitch on I could call my own... aimless and meandering, the people staring at this strange barefooted Englishman.

Stopping to look in a shop window, my eye caught sight of two men—boys, rather—who appeared to be observing me. One of them was very tall, gangly even. He wore trousers that did not meet his shoes and a long, blue-and-white striped shirt. His face was youthful and dark. The other chap was short, though broader in a muscular sense, with cropped hair and lighter skin. Though his eyes seem to be ever-bulging, making it appear he was eternally surprised. His bulbous eyes dug into my back as I did my best to make it look as though I'd disregarded their quite humorous reflections. I found myself staring at a selection of Shisha pipes of gold and purple laid out on velvet cushions. I wondered immediately if the two hawks shadowing me were actually festering over the idea of robbing me.

My eyes flicked between their reflections and the shisha pipes intermittently, and so quickly I wouldn't believe they knew I was expunged with dread and wishing I could disappear. I turned and walked without thinking, but at a steady pace, to give the impression I wasn't running away. A bead of sweat stole my attention as it rolled down my eyelid. The rogue bead stung my eye like I imagine Sulphuric acid might. Curse my meekness and cowardly wilt, clutching my fists. A clear two blocks had passed and I had barged and shoved my way through the crowds to find another small opening, whereupon I began to peruse a store window once more. This particular window was absorbed by an elderly man standing on the other side of the glass who for all intents and purposes could have been mummified. His face was drawn and wrinkled like a prune, with grey straw-like hairs sprouting from his head and chin, and eyes resembling squalid dates. I smiled awkwardly with a nod. He grinned from ear to ear to show a set of archaic, yellow and brown teeth, not unlike a mummified man's. I glanced to my left, praying I wasn't being followed, that it had been my overactive imagination initiating guises for innocent bystanders, perfectly normal everyday folk who may be a tad curious of me at the very most. Not so, it seemed, as out from the steam and sun-rippled air, the two stooges appeared cordially detecting my pause and so too freezing, shamelessly, to peruse the window beside me. This couldn't be happening, could it?

My gaze drew back slowly and I thought about what was happening. Where was I? Could this really be Cairo? I looked up again to find my pursuers floating near a market stall, slyly and most clumsily stealing glances to monitor my position. Once more, I turned and carried on further towards who knows where. And there was the pickle, where in Hades was I running? If this was indeed Cairo, then it would be enormous, more giant than old Jerusalem, a concrete desert full of peril... and the sun would be setting soon. The two scallions would surely wait until I reached a convenient spot they knew of and strip me of my belongings, which was scant pickings at best.

Jeepers. I really knew how to frighten myself. There was no evidence they intended to harm me—not yet, anyway. A thought tapered itself into my mind as my fingers searched the numb crash site near my collarbone, the crash being a bloody, great needle and tubing having been jammed into my heart. To the touch, it panged me and I whispered searingly to myself: "Blackband's spies". They had to be, didn't they?

Ultimately, I decided not to hang around to find out, as I had looked over my shoulder several times now and the two men were certainly following me. One of them appeared to be making pointing signals to someone across the street. I couldn't see who the signals were directed at, only the innumerable bobbing heads of people bustling every square inch of road and pavement. I could run. I was good at that. Really fast, agile and certain, I could lose them both based on their size and shape. But that was pure conjecture, I immediately prodded. My hand pressed over the stitches in my stomach. Who knew what would happen? Would my stitches remain stitched or tear open and deposit my intestines into the street? Adrenaline could do a great deal but carry me where? I could run all the way to Giza and hide inside the great pyramid of Khafre, or chance it to the banks of the Nile and hide in the reeds like a crocodile... chase down a caravan in the Sahara and roam the desert in a brotherly community of Bedouins. I grinned to myself and felt greatly heartened in the soul that I could still jest and romanticize my predicament. This was the Tristan we needed now. However, 'twould do no good to confront them now. Who knew if they spoke English, or if they would even want to speak to me? *Stop thinking so much... I need to think...* the voices in my head clashed.

Before my pursuers could say Open Sesame, my fleet of foot had foreboded even Hermes himself, as the ground was chewed up beneath me. Among man, woman, mule and camel I ran until my heart beat so loudly I thought it must give out.

The Lights in the Darkness

Eventually, after many steps, I skipped around a corner and almost collided with a group of burka clad women. Spinning around, I apologized and continued on along a narrow corridor of stalls and dark doorways that appeared to be made entirely from sand. I slowed as the alleyway dipped like the edge of a valley, offering up a set of ancient steps that appeared to be dressed in mosaic tablets of red and blue. I descended them without haste, observing the intricate artistry that had rendered the decoration of these strange steps. They appeared to tell a story with scripture and strange symbols interceded by colorful figures and temples. The last step bore a gold star that gleamed brighter than maybe it should have. This trail was symbolic. I could feel it in my gut and was ground by the years of sandal, hoof and boot. Yet it still shone remarkably so for the descendant.

Large, waving canopies quivered above my head, broken by portions of the sky. And fort-like window slits in the buildings ran high up, some with mucky faces peering out like Rapunzel, and others with small wooden shutters swinging in a breeze. There were dimly lit archways leading into airy courtyards, with clay pots and large barrels lining the cobbles beneath my feet. Spices from these pots flavored the air with a true pungency and roasted the atmosphere with an aroma that carried them into my mind via all of my senses combined.

Elderly men sat dotted around, inanimate pale figures around every corner, greying whiskers and dusty garments, holding water pipes and small cups of tea and shot glasses of an unknown crimson liquid. The neon lights and shiny motorcars, the social, breakneck hum drum of the high street, with its cries and raucous pace so eminent earlier, were extinct down here. How very alien they would seem here, against the more traditional, social niceties that really instilled a by-gone feeling in this strange place.

I entered another narrow alleyway, furrowed with bags of wool stacked up like the walls of a barracks. The rays of light pierced the holes in the canopies above, corresponding shapes to the broken ground, like golden stepping stones beneath my soles. I followed them, as if crossing a rippling stream, while viewing, rather acrobatically, sometimes more carefully, the building stories that ran three or four high. Wooden-grilled balconies, festooned with the clothes and towels and scarves of unseen occupants, rode the world above me, serving as small, unassuming safe havens to this close-knit hamlet. A strange and sparkling substance loitered in the air from the furthest reaches. Microscopic mirrors reflecting each other, dusting the ground like ashes from an urn turned to the wind. Strangely, this did not disturb me to simply watch them float down, weightlessly, moving horizontally and vertically like fireflies in slow motion.

A window opened above me with a creak and some of the wall came away and fell to the ground as dust. A boy popped his head out and looked at me with a cheeky grin dressing his face, and then a girl of about the same age, maybe eight or nine. Her brown eyes grew upon her face as her smile did, and they both giggled. I thought they must be brother and sister because they shared the same beautiful features. The girl's hair clung to the sides of her face in a wavy mess, curling into the corner of her mouth as though yearning to remain, to not drop below her dainty jawline.

Those faces made me smile. Lights in the darkness. They both offered a wave as I negotiated past a pile of boxes overflowing with old shoes. A cat sprang from one such box and onto my shoulder for a hair-raising moment before spiriting away up the wall beside me. I cried out and covered my face. The animal had spooked me just for a moment, though 'twas long enough to send the little children into fits of giggles, and into the intense laughter only a child can enjoy.

"Oh, you think that's funny?" I asked, brushing myself down and looking around for the frisky feline.

The children disappeared from the window as though they had never been there and a silence fell over the area again. Only the distant, echoic sound of plates clinking and muffled male voices of tradesmen lingered in the air. The black cat, seemingly from nowhere, appeared again in my path and sat strangely relaxed on its hind legs, like a statue. The creature stared as a statue might, its yellow eyes fixed to mine without interruption. The predatory slits at the center of its oval eyes narrowed with suspicion, it seemed to me.

I stooped slowly and offered out my hand. The stoic-looking cat didn't so much as blink but instead sat further to attention, like the sphinx itself. I felt as though the cat was looking *into* me rather than at me. *Curious,* I thought, standing upright again. My feet took a few steps closer and then a few more, but still there was nothing but stillness from the cat. The animal continued to search me with those eyes as I got to within a foot. Stooping down again I stroked its furred temple. All the while, I watched those eyes widen and narrow, widen and narrow, never leaving mine. A deep and tigerish purr emanated throughout its body and ran into my hand with a furry warmth.

There was no collar to speak of, but the cat was immaculate, which was more than I could say for myself. Healthy-looking, too, with long, wiry whiskers shooting out like star trails either side of a dainty nose. The animal sported a fine silken coat that shone without the aid of direct sunlight.

Two children danced out from a swinging door further up the street, they laughed and skipped, as children would anywhere in the world... "Anywhere in the world", I said quietly... *where in the world was this place?* I glanced up for a second only, and, when I stood, the cat had vanished once more, without sound nor trace. The children, however, remained and approached me without the reluctance nor hesitation one might expect. The little girl said something in Arabic, a question quite possibly, though I couldn't be sure. She looked at the boy and he, too, spoke Arabic to his companion, before turning to me again and repeating what the girl had said. The girl laughed and nudged her brother in a revelatory manner and quickly spoke more words in Arabic.

"What is your name?" the girl finally asked.

I doubt that I managed to keep the surprise I felt from my face as the little girl smiled sweetly and awaited a reply. The boy nudged her and muttered something before giggling.

"Hello, little one. My name is, Tristan". I patted myself on the chest, somewhat moronically I decided. "What are your names?"

"I am Theoris, and this is my brother, Amsu", she addressed the boy. "Where are you from?" little Theoris asked eagerly. "England?" she followed up instantly.

"Hello, Theoris and Amsu". I nodded. "Yes, that's right, I am from England. Your English is very good".

"I speak the best English, much better than any of my friends. Though Amsu doesn't speak very well", she taunted him. "Not even in Arabic", the girl concluded, nudging her brother in laughter. The boy clearly didn't compute the criticism and chuckled along with his sister. Amsu spoke Arabic again to his sister. Theoris seemed to be very bright and listened to him while appearing to retain an air of authority a sibling can sometimes manifest naturally. Theoris replied to him in short and then spoke.

"Father has a shop and he likes people to come in and buy things, if he sells things in the shop, it's better for all of us". She touched herself upon the chest. "Me, Amsu, mama and papa". The little girl stood placidly with her innocent eyes. "Would you like to come and see our Bazaar, Tristan. I promise you will like it", she assured me with astute sweetness.

"Children, this is going to sound rather strange, but where in the world are we?"

The two children looked at one another. Theoris broke the silence again. "You are in the old town".

"No, no, I'm sorry... I meant the country, what country is this?"

The children looked again at one another and giggled. Theoris said, "This is Egypt, silly. The city of Cairo". She stepped forward and used her hand to cup her words. "It's the capital, but don't tell Amsu. He doesn't even know that", she whispered. I nodded and she smiled.

"Cairo?" I said. "I never imagined…" my mind boggled. *How did I make it here?* "I'm looking for someone, children... a doctor, goes by the name of Rambo".

"We can help you, Tristan", Theoris said. They each took a hand either side of me and began leading me away. The sun was resting on the horizon like a giant half-orange, spraying the warmest yellow and red into the sky. In the narrow streets, the rays filtered in to create a hot, crimson dusk. We stopped near a large wooden door bearing sizeable hinges and a huge, ferocious-looking head of a lion. And in its jaws hung a ringed knocker, the like of which you would have thought a giant man had created for his own specifications. There was distant shouting from inns and cafes lining the street further down and a couple of mangy looking dogs were savagely feasting on some unidentified morsel in the road.

I pushed open the door with some effort and was greeted with waves of hot-smelling air, raucous laughter and the chattering of a thousand mouths, the clinking of glass and brass, too, and the pattering of shoes against stone. The sounds echoed around the huge temple interior, ricocheting from beam to arch and escaping out into the dying light. Theoris and Amsu took me by the hands into this great and heaving souk, into the spicy, fearsome deluge of people and wares. Stall upon stall dressed the aisles and alleys with golden objects. Pipes, pots and huge brass jars and pottery of magnificent colors and shapes adorned countless cubby holes. The stalactite architecture ran up beyond all, above our eyes, above the stalls, succeeding even our imaginations perhaps. In enormous grand arches worthy of the very finest medieval masonry, this building rose, harking back to a glorious and everlasting market culture from whose ducts this place wept so romantically.

My mind was cast to bygone times, my eyes continually dragged and drawn as the further through the bustling crowds we trekked, the more wonders opened themselves up. Processions of belly dancers fluttered and danced through the crowds on my left, and, to my right was an enclave of colorfully dressed men smoking hookah pipes as deeply as they were conversating. Those pipes stood at least six feet tall and bubbled and chugged and smoked like cross county steam trains billowing out into the thriving alleys. The boy darted forth through the smoke, ducking and diving among the crowds, and the girl tugged at my sleeve and pointed ahead before drawing me further along, and still, her tiny hand clutched my fingers in hers.

There before us, a door appeared through the billowing steam running from a vendor selling meats. A door of black and gold with small windows surrounded by pots, pans, lamps and materials and garments to colour the world. Theoris pointed once more and spoke.

"Our Bazaar, Tristan", she said staring up at me.

"You're not coming in?"

"I have some things to do for my father. Goodbye... for now, Tristan", she spoke like a grown-up but waved me farewell like the child she was. Returning the gesture, I watched her scuttle away between the knees and heels of hundreds of people. I entered the Bazaar with an intrepid turn of a brass knob and a deep breath.

My eyes still harbored flashes of the colour and brightness of the souk reverberating in them when they were met with the relative darkness of the shop. A tinkling from a bell above the door drew my attention, and with it the interior of the shop took my senses in a gust of sparkle and mystery. There was a most agreeable abundance of scents, the like of which I'd never known, while tall, elegantly shaped bottles with stoppers of red, blue and gold—some glass, others metallic stood throughout. Other bottles were green and rotund, with tiny necks and sported old-worldly labels with Arabic dressing in peculiar fonts. The colours, enamoured for each sparkle, reflected and illuminated one another under immense candle light. There was a chapel-like feel to the room, and the bottles and lamps were set behind glass cases along the walls. At the center of the room was a great pillar, lavishly decorated with shelves of perfume bottles, closely guarded and festooned by indescribable trinkets that glowed and gleamed.

"Greetings, my friend. You have chosen well. Please, won't you look around?" a voice startled me, seemingly from beyond a curtain on the other side of the room. A man in a loose-fitting cotton shirt appeared from behind the veil; he appeared to be in his fifties, with silver hair, curled and wavy, still bearing the flecks of the deep black it must once have been. A sturdy frame he seemed to carry easily.

"Hello, sir", I said, still marveling at the many ornaments and baubles that seemed to increase in number with the adjustment of one's eye.

"My shop is your shop, dear friend. Take your time and see what surrounds you. When you spy something you like, just call out and I will be there", he said quite fantastically. His eyes shone strangely with all the colors of the room and his smile beamed as he stood leaning over a creaky banister. One may have noticed so creaky, it must surely have been a place he stood to greet all of his patrons. I frowned and felt a little trepidation. Nevertheless, descending a small staircase, I entered the aromatic cavern. A palace of a cavern, it should be said. The place harked the romantic synergies of the mind, seamlessly reminding me of those rooms you imagine from Arabian tales of cantankerous old magi plotting over a princess's fortunes, or, perhaps, the whereabouts of mysterious and powerful trinkets. Certainly, my mind ran rings when faced with so much mystic charm.

As I sidestepped methodically down the displays and objects, my mind ran into that name once more: Eleanor. The name of names, the ghost of my heart. She had been no less real than the very exotic air in my lungs, though heart wrenching as it was, now I was here in Egypt, 'twas she who seemed like the far-off fairy tale. Out from the many trinkets an object shone brightly and collected my attention without mercy, as though it knew I'd been soothed by its extraordinary visual verve. The piece looked as though it was made of solid gold, dancing with precious stones set to its surface like a crown. A handle protruding as a majestic standard, subordinate to a keeper, falling just short of the swan-like bottle neck. The piece was plugged perfectly by a silver stopper and chain that rested over what looked like a ruby any collector or thief could seldom resist.

It called out to me.

I felt myself scrutinizing its every inch, a feeling of a great power emanated from within, drawing from me a yearning to touch it, a desperation almost. Rather strangely, I felt an overriding urge to possess the piece.

A clouded vision cascaded over my mind and blinded me to my current surroundings, replacing them with one of me grasping the lamp. The intensity of the scene struck me without warning, hastened by more than a little might. I was gasping and alone, clutching the golden lamp against my chest like it was my own fortune, my own heart. My face and hair windswept and sand torn, my eyes bloodied and terrified. What I was seeing. Could it be real? Was I imaging this? Too vivid even for my imagination. I was trapped, danger pranced all around me... the desert... please, no, not the desert again. I felt my eyes squint at the vision for clarity. Pathetically squirming down a mountainous sand dune in the dying sun, clutching this majestic lamp, fleeing like a thief would a jeweler. The apparition continued alongside my conscious thought and drew a creeping, enclosed feeling that threatened to suffocate me. I watched myself slither down the dunes like a dung beetle. Surely I wouldn't be driven to steal this intoxicating piece and become a bazaar fugitive. Interpol's most-wanted trinket thief... Was I, in this moment, rationalizing the means to do so or had I already committed such a crime? My mind was waning from the blood lost, the operation, and that awful poison Blackband had forced upon me. It was all starting to take effect...

Just then, a hand slapped down on my shoulder, and this mirage—this vision vaporized, leaving behind the haunting memory of my hounded eyes, pursued and levied to a bloodshot wilderness. And at that moment, I believe I turned and called out in a manner not unlike anger, "I must have the lamp".

"My friend, it is okay. You're here in my shop". The man was stooped slightly with a hand on my shoulder. "Are you okay?" he asked. "You looked as though you were in some distress".

"I watched myself... saw myself with..." I looked back at the piece and then tore myself away with a stunted shake of my head.

"What did you see, friend?"

"Never mind, it's nothing". The man fixed his eyes to mine, but they bore a family-like ease. I exhaled and rubbed my forehead, partly to break the eye contact he had protracted so seamlessly. Surely, he must now have noticed my invalid physical state of affairs and operating room attire.

"Come, sit down here and take some tea. Sit, my brother." He placed his arm around my shoulders and ushered me over to a green leather couch. I let myself be led after glancing back at the bejeweled lamp one more time. Sitting down, I relieved myself

105

of my satchel and immediately felt a flurry of stars dissipate from within my eyes. I had been close to collapse once more, or worse. "My name is Ibrahim, and this is my shop". He offered me his hand and took a seat opposite. I reached out and shook his hand, watching the reflection of this in the glass table separating us. Shards of tobacco and red liquid had been splashed across its otherwise flawless surface.

"My name is Tristan and I have a story that no one would ever believe".

"Is that so?" he asked curiously, cupping his hands to light a match for the cigarette hanging from his lips. The man shook the match and deposited it into a glass ashtray further down the table. He took a long drag from the cigarette and smoke instantly exited his nostrils before the majority ghosted from his lips and drifted up to a yellow ceiling, implicating a series of fine cracks running out from a dimly lit and most redundant lamp.

"Tristan, tell me why did you come to Egypt?" he asked almost rhetorically. He wasn't finished. "Was it to see our majestic pyramids... or was it to look upon the face of Tutankhamun and his vast array of treasures at the museum". He stood and walked to the other side of the room. My eyes followed him intently. "Maybe it was because you have watched Elizabeth Taylor play Cleopatra alongside your very own Richard Burton, and envisioned the paradise she ruled over". A smile coveted his face for a moment but quickly dissipated. "These are all wondrous elements to my country Tristan, I think you would agree". He held his back to me and retrieving something from the golden walls behind the glass casing. "Especially Elizabeth Taylor as Cleopatra, don't you think, Tristan?" He turned with a mischievous grin and a gruff chortle.

I chuckled uneasily, "Quite".

"But Tristan, something older and truly more amazing, are the scents of Egypt. The ancient scents are the very soul of my country, present and everlasting at the birth of our heritage. They are a homage to the breath of this land and its past". The Doctor spun to face me with a tray of exquisite perfume bottles. He delivered them like a priest at a procession and lay them down upon the table with a careful clink. "Through Smoke", he gasped, exhaling wisps of smoke through his teeth. He stubbed out his half-spent cigarette and began to fiddle with the bottles.

"Perfume, the word in English comes from the Latin: '*Per*', meaning through, and '*fumum*', meaning smoke. The earliest of these scents that would become perfume as you know it now were burned from incense and aromatic herbs, plants and flower extracts". He held one up. "They gave off sweet, aromatic scents through their smoke. Exquisite vapors capturing our souls. Perfume in its truest, purest form, has been intertwined with the very origins of our race, and the land of Egypt for as long as time itself". There was a glint in his eye and, quite possibly, the reflection of a perfume bottle. "So you see Tristan, the perfume is the soul of this country".

Twas certainly in his soul, I pondered as my eyes searched the many bottles standing before me like a proud military troop. Picking one of the bottles up, I inspected it like I had just dug it from the earth... a wonderful object. The only way I could describe the piece, was to allude to a crystallized form bound by a strange purple swirling just visible through an icy exterior, seeming to move like a gas but having a physical element to its being.

The man observed me like a father would a child opening gifts on Christmas morning, a look of marvel on his face, eyes shining with all the colors of the room. I felt around for another and plucked it up. This one became my instant favorite, exuding that ancient Arabian eminence that spoke volumes... the gold bottle had a net covering and a long neck with a black and gold stopper, and across the surface was a series of symbols and silver inlays that seemed to make out a cosmic mural. The object had been the craft of a master, I was certain and shrieked of a mystical life. He removed the lid from one of the bottles and placed it down on the tray.

"Give me your arm, Tristan. You must smell some of them", he insisted, reaching across the table. I didn't resist and offered up my arm. "Is there a girl in your life, Tristan, the girl of your dreams? Someone waiting for you at home, perhaps?" His speech remained somewhat fantastical and dramatic, accompanied quickly by a smell equal to his theater—one that led a hostile revolt against the meandering tobacco. The sweetness grew throughout the room like ivy would a castle wall, clinging and grappling everything. Ibrahim rubbed some on my inner wrist and urged me to take it in. "For the ancients, these scents would have burned in the air at the temples of Memphis, Edfu, Giza and Thebes to signify their purity to the gods. They believed these perfumes held magical powers and became highly adept at their concoction".

He spent a great and deep stare on a bottle he held up like a precious jewel.

"They became masters in their own right and discovered scents and aromas that were truly heaven blessed, bound from paradise, wielding natural powers reserved for the gods alone and not for man". Ibrahim looked at me with a stare falling just short of crazed, but not by far. "You see, Tristan, there are some powers wielded by the concocting of our very own natural elements that do not submit to your western logic and unfortunately are too great a responsibility for man, given his nature".

I felt a mystified look canvass my face, somewhat akin to a child reading his first book, and I replied, most likely as rudimentarily as a child's first words. "What powers do you speak of?"

He leaned in, as though the walls had ears. "There are many stories regarding the properties of these early perfumes and their mystical powers and charms, even ancient recipes for their creation". He showed me the palms of his hands. "Everlasting youth, immortality. The ability to heal the sick. How about the power to make anyone of your choosing love you adoringly for all eternity?"

"Such things are not possible, of this, I'm sure", I offered through a tangible engrossment. "One's heart cannot be swayed simply by a scent".

"Tristan, there is nothing simple about what I say, believe me". He stood and walked to a tray and poured a hot, reddish liquid into two glasses. "Of course, people's beliefs have changed a great deal since those times and perfume now is merely an agent for stimulating the senses and the turning of western heads". He picked up the tray and carried it over to me. "A mere pleasantry of the senses and nothing more… drink, my friend, it will calm you".

"What is it?"

"Why it is tea, my boy, drink. It has many properties", he pressed goadingly. I saw myself in the black of his eyes, lift the glass and drink from the sweet rim without the level of hesitation I'd have imagined. The liquid was warm and sweet but it contained a sour structure that whipped at the tongue shortly after the sweetness, clinging and caressing my throat. Then an extraordinary tingling exploded in my chest that remained for a few moments.

"A special tea containing some very special ingredients, beginning its life as a fine Egyptian red straight from the calyces of the hibiscus Sabdariffa flower. Transformed via jasmine resins and steamed to exactly eighty-eight degrees in the leaves of the flowers of the sun". The strange man took a wistful helping from his own glass and a slight trickle escaped down his bristled chin. His eyes filled with an energy bound from the liquid I felt. He swiped his arm across the insubordinate trickle and so it was absorbed into the dark hair abounding his wiry arms. "You like, Tristan?" he asked, smiling broadly.

"Very peculiar. Certainly unlike any tea I have tried before". There remained a drop in my glass, which I finished quickly, hoping to be offered another. "Very pleasant indeed".

"You shall have another, after which I will show you some more of our perfumes and our fine jewels and lamps. Make yourself at home, Tristan. My shop…" he thrust both hands towards me, "…is your shop".

I did just that, but as I sat back, a whisper called my name. I was as sure of it as I am in my very own name. 'Tristan', the voice whispered. Strange though it may strike a fellow, but the voice sounded like you'd imagine smoke to sound, quietly swirling, and a prolonging of the syllables, as though siphoned through a keyhole. A curious way to explain such a thing, certainly no remedy for explanation in earnest, but this was the way it struck me and the way the word met my ear.

Immediately, my attention was cast and I turned sharply to be greeted by nothing except the perfume bottles that welcomed my entrance. There it was again. "Tristan..." the call came, but this time prolonging further, deeper, like a drug-addled oracle singing her visions. The lamp was calling to me. Could it be the lamp that spoke my name? Impossibly, I believed it to be so. I don't know why I did, but I did, and right then I made the decision to take the lamp away from this place and keep it for myself. The lamp would be worthless to them and would gather dust. No, this was no home for such a wondrous beauty. The lamp belonged to me.

'Tristan, Tristan', the whispering came again. Ibrahim emerged from behind the velvet curtain with more tea. I was drawn to the lamp once more, like a human moth to the sun. There it stood, majestic and willing, singing a sweet tune only I could hear. "Tristan", the voice called once more. Staring into the golden outline, I vanished again.

I was walking in the desert, 'twas hot, so hot. The ferocious heat had blistered my skin and my lips felt dry and cracked. I could barely walk any further, but still I trudged on. The lamp hung from just two scorched fingers. Feet dragging, never leaving the sand, but scraping rather like lazy slugs. There was no life except the birds in the cloudless sky, and my poor vision saw only dark wings gliding the perpetual blue. They circled my position like an endless whirlpool.

Vultures—the rotten vultures counted on my guts for supper. Well, I'd show them. I still had the lamp; the lamp, of course, was mine. I looked back and my eyes burned and my shoulder blades cracked like rigid sheets of sandpaper. There was a figure on the horizon, floating about in the ripples of the heat, gaining ever closer, closer and closer. Attending my plight like the tick-tock of a clock. I attempted to limp more quickly, as though I had somewhere to run. I tried to run, but I couldn't. I tried to skip haphazardly along while my skin peeled off and my eyes began to fail, but it was no use. He had come to take my lamp... come to take my beauty away from me all over again.

I looked over my shoulder once more as I jostled the sands inconsistency, pathetically stumbling and cursing the pursuer before collapsing to the hot floor and burying my pained face in the sand. The lamp fell away and rolled down the dune. I gathered every ounce of life left inside me, didn't seem much, but just maybe enough to move towards the lamp. Each time I moved closer, it tumbled further down the hellish sands. My anguish broke free and I cried out. The pain felt familiar, one of loss. Losing something forever in the deserts of life, having what you love snatched away right before you. I dared not take my eyes from the lamp, but I must look back to see how far the stranger had come. How close now did he draw my doom? I did so with great distress and saw the giant held aloft upon horseback, ragged, black robes fluttering, hooded and swift. He would take the lamp away. But if I could just reach out, touch it once more... I would never let go.

I clawed and clambered with every reserve of my being and soul, crying out to the heavens, getting closer to the precious object. But still it evaded me and still I dragged my beaten spirit. The jagged breathing and wheezing of the great horse were upon me and a metallic jangling rallied against the restless hooves upon the sand. I plucked at the nucleus of my soul and screamed, projecting myself towards the lamp in a final bid to cling on, bursting through the air and falling just short. I managed to capture the handle between two of my fingers, squeezing so tightly that a scorpion's pincers would seldom have relieved me of the precious thing.

My face was buried deep in the sand and stung like the pierce of a thousand hornets gouging at sores lanced by the sun's rays, though tempered infinitely greater still by my own angst. I lifted my head slowly and felt sand particles cling to the moisture of my lesions while others dropped from my face, sprinkling the crater left behind. Another figure, just beyond the lamp, graced a blurred horizon, but the sun blasted my retinas and rallied in waves, so that I did force my glare against its awesome power. The figure began to materialize, omitting a shining light—equal, it seemed, to the sun, moon and stars combined. I wiped the sand from my eyes and looked directly at the figure, feeling the astonishment cripple my speech for the longest time.

Eleanor. As sure as the sun was beating down. There she stood, motionless upon the hot sand. A white dress reflecting light cosmically in all directions, her face, expressionless but exuding a fair and beautiful sympathy only she could portray. Her hair did not blow in the wind, nor did her pure attire, but her soft eyes pierced my pain like droves of morphine, stoking a fire, an energy as hot as these sands that sullied my racing heart. This excruciating pain I would gladly prolong indefinitely if she so wished, if only she would remain in my vision... but cruelly, the devilish snorting and heavy hooves thudded over me, spraying sand into my eyes and blinding me to her face.

The shadow bore down over me like a monstrous demon about to feast. I rubbed my eyes raw and suffered to see her again through the peril that was upon me as a metal blade threw down and drove deep into the sand, slicing across my finger and catching the handle of the lamp. The horseman drew back and dangled my lamp along the shaft of the sword, jousting his prize above me, as if to mock. He raised his weapon skywards, so it slid down to the hilt of the blade. I reached into the air to grapple for the lamp, but it was far away.

Eleanor cried out and raised her arms in grave protest. With her screams, she vanished into the light. The horseman secured the lamp within a large sack tellingly cluttered with others of the same ilk. He galloped away and left me to die alone in the heat of his deeds.

"No, Eleanor, come back", I cried out again and again, beating the sand, cursing manically upon my apparent and lonely grave. There was nothing left. The lamp was gone. Eleanor was gone and I would perish in this woe.

"Tristan, Tristan, can you hear me?" a voice called from the darkness. A hazy vision returned to me. The voice came again, "Tristan, can you hear me? You must try to wake up Tristan". I could feel a tapping on my face. My eyes opened and were met with three faces, two small and one large. A hand reached across and tapped me on the cheek. My head spun and for a moment I couldn't figure out whether I was sitting, standing or lying down. The cracks in the ceiling rang a bell and I found myself lying on a table or bed of a kind, my hands rested against a soft material. The floating faces hovered over me still.

"Father, he's awake", Theoris said with wonder in her eyes and a medley of hair hanging down her face. A very peculiar feeling resided in my chest. A volley of Arabic words jostled between the three before Ibrahim turned his attention back to me and spoke.

"Tristan, you passed out and fell down. You hit your head, but you are okay". He placed a cold towel over my forehead and some icy droplets of water sprinkled across my cheek and neck, triggering my senses. A great thirst grew inside my throat.

"Water, I need water", I croaked.

"Tristan, do you feel pain anywhere?" Ibrahim asked.

"Water, can I have some water? I feel like I'll die without water".

"Of course,". Ibrahim ushered Amsu to fetch some water. The little boy returned holding a jug with both hands, the contents of which went sloshing across the floor. I sat up against a wall and swigged heavily from the jug. Wondrous. The water tasted heavenly and took the entire vessel to quench my thirst. Theoris brought me a plate with a roll of bread and a medley of olives.

"I think I've been in the desert for a long, long time", I said, brushing away droplets of water from the bristles beneath my lips.

"You never left the shop, Tristan", Theoris said.

"I'm sorry for the trouble I must have caused you. You are good people, but I fear it is a curse to know me", I said, chewing the roll and picking up an olive. My breathing was heavy. "I will go, but I must catch my breath first". I ate the olive.

"Nonsense, Tristan", Ibrahim said. My eyes searched the room and found a framed certificate on the wall behind him.

My chewing slowed as I read the name: Doctor. Ibrahim Rambo. The butterflies in my stomach made a staunch comeback and rose through my throat with no small flutter. "Doctor Rambo", I squeaked almost. "Doctor. Rambo, it's you, it's really you?"

Ibrahim looked at his children and then back at me. "I am Doctor Ibrahim Rambo, yes".

"I can't believe I've found you".

"Who are you?"

"A friend of an angel", I said, rooting through my satchel.

"I don't quite follow?"

I handed him the book. "Eleanor sent me here. She saved me". The Doctor turned over the cover and read the inscription. He ran his fingers over the writing and raised his head slowly.

"You are the fearful man".

"That's what they tell me".

"Eleanor, where is she now?"

I bowed my head and the sound of her name spoken aloud sank my heart.

"I see", the Doctor said quietly. "She spent her life looking for you", closing the book. "Did you know that?"

"I don't know anything, Doctor. Only that she was there to help me when no one else could. Will you tell me about her?"

"Eleanor. She wasn't like the rest of us, Tristan".

"No, Doctor. She really wasn't".

"Forgive me, Tristan. I shall return in a moment, try and rest". The Doctor left the room through the curtain. I reached down for the remainder of the roll and an olive and consumed them in peace, though a peace reigned over by an ignited hope. Theoris and Amsu sat on the edge of the bed and watched me like any children would an unusual stranger.

"Tristan, are you sick?" Theoris asked coyly.

"No, I don't think so. I just slipped, that's all. Nothing to worry about".

"No, you didn't. You collapsed, and then you were asleep for a long time", she plucked bravely. "You said you were in the desert for a really long time, too". She was obviously right. I sighed and took a deep breath. "You were talking when you were asleep, so we knew you hadn't died". The girl stole an uneasy glance at her brother.

"Tell me miss know it all. What did I talk about when I was asleep?" Attempting to amuse the little girl. She didn't smile.

"You were being chased by someone and in lots of pain", she replied gravely.

"Well, little Theoris, I can assure you I'm not in any pain, and there is certainly no one chasing me. So you don't have to worry anymore".

"We loved Eleanor, too". She looked at her brother once more, who appeared to be content just to listen.

I sighed again. "I guess to meet her was to love her".

"Where do you think she is now, Tristan?

"Far away from here, Theoris. Far, far away".

Little Theoris bowed her eyes and sighed before lifting her head again, "Do you think she was a princess?"

"Maybe she was", feeling an awful pang in my chest.

"I think so".

I chuckled out my sadness. "Then I guess we are in agreement. She was a princess".

My eyes flickered and an ache struck me in the temple. I immediately applied my hand to the pain and discovered a large bump, while also disturbing a rash of dried blood that flaked and cascaded across my palm. I hadn't registered the gravity of my freshest injury yet, though the dark shadow that now lingered in my peripheral sight supplemented the idea it was pretty nasty. I looked around and saw the bowl and flannel sitting tepid and still. The water was red and the flannel soiled crimson. The children continued to observe me as a spectacle in the zoo. My attempts to move my legs over the edge were ill-advised and I immediately realized my navigation was quite off.

My vision blurred for a few moments before focusing once more to the floor. I dropped my head and sat hunched over, staring at the red in the carpet, contemplating the possibility of lowering myself onto my own weight. Would my legs buckle? Would my vision desert me? Could I even stand up? I took the plunge. My toe tips were greeted with a painful flurry of pins and needles. Dr. Rambo entered.

"Tristan, you are not ready to stand", he cried.

I couldn't feel the souls of my feet touching the ground for the dastardly pins and needles, my legs were not present, my thighs held no sway to my stance and they helplessly gave way as my knees buckled. My body seemed to capsize and my arms flailed to cling to anything. Dr. Rambo captured me and grappled his arms under my own just before I planted my face into the floor. I slumped against his shoulder like an inanimate dummy. The pain in my temple escalated and a claustrophobic panic gripped me like a vice.

"I can't walk", I gasped. The Doctor wrestled me back to the edge of the table and rolled me onto my back.

"Do not be afraid, Tristan. You will regain their use very soon. I can assure you it is quite temporary".

"What is happening to me? I can't walk on my own two feet", I said, becoming lost for words in the furor of my disbelief.

"But you will in time", he replied, glancing towards Theoris and Amsu. They both stared back sorrowfully.

"What have you done to me? I want to know what is happening. I bump my head and now I can't walk?"

"Forgive me, Tristan". He gripped my shoulder, "I didn't know it was you. You must understand it was for the safety of my family that I did this".

"Did what", I asked hurriedly. "What did you do?"

"I removed the use of your legs. There is something else within you, something bad... this thing made itself known while you were gone".

I relented. "Blackband".

"Blackband?" the Doctor replied venomously.

"Yes, Charles Walter Blackband. Do you know of him?"

The Doctor scowled and nodded. "Yes, Tristan. We all know of him". His stare cooled after a few moments and so too did his features relent to a more familiar softness. "Would you care to stay and eat with my family this evening at my home. We can talk more about what I believe has happened to you".

"And how do I know I can trust you?"

"Because Eleanor trusted me, and I think we both know that Charles Walter Blackband is a monster. There are two perfect reasons". The Doctor looked at his children. Their eyes met and between them they spoke a pure and simple truth. "Tristan, all will be explained over an evening meal, and afterwards you will be free to leave with the full use of your legs. This I promise you". He gestured towards Theoris and Amsu. "On the lives of my children".

116

"Well, it doesn't look as though I have much choice, does it?"
I grabbed my right leg and dug my fingers in. Nothing, not a
damn thing. "I want the use of my legs returned, Doctor", I said,
laying my head down like a spoilt child. I was tired and afraid. I
drew my arm across my sight. "I hope you live close by, Doctor.
I don't see myself getting very far without my legs".

There was a shuffling and tapping of small feet and the sound
of a match being lit. I rolled over and saw Theoris and Amsu
standing beside an archaic looking wheelchair, and Dr. Rambo
stood over them, igniting the end of a cigarette, grinning no less.

"My house is not far, Tristan. You will be more comfortable
if you ride in this", he said, shaking the match and tossing it aside.
The children giggled and fought over the push handles of the
chair.

"This just gets better and better", I sighed.

They wheeled me out into the street like a cripple for all of
Cairo to see, or so it felt, and the funny thing that kept occurring
to me as we wheeled away was how I'd ran like the wind, alone
and free to reach the Bazaar. And now, I was leaving in a
wheelchair, helpless, accompanied by a stranger and two
children. The lamp and Eleanor's face danced in the darkness
whenever my eyes closed, and when they opened, they were met
with the stares of the locals, suspicious glances, and amused
glares from every corner of the neighborhood. The ride was a
bumpy one, as I was pushed down a series of passages and streets
teeming with smoke, steam, and people. A great warmth filled
this place, a village-like community. The feeling adorned the air
around them all, as children teased stray dogs and ran through
shutters and up stone steps above our heads. Their laughter
battered the warmth and the glint of their eyes shimmered
throughout the streets, holding hands and playing games.

Theoris seemed to look upon them as just children and not
peers, the way a parent might. Amsu watched them, almost in
awe. I sighed, something I'd done a lot lately, and wondered
where all this would lead me.

"Do not worry for your legs, Tristan. I gave you a mild
tranquilizer that can take away their use for a time". The Doctor

touched me on the shoulder, bowing his head slightly closer. "You will be okay, Tristan".

Theoris slipped her hand into mine as though she knew how I felt, like she sensed my troubles and was offering her sympathies. Maybe she was, in the only way a child could. She squeezed my hand and smiled and gave me courage. I tried moving my legs once more, but they were numb, as though they were not my own. I felt like calling out to the Doctor and asking, demanding, pleading to him that he assure me he was not leading me to danger, that he was one of the good guys. But if he were not, would he have told me? I wagered not and so forthwith held my silence.

We reached a two-story house of sandstone with steps leading to a sturdy, wooden arched door. And a drawn canopy. The wooden shutters on all but one of the windows had been released to sway back and forth. A pair of lustrous trees lined the garden like ushers and a huge pampas grass seemed to reach out to us as we neared.

"Your home?" I asked.

"It is", he gestured towards the path. "You are very welcome. My house is your house, Tristan".

I surveyed the outside and wondered what it would be like inside. Did I want to enter? What awaited me beyond that door, horrors or dreams? The Doctor stopped the chair and the children edged ahead and sat on the steps, staring out like ornate statues adorning the walled entrance. I turned to the Doctor in anticipation.

"You may stand now, Tristan. You are free to walk as you like". He drew his arm across the expanse. "There are no prisoners here. To enter within must be of your own choosing, and to hear what I have to say, you must enter in soul and of your own accord".

I turned back to the two faces on the steps, cold and sweet against an impending twilit breeze. I looked around and dug my fingers into the arms of the chair and wiggled my toes discreetly. Strangely, I wanted to feel the control once more in myself before standing. I wiggled again and again in contentment until a smile almost invaded my face. Amsu smiled and watching this I stood slowly, using the arms of the chair and my feet to elevate myself. I was back. Thank God for the gift I held in such contemptuous ignorance. I felt like I had been granted special powers, as though somehow, I could run faster than before, jump higher, walk taller. "Oh, my... I never thought it would feel so good to walk".

"Tristan, you can walk away as free as a bird..." he pointed towards a dark and lonely road with some daunted figures moving in doorways. "Or you can dine with us and talk of your troubles".

I looked down the dark road and pondered what my 'troubles' were and how deeply they were ingrained. He continued:

"But know this, Tristan. If you walk away then your troubles will follow you. Hand in hand they will walk with you to your doom".

"Eleanor told me the same thing, Doctor. We had vowed to face them together... now... it's just me". I looked up to the sky and secured my satchel strap. "I want to know what is coming".

He stared at me deeply but spoke no further on the matter, except, "Come". The Doctor ushered me forth with an outstretched arm. I did as he asked and entered. We were greeted into an airy hall by a fan spinning on the ceiling and a number of rooms lining the way, rooms with doors firmly closed and others with hanging beads veiling their contents and personage.

"This way", he guided me. At the end of the hall was a set of stone steps that led out into the garden... the sound of water rippled across a jasmine-scented-through-breeze. We advanced beyond the door, where a lush green garden emerged and in the center was a long table set with an array of colorful foods and liquids. Two palm trees seemed to cross each other in a yearning stoop for one another, and all the colors of the rainbow dressed the foliage around the borders of this little Eden.

The garden seemed to be lit artificially, but I could not find the source, and the table, already articulately set, had guests seated who, it is worth noting, stared at me like I had three heads. I was being drawn deeper into the fabric of this place. Theoris and Amsu ran to the table and took their seats beside each other. Amsu was immediately seized upon by a mature woman with jet hair and dark eyes who began wiping his face with a cloth... the way my own mother had done so often in times gone before. My mind wandered to a few of them until a sweet laughter snatched me back to reality.

Little Theoris giggled and looked at me. I was left standing on the top step, observing the patrons of the table. The woman caressed Theoris' cheek and smiled warmly. She turned and approached, siphoning me by the arm and a warm smile to a seat at the head of the white-clothed table. This was certainly pleasant, I thought as I looked around the family, and everyone conversed in Arabic rapidly and sipped wine and tea. An old man to my left eyed me suspiciously. "The cursed boy", he hissed loudly.

I looked at him in shock as a faint but cruel smile dressed his leathery jowls. Dr. Rambo spoke up from the head of the table in his typically assured tone. Trouble was he spoke in Arabic, but he appeared to be berating the old man, softly, then by way of expression seemed to reason and apologize to him... conjecture, of course, but most plausible. The Doctor turned to me once more and smiled.

"Tristan, do not be so alarmed. You should see your face now. Try and be calm, there is some wine beside you, have some".

I looked at the wine jar and then at the people around the table who had once more fixed their attention to me. I poured some into a goblet and found myself still looking around the table as I was pouring. How I must have looked to them.

"Mama, Tristan fell down in the shop and now he is going to die unless Papa helps him". Amsu broke the silence with this quite disturbing, crumbled set of words. Theoris gave him a slap on the shoulder and berated him, quite ferociously for her years. There was a spirit in her eyes and I wondered who these people were and how on earth I'd found them. Why was I going to die? I didn't want to die. I drank the wine in one go and poured another.

A man who I imagined to be very tall was sitting across the table, he spoke. "Tristan, you know something, you look a lot like my cousin. My cousin is a good man".

"Oh", I said, wiping a sleeve across my mouth.

"Yes", he said, nodding his curly head. His smile broadened and he chortled. "He's a good man. You are a good man, too, Tristan. I know it".

120

Dr. Rambo banged his fist on the table and everyone jumped, even the man with the cousin who looked like me—all except Theoris, who giggled at just the right moment. The unassuming, comic timing of a child's joy arrested the suspense and quietened my butterflies. And it made me want to chuckle along, seeing her sweet laughter shame the shocked, weathered faces of the adults.

"The boy is cursed, any fool can tell. Why have you brought him to our home?" the old man repeated with even less tact and a pointing finger. "His heart is dark and haunted".

"I..." the Doctor paused. "*We,* are going to help young Tristan". He looked at the man with the broad smile, "brother". The old man mimicked the Doctor, silently mocking his speech while turning, with great lethargy, to the exotic-smelling food in front of him.

"Tristan, eat something", the Doctor gestured towards the food. "Drink and tell us about yourself".

I was hungry as a wolf but conscious to simply tuck in as suggested. "I don't really know what to say", I mustered unimaginatively.

"Who are you? Why have you come here? Where are you going?" the Doctor prodded.

I looked at my food and then around the table at the foreign faces staring like mannequins in a mock dinner dress set, each void of any tell-tale thoughts or feelings except, perhaps morbid intrigue. I thought about the question for a moment as I looked at my food. A fly had landed just beside the plate. Watching its twitchy animation and fluttering wings, my mind wandered a little. *Well, here goes nothing...*

"Hello, my name is Tristan. I came here because my friend told me about a man, a doctor actually. She told me he was a man who could help me, that the good Doctor Rambo could help solve my troubles". I looked up to the sky and saw thousands of bright stars and a complex constellation twinkling, "to tell you the truth, up until a few days ago, I wasn't going anywhere. I was trapped, wasting away, wracked by nightmares the like of which I wouldn't wish on any of you... until I met my friend, that is". Looking back at the faces, I sighed, "since that day, I've travelled half way to the stars in a plane with no pilot, attacked by scorpions, chased by demons to the ends of the earth, not to mention stabbed, beaten, poisoned, and my heart broken, among other pains too numerous to mention... and you know what? I would do it all again if it meant spending those first few hours with my friend. Just to see her face one more time".

The faces of the family stared wide eyed, some holding forks stationary and with food still hanging from them. I continued unabashed. "You know... you can be saved in a lot of ways. Some might say I wasn't saved at all, that I was simply thrust into troubles deeper still. The way I choose to see it, my friend saved me in the most important way a person can save you. She gave me back something I had lost. She reminded me who I am and what it means, she led when I was too afraid to lead... and in the end, during her final moments, she gave me the hope to fight on, to keep fighting when she knew she would not be around to fight for me". I looked around the faces. "She did all of those things in little more than a day. So you ask me who I am? Where am I going? Well, I say I am Tristan, the fearful man, friend of Eleanor and I am going wherever my destiny takes me". I raised my goblet, "to Eleanor".

The people around the table, except for the old man, sheepishly raised their cups as though they had no idea what I was talking about... 'to Eleanor' was muttered by all and I drank.

Doctor Rambo raised his glass towards me with a discreet look and nodded. He drank his wine down wistfully.

"Do you have family, Tristan?" the woman with the dark eyes asked. She glanced at the Doctor and rested her hand upon his.

"Family?" I replied. "Yes, but they are very far from here and I have not seen them for many months".

"In England?" Theoris asked.

I smiled and nodded, "Yes, little Theoris in England".

Doctor Rambo pushed his plate to the side. "You have had adventures, Tristan, but home will always be waiting". The Doctor looked around the people at the table and then at the dark eyed-woman beside him, who returned his gaze with no small affection. "My greatest adventures are all sitting around me this day – my family, and I needn't step outside this house, my home. You see, Tristan?"

"You are a very fortunate man, Doctor".

"Do you love your mother and father?" he asked.

"Of course, they are my parents", I replied immediately.

"And your brother?"

"He is my brother".

"Then if you were never to see them again, would they not always be with you?" He placed a hand to his chest, "in here?" I nodded and felt a lump form in my throat. "They would".

"Is he like you, Tristan, your brother? the Doctor asked.

"No, he's nothing like me. He's a soldier—strong, brave. I am a very proud brother".

"Maybe you're not as different as you think, Tristan. I am sure he is a good man".

"He is a great man", I was compelled to answer.

The old man grunted as though he had just awoken. "Soldier", he muttered before slurping some soup from a silver spoon like a dog might. I gave him a look, but no more.

"Family is everything, Tristan. But some people are destined for things that remove them from their loved ones. Purpose takes us from our families, sometimes forever, sometimes for a while". He looked around the table and then back at me once more. His eyes held a contemplation I could not know. "Do you understand my meaning, Tristan?"

"I believe I do".

Theoris giggled and mimicked my words, grappling and swinging from her mother's arm.

"Let us eat now and converse of things that do not muster such puzzlement and intrigue", the Doctor chuckled.

We talked, one and all, over dinner and wine, in laughter and in story. Even the old man at times. After dinner, most of the family retired into the house and Dr. Rambo's wife, Medea, cleared away the plates and condiments without a sound. There were obliging nods of appreciation as she did so and I myself thanked her quietly. The old man stayed seated as did the Doctor.

"Doctor, could we…" I began, before he impeded my speech seamlessly, as though awaiting my questions.

"A glass of brandy?" he offered in his most charming manner yet.

"I trust there will be no more potions of immobility?"

The Doctor smiled and shook his head. "You have my word, Tristan".

"Then, why not?" I relented. "Thank you", stealing the slightest of momentary glances towards the old man. Medea had already breezed out from the house carrying three bottles of a clear liquid and three glasses. She set them down and embraced the Doctor with a whisper in the ear, to which he simply nodded and spoke a few brief words in his native tongue. She turned to me. "Sleep well, Tristan".

The Doctor poured some of the clear liquid into a glass and slid it along the table like a pistol in a game of Russian roulette. I was gambling now, but nothing stopped me from sipping and wincing at the flavor. I was still awake. I could feel my legs. I was alive. No bullet in the chamber this time.

The old man stood gingerly and sat closer to me. He coughed gruffly and summoned all manner of phlegm from his throat. Raising his glass, his eyes locked to mine, he downed the drink in one, lowering the glass slowly, never letting his cold stare stray, a trickle ran down his bristled chin.

"You like?" the old man grunted, as though a scarab was lodged in his throat.

"It's… unusual", I hesitated. "But pleasant", I lied.

The Doctor laughed out loud, rendering a skip of my heartbeat absent. I don't think it showed. The wings of butterflies fluttered about my intestines, fanning them in a taunt of flight. I seized the bottle and poured myself another glass until it overflowed and immediately swigged down half. *Easy, Tristan. Hide your fear.* The brave one yielded the wise words even before the wicked taste of this firewater had cooled.

"Come, Tristan, you are in my company". The Doctor gestured a hand towards the house, "my family's company". He raised his glass towards me. "You should feel no fear here".

The old man released a phlegm-spangled choke of laughter and poured himself another drink. A fly landed on his lip as he poured, but he made no attempt to remove it, instead, he visibly savored the next sip.

"I feel no fear, Doctor", I said, very much in white lie territory. "Good, Tristan. Glad to hear it". He thrust his glass towards mine. I obliged and the glasses chinked against the sound of the water fountain that was around here somewhere.

The old man raised his glass, too, and looked at the Doctor, and then he looked at me with his drink sodden chin. "To the boy, Tristan and his cursed heart". He toasted the sky and then took a healthy swig from the glass. "May he live to find his fears", he concluded bitterly.

I looked at the Doctor in the lamest of protestation, but he simply quelled this by winking and raising his hands in an appeasing fashion.

"Father, come now. The night has drawn". He stood and rounded the table. "It is time for your rest". The Doctor sat down beside him and pushed the bottle across the table, out of his reach and then removed the glass from the old man's decrepit fingers. He offered no resistance. The Doctor helped him up. An apparent stupor had now set about the old man and he shook his head, as though he was as surprised as I was. The old man looked at me in the strangest of ways and muttered these words...

"Boy, go well into the night, brave soul". He blinked a couple of times and a sinewy string of saliva dangled from his lip before breaking and falling to the stone floor. I was quite dumbstruck. The Doctor led him away. I took a drink and looked up at the stars. I felt calm and realised that my family could see the same stars as I right at this moment. Twas all I could ask for.

The Doctor returned after a while and sat crossing his legs; he arranged his trouser leg at the seam. And then he lit a cigarette with a match. The smoke ghosted his features causing him to wince a little.

"You know, Eleanor once sat exactly where you sit now". "Right here?"

"Right there", he replied. "Full of life. She was just a girl, a young lady, one single life... but she gave you the impression she had lived a thousand. Theoris and Amsu, of course, they loved

125

her from the moment they laid eyes on her. Medea, my wife answered the door one evening and there she was, stood on the step, small rucksack in hand and a smile across her face. It was strange, but my wife invited her in even before any words were exchanged. Needless to say, very soon, after words were exchanged, we found her to be a delight and welcomed the girl to stay".

"Who was she, Doctor?" I asked.

"Who was she? Who is anybody, really?" The Doctor said. "All I know is that of all the dark forces I have seen and heard of. Of all the dark places in this world and the next, this young lady was one of light, a bright light from a place…" the Doctor paused and looked up to the stars. He looked back and shook his head, faintly, "…well, from a place people don't usually come back from".

"I knew her… I mean before…"

"She knew you, Tristan. Before she ever met you, she knew you. Eleanor spoke of this many times".

"The strangest feeling..." a lump in my throat threatened any more words for the moment.

"One night, Eleanor was putting the children to bed and they asked her to tell them a bedtime story. Eleanor told them she knew lots of stories, but the one they would really like was her favorite story. I had been passing by the children's room to join Medea for our evening tea when the beginning of her story made me stop and listen".

"Do you remember it, Doctor?"

"You wouldn't forget it".

"Tell it to me".

The Crossing of the River Goddess

"Once upon a time, there lived a girl they say came from a great river. She could not see the world for the stars, nor could she remember ever being a child, or even growing up. The girl wandered the realms with her band of sisters until one day, after many adventures of which she did not remember the beginning— she became separated from her sisters for all of time. Scattered to the wind were they throughout the lands and seas, never to live as they once had, walking paths very differently to one another and evermore further from the purpose of their creation. The girl's spirit was captured by the vision of a boy in a time and place very different from her own, a time and place very far from her own. This made her so very sad, as she knew he would always remain no more than a figment of her memory, a memory never lived, but missed out on in some cruel trick of the fates. So powerful was her vision of the boy, most days, it would consume her cheerfulness, completely crushing the amazing light that once shone from within her.

"Her light, she feared, would be nothing more than a dim pinprick across the time and space separating them. She believed it was her light that shone for him and no one else, and that it would be of no earthly use unless it was cast upon the path the boy was struggling by.

"Perhaps it was the gods themselves who couldn't bear to see such a light, such a fire reduced to a mere flicker, a flicker now threatening to extinguish itself evermore with each sundown. For one day, the Olympian Hermes, while disguised as an angel, visited and told her of a flower that existed that could lead her to the boy. The girl from the great river broke down and wept that she may actually find him after all her wanderings, all her efforts to break through to him would not have been in vain, and she might one day shine her light upon his path.

"The girl asked of Hermes: 'What flower do you speak of?' The winged messenger told her about a lotus flower that could make her like them. She could be reborn a mortal, but only if she could steal it away from an evil sorceress, a true demon known as the Eater of Hearts. The girl from the river felt no fear, she felt no qualm in setting to her task almost immediately, for she had only to compare the cold and sad meanderings she'd wallowed in for so long. What could the Eater of Hearts do to her that would be worse than this mournful sadness? Now, she had been presented with a chance to find the boy, a chance to live beside him in the world for as long as the fates would allow.

"The girl asked of Hermes: 'Where will I find The Heater of Hearts. To which realm must I travel?"

"Hermes replied: 'The Eater of Hearts remains banished from the Duat Halls, languishing in the underworld, lying with the slithering and the wicked in wretched Tartarus. Though even if you were to steal upon such a place and steal away such a thing... you must know that in finding the boy, your destiny is to watch him die. This is the will of the fates'.

"The girl recoiled and swore blindly. 'I never shall, never...' the immortal girl felt a burning deep within her. 'No', she cried, 'you are wrong... the fates are wrong'.

"But Hermes shook his head... 'The fates are never wrong, child. You will see him close his eyes for the last time'.

"The girl would never believe it. She believed in her heart she could never let that happen. 'I will help him. I will save him from the horrors that await him'. Her words were driven and furiously delivered.

"Hermes replied, as if fencing with her: 'Such anger. Is it only this fury bubbling beneath such a pearly exterior that drives you towards him?'

"The girl calmed her tone, for she was also an eternal one. She breathed and suppressed her fire. 'Do not mistake my light for anger. It is my light I have buried so deeply within that now flows forth. No such light could ever harm him. He is the one it shines for'.

"Hermes had heard more than enough... 'Where you are going, there will be a great need for light'.

"The girl traveled to a place she knew. A place of darkness. A place where if you were to step upon the precipice of gloom, the edge of the reasonable heart, the very last point of logic, then the remaining vestiges of hope, should you enter, shall leave your body and soul as you make that meander beyond. But not this girl. No, she felt a tepid joy that continued to simmer wildly as she approached the place of despair for a multitude. Hades.

"The girl came upon the great Cerberus, guardian of the underworld. She did not shine her light upon the ferocious beast, but instead sat, so the story goes, three cubits from the gnashing jaws of the hound that bore three heads. For three days she rested upon the burning ground, watching the animal make dash upon dash towards her. Teeth bearing themselves and still hanging with the flesh and sinew of great and brave heroes that came before. Many times, the beast quarried the depths of its rage, each time the gaping jaws were primed so comfortably to consume the girl's skull between fangs that reeked of the dead. But, alas, the great Cerberus would be halted by a force that placed the beast to a falter, a stumble, and finally a crashing down to the hallowed soil of the gates she had guarded for an eternity.

"What the guardian of Hades could not have known, rather, what the creature could not have remembered, was that the girl had visited the river Lethe before she'd befallen the gates. For the souls who have heard of the Lethe, they will tell you, its waters are the essence of oblivion, the place that drowns the memories one holds and seals the final steps to complete forgetfulness. The branch of the poplar tree the girl had soaked in those waters had been sprinkled upon the sleeping beast's crowns of unkempt fury, and also the ground around where she now sat. The spirit of Hypnos, conjured by the waters of the great Lethe, had made the formidable beast nothing more than a slumbering, three-jawed mound of furious wheezing. The girl approached the beast and knelt before her. She leaned into the still-pricked ears of the highest head.

"She spoke softly: 'Do not fear, great Cerberus, for you will remember again... but first I must remove something from this place. Something that does not belong here. You shall wake one day and resume your duties'. The girl stroked the brash fur of her crown. 'Sleep well, great Cerberus'.

"And with that, the girl entered the cave that would lead her to Tartarus, the most heinous of abodes. A place, they say, even dreary Thanatos did feel a chill in the air. Though the girl knew the underworld intimately, Tartarus was the dwelling of despair itself, the cauldron of which only misery, demise and eternal suffering did stir beneath the broil of divine retribution. For even the wiliest, the most cunning beings, the bravest, far hardier and grizzled heroes and villains... non shall fare any better nor slight the path with advantage of their bold standing. Those sent here shall wither and languish at the behest of whatever foulness did exercise dominion. When one approached this place, it did not serve to imagine quite so fervently.

"Nevertheless, the girl ventured beyond the great divide and by way of vast and winding tunnels she wove herself, and from her origins she summoned the bright light she had been saving for him, using it now to illuminate her own path. For three days, she wandered the tunnels, hearing screams and cries of agony, voices not convincingly human. At times it was silent, but not the silence you experience when in a quiet place, no, this was a silence that grated against your nerves, a silence that screamed in your face until you wondered if the existence of anything remained. Had all things vanished and ceased to be? Was my consciousness real?

"The light she possessed did pierce the darkness, though it created the terrible shadows and visions that seemed to all at once loom over her. Towering creatures with elongated arms, their tails whipping against the dripping walls but never quite reaching her. The tunnel closed around the girl with such figures so tightly, that she drew in her arms across her bosom and kept her stride dainty, feet stepping in single file... and yet the monsters served only to scare but not touch the girl. She braved many hours, many days in those lonely tunnels, the forlorn passages of Tartarus, constructs of the mind, perhaps, or possibly the very shades of a journey absent of hope. A vigil of sorts for the desperate and despicable among us, paving the way to further, greater horrors of the mind and flesh.

"Still, she feared not a single step, for her journey was not paved with hopelessness, but one of pure hope and veiled excitement. An excitement she would not let sprout and flower too soon, for Tartarus would not let her go so easily, she feared. One does not venture to Tartarus and return without a fight. Upon the end of the tunnel, she fell upon a black hole in the ground, where it appeared all the other paths stopped, and the conclusion of each surrounded the chasm like the moments of a sundial. The fall of Tartarus... the girl had learned of this many moons yonder, before this endless night. The fall of Tartarus was not the destruction of a place... but the literal fall all souls must make before their final place of bloody reckoning. Some said the fall was equal in distance as the heavens were from the earth. Others spoke of a bronze anvil dropped by Zeus himself taking nine days to reach the lowest pits of Tartarus, the lair of the most ghastly and rampant beasts, to which even the Gods did strive and suffer to shackle in times gone before.

"The girl stepped upon the precipice and breathed in the air of this void, stretched her arms outwards like an eagle to soar and let herself drop into the fall of Tartarus. In silence, the girl fell. Some say for nine days, just like the anvil of Zeus. Others say it was much longer.

"For how long she fell, no one will ever truly know, but her light shone so brightly when she reached the bottom that all things present took themselves into the darkest corners of that place. The shooting star, traveling fastest of all down that awful trench, did hit the black lake. The pool used to capture the unfortunate after the fall. A pool sitting serenely at the bottom. No longer did the surface stay calm, but a great splash pierced the tranquil black mirror and sent ripples that morphed into waves crashing over the grey silt mounds of the shore.

"The girl stretched her limbs out from her fetal form and swam to the surface, allowing only her forehead and eyes to emerge above the water line. She scanned for signs of life, signs of the threat that must be lurking in every crevice of this... the lowest of realms. The last of the frothy surge of ripples tapered to a calmness as she breast-stroked her way to the edge of the black lake. She climbed out dripping wet, jet hair clinging in winding columns to her snow-white cheeks, and the rows of unkempt freckles hiding behind them, secreting droplets of water that stubbornly did not roll from her shimmering skin. A howl snagged her attention, a long and lasting howl from the jaws of a hungry wolf.

"Now that the furor of the black lake had receded, the sounds of Tartarus slowly came to being once more. The nattering and gnashing of teeth echoed the pathetic moans of tortured beasts, toppled to shells of creatures. Whittled down long since from the days they must have snarled and roared. Tartarus was all-consuming of these eternal beasts, these wicked forms of depravity. Made nubs of them, senseless, toothless, cumbersome nubs to be stepped beyond while holding a free hand over one's nose and mouth... but there were others down here, others who endured the wickedness and zealous evils. Made not into nubs but remaining, even growing to be more vile, more wholesomely cruel. Yes, there were a few monsters destined for this place. Those who yearned for Tartarus.

"A wolf emerged from a dark hole in the wall and paused, part of a rib cage hung from its bloody jaws. The eyes set upon her for a moment. From whence the wolf appeared, so too did a staggering figure barely containing his dangling guts, close to his torn sternum. The man festered to call out to the wolf for the return of his anatomical belongings, though the wolf simply plodded on, bound for a place to strip the bones without hindrance. The girl knew she mustn't let such things quarry her mind, she mustn't let the place where her heartstrings might reside be played upon while a guest in Tartarus, for she knew those who dwelled down here had been of foul deeds in the world above.

"The girl stepped upon the ashen mounds and crossed a smokey plain of black coal that made the sound of egg shells breaking. On the other side she was met with a fissure in the grey rock, one that ran high up into the darkness like a black thunderbolt. The girl peered in and felt a coldness upon her face unlike any she had felt before. Undaunted, she stepped through and took more steps, into a darkness not seen before in the realms above. Once more, she summoned the light from where she imagined a heart may be and lit the way before her. Upon the sodden walls were the bloody entrails and crimson smears of the takers of this path. Red hand prints borne by struggle dashed the rock, and others were made from the sharp appendages of creatures one would not want to encounter in such a dismally cramped crevice. Still, the girl loitered not and followed the shining light she imbued from her every pore, as many hundreds of steps became many hours of endeavour. And when she believed it must go on, for as many days as she had fallen upon this place, she came upon a cavern, dark and dank.

"Her glow spread outwards, reaching forth all around her, and yet the edges of this world still escaped her. The girl crouched down to the black sand and closed her eyes. She listened carefully and began to hear the prisoners of this place. They were all around her. She summoned her strongest will and sent illumination to the furthest reaches of whatever cavern, whatever darkness had besieged her light before now. With the light came the sounds of the awful things down here, the sounds of the underworld sobbing and wailing, gnashing and retching.

'Stop, child', a voice emerged.

'I am no child, you are mistaken', the girl replied.

'No, you are not a child. I was wrong to call you by one'. The woman appeared on the edge of the light. 'But maybe it is your desire to become one', she spoke softly, edging closer. 'Am I mistaken once more?' the woman asked the girl.

'What do you know, stranger?' The girl advanced with her light. 'What would one unfortunate bound to Tartarus know of my desires?'

'Don't listen to her. The witch killed her own children', a sly voice emerged from a cave to the left of the girl.

'Who speaks?' the girl replied quickly, casting her arm and shedding light across the way as an arrow might spring from a bow. The woman on the edge of the light drew herself closer and approached the girl. Her face was shrouded by a low bearing-hood.

'Do not come any closer, woman. I wish you no harm, but it is all you will find with another step', the girl told her. The woman froze and dropped her crimson hands. Droplets of blood ran from her fingertips in streams to the ground. She raised her head slightly, though a shadow remained akin to her features.

"She spoke again: 'Child, I do not deny what the voice of the cave tells you, for how else was I to get here? How else would one be sent to such a place as Tartarus?' The woman began creeping forward once more.

"The voice from the cave came again, shrieking this time. 'She murdered her children. You must kill her. You must kill her now'.

"The girl brandished a palm of pure and brilliant light towards the woman in the hood. 'One more step and I will end you'.

"The woman froze and lifted her bloody hands towards the girl. 'Listen to me, child. I can help you steal away that which you seek'.

'Kill her, burn her with your light', the voice from the cave emerged even louder, echoing throughout the bleakness. 'She must be burned for her deeds'.

'Of what deeds does the voice of the cave speak? What did you do?' the girl asked the woman, whose hands began to tremble, and the droplets of blood at the tips of her fingers quivered and cascaded far more frequently for it.

'Child, there is only one way to Tartarus for such as I up there in that cruel world. Now my darlings are picking fruit in the isle of happy souls, for their mother hath released them from a greater suffering still', her voice rasped. 'The flower of light does not belong down here. Not like this, never like this'.

"The girl felt a pressure inside of her, a rush that pressed against where she believed a heart must be. And heartstrings, if she imagined what they might have been, then she felt them being plucked—nay, dragged upon with great force. 'What have you done? What have you done, monster?' the girl cried, as she drew towards her with a light that threatened to ignite into flame. But as her rage illuminated further the dripping gloom, a voice petered out to a yelp, withering to a whisper behind a strange glow across the stone and bone-strewn way.

"The woman in the hood cowered to the floor and rose her arms for mercy, but she immediately witnessed the voice did quell the anger about to be met upon her. 'The boy', said the witch.

'What boy?' The girl asked. She didn't wait for a reply, but wandered over to the mysterious glow across the way. The witch followed her with bloody hands and an uneven step.

'It's you', the girl whispered, stopping before a very peculiar sight. A three-dimensional cube, transparent, but it's sides and borders buzzed with a blue light, pulsing with an electrical energy. What was more peculiar, stranger still, was what was contained within the cube. There within was a space, an abode of sorts, a place certainly at odds with the dank desolation of Tartarus. For within this other place, lay a boy tucked up neatly in a bed, surrounded by all the things not seen down here, not anywhere. The boy was pale, sickly looking and showed signs of a strong and rueful fever, and his breathing was crackled and laboured, as though his lungs were filled with smoke.

'The boy', the witch muttered, carefully stalking beside the girl.

'He's not really here. He cannot be down here in this place. It cannot be', the girl said, not once removing her eyes from the boy.

'It is so', the witch replied. 'He's here for you. Every night he returns, searching for you in his nightmares".

'I don't understand', the girl said, wandering closer to the boy. 'He could not know of this place... there are millenia between us. This is not his world'. She gasped as a series of dark shadows neared the edge of the boy's dwelling. The boy began to breathe quicker and he rose from his back and clutched the bedclothes against his chest, trembling, shooting terrified stares all around the room. A woman appeared beside the boy and laid her hand upon his chest and another against his cheek. She seemed to soothe his panic with her touch and she goaded him back down to his pillow. Lowering his head against the palm of her hand, 'There, there, my darling boy', she said softly, 'there's nothing to be afraid of. I'm here now'.

"The girl clambered beyond a gathering of rocks and halted just shy of the electrified field the boy lay behind. She could see the hounded look in his eyes, that look of terror pained her where she imagined a heart might be in her own chest.

'They are here, mother. They have come for me', the boy gasped, clutching his mother's arm. 'He has sent them here'.

135

'There's nothing to be afraid of, my poor boy. It's just a bad dream'. The woman gathered the boy up into her arms and cuddled him close. 'It's just a bad dream... it's just a bad dream'.

"Though, just as the boy feared, a shrieking laughter did belt out into the electric air and the boy shuddered into his mother's arms and clung to her tighter still. Two faces appeared, the faces of girls glowering into the boy's window with the eyes of jackals. Their lips scimitar-like, dripping crimson droplets from ever-broadening grins. 'Tristan, Tristan', they cooed, slurring and drooling blood upon their own words.

'Dad', the boy called out and reached from his mother to meet the hands of a man who had appeared near his bedside. The boy's father sat beside him and held him by the shoulders.

'You're alright little man, I've got you now', he said and hugged him close. The boy grappled his father and dug his fingers into his back, and he began to weep over his shoulder, still watching the ghouls blighting his world. The boy closed his eyes tightly.

"The girl shoved aside the witch and seized at the walls of the cube that held this peculiar scene. The electrical seams, flared by her touch, drove her back. But some of her light exceeded the boundary and lit up the room, casting a momentary glow upon the little family... only for a second, but it was long enough. The boy had seen her.

'The boy's eyes. He saw you', the witch crowed excitedly. 'What will you do?'

"The girl reached for the electrical current but did not touch it, instead, she placed her palms almost upon it and felt the warmth of the boy. She followed the edges of his world and circumvented the scene under the guise of a swell of light, until she fell upon the two girls who tormented the boy so. 'Sisters', the girl whispered. They looked upon the girl at once and did nothing to quell their raging glances upon her.

'Sister', they hissed. But their words fell upon a light she imbued as the girl screamed her sorrow for the boy against them. And their faces, their long, spindling locks, were drawn back with a force that carried their flounder against the rocks and back into the dark. The girl turned to look upon the boy once more, but she could see he had been settled by his mother and father. His eyes remained fixed on hers. He, and the dwelling began to flicker and fade from this place.

"The girl walked into the dank remnant of where the vision of the boy's realm had occupied. Nothing left but black silt and sullen rock, creeping vines and creatures that scuttled with haste at the touch of her presence. She stooped and knelt where the boy would have lain.

'Witch, who speaks from the cave? Who is it that wishes you burned?' the girl asked, allowing a handful of the black sand to run between her fingers.

'The Eater of Hearts speaks from the cave. She who was banished from the Duat', the witch crowed, clapping her bloody fingers excitedly. 'She has been hiding what you seek down here in lowly Tartarus'. She crept behind the girl as she spoke.

"The girl had allowed her light to dim and invited the witch to get within touching distance. 'You said you could help me find that which I seek', the girl said.

'I did, child'.

'Tell me, witch, how would one best approach the Eater of Hearts?'

"The witch drew herself behind the girl, wound her spindling fingers to rest upon her shoulders and whispered into her ear, 'One would enter the cave and take it from her, one with powers such as yours. She will not behold such a light as your own, dear child'.

'Indeed, well-meaning witch', the girl replied. She walked towards the cave and, on reaching the entrance, looked back. The witch gave a gleeful chuckle and urged her forward, waving her bleeding claws like a doting mother would her child.

"The girl turned once more, to the cave entrance and stepped into the darkness. The girl knew what would happen, she was all too aware of what the witch's intentions were. Or so she thought. For all at once, the cave fell around her and sealed her in beneath a medley of rock and soot. The cackling of the witch followed the crashing of the rock and continued when the stones fell silent.

'Child, did you think I would let you visit on me and take that which is precious', the witch called through the rocks.

137

"The girl smiled to herself and bit her lip, anticipating how she would play her so. 'Oh, kindly witch, you promised you would help me take that which I seek. For I would then go to the boy'. The girl paused and almost released a chuckle, but she relented. 'Tell me, witch. Why do you trap me so?' The girl was almost certain that in her snorting revelry the hag would not be able to contain her gloat, and her parading of the flower would be forthcoming... but it was not so... that moment the girl anticipated did not arrive and the darkness accompanied the silence to cast a cold chill upon her immortal being.

"For moments longer than she'd hoped, nothing stirred. And then a wart-ridden beak protruded from the darkness. A long and shiny nose upon a face that bore black eyes, dead eyes that drilled into her with gasps from the blackness. Before the girl could move, the figure slapped a palm across her bare forearm and cried insanity. Grey, draping locks fell across the girl, rancid like the damp fur of some infernal hound. The girl felt her arm began to sizzle and burn, fizzing and steaming like a geyser about to blow.

'The Hex has you now my child. Wherever you go, I will find you', the figure cried in sputum across her face. The girl quickly imagined where her heart might be, or one's heart might be. She thought of the boy's heart and her fury broke forth in such a way that it brought about a light even she had not yet summoned before this day. This deluge of light swallowed the darkness like a monster of the abyss might consume the small creatures of the lagoons, absorbing the blackness as though it had never been present. With such light, she expunged the rocks that blocked her way like breadcrumbs brushed from the chest of a Titan.

"The girl cried out so loudly, so deafeningly, the creatures of this place wept and her screams guided the light like a hail of spears upon them all.

"The underworld seethed and heaved as the light forced the walls of Tartarus to expand and betray the vines and roots, wonderful in their colours, were they that ran throughout the walls and beneath the black sand. The girl swept away the wart-ridden Hex, who grappled her arm so tightly, and looked up in wonder at the system of sprawling nature that so enlivened this place of once-colourless woe. This nook of notoriety where nothing lived now had the veins of immortality running through it... and who knew what they would bring with them. The girl had found that which she was seeking. The Great Sun Lotus had been unearthed. She knew she had found the way to the boy.

"The girl saw that the electrical currents running through the vines of the flower were not in nature the same as her own light, of which was now emblazoned throughout this chamber. But that it was something else. She ran near where the charge had reached down and discovered that, once again, the boy's dwelling was actualizing before her. The girl stood outside the boy's room once more and her nose almost touched the buzzing hue of electricity. The boy was flat-out in his bed, sickly looking and clammy. And once more she all but touched upon the current and felt the boy's warmth upon where she might imagine a heart should be. She wondered on his heart and imagined she could see it beating beneath his chest, a chest that was working so hard to produce such stunted breaths. The boy's eyes opened and he sat up.

"He was afraid and a great roar went up that seemed just for a moment, to distill the great light from this place. But the light endured and the boy's eyes widened and she thought she saw in his eyes the thing he feared most of all. The sounds of pigs being butchered in their droves splattered the airwaves, the squeals so incessant, the boy fell from his bed and clasped his hands over his ears. The snorting of a great creature and the thumping of hooves made the airwaves vex with stench and pomp—some demon of magnitude was within the vicinage of this unholy place and the hellish sauntering was growing ever greener.

"The girl felt the rumble before she heard it, as tremors began to split the light into rays across an ever-growing darkness above. Her eyes followed the intricate ley lines of vines and petals glowing through the walls. She saw that they ran all around her and beneath her feet. She dropped to her knees and dug her fingers beneath the grey silt, driving her rigid fingertips deep beneath sharp grains that seemed to flow like a great and dark sea, hiding the life and color that writhed beneath.

'No, child. You mustn't take it', a voice cried behind her, and the screams that followed pierced even the bellowing of the butchered pigs. The witch with the bloody fingers who had so gently talked the girl into entering the cave, she now drew back her veils and revealed herself in all of her true horror. Climbing out from the shadows of her ragged garments was the screaming and bloodied Eater of Hearts. The beast herself now stood, transforming from a wretched skeletal shell into a monstrous clapping of claws and gaping jaws.

"The girl flung herself to the floor and began digging harder. But the sand with every stomp, every reverberation, each collusion with chaos by the beasts that now approached her, caused the displaced sand to shift back and cover her hands. She looked up at the boy in his abode. He was staring at her. She stared back.

"The boy raised his hand and flapped his fingers back and forth against his palm. 'Come here, we must hide from the monsters', he whispered loudly. The girl stood and made haste for the boy's little abode with the electric walls, but she was cut down by the claws of the Eater of Hearts. Her light did much to blind and hinder the creature, though cling the beast did to the girl's ankle with a crunching severity, and cry the girl did for the pain that now ran through a place she imagined a heart might belong.

"The girl looked up at the boy once more. He looked back with swelling eyes. The girl opened her hand and reached out to the boy. He began to run. The boy passed through the electric and beyond his dreams. The nightmares would now be able to meet with him in this reality. The boy had breached the boundaries of his dreamscape. But he knew that somehow and still he came for her. He ran and ran, holding his hands out towards the girl until he stumbled to his knees and their fingers met and entwined themselves, as two flowers might in a tangled embrace. The girl felt a warmth within her. She felt a surge of light come from a place she imagined a heart might be, and this was enough to ignite the terrible shackles binding her legs. The unsightly beast squealed and roared as its bloody pincer was sheared off in the great light. They both ran away, the boy and the girl making for the electric abode together. But so too did a multitude of beasts and gorgons in pursuit. The rabble of devils frantically made for the boy and the girl, and on their heels, they blithered their salivating tongues and primed their rancid claws. The ground between the boy's haven and the pair was growing ever smaller, but so was the territory left without a ghoul of distinguished fervor, each gnashing and reaching out for them in hungered desperation. The boy breached the electric field that separated him from this world, but her hand slipped from his and the girl faltered just shy of safety. The girl stared at the boy through the blazing hue of electricity and at that moment felt a greater trepidation for the confines. She was afraid for him.

"The girl knelt to the ground and pained herself, digging to the furthest trenches of her being to summon a light so bright all of Hades would not sustain such a force. The sorrow she had felt for so long had crystallized where she imagined a heart might be housed—a heart she had been deprived of all her life. The ground began to tremble and a swell of light began to emit from her eyes and the beasts bearing down did slow at the sight of such wonder. Though, one giant did no such thing, but instead burst beyond the tapering horde. A megalithic bundle of steel and chains, snorting and squealing like a stuck pig. This giant thundered forth and reached towards the boy with a hand, bound up with iron filings and shards of steel, fluttering to the ground like a hail shower. The boy made one last meander into the damned realm and dragged the girl through and over the precipice of his mind and into the safe zone. But as he did so, the razor tip of the giant's finger nicked at his wrist and left a smear of blood that trickled into both worlds.

'Your hand', the girl cried, seizing his arm. The boy drew his arm away and hid it behind his back. He rose his other arm slowly and pointed beyond the walls of his room. They both stood and peered at the collage of faces, a mass of bodies and limbs, some humanoid in essence, others wickedly distorted and insect-like... their eyes were wide and unblinking, rising up in a towering wall of staring that spoke no words but reserved dominion for every fear one's heart did hold.

'I have to go back out there', the girl said, turning to the boy.
'Not if we go together', the boy replied, placing his palms

upon the electric wall. The girl watched him and followed suit, placing her own hands upon the wall. She felt a buzz, a warm sensation within her chest. The boy closed his eyes and started to push against the walls of his dreamscape, much to the dismay of the monsters outside, who began slowly to be bartered backwards by whips and cracks of electricity reaching out and striking them as they fought among themselves for room in the dirt. The girl pushed against the wall and together they began to move the boundaries of his room forward, gradually driving the ravenous horde apart and moving ever closer to the spot the girl had been digging.

"The squealing of pigs rose from the monsters fizzing about the boundary wall, and the giant upon the horse crashed through them all. The boy's eyes opened as wide as they possibly could. He removed his hands from the wall and clasped them over his ears once more, halting their progression through the mob. The boy crawled away into the corner beside his bed and started rocking back and forth with his head buried between his crossed legs.

'No, no, no, no', the boy repeated over and over again.

'It's okay', the girl tended to him, wrapping him up in her arms. 'He cannot hurt you here, they cannot come in'.

'Let us in, dear sister', a voice screeched from the window on the opposite wall. 'We are cold out here. We wish to come in from the cold'. A pale and drawn face of a girl hissed against the windowpane and drew a sharp finger nail down the glass. The electrical current seized upon her hand and she screamed her fury upon the panes, striking the window repeatedly and being painfully zapped each time. Another pale face, that of her sister, appeared beside her and drew away the wailing banshee before she combusted entirely into flames. The boy burrowed his face into his hands. His dreamscape was closing in around him and his nightmares were verging upon his sanity for those moments.

"The girl rested her forehead against the nape of his neck and whispered, 'They cannot come in here, not now'. But just as she released a deep sigh against his bare skin, she saw the world around her begin to flicker, and, little by little, the boy was becoming translucent.

142

"The boy brought his hands up before his eyes and witnessed the phenomena. 'I'm leaving here again. I don't have long left'. 'I can protect myself. My light will destroy them all...' the girl started, but the boy interrupted her.

'No, you must find it before I leave here'. He looked into her eyes. 'It's your only chance of leaving here... your only chance of finding me'.

'How do you know this? How did you know I was looking for you?'

'How did you know to look for me?' the boy replied.

'I just know', they both said simultaneously, and in perfect unison, 'I've always known'.

"The boy seared through the moment. 'There's no more time', he led her back to the wall. The giant was standing inches from them with nothing but the blue haze to separate them. The boy didn't look directly at him—he couldn't bear to—but the squealing and snorting continued and the plate armour of the goliath shone against the flickering of a current that ran thinner and thinner by the second. The girl and the boy began to push against the wall and it started to move forward again, towards the hole in the ground. Begrudgingly, ever so begrudgingly, the giant took steps backwards as the wall approached him, remaining very close but never letting the current touch him. He was waiting for the walls to fail. He was anticipating the boundary to falter before the boy had completely left this place. The girl didn't know if that was possible. There was much she had not known before she came to this awful place. The electrical field flickered again, and, for a series of the briefest of moments, there was nothing standing between the massing of creatures and them both.

"But the pair had pushed so fervently that the shallow ditch the girl had clawed out was now beneath the boy's room. The din of wailing, the horrified screams from the patrons of Tartarus, grew louder when they saw that the ground was swelling, and that which the girl was seeking began to glow so brightly. The boy and the girl both dropped to their knees. The boy looked at the girl and smiled. She smiled back.

'That which you seek, you shall find'. The boy's eyes wandered her own.

'Is this a dream?' the girl asked.

'I can never tell'.

'What do I do now?'

'Dig', the boy said, watching his hands disappear and reappear. The girl began to dig quickly and as she did the light from her hands began to grow, until the threads and vines and leaves of many colours flooded the room. One such vine entwined her arm and the burgeoning buds began to flower and cause great bursts of colour and chaos. She reached down with this arm and rescued that which had been buried in Tartarus. Something she had been seeking for so long. The Great Sun Lotus.

"The boy touched her shoulder and she met a gaze that vanished with a gust of foul Tartarus air. He was gone, and so too was his abode with the electric walls. The girl climbed to her feet and looked around. She gyrated the scene slowly, feeling the gritty sand mingle in between her toes. The sea of beasts crawling over and beneath one another made their cruelest noises, some writhing with ignorant giggles, others growling like cornered wolves. They could not know the wrath. The girl smiled at them sweetly, an assassin of this dark place with the light of innocence and rebirth. She dropped to her knees and made a shell of herself upon the black silt, cradling the flower against where she imagined a heart might beat. She closed her eyes, and, in the darkness, just for a moment, she saw the boy's face. 'I will find you', she whispered.

"The throng of creatures roared forward and over her. Tartarus became light itself and the explosion was said to have blown an infinite gorge through the many levels of Hades. Some say even the sun managed to steal down a beam of light after the mushroom cloud had cleared. But what was certain was that the girl was no longer there. She had been recast. She was reborn into the mortal realm".

.

The feeling in my heart was one of dreadful pain, and within the searing revolutions of aching there fluttered the good butterflies she had instilled within me that day in Jerusalem, battling their wings against the violent storm that began with her passing. How bittersweet 'twas to hear this tale and how ferociously this awful feeling now fought with the wonders of her and all that she was. My throat was almost completely closed and the heavy lump was forcing my eyes to well.

"She told that story to the children?" I asked.

"She called it... '*Our story*'. One can now imagine why. She desperately hoped it would not be the end of your story".

"I remember the horrors the night would bring me as child, those places of darkness I would descend... but how did I forget her. How did I lose her?"

"Time is not always linear, Tristan. It may be that neither are your memories. However you interpret the story, it seems you both are inextricably linked in a way ignorant to the annals of time, existence and the metaphysical realm".

A tear threatened my eye—a well of them, actually. "But I couldn't save her".

"I don't think you were supposed to, Tristan".

"But..." I leaned on the table and seized my forehead, rubbing at the impending ache now erupting in my mind. A warm sensation ran through my sinuses. "If not, then why..."

What was this? I leaned back and touched my lips. Moisture wicked at my fingers immediately and further trickles ran down the back of my hand and into the hairs on my forearm. Twas blood and plenty of it. My hands seized the rims of my nostrils and they were met with a disturbing volume of blood. The blood flowed down my lips and into my mouth, and as I spluttered, my breath drew wildly inwards, evoking from my throat a desperate croak. My hands became saturated and a shimmering estuary had formed around my feet.

I choked out a plea for help. "Oh, God", my words spluttered. "Doctor Rambo", tasting the bitter iron. "Doctor, I'm bleeding, Doctor". My knees began to tremble, violently, and so too did my hands. My vision blurred further still. The world appeared to me from behind a murky window, stained and shimmering and chills ran through my body like jolts of electricity. I tried to stand, using the table as support, but my senses would not allow it. My eyes wept upon my cheeks and I rubbed the backs of my hands into them, creating a darker world.

"Doctor, are you there? Is anybody there?" The shadow of a figure emerged and advanced towards me. Hands grasped my arms tightly.

"Tristan, it is okay".

"I can't see you, Doctor. I can't see anything". I strained my sticky eyes in an attempt to make out his face. Only the outline of my crooked fingers trembled before my clouded vision.

"Tristan, try to be calm. Try to calm yourself. You are going to be alright". The hands around my shoulders squeezed as my spine juddered and swayed. "Tristan, whatever lies beneath is attacking your central nervous system. You must fight. I need you to fight", the voice urged. "Medea, please hurry". His tone frightened me. The assured tone of the esteemed Doctor was now entirely absent.

"What..." I struggled to speak coherently. "What... is happening?" The breath was stolen from my chest suddenly and then returned like a gust of wind. "What is happening to me?" I trembled out in epic seizure. The sound of hooves resonated around me and the brutal neighing and snorting rushed my ear drums. My world twisted and warped itself around and around like a kaleidoscope of horrors and my temple began to burn as a bonfire.

"Tristan, stay with me, stay with me", the voice pleaded, holding my hand in two clasped ones. "Medea", the voice boomed above the crashing hooves. Medea's voice emerged, spinning frantically in Arabic and meeting my ears in panic. Only the pure and natural nurture in her voice stopped me tipping over the edge. My mother's voice. My mother's voice had drawn me from the darkness and the flames as a child. Now the memory of her voice had my demons relenting into the shadows.

"Tristan, drink this, it is a tincture of the lotus flower. You must drink or you will not come back", Medea's voice, soft and motherly, resounded and I could feel her breath on my face. I felt the liquid pour into my mouth and trickle down my throat with an intense tingling.

Moments later, everything faded to black and there reigned down the silence of peace. I was dead this time. I knew it.

The sound of children laughing and of women in song. I was going to another place now. The blood, the pain, the anguish was all gone. Things of the past. Where now would I end this journey? What was waiting for me out there?

Light met my sight, intermittently, light and darkness, light and darkness. My conscious thought played its hand and dragged me back into the real world. My eyes opened with the resistance of two noble and stoic oysters. They stung with debris and I raised my hands before them and saw that they were still and calm. Doctor Rambo and his wife knelt before me, ashen-faced. The Doctor's eyes widened and his mouth became a great smile, stretching from ear to ear. Medea smiled more conservatively, though she soon closed her eyes and let her gaze drop to the floor.

The Doctor grasped my shoulder and laughed heartily. "I knew it, Tristan, thanks be to God. I thought we would lose you". He rapped in more laughter, "I knew you could do it, Tristan. I just knew you could".

Medea raised her head and released chuckles akin to relief. She bore a warm smile. "Are you okay? How do you feel?" she asked, wiping a newborn tear from the corner of her eye.

"I thought it was all over". My eyes closed and opened again. "But I'm still here".

I may not have been dead, but to live and feel just like Frankenstein's monster, fed potions and bled out like some horrific experiment. The awful inkling I'd been sewn together from many different parts, maybe even different souls. Death may be favourable to such a creature.

"Come, Tristan. We will clean you up", the Doctor said heartily.

The Legend of Blackband

Medea and the Doctor led me down a hall and into a room where a roaring fire and a semi-circle of wicker chairs with a scattering of cushions gathered my attention. Against the wall was a chesterfield sofa with bedding and a pillow. Ornaments and framed pictures stood along the mantel piece and a real homely feeling cleansed the room. A large plant sat in the corner, truly reaching and green, and beside a tall statue of a cat appeared to be staring, just as all Egyptian cats do. I was placed down upon the couch and coaxed into a sprawl. My limbs had not regained full functionality and felt as stiff as wooden planks.

"Thank you", I struggled.

"Just relax, Tristan. You will need to recuperate, regain your strength. You lost yet more blood", Dr. Rambo said, reversing and planting himself into one of the wicker chairs. "Where to begin", he spoke within himself, it seemed.

"How about the beginning, Doctor. That usually does the trick". I surefooted my tone, though my voice was strained and crackly. Most likely, coagulated blood clogging up my insides.

Medea returned with a large bowl of steaming water and placed it down beside me. The glistening surface was scented and a cloth was swirling beneath some petals of a kind. She looked at the Doctor who gave her the slightest of nods. Medea sat herself beside me and motioned for me to remove my satchel. I did so with no small degree of stress.

"The top, too, Tristan. You must be clean", Medea said, squeezing the cloth so tightly, an unbroken chain of water droplets sprinkled down into the bowl.

I did as she asked and removed my top to reveal the wild streaks of dried blood running down my chest. Medea and Doctor Rambo did their best to stifle a heavy consternation, for one surely mustered at the sight of the mockery of stitches and wounds lacing my torso together. Medea would do less than her husband to hide her horror. She exhaled sharply and looked at her husband with a yelp. Doctor Rambo's eyes met Medea's for a moment before moving to mine.

"Blackband did this?" he asked.

"Not exactly". I pointed to the mishmash, "the stitches are his handy work, yes, but the wounds are from the plane crash".

"Plane crash? What plane crash, Tristan?" Dr. Rambo surged.

I raised my finger to my collar bone, which was still quite numb. "This, however, is entirely Blackband's doing. He cut me open and poured poison into my heart. There was nothing I could do to stop him".

Medea dropped her head and her locks trembled with an apparent angst. "Monster", she muttered with great scorn, and followed up with a string of hateful-sounding words in her own language. The Doctor spent a glance upon her and then turned his attention to me once more.

"Tristan, you must tell me everything. Start from the beginning".

"Doctor, it is I who needs answers. Eleanor told me you could help me".

"I can help you, Tristan. But you must first tell me where you have been, so I may know where you are going".

"Very well, Doctor".

So I did as the good Doctor asked. I told them about my nightmares and the creatures guarding the walls of Jerusalem, how I'd met Samuel and found the house that was built on love. How Eleanor found me, how she had saved me. I told them about Baal, the purger of souls and the plane crash in the desert. When I had finished, the Doctor dropped his head, rubbed his eyes and said simply, "Remarkable, truly remarkable".

Dr. Rambo stood and walked over to a brass trolley stacked with an assortment of crystal decanters bearing an array of light-to-dark liquors. He removed a glass stopper from one of them and poured a large measure into a tumbler. He raised it to his lips, but before he drank:

"So, it has begun". He consumed the contents in one gulp and held his sleeve over his mouth to absorb any remnant.

"Doctor?"

The Doctor continued. "Blackband is an evil man, a man of darkness". Medea began cleansing around my eyes softly. "He is very old, Tristan. Older than any man you will have known". He strung out his words theatrically. "When I was a boy, people would tell stories about him, stories that their fathers had told them, stories told to those fathers by their own fathers long ago".

Medea rang out the cloth and I watched as crimson droplets fell upon the surface like raindrops, turning the water closer to the colors of the petals.

"What kind of stories?"

"Some say he was present for the discovery of King Tutankhamun's tomb, that he was one of the band of archeologists first to touch the treasures". His eyes glinted in the firelight and he leaned forward. "Some stories tell of him becoming crazed at the opening, driven mad by the riches and his own greed. Other tales paint him as a rival explorer who lost his mind upon failing to locate the tomb".

"Mr. Blackband?" I said. "Surely he couldn't have been much older than your own children, Doctor", feeling a creeping engrossment.

"Indeed, and yet, there are stories that predate the opening of the tomb, his quests for treasure were known from here to Aswan and beyond since the turn of the century".

"Then it cannot be the same man. The Blackband I know is old, yes, but not that old".

"On the contrary, Tristan—the stories seem to have originated from an even earlier tale known only as Charlie & Delilah. The story of a young nobleman from England who came to Egypt in search of the secrets of this land. The man's name in the story was Charles Walter Blackband". I felt my eyes widen at the mention of his full title.

The Doctor continued unabashed. "This wealthy landowner was never without his wife, a noble and enchanting woman of unknown origin. Her beauty, they say, parted the masses in Tahrir square. Some believed her to be the reincarnation of a goddess, some said she was from another world, while others spoke of her ability to sway the hearts of men. Their story tells of a time early in the last century when the great ship Titanic had sunk".

"Nineteen-twelve", I whispered through a growing enchantment.

"Blackband was a young man full of wonder and adventure. He wasted no time in beginning his expeditions throughout the entirety of my country, from the far-reaching Alexandria on the Mediterranean down to Luxor and beyond". The Doctor lit a cigarette. "Hundreds of workers followed him, engaged, enthralled by his promise of riches".

150

Medea methodically wiped away and cleaned the blood from my neck and chest, rinsing every so often.

"Charlie, the man in your story is Charles Walter Blackband, the same man who operated on me today?" I asked.

"I believe the old man you speak of to be the Blackband in the story, yes", he answered, taking a drag from the cigarette and exhaling deeply. I didn't reply. I knew the Doctor would continue. "His wife followed him on his arduous expeditions. She was a real lady of the time, a quaint and curious woman. But it is also said she was his equal in social stature and just as thirsty as her beloved Charlie for the riches he sought". The Doctor tapped out his cigarette and exhaled again into the air above him. He stood and approached the liquor canteens once more.

My eyes followed him.

"Delilah was known to fervour after the perfumes of Europe and beyond, taking a particular interest in the source and concoction of the scents so eminent in Egypt at this time". The Doctor poured two small measures and replaced the bottle. Picking them up, he turned and sat down again.

He remained holding the glasses and seemed to be mulling. "She would surround herself with these scents in their beautiful, ornamental bottles, transporting many case-loads throughout their travels. They visited countless bazaars, evermore obsessed with finding particular formulae made from a certain Lotus flower that was to be found only in myth... or so it was believed", he smiled and the light made his features converge with shadows.

"Could this Lotus flower be the same one from Eleanor's story?" I asked, suspecting only a fantastical reply.

"I believe it is, Tristan. The Great Sun Lotus". He waved his hand forward. "It has been called many things, and much has been attributed to its wonder since the stories began, but both Charles and Delilah believed very much in the existence of such a flower. They believed it could bestow eternal life upon anyone who possessed it". The Doctor's speech trailed off slightly. He handed me one of the glasses.

"And what do you believe?"

"Me?" the Doctor shrugged, "I have learned to keep a very open mind on such things... if you understand me, Tristan".

"So what happened in the story? What happened to Delilah?"

"Walter and Delilah were said to have grown tired of searching the Bazaar's and antiquarians of the day, grown impatient from digging for what no mortal man possessed in the bustling markets and dark, labyrinthine holes of Cairo". The Doctor lit another cigarette, sat back and crossed his legs. I sipped a little of my drink and subdued a cringe that welled in my cheeks.

"They themselves went in search of the Sun Lotus". He swept his arm outwards, as though pointing in the exact direction. "But this time, they chose to seek out the wonder in a place many never return from... the vast sands of the Sahara". The Doctor lowered his arm slowly. "Into the desert, they ventured with men and camels, a great caravan that saw crowds of people wave them off like soldiers going to war". His eyes glistened and he took a sip of liquor from the glass.

Medea had finished cleaning up and left silently closing the door behind her.

The Doctor swallowed a contented gulp, closing his eyes momentarily in stark appreciation for the drink. "The rest of the story is very much hearsay and myth". He raised his forefinger, "but as the caravan slipped away, snaking deep into the desert that day, many believed a demon followed them. People of the time recalled seeing the shrouded figure of death chaperoning their souls to meet with his sly scythe. They spoke of a giant upon a great steed, one that stalked them deep into the sands to prey on their souls. Stories of this dark rider have been circulating for centuries and some believed it was he who ushered them that day to a demise of unspeakable horror".

I felt a brazen fear grip my insides at the mention of this dark rider. "Demon?" I asked with oblique caution but riddled with an all-too-upstanding dread.

The Doctor continued. "This demon is said to stalk the hearts of mortals... hate, love, greed, fear". His brow rose unquestionably high at the mention of that word, fear. "My father and his father, and his father before, each spoke of such a ghoul. There are tales from here to Petra of its plight, feasting upon the desires and inhumanities of *man*". The Doctor chuckled, but it tapered quickly and he seemed to ponder deeply again. "Inhumanities... a strange word to use for defining our own actions as human beings", he strayed mistily. "Wouldn't you agree, Tristan?" The Doctor regained some of his verve and his eyes rested upon me.

"Doctor, what happened to the caravan? What happened to Delilah and Charles?"

"Three years later, nineteen-fifteen, three men wandered out from the desert and told a story that many dispelled as the ramblings of madmen, the ravings of desert drifting lunatics with grandiose delusions". He sighed and ran his hand through his rough hair before letting his arm slap back down onto the arm rest. "They were cast aside and branded as fools, denied the recognition of ever being part of the original caravan of nineteen-twelve. Two of them were dead within days. My Great-grandfather was the last of them, the sole survivor... or so he thought".

"You're Great-grandfather was part of the expedition? I sprang forward.

"He was".

We both sat in silence for minutes, it seemed. In this silence, we drank some more.

"Doctor", I enquired, tentatively.

"Yes, Tristan".

"What became of him? Did he tell you where he'd been for those three years?" I spewed my questions. I regretted the practice immediately. The Doctor chuckled once more and frowned. "I apologize, Doctor, it's just that..."

"No, Tristan, not at all. We are here talking so we can help you. Do not lose sight of this". He gestured his palm towards me. "After all, you have trusted me. Now you must learn what is out there waiting for you, Tristan".

He gravely reminded me this wasn't just a fairy tale for a weary traveller, but a story that concerned me in a very real way. Doctor Rambo stood again to venture for another drink and returned with two more glasses of the same liquor. I could smell its pungent approach.

153

"The caravan", he began, settling himself down with a sip and the lighting of another cigarette. "The caravan, needless to say, was neither seen nor heard from again. By late nineteen-fifteen, my great-grandfather was all that was left of the expedition for the fabled Lotus of the Sun. He kept his story close to his chest from then on. Most of the time, he denied he'd ever left Cairo, often simply to save himself the bother and persecution some lay at his door. The Blackband expedition of nineteen-twelve was a taboo in some corners and in others a hotbed of fevered speculation and a curiosity that still bears fruit, to this day".

"What happened out there? Did your great-grandfather tell you what actually happened?" I asked again.

"He spoke of them reaching an oasis—a lush, green oasis bearing all manner of flower and animal, a place where crocodiles, hippos and big cats roamed over fertile land that lay on no map. Fresh water sprang up from the sands like foraging fingers, becoming gushing, unquenchable fountains. And lotus flowers congregated up and down the banks like groups of maidens quivering in the breeze". He took a drag of his cigarette, "his precise words".

"The Sun Lotus?" I asked with anticipation. My lips felt dry and I could taste my own blood again.

"No, not the Sun Lotus. He told me Blackband went galloping into the waters and threw himself from his horse amid the Loti, tearing them from their brittle stems and gathering, gouging them into his pockets". The Doctor shook his head slowly. "Very much like a greed-filled madman. My great-grandfather always felt they were in grave danger with Blackband. He said his eyes held a dark glow, one that left him in no doubt he would stab you through the heart for the Sun Lotus".

"Where was this place, this oasis?"

"No one knows. Such a place has only ever been mentioned in legends and myth: no path remains, no route in or out. To you and I, Tristan, this place simply does not exist", he replied, swirling the remnants of his liquor around the glass. "According to my great-grandfather's recounting, Blackband was visited by the dark rider and offered the Sun Lotus in exchange for the soul of his beloved Delilah"

"Never", I gasped.

"Unfortunately, Tristan... the legend goes that during the night of the second day at the oasis, the demon upon his steed entered the camp at a steady trot, flanked by two rabid jackals". Dr Rambo stretched out his hands and fingers. "Monstrous things, monstrous... my great-grandfather said he could hear the snorting of the devil's beastly horse as though it were fire in his ears". He paused as if to recollect, "and the metallic jangling from two large saddlebags slung either side of his mount... that same sound would keep him up at night many years later, when the moon was at its palest".

I listened with wonder and horror, for this horseman was all too familiar. It could have been a coincidence, couldn't it? I had to hear more. My engrossment had dissipated my considerable fear, for the moment, at least.

The Doctor continued holding an empty glass. "My great-grandfather remembered being bound, frozen, he dared not but avert his eyes. The jackals prowled close by in hungered grumbles, growling like no beasts he'd ever heard. He recalled no more after that, or maybe he chose not to". The Doctor placed his glass down and looked right at me, a gravity enveloping his features. "The next day Delilah was gone", he clicked his fingers away from his lips, "vanished into thin air".

"What happened to her? Did Blackband trade her soul for the Sun Lotus?"

"It is believed he did indeed make a trade, though not for the Sun lotus in its entirety, but a solitary petal from the lost Sun Lotus... some say he was tricked into believing he could save Delilah from a terrible fever set upon her, not two days before. A fever that was beginning to take her away.

My blood ran cold with those words, *solitary petal.*

"The people of the caravan demanded to know where Delilah had gone, for they had become fond of her. Blackband told them not to concern themselves with such matters and ordered them back to work".

"The solitary petal?" I whispered.

The Doctor's eyes widened and he continued. "Blackband drew a perimeter around the largest tent in the camp and warned that no man, woman or child should go within two hundred yards of his markings. He told them that whoever did would be shot where they stood, without exception. The people believed he was keeping Delilah hidden away in the tent because she was poorly or even dying... but this was no longer so".

"How do you know, Doctor?"

"Some of the men from the camp, including my great-grandfather, decided to find out what was going on. They waited until after dark and made for the forbidden tent. Blackband, of course, had a number of his mercenaries guarding the entrance. Men ordered to kill on sight".

"Did they fire on them?" I asked in haste.

"On their approach, my great-grandfather told me two bullets whooshed by his face in quick succession, like the cracking of a whip. Whatever was in that tent, Blackband was prepared to kill for with extreme prejudice", the Doctor said with an assured conviction. "The people turned back and retreated to the camp, deciding it was too dangerous, the men had wives and children to care for, and after all, the people loved Delilah, but no one wanted to die out there in the cold, dark desert".

"I don't blame them a single bit, Doctor".

"However, the morning brought bloodshed. Blackband was said to be furious, and to the horror of the camp, he ordered five men to be executed for breaching his ruling".

"No".

"Blackband's small attachment of men stood with their guns trained on the people who must have numbered a hundred and more. His mercenaries demanded the ones responsible for the incursion step forward and pay for their disobedience. My great-grandfather listened in horror and prepared himself to step forward, but before he could, a man beside him grasped his arm and gestured towards some of Blackband's men. '*Look'*, the man whispered. The eyes of those men carried uncertainty—fear, even. He recounted, one of them began shaking like a leaf in a hail storm... bang", the Doctor cried.

I nearly jumped from within my skin. "Did they fire?" I asked, wiping spilt liquor from my thigh.

"The foolish coward pulled the trigger and sent a bullet fizzing into the crowd. It is not known whether or not the round took a soul with it, but what is certain is that the crowd seized forward like a swarm of locust in the desert heat. Many of the mercenaries were beaten to death, screaming for their very lives, screaming for a mercy that would not be granted".

"And what of Blackband?"

"A few of the surviving contingent retreated with Blackband to the forbidden tent, where they dug in and fired on the people once more. Blackband was said to be heard screaming, '*Get back you dogs, I have the Sun Lotus'*. He entered the tent while his men continued to fire into an unstoppable wave of fury that would bring only death to them, and yet, on the strict orders of Blackband, they stood fast in the face of certain doom".

"So how the devil did Blackband make it out?" I asked, leaning forward and immediately feeling my stitches crease. I absorbed the pain, but more so the crippling fear of them splitting open.

"The crazed Blackband emerged from the tent holding a clasp of woven leather, and from this clasp a glowing petal ignited into flames before the people. He swore he would live forever and that he would kill them all for their treachery. My great-grandfather told me his eyes turned as black as night and his skin drained to the color of snow. The crowd rushed forth, tossing him around like ravenous crocodiles would a wilder beast".

"But they didn't kill him, did they, Doctor?"

"No, Tristan, they did not. It is said an almighty thunder cracked the sky, striking silence into all living things. Complete stillness, Tristan. Shock reigned and everything fell to a complete stillness. My great-grandfather said the sky turned black as though nightfall had come all too soon, but there were no stars, no moon". Dr. Rambo looked to the ceiling and raised his fingers before him, as if remembering. "The air turned as cold as ice, so cold you could see the breath before your very eyes... then a howling wind began to tear trees from their roots, horses were blown into the great beyond, never to be seen again... Tristan". The Doctor leaned in towards me and his eyes narrowed, "he swore to me the desert quite literally turned itself inside out, until

157

everything, absolutely everything, was buried deep beneath its sands".

"Just like that, they were gone, Doctor?"

"Indeed... frightening stuff if you believe in the Sun Lotus", he said, lighting another cigarette.

"So if your great-grandfather made it out with..."

"Azeem and Hasham".

"Then how did Blackband get out, Doctor?"

"No one knows, Tristan. The particulars of his escape remain shrouded in mystery, for when the storm had receded and all was laid to rest, they left Blackband crawling around like an insect, scraping about in the dust. He was clawing beneath the sand, dribbling and muttering, speaking only gibberish. My great-grandfather told me Blackband had lost his mind, that he was driven to madness by the loss of the petal... or maybe by his beloved Delilah".

"But he did get out, Doctor?"

"That man you met today, Tristan. My great-grandfather swore on the lives of his children was the same man who led them into the desert".

I didn't reply immediately, instead I simply stared and ran over things in my head continuously, over and over, until a dulcet ringing smothered the thoughts of the dark rider, Charles Walter Blackband and the mysterious Delilah.

I looked at the Doctor, "The solitary petal".

"Plucked from the flower itself".

"Doctor, I have come across two such petals in my life, both have saved my life..."

"The petals from the lost Sun Lotus are believed to extend life by many years, sometimes even enhancing a person's senses or abilities".

"The very first time Eleanor found me, when I was a child. There was a witch and she stabbed me here", I pointed to my fresh abdominal wounds. "I was dying... but Eleanor, she fed me a petal from an old and withered stem".

"Remnants of the lost Sun Lotus", the Doctor interjected, eyes wide with a growing anticipation.

158

"But Doctor, was it really lost after all? What if Eleanor somehow took it with her from Tartarus... the bedtime story. Am I to believe these petals came from the same Lotus flower the Eater of Hearts kept hidden in Tartarus?"

"Tristan, you must now work on the assumption this bedtime story was not just a story".

"She too, Doctor, consumed a petal from the stem... I'd always believed it was just a dream... but when she died in my arms in Jerusalem, that same petal was all that remained of her. Without it, I'd never have survived the plane crash. Those petals have been keeping me alive my entire life".

"Blackband endures to this day from the essence of the petal he lost in the desert", the Doctor said.

"Yes, but its essence alone does not last forever. Forever requires the Sun Lotus in its entirety". I surged forward, unrewarding of my lesions. "He means to recover it once and for all, surely", I said, with a burgeoning conviction. "The dark rider must have acquired his own petal from the Sun Lotus in Tartarus just before Eleanor blew the place wide open".

"Sounds as if someone is starting to believe".

"And the Hex, the witch who marked Eleanor's arm in the cave. That's the same hag who imprisoned me in Crete when we were children... she must have found Eleanor".

"Yes, Tristan. You are beginning to unravel the mysteries... but we must now talk about how we can help you with your problem", the Doctor said calmly. An air of ease about him prepared me to listen.

"Am I beyond help, Doctor?"

"Fortunately not, Tristan. But I will not lie to you. What must be done you must do alone. Only you can face down and overcome what lies ahead". The Doctor smiled as if contemplating his next words. "Theoris is very fond of you, more so than any of the lost souls before you. But she is frightened because she senses a great fear inside your soul, a terror that grips your heart, one she fears will eventually defeat you. She told me your path will be cut short by the very thing growing inside you". The Doctor spoke like a doctor bestowing the news of a terminal illness. Maybe 'twas just that.

159

"She may be right, Doctor". I was scared again. Damn this insatiable cowardice. A drop of blood ran down my lip. The warmth sat on the tip of my tongue and reminded me that many more would follow.

The Doctor noticed this and gestured with honorable subtlety.

"Tristan, you must be told the truth. Theoris sees all lost souls for who they really are, inside and out. So you must know that she also sees a strength, one that is greater than your fear". The verve in his voice rose considerably. "Though it is one plucked at and beaten down. Destroyed by self-doubt, weak will and self-deprecation". Words motivational in their harshness, one might garner, or at least hope. I wiped away the blood and agreed silently with most of what he was accusing my mortal soul of being.

"What must I do, Doctor?" I asked, holding a tissue to my nose. I needed to be alone for a while, to sit alone. Walk, dammit, a brisk walk away from the madding crowds is what I needed. I wasn't going to get that, though. I knew. A battle to the death with a conniving, hundred-year-old, tomb robbing, wife trading demi-mortal. Well, okay, if that's what I had to do to show my soul in a more respectable light... so be it.

"Tristan, a poison has been administered to your body that, as I explained, will eat your soul. We know that much".

"Which I'm not thrilled about", I interjected with some veiled humour. The Doctor only nodded and continued. "But it is my belief that this is for the purpose of controlling you". The Doctor approached the door and turned just before opening it. "I do not believe he means to kill you, Tristan, not yet at least... there's something out there he must believe only you can find.

"Doctor, he means to use me to recover the Sun Lotus".

"I'm afraid, Tristan, it's beginning to look like precisely that". He turned the handle and opened the door. "Get some rest now. Tomorrow you can change things. I will help you... *we* will help you, Tristan".

Beyond the Figurehead

The Doctor left and I listened out for the turn of the key in the lock. There it was, right on cue. I was trapped here, but that was a comfort somehow, after all, I had the Doctor and his wife watching over me, and let's not forget little Theoris and Amsu. No, I was not alone... for now.

I lay back and stared into the eyes of the tall cat standing watch over me, its gaze cold and steely, but somewhat comforting, as though harbouring an immense knowledge, a truth. My eyes began to droop and I felt myself fighting the dream-like feeling now enveloping me—you might know the one—that feeling, when it is just possible to have dreams but be awake. And knowing neither what is real nor what is not... truth and untruth, dreams or life. A state in which reality and fantasy play in a garden together, hand-in-hand, like children, entirely disregarding of the world and its laws...

My eyes opened and were met with a cool breeze that fluttered about my hair. A vast and endless night sky spread through the atmosphere, the sounds of creaking wood lurching to a methodical pattern clung to the night, and the light splashing of water swam all around me.

I'd not the faintest idea where I was, but it didn't matter for some reason. I hadn't the faintest idea what I was doing, though a shadowy purpose stalked. My line of sight rose and lowered over and over like a giant seesaw, each time being coupled with the sound of water cheering into white crest. The dulcet clanging of a bell rode the breeze and ceased sporadically before spluttering out its lame metallic clink again. I was sitting on hard wood, cedar or oak and my left arm wrapped around a rope running alongside me.

Before me was a great and lustrous carved figure of a woman reaching out into the black sky. She was naked from the waist and beautifully shaped, with long, waving tresses that fell about her snow-white shoulders. Suspended in a frozen moment, one of her arms was pointing into the darkness, or maybe beckoning something out there in the great beyond. The figure was powerfully feminine and commanded my attention with all the vigor of a living person. I stared at her for long moments and wondered how beautiful her face must be, but the bell clanged more vigorously than it had before and I suddenly became aware of myself.

Above the woman, a lengthy beam stretched out beyond her reach, obliquely skywards like a great and thrusting spear. A spontaneous flapping met my ears as the winds picked up, and zipping gusts now slapped my face with a zealous freshness. Looking upwards, to my astonishment, I saw sails riding atop the great pole, shuddering and clapping in the wind. They wrestled and harnessed the power of nature, and beyond them countless twinkling stars moved from side to side in the sky as the ship brushed úp and down the surfing waves. I was aboard a ship, nay, a galleon. The moon and the waters seemed so real.

I was sure if I were to fling myself overboard, I'd be submerged by the choppy waters. Could I really be aboard a ship or was this another dream? I really couldn't say, but I could feel my sweaty palm grind against the spindly rope hairs, that kind of detail I'd never experienced in a dream before, nor had I ever felt an atmosphere and breeze quite so tangible in dreams as the one that now teased at my hair and cheeks. Come to think of it, I had never mused consciously with myself during slumber or otherwise, over whether I was in the real world or some cheese-or liquor-induced wonderland. That is exactly what I was doing right now and the world around was just too real to be my imagination.

The darkness fell just short of all-consuming, as I could see the endless sea of sand roving far away. Mountainous dunes as far as the moon could run and as far as it's light would allow my naked eye to roam. A shiver ran down my spine and I wondered why I was here. Why was I aboard a ship in the middle of the desert with only the stars and the beautiful woman, the beautiful figurehead who commanded the prow of this ghostly vessel? Why could I not remember boarding her? And where was my... I looked down and patted down my person, drawing my fingers across the satchel that clung to my hip. How close to reality could this illusion, this dreamscape, come to fooling me completely. What if I really was sitting here? What if this was actually happening and the place before now was the dream I had awoken from? I felt my palm again and found it to be red and sore. Rope burns... *'too real'*, I whispered. I even licked my palm and tasted that salty twang you'd expect.

This was real. You can't die in dreams, people say. You will always wake up just before you perish... won't you? Real life was, of course, very different—you can die at any moment, as I had been reminded countless times. I couldn't treat this here and now like a dream, in case it wasn't. A chap could get himself seriously hurt that way, or worse.

I took a deep breath and looked out over the course of the river before me. I wagered it to be the Nile. This river could only be the great Nile.

A soft female voice emerged behind me, like a spirit on the air, the slight creaking of wood. "What do you see, Tristan?" the voice asked.

I turned only to find the statuesque cat staring me down. My eyes darted around in their sockets, though, failing to focus on anything sharply enough to recover my mind entirely. The Doctor's house quickly constructed itself around my thought pattern again, as though caught unawares, caught short between a void or chaos that sat between dreams and reality. And there I was once more, lying down in the little room with the cat and the locked door. I grasped at the blanket and patted around my person like a lunatic, flashing my sticky eyes around the room, sweating profusely but feeling a chill rush over me as though I was high upon a mountain summit. The cat, unflinching and stern, looked on in mute amusement, or perhaps, morbid curiosity.

Incredibly, the morning had made stay with the world outside. I felt as though Dr. Rambo had only just bid me goodnight, and yet there was a powerful sun emerging in the east, bringing forth a new day. Instant trepidation for what was to come. The all-too-familiar taste of iron filled my mouth. I was beyond hoping this was all just a nightmare. The scrape of a key entering the lock from the outside took my attention, turning slowly. The Doctor entered with a tray and a smile on his face.

"Good morning, Tristan. How are you feeling today?"

"Good morning, Doctor. I don't feel as though I have slept. Morning came so quickly I can't believe..."

The Doctor broke in before I could finish. "Tristan, you have slept for many hours, I can assure you. Medea checked on you several times and each time you were in a deep sleep. In fact, she feared you had fallen too deeply into your sleep". He placed the tray down. "Medea told me she was sure you were dreaming". He finished in a manner almost asking of a question.

"Perhaps", I muttered, choosing to keep the vision to myself.

"Tristan, a bath has been prepared. You will bathe and join the family for breakfast. Some clean clothes await you also". The Doctor placed the tray down carefully, "drink this tea, the family shall await you in the garden".

"Thank you, Doctor. That's very kind of you, but..."

The Doctor interrupted once more, anticipating my polite protest. "Nonsense, Tristan, drink your tea and I will see you shortly". He left, closing the door behind him.

The turn of the key in the door was not forthcoming.

I reached for the tea and poured some into the glass, where a leaf at the bottom swirled to the top in a circular motion. I took a few sips before placing the tumbler back down on the tray.

The bath was a welcome comfort. I stretched myself out and let my face be engulfed by the soothing water. My skin prickled with the heat of the water and my lesions and wounds immediately pulsed and throbbed, begging to be remembered. I wouldn't have minded staying in this bath forever, 'twas the most peace I'd felt since I held Eleanor's hand in mine.

Yesterday had been long and frightening, drawing from within all of my frailties. My mind had withered. I was back now and I was ready, ready to take back my soul. I listened to the absurdity of my vow, and, pinching my nose, plunged myself back beneath the water line.

I wrapped myself with a towel and opened the door into the hallway, peeking out to check the coast was clear. Appeared to be, though, I could hear the laughter of children and the chatter of adults, the chinking of plates and the barking of a dog. A warm breeze fluttered its way down the hall, carrying two flower heads and stems of grass in wisps that seemed to collude against one another in a race for the outside world.

Jasmine in the air brightened my mood, giving me a little courage of the senses.

I stepped out, carrying my clothes in a bundle and darted back into the room I had slept. Fresh clothes had been placed on the chair and the couch cleared of the blankets. I seized the clothes and held the garments against myself. The shirt was light but tight-fitting and the sleeves fell short of my wrists. The slacks were comfortable and three simple buttons around the waist allowed me to amend their fitting. A pair of brown sandals sat precisely under the table. I placed them on and they covered my toes with a zigzagging weave of leather straps. I hoped I wouldn't have to run quite so fast or far today.

I walked through the hall and out into the garden, where the elements I sensed when tiptoeing out from the bathroom were to be found. The faces of the people turned towards me just like the night before. I grasped at the material around my neck and expected billows of steam, such was the now-repeated social awkwardness that spanned my being once more.

"Tristan", Theoris cried with joy. She ran to me and hugged me around the waist. Amsu approached more hesitantly. I rubbed his mass of tatty hair like you would a dog. Sufficient enticement, it proved, as he followed his sister in, hugging me around the waist with more than a little more thud than Theoris.

"Tristan, I see you found the clothes I prepared". The Doctor motioned his hand towards the table. "They are to your liking?"

"Thank you, Doctor. Very comfortable, they fit just fine".

"Good, Tristan, good. Now come, sit and eat breakfast with us".

I looked about the table and saw the Doctor's wife, Medea, sat beside him with a hand placed on his. The Doctor's brother sat grinning and holding a glass of something chilled. And, of course, another figure sat with his back to me, 'twas none other than the old man. I wondered what sort of reception I'd receive this morning. Theoris and Amsu drew me by force to the table and I let myself follow like Gulliver among the tiny people. Theoris and Amsu quickly took their places either side of me, giggling and nattering as always.

The old man grunted and looked up from his food, holding a piece of bread and cheese. He made a sound I can only describe as '*Hmmpf*'.

"I see you are still alive, boy", he crowed.

"It appears so. Takes a lot more than a curse to finish me off... doesn't it, children?"

Amsu laughed out loud and nodded. Theoris smiled and nodded, too. The old man rolled his eyes. "The boy thinks he's funny. Keep smiling, boy".

"I shall, good sir. Now, what are we having?" I asked, mustering all my happy thoughts. Theoris was already distributing food onto my plate and Amsu was chuckling away with crumbs festooned about his curled lips. Medea stood and approached. She picked up a canteen and poured me a glass of water, accompanied by a warm smile.

"Did you sleep well, Tristan?" she asked.

"I did".

"You look much better. Eat plenty now, won't you?"

"Thank you". I picked up some bread, and ate a piece of cheese. Theoris watched me. She was reading me. I winked at her, but she didn't smile. Amsu was studying a bug that was moving slowly across the table, staring much the same way at the creature as Theoris was observing me. I gazed up into the sky and saw a flock of birds cross the sun in majestic flight. One of them broke formation and circled above us, calling out with an echoic screech.

"Doctor".

"Yes, Tristan?"

"What am I to do when I meet Mr. Blackband?

The Doctor looked at his father and then his wife. "You must not do anything except, listen, allow him to reveal his intentions. You must allow him to reveal what he wants from you", the Doctor said. "It is very important for your own welfare, Tristan, that you go along with his treachery and his wishes. You must

167

discover through listening how you can aid yourself". The Doctor looked at Amsu and then at Theoris and then back to me, "I am in no doubt he will use this affliction to force you to do his bidding. This is only the beginning for you, Tristan. I am afraid you have a long and dangerous path ahead before you can rid yourself of the deathly curse that lives inside of you". The Doctor spared nothing in his words.

"I expected nothing less, Doctor".

"Be careful what to expect, boy. You will do well to lose that tone", the old man said with a grunt. He wasn't finished. "Boy, you are going to fear for your life more than you ever have from this day on. You'd better not apply this whit in the company of Blackband, else he'll crush you like a bug under his shoe". A subtle smile curled around the edge of his lips. I stared at the old man without anything to say; I didn't want to antagonize the old fool any further than my presence obviously did.

"Tristan, after you finish breakfast, there is something I would like to show you", Dr. Rambo said, lighting a cigarette.

"Nobody is going to crush Tristan, I won't let them", Theoris chirped.

The old man grunted.

"Of course not, Theoris. However, Tristan is perfectly capable of looking after himself", the Doctor said to his daughter. He turned towards me. "Probably to a far greater degree than he is yet aware".

We ate and basked in the sun, feeling as though I was having a last meal before execution, well, maybe not quite, but there did hang an eerie finality to the otherwise pleasant atmosphere this garden held on a lovely morning.

"Tristan, follow me. There are a few things you might find useful".

I followed the Doctor into the house and, down the hallway, he opened a door into a room of considerable fragrance. The scents fell all around me as I wandered through the sweet air that filled my lungs. There, over by the wall, was what struck me to be one of those science experiment tables, one worthy of Dr. Frankenstein himself. Beakers and tubes of rubber and glass filled with red, blue and green liquids running through them, some of them bubbling, others sitting turgid and suspect. Two stone cats in opposing corners of the room, tall and stout, they looked on silently. Doctor Rambo approached a mahogany cabinet and turned a key to the lock. He removed a wooden box with golden hinges.

"Come", he said, carrying the box in a careful manner.

I followed him, but not before taking a glance back at the strange-smelling laboratory and the cat guardians that roamed it. Closing the door, still peeking through the gap, until the vision was extinguished. The Doctor led me down the hall, back to the room I had spent the night, and as we entered, two black cats darted between us, continuing along to the bottom of the hall. The first trundled through the doorway and into the street, but the other paused and looked back, watching me for a moment. Doctor Rambo made a tutting sound and opened the door. I motioned to follow but felt compelled not to break the stare of the cat. The creature remained for a few moments before it raised a paw briefly and ghosted out through the doorway.

"Tristan", the Doctor called.

"Did you see that, Doctor. The cat?"

"Tristan, sit down, I have things to show you".

I looked again and saw the tiny dust particles wandering about in the sun, rays flooding in through the open door like angelic javelins, ushered by the laughter of children dancing around the sunlight. My senses were saturated by the almost supernatural themes of this place.

"Tristan, there is something I want you to take with you. Some elemental aids to assist you along the way", the Doctor said, taking great care in his actions as he opened the box.

"What kind of elemental aids, Doctor?"

Inside the box were four small vials. One was blue, another red, a green one and a purple one. They nestled snugly in black velvet compartments.

"Tristan, you may be alone when you leave here, for it is your journey to make. I have great confidence these vials can help you, but only if you use them correctly and at precisely the right time".

I looked at the Doctor and then back to the vials. "What do I do with them, Doctor?" He removed the red one and held it up to the light, causing it to sparkle translucent.

"Listen very carefully, Tristan: The red vial is an elemental potion that combines the fury of man's heart with the fire of the sun. You may administer this vial to any known material, substance or metal and it will dissolve such within approximately fifteen seconds. Oxygen is the trigger, so do not under any circumstances open this vial unless you mean to use it". He looked from the vial to me. "Do you understand me, Tristan? If you get this on your hands, you will lose them".

"But, Doctor, how..."

The Doctor interrupted me seamlessly. "Do not ask how I got this wonder inside the vial", he said, pointing at me.

"Ah..." I relented.

He replaced the red vial and removed the blue vial, holding it up just as he had the red one. "The blue vial will kill you", the Doctor said, quite nonchalantly.

"I'm sorry, Doctor?"

The Doctor looked at me again and continued. "Drink the contents of the blue vial and it will kill you. To all the world you will be dead. No breath will leave your body, your blood will no longer flow and your heart shall not beat. You will be cold and still like the desert at night".

"And why, Doctor, would I ever use this vial?"

The Doctor's icy expression turned into a smile. "Because Tristan, if you take the green potion within the hour, you shall be resurrected. Your heart will beat again, your blood will flow and you shall be whole once more", he said, picking out the green vial.

"Doctor, as glad as I am to hear there is a reversal potion... the real question is why would I want to die even for an hour? Even for, as you say, the green vial to bring me back", I chuckled agitatedly. "Doctor, I don't think there will ever be a time in my life when I want to kill myself, temporarily or otherwise. In fact, I know there won't".

"Because the one who instructed the creation of these vials did so with your sole interest at heart".

"Eleanor", I relented in my tone, once more feeling that dreadful flutter in my stomach.

"Tristan, these potions were created to help you. I cannot tell you how they can help you. I cannot tell you how you will choose to use them". The Doctor replaced the green vial back into the pocket, "because in truth, I do not know. But these vials are yours to take and wield as you see fit... I ask only that you carry them in your possession at all times, and if you do not fall upon good reason to use them..." the Doctor shrugged, "so be it".

I looked at the vials and sighed. He was right, of course. What harm could it do to have such things. Maybe I'd show Blackband what it's like to be cursed by slipping a little of the blue potion in his fancy tea. *No, Tristan, you mustn't think such things*, I thought... *But why not?* another voice spoke just as prominently. I shook my head and concentrated on the vials.

"What does the purple one do?"

The Doctor simply smiled. "This one, Tristan, is what I call an implosive super reactor".

"What on earth is an implosive super reactor, Doctor?"

"Trust me, Tristan... let's say you were to come across an immovable object, the contents of this vial shall become the unstoppable force for which you will use to counter it. The effects born of this potion upon its target will be the comprehensive reversal..." the Doctor made a tight fist from his open hand, "the complete implosion of all cellular matter straight to the very core of each and every atom present of its being". He closed the box, stood and approached the decanters on the trolley behind him. The box sat there on the table, like a beautiful orphan.

"Doctor, how am I to carry such a destructive force. It is not my place to cause such chaos. And what if such a thing was to fall into the wrong hands", I raised my hands before me, "what if these are those wrong hands, Doctor?"

"Eleanor decreed that you should have these elements. She may not be with us now, but she entrusted them into your possession, and, more importantly, Tristan, your good conscience and judgment. Of which, I might add, she was unflinchingly certain of".

The Doctor began pouring a drink.

My heart sank and the eternal butterflies flew sharply around my stomach and chest cavity, such was her kind sentiment, a truly bitter pill to swallow in the face of her stark absence. "Tristan, she believed in you so that you may believe in yourself. I can think of none other better suited to decide the beneficiary of such powerful weapons. Besides this, Tristan, you may yet find yourself in a place where you have a great need for them". The Doctor poured a second drink. "Go ahead Tristan, take them". He took his drink back in one go.

I opened the lid and ran my fingers along the glass of each vial. Such chaos and power in such a tiny space. Closing the lid over, I placed the box carefully into my satchel. Who knew what horrors those vials would be called upon?

"Doctor, there is something else. One of the lamps in your bazaar. I don't know if it means anything, but I'm very drawn towards it. I feel as though it spoke to me".

"I recall".

"I'd like to buy it, Doctor".

Doctor Rambo turned around. "Nonsense, you shall take the lamp at no charge", he returned to the chair beside me and sat down. "If a lamp speaks to you, then Tristan, in my experience, it already belongs to you". The Doctor lit a cigarette. "Unfortunately, I have nothing to tell you of the lamp or why it affected you in such a way".

"That's very kind, Doctor".

He frowned before exhaling a cloud of smoke. Of course, I hadn't entirely enclosed to the Doctor my visions or that I'd encountered the dark rider within them. However helpful he had proven, I decided to keep some things close to my chest. The Doctor and I sat for a few silent moments before he spoke. "Are you ready, Tristan?"

"I am, Doctor".

The Doctor gripped my arm and gave it a comforting squeeze. I closed my eyes and opened them again. I was still here. Still alive. Something I felt compelled to tell myself.

I stepped out into the garden and felt the sun beat down upon my face. Children ran and danced around chasing dogs, flying

172

kites, and throwing balls to one another. The wheelchair I arrived by was being pushed recklessly around with a young boy inside clinging to the armrests for dear life. To be a child once more, I thought. I'd have given anything to go back. "Come", the Doctor said blinking into the sun with an outstretched arm. The road ahead beckoned. I joined the Doctor, but looked back more than once to watch the house of wonders disappear along with the children of the old town, and vanish they did through smoke and canopies.

Inside the bazaar, I approached the place of the lamp, fully expecting to be spoken to again, anticipating my return to a dangerous place... not this time, not a whisper. The lamp had seemingly won me over the first time and felt it not necessary to play any further subterfuge. Stranger still, I appeared to be personifying a lamp merely because I was under the illusion the thing spoke to me. But the lamp was bequeathed to me and I would be taking it into my possession. The Doctor kindly opened the glass case with a silver key.

"It's all yours, my friend. May she serve you well".

"Thank you, Doctor".

The lamp wore a small leather strap, fixed to the bottom by a ring and the same could be found at the neck, suggesting to me it had been carried in a bygone time. I looped the strap over my head and across my shoulder so it hung against my waist opposite my satchel. On securing the lamp to my person came a feeling of being ready for what was to come, decorated with this strange arsenal of which may have no use whatsoever.

A drop of blood ran down my lip and an awful pain in my head erupted. If you have ever experienced brain freeze from ice cream, well, let me tell you, it was nothing like that, 'twas infinitely worse. I felt myself stumble backwards but managed to grasp the rail while holding my forehead and bearing a quite astute pain, one that threatened to overwhelm my vision and consciousness.

"Steady, Tristan", the Doctor said.

173

I lowered my arm, feeling the darkness inside retreat to whence it came. "It's gone, Doctor, it's gone. I think I'm going to be okay".

"Here, take this", he passed me a handkerchief, "you're bleeding again... look at me", the Doctor instructed. "Just as I feared. Your eyes have begun the transition". He pulled down the bottoms of my eyelids and squinted, a squint that soon became a grimace. "They will likely return to normal in a moment, but eventually they may not.

"What transition, Doctor?"

The Doctor grasped my shoulder. "Tristan, it is best you don't look at them". He withdrew and went to a drawer in the wall. "You will need to wear these. It is best you keep them on until you reach Blackband". The Doctor placed a pair of dark sunglasses over my eyes.

"Doctor, I want to see my eyes", removing the glasses. I marched across the shop in search of my reflection. "Please, Doctor, a mirror?"

The Doctor made stay for a moment and he looked at me with a sadness in his eyes. "Very well", he motioned forwards, "but do not be afraid of what you see, I warn you now". The Doctor returned to the same drawer and rummaged a little before removing a hand mirror. "Before you look, just remember..." he began.

"Doctor, the mirror, please".

He handed me the mirror and folded his arms. I raised it up to my face and wasted no time in looking. My eyes were absent, replaced by vile pools of oil, swirling and twisting like serpents, and the whites had succumbed to the dark matter moving through them like ghosts behind jaded panes of dirty glass. I could hear whispering coming from my eyes, those eyes of darkness did not belong. I dropped the mirror and scrambled to put the sunglasses back on.

"Doctor, they are not my eyes. Where have *my* eyes gone?" I surged forward in tandem with a pocket of rage that bubbled from within my chest. "This cannot be".

"Do not be afraid, Tristan. You know what does this to you". The Doctor injected a fresh sternness into his tone. "I have told you of the burden you now carry and what you must now do", he picked up the mirror and stepped closer to me. "Don't let these things frighten you. Do not let them crush you, do not let the fear that you hold inside win". Gripping my shoulder, he leaned in to the lenses of my sunglasses. "If you do, then that which haunts you will consume you before dusk. This I can promise you". The Doctor concluded his warning with a gravity that touched my very soul. "You must pull yourself together".

My body loosened ever so slightly with the Doctor's words and an immense tautness left me. I removed the glasses slowly and watched the Doctor step black. Raising the mirror once more, and with a deep breath, I gazed into a demonic set of eyes I would never call my own. The eye of my mind stared into those awful eyes as if facing down an adversary—a physical adversary that meant me harm. The moments passed and I blinked not once as I met this foe with a steely fixation, one I meant to counter my sickening fear with, and so turn inward, turn it against the entity behind those awful peepers.

Slowly, but surely, the blackened swirls faded, beginning to disperse with a purity that shone through. Black turned to grey, and beyond the pollution my pupils began to grow into expanding ripples like those of a serene pond, disturbed by a pebble, resonating outwards, drawing the blue of my true eyes back from the abyss. My heart filled with life and my chest beat like a carnival drum, yet I would not let myself blink or smile until my eyes had fully returned. Not until I could see my own soul again.

The whispering subsided and my eyes twinkled as if in gratitude for their revival. I continued to stare into the mirror even beyond full recognition of myself, and only until the Doctor's hand tightened around my forearm.

"It's over, Tristan, it's over", he said, in little more than a whisper.

I felt the Doctor's hand and recognized his assuring nature as clearly as the words he spoke, and with that my eyes closed over. I opened them, knowing in my heart my own blue eyes would greet me. I'd beaten the entity for now, with the very strength the Doctor and Theoris had spoken of. Something told me, however, this was a preliminary victory to neither be swept away by nor preach of, for there would be more questions asked of my fabled bravery. The blue in my eyes sang to me for those moments and I watched them as my father had looked upon me as a child.

"Thank you, Doctor. I must leave now".

The Doctor swept his hand into mine and we embraced in genuine respect. He began to speak, "Do you need..."

"I know where I am going, Doctor. Please say goodbye to the children for me... I will miss them".

The Doctor merely smiled and gave me a sincere nod. I smiled back and walked towards the door. The bell tinkled with the turn of the knob, just as it had on my first arrival, and the sounds of the crowds rushed in. I'd not made ten paces, and, knowing the Doctor would still be standing at the door, I decided to ask him one more question. "Doctor, whatever happened to your great-grandfather, did he ever..." My words were halted and my tongue frozen. I laid eyes on the Doctor, and standing beside him - the old man.

The Doctor gave me a subtle nod. "Why don't you ask him yourself?"

The old man smiled, and he raised his hand. "Go bravely into the night, boy".

I wasted little time in exonerating the wave of astonishment from my face with a warm smile, a chuckle and a nod. I raised my hand in farewell and we parted ways. Probably forever.

The Light of the Lantana

The sunglasses gave the world around me a rose-tinted view of everything, a literal one, the fiery characters, the smoky holes in the walls and the raucous language that jolted my sides all seemed to bounce and fade from the shade screens. Things looked quieter and warmer, but clearer, if that were possible, and oddly felt as though I was in a bubble, observing the world but not within it somehow. I chose my path with confidence and left the bazaars and stalactites behind for the hot air in the streets of Downtown Cairo. I had an appointment to keep and the clock was ticking. The hands of time would wait for no man, much less a cursed one.

Car horns and the sounds of people shouting flooded my ears again. I stopped, looked around and pulled my glasses down slightly to read the address Dr. Rambo had written down for me. *Zamalek Street.*
Zamalek Street could have been a canal on Mars for all I knew. The time was approximately 12:30 p.m. as I began the long walk, through smoke and cars, people and camels, until Zamalek Street appeared, behind the swaying of a green tree. 13:52 p.m. and I had arrived at Charles Walter Blackband's Bazaar.

The shop windows were blackened, as was the façade of the building, and the only animation, a golden scimitar and lotus flower above the door. A small sign hung behind the glass that read, 'Open'. The gates of Hell didn't have to be actual gates of fire, did they? Placing my hand on the glass, I pushed open the door and entered.

The interior, I noticed now I wasn't floundering blindly, was similar to Dr. Rambo's Bazaar, with trinkets and jars lining the walls and mystical pots and pouches abounding the many crevices. I wandered in further and found what had so obviously been waiting for me all along. Mr. Blackband was sitting behind a large wooden desk, his legs crossed, nursing a cup and saucer.

Flanking him were none other than the very two stooges who had stalked me along the streets of Cairo.

A presence behind me tickled the hairs on my neck. Beginning to turn, I saw a large man emerge from the shadows to stand over the doorway, his frame blotting out my only means of escape.

Blackband placed his cup and saucer down and removed his fedora. "The prodigal son returns. Would you take some tea?"

"No, thank you". I fingered my satchel strap, feeling the outline of the box of vials within. "You see, there's something not quite right with me, strange things going about my head. I'm not myself at all, I'm afraid". *What the hell was I blithering about?* I thought. *Listen to what they have to say, dummy.*

"Why, whatever could be the matter, dear boy?" Blackband asked, giving the slightest of nods to the lanky henchman on his left.

"I was wondering if that was something you could help me with, Mr. Blackband".

"Afraid not", he stood lethargically with the help of his cane. "The heat, maybe?" He began to edge around the desk, "the food, perhaps".

"I see. And there was me thinking you were expecting my return. Well, I'll be on my way if you don't mind", attempting to force his hand.

Blackband spoke out in Arabic quickly. A shuffle emerged from behind me and a huge pair of hands planted themselves upon my shoulders with brutal force. I didn't say a word, didn't even flinch or struggle, as I knew this was the way it must be. The two scallions grinned and stood in preparation to charge me. Blackband gave the foreign order and I was projected towards two adjoining doors. The doors were dragged open by Blackband's men and I was pushed through them hastily. They were immediately drawn to a close behind me, extinguishing any chance of escape. I felt no fear... I would not allow it. Not now. Not yet.

A wide corridor opened up and Blackband spoke again. "Tristan, you are a remarkable young gentleman, this I grant you, but you seem to be arranged in a way unbecoming of a man in your predicament".

"What predicament is that, Mr. Blackband?"

I'd stopped myself from wondering where I was being taken, what danger I may have voluntarily walked into, instead choosing simply to march along to the jig of my fate. One of the boys advanced and opened a door that creaked like an old trap hatch... a cellar door. The musty, damp air escaped into the hallway and ran through me as callously as Blackband now stared.

He stepped forward and pointed. "Send him down".

"Mr. Blackband, what do you want from me?" I asked, being led through the doorway.

"In good time. All in good time, dear boy". We locked eyes, and, with a hobble, he closed the space between us. "Though I must return the sentiment and ask..." he drew closer still, and his eyes narrowed. "Who have you been talking to, boy?"

I said nothing, but stared him down with a quite brazen defiance, one he would surely have cared little for.

The old man began sweating profusely and a bead ran down the side of his face, it's tickle appearing to cause him some agitation as he mumbled something incoherent and backed away. "Throw him down", he said coldly, as wheezing breaths made his eyes dart like pinballs about my face.

I braced myself. Inside, screams of protestation sang through my bones, but I knew it would do no good. I stared at Blackband, feeling a pang of fear inside—acidic, treacherous and dreadful collapse onto my lungs. And yet I remained silent. A rough hand grasped my neck and squeezed tightly, causing my eyes to screw up. When they opened again, I watched the rotten steps propel towards me like a kaleidoscope of swirling grey. A chilling blunt smash drilled into my head with thunderous resonation and the cold, savage drag of my face hitting the steps over and over tore a nauseous horror into my loins.

The lights went out like the flicker of a match in a hurricane.

The shoreline in the distance crashed against the grey sand with ghostly, echoic waves. The clouds above, ever darkening, seemed to close around me like impending devils. Raindrops fell so lightly, so crisp were they you could barely see them, but all was drenched and the relentless trickles had saturated my being, running down my face like slithering serpents.

On this beach stood dozens of people looking out to sea. They did not stand together, but alone and still. Some of them submerged from the waist down, yet they did not move, instead remaining motionless and without struggle. Void of preservation, they continued to be swallowed up by the crashing water. There was something so familiar about this place. I had the strangest feeling I'd been here before... but when? I wiped my eyes and looked out into the distance and wondered why the people did not move in the face of the tide, why they stood so still and lifeless and...

The dark rider's steed stood at the edge of the waves, as still as the silent people, a raw steam cloud billowing from the great horse's muzzle, rising up beyond the horseman like a ghoul who had ridden from Hell to meet the rain.

I froze and could only watch the huge figure loom on the edge of the shore line, as waves crashed and advanced around the titanic hooves of the great beast. The rider's eyes, I swore, glowed from within his black visor, crimson beams of despair glowing like lightning bolts doused with the blood of mother nature. Without warning, he sparked into life and sheared across the thick reigns of his mount, causing its front legs to climb into the air above and cry out a deafening screech.

My limbs trembled... but not my feet. I stooped down and clawed at the sand that clung to my ankles like cement paste. My feet had sunken beneath the sand, bound and rooted solid.

The dark rider began galloping along the shoreline towards one of the figures, unsheathing a huge broadsword from his saddle. He thrust the blade skywards, his robes fluttering madly in the wind. The great horse snorted with rage and violent energy as its pace increased. *Why don't they move? Why don't they see him?*

"Hey, get out of the way", I waved my arms frantically as the rider continued to pick up speed, beginning to zero in on a lone figure. The demon swung his blade, circular, over and over in great revolutions that sliced through the rushing winds. "He's coming. Turn around, look behind you", I cried, waving my arms wildly. "Run", I screamed, louder still. There was nothing. I looked down and strained to free my feet, clawing at the sand over and over like a rabid hound digging a hole. The rider's arm swung upon the figure from high above. My arms reached out in defiance, though limp and with futile consequence. The great sword severed the head from the poor soul as cleanly as though it had not been there, dropping into the salty up-rush and rolling beneath the white crest of a shore wave. My eyes closed and I groaned.

Who could truly say if my tumult of tears were shed from the ducts in my eyes or from the clouds above? But my fear had burst forth and was running around this beach free and untamed.

I was next.

My ankles gradually began to sink beneath the sand as its consistency loosened, becoming a sloppy quicksand now chewing me up inch by inch, the way a beach succumbs to the tide. The rider clopped boldly along after the sprint and seemed quite aware that I wasn't going anywhere.

He was savouring the hunt, stalking me patiently. Gasps began to escape me in stunted breaths as my knees disappeared beneath the mix. The more I squirmed, the quicker the descension, but there was nothing to grab, hold or pull. Nothing could stop this now. The rider began to gallop towards me at a steady pace, saddlebags jangling and his chain mail ringing out above the wind with each advancing stride. He picked up speed just like before and drew his sword skywards. My death was to be held forthwith, suffocated beneath the quickening sands or beheaded by the devil. Whichever bore most haste. My thoughts clouded with fear, confusion halted the functions of my mind and terror reigned supreme. Watching the rider come towards me with such anger and fury boiled my blood but froze my mind in equal parts. The demon who stalked the annals of my consciousness so meticulously was upon me. In plain sight, the devil swung high into the air and brought down his blade.

"Wake up, wake up", a soft female voice whispered in my ear.

My eyes opened slowly and for a moment I saw nothing. Sticky eyelids fluttering wildly, and with each, things became clearer. Rusted bars, wavering and parallel, and behind them, a face shining through. Snowy and pretty in the dim light, she was with dark locks straddling wildly the sides of her face. Insubordinate blades, cavalier and winding, converged over her eyes. Her mouth slightly ajar and a sharp cluster of shiny hair rested on her bottom lip. The girl's eyes glinted as if to ask a thousand questions, but she did not frown.

I hadn't moved more than an inch when my head burst in excruciating pain, forcing me to stop. The voice whispered again. "Try not to move". She placed her hand gently upon my face, "that fall could have killed you".

I did as she asked and lay there, looking up at her face. The bars between us steadied, and the rusty iron sharpened into focus. The girl was kneeling down against the bars with a hand reaching through to me, stroking my hair. Her hands were bloodied with smears and coagulated droplets, glinting upon her palms and finger tips. Surely my own sanguine fluid had flowed once more, as I could taste iron in my mouth and my body was limp and useless. My jaw and cheek throbbed wildly and my nose felt numb, for there, swimming in my saliva were tiny stones that must have been chips from my teeth. I allowed my eyes to scout a little without moving. My prison appeared to be a cage or cell of some kind, with scatterings of hay on the floor. A dim light crept down from a cloudy bulb hanging from the ceiling. The girl, I presumed, was in a cage, too, although a grasp of my surroundings couldn't yet be trusted.

"That fall would have killed most people", she said, tilting her head. "Who are you?"

"Who am I?" I sighed. "That's a very good question".

"What's your name?"

I wiggled my toes and felt relief I could do such a menial thing. I moved my legs, only slightly and felt my body awaken. A little strength flooded back into my veins, but the discomfort was stark and revealing. The girl continued to observe me without speaking. I reached for one of the bars and grasped it tightly, dragging myself up and forcing my legs against the cold stone. I leaned my back against the bars along the wall behind me and groaned out loud. My face felt like a balloon and there loomed shadows of bumps and blood spots in my periphery.

"Be careful", the girl reached through the bars as if preparing to catch me. I attempted to touch my face. "I wouldn't..."

My fingers lay themselves upon my face and were met with a very disturbing sensation. Flakes of dried blood fluttered down from my forehead and the cold air jabbed intensely at an open wound I dared not disturb. "Tristan", offering a trembling hand towards the girl.

She reached through the bars again with a smile, this time, "Elysia". She held my hand and her touch halted my trembling. For a moment at least.

"Pleased to meet you, Elysia".

"You are too cold, Tristan". She squeezed my hand and clasped her other one over mine so it was sandwiched between hers. "It is not good for you". She began rubbing them together.

I watched her face as she did this. The fate of my belongings sprang to my mind like an excited sprite. "My vials, my lamp", I began with a spring that quickly morphed into a sting, causing me to freeze with a hiss for my ailing wilt. "My things, I need them to survive. I must have my things". I looked down and found my satchel wrapped across my chest. My belongings remained inside as I'd left them, but they must surely have taken a battering in the fall. I didn't want to check on the vials in case they had broken.

"They dragged you with the lamp strap by the neck, but it snapped", the girl said.

"My neck?" I stammered, grasping my throat and feeling my mouth widen into a grimace, "snapped?"

"Not your neck, silly, the lamp strap", she chuckled. "They left it over in the corner".

Silly? I thought, *silly, indeed, you bloody idiot. If your neck had snapped, you'd be dead... or maybe not dead but walking dead, possessed and deformed but still walking,* a voice said. *Cripes, stop thinking this instant, Tristan,* another voice interrupted.

Sure enough, the lamp stood on a wooden table with the strap hanging loose over the edge. I touched upon my neck and found the skin to be rough and irritable but couldn't remember anything beyond being shown the cellar steps.

"I screamed at them to stop, that they would kill you. But they did nothing but laugh". She gripped the cage bars tightly. "They wouldn't laugh at me if I wasn't in this cage".

Who was this feisty, mysterious girl? Her hair wound about the metal bars and she drew her face between them.

"Really?" I said with a strained smile.

"Really", she replied. "But I am, aren't I?" The girl slumped back against the wall and crossed her legs. "Are you okay?"

"I'm okay... are you okay?"

"I'm okay".

"I can't feel my face or my legs, and I think I've lost half the blood in my bones. Aside from that, I'm just dandy".

She said nothing, but she did smile. The girl wore only what appeared to be a night gown, gleaming white, frilly-ended sleeves hung over her knuckles and her feet were bare and blackened on the souls.

"You must be cold. Where are your shoes?" I asked, gesturing towards her feet. "Would you like to wear my sandals? Probably not very warm, but they are quite new. I was only given them today".

She looked at my feet and drew her legs back so her knees touched her chest. "I don't wear shoes", she said matter-of-factly. "I wear boots when I'm aboard my ship, never shoes".

"Well, if you wear boots, where are they?"

She gave me a scornful look and drew herself towards the bars once more. "Do you always ask strangers silly questions? I think it's quite obvious that given what I am wearing, I wasn't planning to be on land, or in this rancid cage". She looked at the cellar stairs and then back at me with a more agreeable expression. "I was kidnapped from my quarters".

"Sorry, I was just curious. I'll be sure not to ask anything more… stranger".

Elysia knelt in the hay facing me and rested her weight on her left palm. "Oh, you are a big baby, aren't you?" she chuckled.

184

"You have more questions. I can see it on your face, that grumpy-sour face", tossing a piece of hay through the bars.

I attempted to remain sullen-faced for two reasons—foremostly, because I was that way inclined when snapped at, and secondly, with these injuries, laughing and smiling hurt like Hades. "You'll forgive me if I don't join you in laughter, my face is rather battered and the cause of great discomfort", I sniped, grossly overdoing the tenderness.

"Oh lord, help him, blimey", she cried in laughter. Watching her sent a smile rushing to my face in direct contempt of my efforts, stretching my wounds to cracking point. I yelped as they creased, further fueling her amusement.

"Do you know why you are here, Tristan?"

"You wouldn't believe me if I told you".

"Don't be so sure of that, Tristan", she replied, as if implying a great deal more.

I didn't doubt the implication. If she, too, was languishing in this basement, then she probably knew something of the world I'd been dragged into.

"Well, to cut a long story short, I'm cursed, cursed rotten".

"Cursed?" she edged closer.

"I was *bestowed* with a curse the moment I got here and now I live in its shadow", breaking into halfhearted laughter. The very words still sounded ridiculous out loud.

"What kind of curse?" she asked, sweeping the hair from her face.

"The kind that makes you see things, hear things, things that aren't real but feel very real". I looked up to meet her eyes, gauging her thoughts. They only begged me to continue. That scared me, in truth, as my mind was conjuring thoughts I'd been trying to suppress. "The kind that makes you bleed until you have no more blood to give... the kind of curse that's going to break my soul into tiny little pieces and leave them to rot in the underworld..." I could feel my bruises, cuts and overall ashen expression swelling and stinging further with each word. I looked up with a smile, "Do you know the one?" I asked, exhaling with muted laughter.

"I have heard of many curses, even yours". Her tone was unceremoniously low. "Sounds to me a lot like Cowards Debt". She looked at the floor and then back at me. "It can do frightening things to a person before long".

I have…" pondering for a moment on what other terrible things it might do to me. "I have already experienced some pretty awful things... you say you have heard of this Coward's Debt? What else do you know of it?" I asked edging closer. "Can it be cured?"

"I have never heard of a cure for Coward's Debt. It will kill you… eventually".

I lunged forward, grasping the bars, and my hands clenched around her own. She didn't flinch. "That cannot be. Doctor Ra…" I stopped myself before finishing his name.

"Doctor, what doctor?" Our faces were close and I could feel her exhalations never once heightening in the face of my close proximity.

Ironically, the thought of dying from a curse called Coward's Debt terrified me, though it angered me equally. My body was tensed, and the pain frozen out.

Without removing her stare from mine, she spoke. "Tristan, your hands are too tight. You're hurting me".

"I won't die". The feeling inside of my consciousness being hijacked rose like a shadow at dusk, but I fought it back somehow. I looked at my hands upon her own, immediately releasing them.

"I hope not, Tristan", she said softly. Elysia backed away a little and an alarming look converged over her pretty features. "Your eyes, Tristan. Your eyes are…"

I slapped my hand across my eyes and slid away to the other side of the cage like a snake, snatching away at my satchel, unable to release the locking mechanism for the tremble of my fingers, gasping with frustration at my failing plight... I couldn't let her see those eyes.

"My sunglasses, I need my sunglasses", muttering intensely. I had become a jabbering wreck and couldn't open my satchel. My fingers would not work, but instead threw crooked shapes and trembled so.

"Tristan", Elysia called.

I wouldn't let her see those eyes. The fury that was growing inside me, I wouldn't let it have the satisfaction.

"Tristan", she called a little louder.

Put the glasses on, Tristan, you fool, just put on the glasses. Why can't you open the satchel, you damn fool?

"Tristan", she cried out, louder still. Much louder.

I froze at the ferocity of her cry and clutched my satchel tightly, still covering my eyes with one crooked hand.

"Come here to me, I will help you. I won't look".

I felt her delicate tones wash over me and I turned slowly. Parts of her visible through the slits of my fingers, beckoning me with her arms through the bars, and behind her searching hands, her hair clung wildly down her face like winding columns of black fire.

I approached her on my knees, edging slowly but still maintaining my mask until I felt her hands touch my face. I tried to close my eyes, but the thing inside wouldn't allow me to. The affliction desired my sight. It wanted to see what I was seeing.

"Tristan". She played her fingers upon my temple.

"Yes". I replied meekly.

"Look at me..." she whispered, and I felt her breath flow through the gaps in my fingers. I felt weak.

"I can't".

"Yes, you can, Tristan. You can look at me".

I dropped my face and my hands fell to my knees. She held my head in her palms. I was shaking now and it felt as though this parasite was trying to tear me open from deep within.

"Tristan, I want you to look at me. I want you to look into my eyes right now". Her voice cracked slightly. "Tristan, please".

I was fighting a raging battle behind the very lenses of my eyes and it was a battle with everything to lose, 'twas a battle for my soul. I looked up slowly and met her gaze. Her palms closed over my cheeks and she stared deeply into my cursed, black pools. Elysia's face matched that of a ray of heavenly light, piercing through the clouds like a great spear against my darkened landscape. Combatant in nature was her stare, steely, pure and imperforate in its engagement with my darkness. She stared at

187

me longingly for moments, not relative to the real time outside of our cages... then, just like that, she spoke:

"Your eyes have brown in them". The intensity of her stare receded and she looked upon me instead of into me. A slight curl at the edge of her lips only suggested a smile. Elysia meticulously observed the rest of my face for a few moments, but soon returned her eyes to mine and dropped her hands away. "It has gone away for now", she said, drawing away and sitting with her legs pulled up to her chest again.

I didn't know what to say nor I suspected how I would say it, if indeed I knew. But what I did know was that I stared at her face for a little while, completely unaware, or at least un-regarding of our quite dire surroundings, for their dilapidated stench was sweetened if only for a brief time.

"Thank you", was all I could say. She had helped me, I didn't know how, but it was probably to greater degrees more than I'd ever know. She wiped away a tear from one of her eyes, though I chose not to question it. I sat down and mirrored Elysia, drawing my knees up to my chest.

I opened my satchel, removed the sunglasses and placed them on my face. "So there's a bit of brown in my eyes?"

"A little, but not a lot. Mostly they are blue".

And just like that, a creaking sound and the turn of a key broke our dark little world up into pieces of uncertainty. A warm light danced down the dusty steps, like children escaping class at the sound of the lunchtime bell. The end of a cane stamped down upon the top step and two expensive-looking leather shoes shuffled alongside it. Blackband and his merry men no doubt.

The old man descended the stairs slowly, with a distinct number of other, nimbler feet negotiating his cordial lead. I looked at Elysia. She looked at me, but not for long.

Elysia darted forth and clung to the bars, pressing her face against them, she didn't look even a little scared. I dropped my head and once again took comfort in the shady world behind the sunglasses.

Twas to be a time for listening. Doctor Rambo had told me so. Listen to Blackband he told me. The great oaf who threw me down the stairs arrived behind the two louts that chased me through the streets of Cairo, and before them stood Charles Walter Blackband, leaning on his cane like some horrifically reanimated Fred Astaire. He spied my lamp, removed a handkerchief from his top pocket and picked the thing up as though it were a dead rodent. The old man snorted as he inspected my treasure and gave off a sly chuckle before placing it back on the table.

The large buffoon who'd almost killed me spoke. "He carried the lamp around his neck, master, he believes…" but he was cut short by Blackband, who did so by placing a finger in the air. The tall chap drew a chair from the darkness and placed it directly facing our cages. Looking up, he grinned and winked at me.

"Who are you looking at, hmm? You gangling shrimp", Elysia scolded, rattling the bars. "How about you open this cage and I'll carve you up like one".

The chap's uni-brow dropped like an apple from a tree and he appeared hurt, shooting a look towards Blackband in protest. The old man merely raised a gloved hand to shoo it away. Blackband sat down and crossed his legs, removed his hat and gave it to the stocky henchman to his right, and began, finger by finger removing his gloves.

He leaned forward and squinted, and a smile whipped at his sagging jowls. "Is that you in there, Tristan?" Blackband looked at his henchman and then back to me, "it's hard to tell behind your pretty sunglasses and those quite beastly-looking abrasions".

Blackband rested the gloves on his thigh and clasped his hands together. Thin, wart-ridden fingers, resembling twigs from an ancient oak, the backs of his hands bore blotches of grey and black, interlaced with bulbous veins of red and green. His fingernails, a cloudy yellow and chipped and frayed like a hell hound's claws. The gloves in June made sense to me now—he was older than the stone of the Sphinx. Doctor Rambo was right. This was the Blackband from the stories.

"Do you know when I first came here, Tristan?" he gestured with a crooked hand, "to Cairo... to Egypt?" I didn't know if it was a rhetorical question or not. I said nothing. Though I looked on defiantly and waited for something more, if I am honest, I didn't have the slightest inkling on how to conduct the impending conversation. What I could and couldn't say? What I knew and wasn't supposed to know... annoying, to say the very least. Blackband looked at his companions, minions more to the point. Each of them grunted in a variation of octaves. He leaned forward and the chair creaked. "I know where you have been, Tristan. I know who you have been talking to", he said.

I removed the sunglasses and prayed my eyes were as they should be. "I was in the hospital".

Blackband glared for a moment and then sniggered with a wheeze that whistled from his nostrils. "Poppycock, boy", he said. "Never begin a conversation with a lie, you must always garnish deception with a little truth, and I say you just told your first truthless lie".

"I don't follow, Mr. Blackband".

"You will, boy. You will", he replied and leaned back. "Young man, you have not a penchant for lying as I had suspected, but that was truly pathetic", he chuckled briefly and wiped the edges of his mouth where a blob of foamy saliva had formed.

The gangling shrimp, as Elysia had mercilessly labelled him, recovered a wooden pole from the shadows. I was beginning to dislike him particularly.

Blackband continued: "Do you know what kind of trouble you are in, boy? Do you have even the slightest fathoming of what is going to happen to you if you don't listen to me?"

I almost laughed out loud. I'd heard this before. "I have a feeling you're going to tell me".

"Where have you been since yesterday afternoon, Tristan?" He quickly raised his hand and closed his eyes. "Do not say the hospital, I beg of you, because I know you have not", he opened his eyes again. "I warn you only once".

"I don't remember—it may have been the hospital", I stuttered.

Blackband tutted and sighed with a shake of his head, "Tristan, Tristan..." he nodded once to his right. The tall chap drove the pole through the cage and into my chest. My breath left me and the blunt edge deflected off my ribs and gouged into my stomach.

Elysia sprang up in protest and reached through the bars in an attempt to reach me. I grasped the pole clumsily, but he twisted and wrenched it back.

"Stop this. Stop this now", Elysia cried. She tried again to reach out, but I was beyond her grasp. The girl seized the bars to her own cage gate. "Listen to me, you stop this now or so help me, you'll be sorry". The tall man laughed in her face, crashing the pole along the bars and over her fingers. She neither flinched nor blinked. "Damn you", she cursed with fire in her eyes.

The old man shook his head and spoke again. "Tristan, if you had been in the hospital, you'd probably be dead now", he said, waving his finger as though addressing a small child. "Besides, I had my people search the hospital and they did not find you". He paused and sighed. "I know you are lying. You will find soon enough that it does not pay to deceive me... but you cannot know precisely what I'm capable of doing to you, so I will give you another opportunity to come clean".

"I can't remember where I've been, this curse..."

"Oh, come now, Tristan", he elongated my name in a revelatory nature and a grin cropped from his ancient lips. "Don't fence with me for you will lose. I have asked you as politely as one shall and you have chosen, much to my dismay, to mislead me". His smile turned into a dark grimace, sending shadows running over his face like a pack of wolves, and his yellow, archaic teeth appeared to sharpen. "You have one final chance to acquit this foolhardy charade and disclose your whereabouts yesterday between..." he looked at his watch and then back at me, "4:30 in the evening and the moment you returned".

"Tell them the truth, Tristan", Elysia said, pressing her face through the bars.

I expected the wooden stick any moment now, whether I answered or not, the dorky lad was waving it about like a pole jumper and his eyes were set firmly upon me. I didn't want another of those in the ribs, but I couldn't betray the Doctor and his family.

"Mr. Blackband, I don't believe I owe you any answers until I am released from this cage", I looked to the cage beside me, "Elysia, too". Blackband chuckled. "At least not until we are treated something closer to human. I have been violently ill, that is no lie and I have had problems with my memory of late, nor is this a deception, but..." I paused as Blackband gave a slight gesture with his hand. "I'd like..." I trailed off, watching the lout with the pole. He reached onto a shelf beside him and withdrew from the shadows what I can only describe as a saber, and proceeded to attach it crudely to the end of the pole. My stomach churned up, just as it had so often of late. I fought to subdue the feeling, but a saber?

Elysia reached through and grabbed me by the scruff of the neck. "Tristan, tell them where you have been or he is going to stick that thing in your gut".

"I..." only part of the word escaped me in truth, before the pole emerged through the bars and sped towards me like a cruise missile. I arched my body like a terrified cat might, watching the blade run into the wall behind me with a dull thud. I grabbed the pole and immediately protested. "Are you trying to kill me with that thing?"

"What do you think?" Elysia cried.

The boy wrenched back, but I hung onto the pole and forced it against the bars. He grappled away viciously while I used all my might to keep a tight hold of the dangerous end. Elysia, meanwhile, was shaking the bars and screaming for them to stop, gallantly attempting several times to reach the pole in vain.

Blackband sat watching the struggle. He appeared to be enjoying himself, and his dark features grew as the boy strained some quarrelsome Egyptian words from his mouth in shards of spit, and with them he wrenched the pole back out. I recovered myself quickly and backed into the corner, regrettably like a rodent probably would. The stabbing device came once more like a snake attacking a wounded prey, slicing across my right arm.

"The next one will kill you, boy", Blackband said.

"Tell them", Elysia pleaded.

"I don't remember".

Blackband shot an apparent command in a foreign tongue, and the large man quickly joined his lanky companion in seizing the pole and together they wrestled it from my grasp instantly.

The old man shook his head and spoke. "Your foolishness knows no bounds it seems—you'd sooner die than tell me where you have been?" Blackband looked at Elysia with a neutral softness; he smiled faintly and removed his spectacles. His pupils dilated and turned black. "Kill the girl".

The boy grinned maniacally and released a disturbing chuckle that suggested killing, to him at least, was a pleasurable experience.

"Okay, stop, I'll tell you", I cried, feeling this was no time to call his bluff. I couldn't say if I believed they would kill her, but I couldn't watch them do to Elysia what they were doing to me. Myself and the strange girl in the cage beside me were in a cellar at the mercy of four lunatics brandishing a lethal poking device, the like of which, I would wager you'd find in an eighteenth-century zoo for dangerous primates.

This was getting out of hand now and more blood had been drawn from me over the past twenty-four hours than it had in my first twenty-four years. I would have to tell Blackband where I had been and then maybe he would get on with his wretched ultimatum. I had to remember the curse. I was here for the curse.

"A doctor took me in after your men had chased me through the streets". Elysia listened as our captors did.

Blackband sat back and made a triumphant humming sound. "The doctor's name, boy?"

"Doctor Rambo, his name is Doctor Rambo", I said, dejectedly.

"Doctor Rambo, of course. Doctor Ibrahim Rambo. Alas, I know him well", Blackband smiled. "Now we are making progress. I don't want to hurt you, Tristan, but if you insist on forcing me to".

"There is no need to hurt anyone else", I said. "Give me your word, you won't hurt her".

"I can look after myself, thank you, Tristan", Elysia said. I fully expected such a response.

"We are both caged in a basement. How so?" I looked at Blackband. "Do I have your word?"

193

Blackband motioned to speak, but for another interruption. "I told you Tristan, I was kidnapped while I slept. What would you have me do?" She advanced towards the bars again, "not sleep?

"Of course not. I am just trying to help us both. We are in a bit of a pickle, wouldn't you say?"

"Yes, I would say, but if you had told the truth in the beginning, you wouldn't have gotten hurt".

"Wouldn't have gotten hurt?" I advanced towards her and gripped the bars. "What do you call being thrown down those steps, and then strangled with..." I paused, before my tongue ran away with me. "Anyway, I was protecting my friends. But now I'm trying to protect you, so whether you approve or not, I'd much prefer you kept it to yourself".

"Fine", she replied, and retreated back, folding her arms. Her bottom lip trembled with an anger she was working to quell, though nevertheless apparent beneath a thinly veiled expression.

Blackband burst into laughter, as did his henchmen. "If I may?" he said. "You really have no idea who she is, do you? There is very little I could probably do to harm this particular girl..." he looked between us. "However, you have my word, she won't be touched. You also have my word that if you answer my questions honestly and promptly, you will leave this basement without any further injuries". He scowled suddenly. "But if you do not, Tristan, you will not leave here alive".

"He's walking out of this basement with me on his own two feet", Elysia said with a steely stare.

Blackband returned with a chuckle into a handkerchief, as though suppressing a cough. "Let's hope so".

"You have my word. Ask what you will". I looked at Elysia apologetically, seeking some solace in her eyes... her lip trembled no more and her eyes had cooled.

"Now, tell me, Tristan. What did you learn from our mutual friend?"

"He's no friend of yours, believe me. I know everything: the desert caravan of nineteen-twelve, the quest for the Sun Lotus. Doctor Rambo is my friend and he kept me alive when that thing you injected me with started attacking me". Elysia moved towards the bars again to listen. "He told me you were the only person who could remove this curse if I did as you asked".

"Ah, the curse, the curse, the curse... Cowards Debt", he sighed.

"What have you done to me, Blackband?"

The old man smiled to himself and glanced upwards. "Coward's Debt: the consumption of the soul by execration of the flesh... he who shall walk through the valleys of darkness, never once opening his eyes, never once feeling the warmth of the human spirit, nor his fellow man, for he shall venture forth, bound to regret and anchored solemnly to his fear. He is the one you shall not go thither, for he is the one who greets his fear with an all-too-mighty cheer. Go thither from he instead, this awful creature and look back not once as he wanders into the darkness", Blackband recited like a poem, the curse's cryptic consequence.

"I don't understand", I said pathetically.

"Your soul, my boy, will be consumed in sadness by a spirit empowered by your very own fear. Your body will be decimated piece by piece, until you are no more—every part of you, every atom of character, everything that embodies you as an individual will turn in on itself and die. Finally, your soul will be spat out, regurgitated, into darkness, into the underworld, where it will wander, spewing impurities and hatred and fear among the lost souls of the wicked".

"I'm not wicked, I've never hurt anyone".

"Matters not, boy, your soul will see the depths", Blackband chuckled.

"How can I stop this?"

"Stop it?" He burst into fits of coughing, laced with sniggering. "You cannot stop it... not unless..." he faltered. Blackband gestured with great lethargy to his right, "Anum, prepare us some tea, will you".

The large man nodded and clunked his way up the stone steps, closing the heavy door behind him.

"Unless what?" I asked hesitantly. Elysia only stared at me. I couldn't say what ran through her mind, but she seemed pitying, and a sadness crept from her eyes.

"Do you know how old I am, Tristan?" Blackband asked.

"Not exactly".

"I was born January 24th 1875. Which means this old bag of bones you see before you are one hundred and thirty-two years old. I am dying, albeit very slowly. You see, I held a petal from the Great Sun Lotus, a single petal, in my hand, all those years ago...." holding up his decrepit fingers as though cupping the flower. "I held the promise of eternal life in my hands for those few moments..." he blew on his cupped hand. "Then, it was gone..."

"Where did it go?"

"The mutinous hoards I'd fed. The unwashed peasants I had paid so handsomely returned their gratitude by overrunning the camp. They tried to take it from me but they could not". He rose his gaze and his eye glinted. "Even as the filthy rabble bludgeoned and beat me, my body remained impervious to harm". Blackband wiped his forehead with the handkerchief. "Of course, my personal guard were torn to pieces, savagely beaten and slain before my very eyes, and yet I remained. That single petal protected me from certain death... Tristan, can you imagine what could be accomplished if one were to procure the whole flower?"

"The storm..."

He set his dark eyes upon me, and his lips drew in tightly. "The storm, indeed. You have heard the story... Doctor Rambo no doubt enlightened you during your little visit".

The memory was a painful one, 'twas clear. I thought at that moment, the loss of the lotus petal, the loss of immortality and divine power, was akin to the loss of a great love to any other man. These things mattered to him far more than any person, though. The Sun Lotus and its fabled powers could never fall into the hands of Charles Walter Blackband.

Twould be the end of you and I forever...

"Yes, he told me everything. The Doctor told me how you exchanged the soul of your great love, Delilah. How you sold her soul to a demon to extend your life, like she was currency, like she was coins or jewelry". I sensed a deep-seated anger bubble up within me, stemming, I felt, from the absence of Eleanor. "The people loved Delilah, that is why they revolted", I felt my tone grow with passion. "You punished them by decimating the families of innocent men and women, you condemned those people to death because they cared for the woman you had promised to protect".

Blackband launched himself forward, thrusting the cane into the cage. His face creased demonically and his eyes pierced me like laser beams. "That's enough, you impudent scamp", he roared. "You know nothing of what you speak", he boomed louder, jabbing his cane into my shoulder. I grabbed the cane and wrestled it away. "You would do well not to anger me, boy".

Blackband drew the cane back and slumped into the chair. His zeal subsided and he wheezed heavily, holding his temple in exhaustion. His lanky henchman drew back his saber and cried out. Blackband didn't look, but roared a command to cease the impending assault, "Fallback", waving his handkerchief in the air.

I braced myself for the killer blow. Thankfully, the boy froze and shot me a look that assured me of his disappointment. I had almost dug my own grave. I felt my body being drawn towards Elysia's cage to be near her, another soul. Feelings of mortality rose up inside mine and I thought of death, of not leaving this cage, this basement. Blackband had said earlier about not seeing the sun again. A chill scurried down my chest like a tottering centipede. I had to leave this basement. She and I both.

Elysia placed her hand in mine. I closed my fingers over hers and looked up to see her smiling. Blackband drew his arm in slowly, the handkerchief dangling like a white flag in the stale draft. He raised his head and a sombre but resenting look danced about his features like trolls on the dark, mossy moors.

"You know nothing of love or sacrifice. I loved Delilah with all my heart. Delilah was my wife... my one true love". His hands sat trembling on his lap. "Delilah was sick, she was dying. Struck down by the Typhus".

"She was dying?"

Blackband shook his head slowly, sadness flooded his eyes. "Her mind clouded and her body became racked with this rotten", his hands turned to fists and clenched, "...this rotten affliction that slowly drew her further and further away from me. We had

197

sworn that death would never smile upon our souls, that we would forgo the reaper and seek out immortality". Blackband's hands fell limp again on his lap. "Death had come for my Delilah. I could not accept she was going to die; my very soul would not accept it".

His eyes had filled, shimmering in the cold. But they would not spill over—a coldness, a hardness, perhaps would not allow this final step. "If I could become immortal and everlasting, then I could bring her back and together we could live as we had envisioned... I would..." his anger bubbled up again but quickly dispersed itself to become a mutter... "I could destroy the typhus that ravaged my beautiful wife". He stared with conviction. "Destroy the devil who took my Delilah to the abyss. I would find her again and destroy all that stood before us". Blackband was staring at the stone floor. He paused for a short moment.

Elysia and I both looked at each other and I wondered what to make of this human story. The evil so apparent had been diluted and I felt conflicted over Blackband for the first time.

He spoke again. "I would have watched her smile each day, never changing, for a thousand years".

"What happened to her?" I braved.

Blackband's stare remained rooted, but from this stare a single tear dropped to the stone floor. Tiny was the tear, but it held a hundred years of regret and misery. His heart, I could see, had broken long ago and hatred now lived in that tear, and evil was born from the ones that came before.

The old man spoke as though under a spell. "Delilah", he looked up eerily. "My beloved has spent one hundred years drifting in the void, a century of darkness. So many years in tempestuous agony brought on by the one who should have saved her from the horrors she must have now endured". His words carried a gruesome reality. "Delilah would no longer be the Delilah who left this world all those years ago".

I felt the destitute rawness of what had happened to poor Delilah. Where had she gone? Where was she now? What horrors must she have endured? Drifting in the void... I was racked with visions of a beautiful young woman, ravaged and scorched by typhus, floating through the darkness, wallowing in Hell and calling out for her love. My hand tightened around Elysia's, maybe too tightly, but I could see a haunted face in my mind's eye and it sent me cold and afraid. The Coward's Debt would be coming for me soon. Would my fate mirror Delilah's? I felt it would.

"All of you out. Yalla imshi", Blackband cried, suddenly, waving his hands in a sweeping motion. The henchmen scurried out while the biggest man ushered them. He fired me a final snarl before he himself followed the others up the stone steps. Blackband sat back again and crossed his legs, sniffing and dabbing his eyes with the handkerchief. His face turned cold again, emotionless, and then he smiled.

"Tristan, you are going to find the Sun Lotus and bring it back to me Because if you do not, you will find yourself in a place of unspeakable horror. Your fear will burst from your heart like a dagger, anger will consume you and rage will destroy those around you. The blood in those veins will flow from you in ways you could never imagine", he chuckled. "Your mind will be so lost, you'll be neither human nor beast, you will speak no more and your name you will forget... your very flesh will peel from your bones and turn to dust. Your dismemberment will become such, even the vultures will fly beyond such measly offerings".

I listened in cold terror, because I imagined it so. What happened at Dr. Rambo's house was just the tip of the iceberg and the true nature of this curse was still to show itself. I was a goner—not just a goner, but a goner in the most horrible way. I wanted to leave now and run all the way to the damn flower. I couldn't, of course.

"If you should fail in bringing me the Lotus flower, your soul will be chewed up and submerged beneath the miserable waters of human fear and loathing, for take note, this world holds no terror..."

"Enough. I think we get the idea", Elysia interrupted.

"I want to bring it back, but I don't know where to look?" I felt a crushing pressure on my chest. "Of all the people and all the places on this Earth", I said. "I am just one man. How can I find it? Tell me and I will try?"

"I might know where to start", Elysia said.

I looked at her. "You know how to find the Great Sun Lotus?" Blackband began placing his gloves back over his yellow fingers. "Your task, Tristan, dear boy, is convincing your new friend here to help you", he said, smirking. "What say you, girl? Will you help Tristan on his journey? Will you give him a fighting chance?"

Elysia peered through the bars. "I will help you find what you seek, Tristan".

Blackband frowned and slipped the last of his fingers into his gloves and placed his hat upon his head, tilting it slightly to the left. He chuckled under the shadow of the fedora tip and muttered, "Indeed".

"Well?" I practically choked, turning to Blackband and peering out between the bars.

He looked from me to Elysia and back again. "Tonight you will stay put. Embarkation will take place tomorrow at zero-six-hundred. Should you during the night, suffer from another attack..." he frowned and rolled his eyes. "Well, let your pain be your inspiration". Blackband waved his finger back and forth. "If, of course you fail in recovering the flower, do not bother to return... for I very much doubt you'd last the journey", he said coldly. "I have faith in you Tristan, my boy, great faith". He tipped his fingers at the edge of his hat and struggled upwards on his cane, tapping his way to the steps and ascending them like a harmless old man. But, of course, he was anything but.

"Blackband", Elysia called out, drawing the damp hair from her eyes. He halted on the stairs and turned. "You will pay... with blood".

"That's the spirit", he chuckled. "I suggest however, you vent any blood lust on finding my Lotus flower, for you will need all you have". He left through the cellar door and slammed it shut behind him.

The turn of the mechanism in the latch finalized my second evening under lock and key. I sighed and slumped back against the bars of the cage. Now he was gone, each of my wounds and cuts came into a perfect starkness, and my head throbbed in tandem with my beating heart. I felt disturbed by the thing inside me that even now must be working to tear me apart.

"How do you feel, Tristan?" Elysia asked, peering through the bars.

"Afraid every time I blink, each time my eyes close, I wonder if it is going to be for the last time". Never one to dress up the truth, even to strange girls in cages. "Though I know it won't be... because my limbs haven't fallen off yet. Maybe my eyes should close and stay closed", attempting a dark humor that sank like a lead balloon.

"Tristan", she tutted, "I can cut them off for you if you are in such a hurry to die". Elysia had registered my attempt at humor. "Besides, you have a chance to stop this. Come morning you will be ready to go out and find the Sun Lotus". She tugged at the bottom of my trouser, "isn't that right, Tristan?"

"Will I?" I replied. "Who am I really? Just one man". I dug at my abdomen and cursed, "I am not an adventurer or a soldier, least of all a hero. I'm not tough, not even in the slightest. I am a coward with a curse, that's all". I felt a wave of hopelessness inside. "Coward's Debt, he called it, you heard him. They made a curse just for people like me". Crumbs, I couldn't tell if it was me or the curse talking, 'twas unsettling in a way I'd never felt before.

Elysia's face shone stern and her eyes chastised me. "If that's the way you feel, then why don't you just sit around in your little cage and wait for your arms and legs to fall off? Just sit there and wait to die like a helpless, wounded animal", she spat her words at me with violent hand gestures. "You're right, you are a coward. You sound like one so much I can hardly believe you made it this far. How did you anyway?" She sent her words with venom, "how he thought you could find the Sun Lotus, I don't know". The girl slumped back and drew her knees in again. "I won't help a coward. I can't".

I listened to her words and felt a dark chasm open up inside my mind, one that seemed to swallow my thoughts, and void thought transactions enveloped me in a darkness that superseded any logic.

"Help me", I felt myself whisper. I stared, trance-like, at the hay, feeling a growing wish to die. I wanted to end this awful anticipation, the wait for a horrific demise, explained to me in full technicolor. That was all that lay ahead for me.

Why wait?

I could end this now by taking the blue potion, then no one could tell me how awful my death would be, or where my soul will spend eternity suffering. I could simply drift quietly away... This quest was not mine to make and I didn't ask for any of this. Anger erupted inside my chest for the turn of events that had befallen my journey.

Flashing images of my own face broke through the darkness deep inside my mind, calling out silently. My own image struggled against this vat of black oil, constantly drowning me before I could focus. I looked down and opened my satchel, taking out the box of vials... again, my anguished face rose from the swirling darkness, enveloping my thoughts, swamping my mind... I opened the box with hands that led themselves and my sight became blinkered and fixated to this one vial. The blue vial. The one that would end this mockery and fear.

I took it out and held the glowing tube before my eyes. *'Drink of this and forever hold your silence'*, a voice whispered in my head. *'Do not be afraid, there is a place in heaven that awaits you so'.*

"What is that, Tristan?" Elysia called from the darkness. "Tristan, you answer me right now", her tone rose. "Tristan, your eyes", she gasped, crumbling into alarm, "Tristan, come here to me".

My face screamed silently in my mind and a figure wallowed and fought in a sea of black oil, wildly kicking and screaming but drowning in the sticky black waters of my imagination.

'Drink and take your place at the table of peace, free thyself', a voice whispered slyly into my ears.

"Tristan, your eyes", Elysia cried. "Come to me, Tristan, put that down and come over to me".

I could hear her words, but they meant nothing, as though spoken in another language. My mind was consumed by the thought of opening and drinking the contents of the vial. The figure waded again in the ocean of black, struggling to stay afloat, thrashing in fury and panic. A humming began to resound in my ears that shook my very world as the vial sat trembling precariously in my hand. Beads of sweat began to drip from my face like rain drops upon the hay beneath.

"Tristan, come a little closer to me, just a little closer", Elysia strained, her arms outstretched, face pressed tightly against the bars. Her proximity bore no effect upon me, 'twas inconsequential; my mind was lost. "You don't know what you're doing", she gasped, stretching her fingertips to a point of tremble.

The humming grew louder as I began twisting the silver lid of the vial. The vial stood fast against the shredding of the drone, but the ringing rose to a deafening climax, almost a roar. Elysia's fingertips all but brushed the vial in desperation as she pleaded for me to drop it. Twas my way out, the voice had said, my path to peace. 'Drink it', the voice hissed angrily.

Just as I placed the vial to my lips, an explosion of screaming emerged from the black sea of oil, and my own image fought beyond the tide of cursed sludge, crying out so loudly my eyeballs rolled over and my fingers straightened like sharp knives. "No", my own mind and spirit emerged over the black void, crushing its power. And then a revolting pain struck me in the temple and knocked me sideways.

The vial dropped and Elysia screamed, "Tristan".

Darkness reigned.

My eyes opened and were met by the rusty ceiling of my cage. Orange flakes of corroded metal dotted the ceiling like countries on an atlas. I remembered exactly where I was this time.

"Tristan". I felt a tugging on my leg. "Tristan, wake up", Elysia's voice rang out impatiently. "Tristan, what is wrong with you?"

I rubbed my eyes and sat up slowly. "I... I don't know. I think I tried to kill myself". Those words sounded so awful when spoken out loud. Elysia peered through the bars, clutching them so her knuckles ran parallel with her shiny locks. "It wasn't me, Elysia, you have to believe me. I would never do this. Something was telling me to drink from the vial, something inside".

Elysia looked into my eyes and exhaled with a shiver. "Tristan, if you ever try that again, I swear to you I will kill you myself. Do you hear me?" She shook the rust from the metal, "bars or no bars", beating her chest, "I will kill you, Tristan. This is not over. You have a life, a path to walk before you die". She punched me in the thigh and ground her teeth. Her eyes met mine and her bottom lip quivered with anger. "Why would you not even want to try?" The girl's eyes carried a powerful fire I had never seen before. "You are alive, you just have to keep living". Elysia clenched her fist tightly, "you must hold onto life".

"I'm sorry", I offered in wonder of her heart.

"Don't be sorry, Tristan, be strong. We will be free in the morning and where we are going there will be many things that may cost you your life, but this cage is no place for you to give it away so cheaply. I will show you the way, but you must choose to follow".

"I will follow", feeling a great shame. "I want to live".

The girl gazed searchingly, and, brushing a lock of hair from her eyes, she spoke again. "Lie down now". Her eyes lowered to the hay and I followed them, placing my head on a clump beside the bars separating us. Elysia did the same, and, facing me, lay herself in a fetal position. "Take my hand". I placed my hand in her palm and she closed it over mine. "Rest now", she whispered. I felt peace in that moment and let every muscle and sinew in my body go to lay dormant of worry in this dungeon. A dungeon of new hope.

"Tristan", she whispered.

"Yes".

"Would you like to hear a story?"

"I would".

"Where I come from there is a tale of a great stag, a stag of stature and might and spirit and soul", she squeezed my hand ever so slightly, "but the Stag, for all its bluster and agility, was alone and sad. Loneliness followed the stag like a child it could not leave behind. You see, this stag was born without antlers and so had no hope of ever becoming anything more than an outcast. Without antlers, this great animal would never realize his birth right nor could he ever live as part of his nation or bask in the

204

magnificence of the animal he had become. For a stag without his crown had no call to arms, no identity, no place in the world", she spoke almost as if reminiscing.

Feeling my eyes drooping, I endeavoured to listen beyond my growing wilt.

"Life was a wandering journey for the stag, in a world he felt he did not belong, feeling no kindredness to any living thing. The poor stag roamed the forests and fields until a hind appeared atop a hill... tall and proud, the hind said unto him: 'What do you want, tall hind?' to which the stag replied: 'I am no hind, though I am no stag either'. The hind looked at him: 'No?' the hind asked, 'then what are you?' The stag was ashamed, standing at the bottom of the hill, seemingly unrecognized by one of his own. He kept his head down, closed his eyes and began to back away: 'I am nothing kindly hind but a monster, I shall avert my eyes from your beauty'.

"The stag began to turn, but before he could, the hind said: 'No, you are no monster, follow me and let me show you who you truly are and what you can be'.

My eyes were closing and the story felt more like a dream as I drifted in and out of sleep. Elysia's soft voice continued weaving itself into my slumber.

"The stag looked up and saw that the hind was engulfed in a rainbow of colors that blinded him, and the hind, glowing in all of the colors, said: 'Follow poor and mighty stag and become what you have traveled so far to find'. The stag climbed the hill like a giddy fawn and entered the melody of colours with a leap of great faith. The two animals shot up into the sky in a golden stream of light that lit the heavens for millenia... on a clear night, they say you can still see the two wondrous creatures dancing around each other among the stars, always reliving their first meeting upon the hill... the stag without a crown and the rainbow hind".

I awoke frozen with aches from head to toe, 'twas was no exaggeration to say that for at least a few minutes I could not physically move, such was the state into which my limbs had been beaten. I tried to roll but could not. I attempted to straighten my leg, but it just wouldn't budge. Instead, I looked upon Elysia, who was curled up, still clutching my hand. Her face was peace personified and her slow breathing flowed out onto my face. I lay and watched for more than a few moments and wondered greatly who she was. My head felt like someone had taken a bat to it and my throat was dry, as dry as a desert at noon.

The gate to my cage was open. I hadn't immediately noticed. And so, too, was Elysia's gate, ajar. My joints pained me, but I managed to force out my leg, and for my pains my foot edged over the threshold of freedom and breathed life into the rest of me. I looked back at Elysia, her eyes shone, wide and fiery. White hot stars. She stared back for a moment and then spied the open gates springing up and emerging from the cage like a shiny pearl from a weathered oyster. The girl stretched her limbs out to their tips and shook her wild mane, standing there for the first time before me. Athletic, free moving and tall for a girl. Her eyes stored something I could not explain—no words I could muster, nor inkling, I would figure. She neared and began to stoop like a giant angel, towards my curled, pathetic body. "Are you ready to leave this place?"

"Elysia, I would love nothing more than to leave this place", I said with a heartening chuckle. Then, with great determination, I forced all my limbs out until the pain pelted every joint like hot coals. Elysia entered my cage, hugged underneath my arms and heaved me out with surprising ease. She was strong. Really strong. I dragged my satchel behind me and limped out with Elysia as my crutch. I'd have to snap out of this treacherous condition or my journey would not lead far.

There was a tea set on the table, beside a jug of milk, and there also sat some bread and butter and tomatoes and olives.

"Here, sit". She placed me down and took a seat facing me. I bit into a tomato like I would an apple, but quicker, like a hungry dog, then a piece of bread I scoffed down, spilling crumbs across the table. Elysia followed in a similar fashion, eating a tomato and causing it to burst down her chin. She stuffed some olives in, too, and we both broke into laughter. She wiped her mouth with the sleeve of her gown and we continued like hungry children in a candy store.

"Tea, miss?"

Elysia's mouth was full, but she nodded incessantly and made a 'hmmm' sound, wiping her lips away of sesame seeds. I poured the hot tea into two cups. Elysia placed her hand over her cup and made a tutting sound, and then proceeded to pour the jug of milk on the floor.

"Milk ruins a perfectly good Egyptian tea", placing the empty jug down, and we laughed again as we raised our cups and chinked them together over the dainty feast. Freedom from our cages instilled a spirit so blatantly lacking in captivity.

We ate a little more and then I looked up the passage steps towards the large oak door, where a tiny stream of orange light had invaded the grey dominion of our cavern.

"The door, the door is unlocked", I signalled Elysia. She held a morsel between her finger and thumb, it dropped to the floor and she began chewing very slowly. Elysia darted from the table to the bottom of the steps and began ascending them slowly and stealthily. She turned to me and placed a finger over her lips and then skipped up the last few steps with the agility of a leopard. I waited with bated breath and an overwhelming sense of anticipation. She returned quickly down the steps and held her finger over her mouth again. I obliged her with silence and tried to stand the way she moved, but I broke down and clambered her shoulders and arms.

Elysia whispered into my ear, "Tristan, your lamp". I seized and gouged the lamp beneath my armpit, wrapping the strap around my forearm. We began for the steps, but I was compelled to stop.

"Wait, I need to do something", I whispered.

"What is it?" she whispered back.

I limped over to the corner, feeling around for the wooden stabbing device that lay in the shadows. I found the rotten thing and stepped back a few paces, drawing my arms away from me. Elysia broke into silent animation and began waving for me to stop, but on failing in her attempts, she turned her cheek as I swung, crashing the pole against the corner of the brick wall and severing it in half. I looked at Elysia, who stood and smiled. She nodded. She understood.

"Come, Tristan, we're leaving", she whispered, beckoning me to her shoulder.

I hobbled over and put my arm around her and together we climbed the steps, stopping only at the gap of hot light. She quietly pushed open the door.

Elysia advanced first and popped her head around the corner and back again. We walked out into the hallway where the sliding doors had been drawn apart. Where was Blackband? Where were his henchmen?

I prepared myself to be thrown back down the steps; the next time would certainly kill me. No one mustered as we entered the inner sanctum of the Bazaar and its wonders that sparkled. The counter was unmanned and the shop appeared empty. We both stood, clung to one another, our eyes searching the walls like children. Elysia looked at me and winked. She removed my arm and guided me to the wall.

"Wait for me", she whispered, and then went to the cash register. Elysia opened the drawer and removed the monetary contents in swift grasping hands; she looted it to the last Egyptian pound and returned to shove it all into my satchel.

"Elysia, what are we doing?" came my whisper, but riddled with alarm.

"Do you think you owe him anything? You could be dead now because of that devil".

"I know, but this is wrong. We need to leave here, don't we?" Grabbing her hand as she shoveled more cash in. Elysia looked me in the eye and our clasped hands rose between us, full of notes, our noses almost touching. Her eyes burnt like star fires again.

"Tristan, you tell me this is wrong". Her sweet breath cleansed my wounds and she shook our bound hands, "you tell me this is wrong and you mean it, and I will stop".

I swam in her pupils searchingly and for moments not long enough, before releasing her for fear of losing myself in their infinitum. Her eyes relaxed and she lowered her hand to deposit more money into my satchel without breaking our gaze. I stood mesmerized and convinced. She turned and wandered the shop, sometimes as though walking a tightrope, others, like she was playing hopscotch, a carefree eminence oozing from her every step. She picked up a golden necklace from a cabinet and turned to face me, her smile gleaming against the precious bumblebee coloured citrine stones.

"Do you think this would look nice around my neck?" she asked.

I was lost for words.

She turned and drew her hands over her shoulders, holding the fastener and chain behind her for me to link them. I did so without hesitation. She turned to face me again.

"Yes?"

"Striking", I exhaled.

"Then it is mine", Elysia said with a smile that could light a candle—nay, a room ablaze.

She turned again and picked up a glass ashtray from the table beside a pillar that danced with sparkle and color. I didn't bother to protest as she stood over a cabinet full of jewels, ashtray in hand. She smashed through the casing in a remarkably muffled shattering and scooped the jewelry and broken glass from their displays. Turning to me, she held up the loot in celebratory fashion and smiled from ear to ear.

"Tristan, these belong to us now. These we take and the money in return for kidnapping, trying to kill you and locking us up in those rotten cages". She looked at her clenched fist and lowered it. A small gold ring she plucked from the colorful mix. Elysia inspected it closely.

"This, Blackband... I will kindly spare you as reparation for the food and tea", she said, tossing it over her shoulder. "After all, Tristan, we are not monsters".

"Certainly not, Elysia".

She returned to me and crammed yet more into my satchel and supported half my weight again. "Now we can leave, Tristan".

My leg was in a great deal of pain and my head felt as though it was filled with air. But as though my heart had been so illuminated, I smiled widely as we made for the door. Elysia turned the handle and the world flooded in like ants infesting the quietness—car horns ablaze and shouts and cries and the heat punched my face like the old cellar steps had. We both stumbled out into the direct sunlight, and the rays stung our eyes and we recoiled and covered them like you would imagine vampires might, emerging into a full and coarse sunshine. She wasn't a vampire, at least, for she didn't combust or turn to dust, but instead led the way beneath a shielding hand, towing me along with my odd steps and limps.

We were knocked from pillar to post by passing people who barged and ignored and dissented us for our apparent invalidity. Elysia scowled and shoved them back in her own domineering style. I opened my eyes, but the world was so bright and chaotic, I closed them again. How we must have looked to the people on this hot morning.

"Don't look now, Tristan". Elysia squeezed my torso and began to heave faster.

"Don't look where?" I asked, looking across the street.

"I said don't look now. Don't look", she reiterated. "What I didn't say was look across the street now, Tristan".

"Ah, too late"

Blackband and his merry fellows were stood on the other side. The men to his left prepared to advance towards us, but as they did, Blackband impeded them with his cane. Another tall man began stepping out to Blackband's right side. Astonishingly, Blackband drew a long blade from within his cane and drew across the man. He stopped obediently. I froze and watched as the old man's eyes met mine, a wry smile forced his features and he stepped out among the traffic, leaving behind his doting rabble.

"Don't stop, Tristan. Have you lost your mind?" Elysia shunted me. "We have half his wares in your satchel".

"Wait a moment", I replied, keeping my eyes firmly on Blackband.

The old man walked direct and true into the perilous lanes, stopping the traffic as screeches and wails of emotion broke from his path. Elysia observed the scene, still holding me around my waist. A feeling from her close proximity led me to believe she was preparing to pounce forward.

Blackband reached the curb and sheathed the blade into the cane once more. The old man raised the walking aid above his head and threw it through the air. I caught it in the palm of my hand and hesitated not in wrapping my fingers tightly around the antiquitous shaft.

"Return my cane to me along with the Sun Lotus, and you shall retain your soul".

I nodded and watched as he allowed himself to vanish into the crowd, swallowed up by the growing hordes of feet, hands and bodies. Elysia guided us slowly backwards until he was completely out of sight. We took knocks and shoves for our troubles, but we persisted. We had to be sure.

Elysia looked at me and then rested her head against mine. She laughed and her breath ran down my neck like a stream of fluid anesthetic. "How did you know?"

"I didn't". She frowned expectantly. I smiled. "What now?" I asked, placing the cane against the floor.

"Now we head for my ship", she replied. "She's moored on the Nile two miles west of here. Do you think you can make it?"

"Well, I do have Blackband's cane so the walk shouldn't be a problem". I hobbled away from her. "But do keep up, won't you?" I glanced back in time to see her greet me with a broad smile.

"Then we shall venture for my ship, though I will need to stop at the shoe market. The soles of my feet are burning like the fires of Hades". Elysia grimaced and danced over to me on tip toes. Throwing her arms around my neck, she yelped, "I think I may have to run, Tristan, for I fear they shall melt".

Elysia took her arm away and skipped and danced to the shadow of a tree that wavered a cooling shade along a few yards of ground. "Come, Tristan".

I placed my weight onto the cane and followed too quickly, too giddily, almost falling flat. Elysia chuckled and turned to run to the next stretch of shade with all the animation of a colorful painting, jumping from one step to the next on the balls of her feet. I laughed while I sped along behind on my cane, feeling so damn glad I was out of that putrid basement and so damned wanting to run, too, alongside this strange girl. The hobble would have to do for now.

Elysia danced along the edges of the road and around cars like a nymph in song, before darting into a store overflowing with baskets of shoes and sandals as plentiful as there was sand in the

211

Sahara. Truly, they abounded, every inch of the shop spilling out onto the pavement, almost as though the premises was balking its wares from a full belly within.

Elysia's head popped out across the sun and shade threshold. "Are you with me, Tristan. Where are you?"

I was sweating profusely and dawdling along, and let me tell you, making full use of the cane. My pace had lessened, considerably, but I reached the shop to find Elysia attempting to drag a huge leather boot up her leg. I watched her for a few musing moments and then intervened.

"How about these? I like these", I said, digging out a pair of brown sandals beneath a hill of boots. Elysia stopped what she was doing and looked at them. She discarded the boot and approached me. "You like those?"

"Yes, I do. I think they would look splendid".

Elysia looked at me with a straight stare, then broke into laughter. "You think they'd look splendid, do you?"

I nodded smiling.

"Okay. You can buy them, Tristan, if it pleases", she said, slipping them on while using my shoulder to support herself.

"Though I do recall you saying you only wear boots", I chanced.

"Then Tristan, as we are on land..." she glanced up and swept a lock of hair from her hidden eyes, "I shall make an exception".

I rooted into my satchel and relinquished a fist-full of the stolen notes, passing them to a man digging among some heeled shoes. He took the crumpled currency and muttered something inaudible.

Elysia stepped out. "Come, my ship awaits".

I followed her into the streets with looks and stares aplenty. I was back in the running. Back on my adventure. I was no one's prisoner now. I didn't want to live forever, if I'm honest, but neither did I want to die today.

And together we took the bustling path among the crowds until it felt as though the sun would burn through my garments, into my skin and onto my very bones. The great many cuts and lesions that dressed me so painfully became a constant, a droning, aching reminder of my predicament. Elysia led on, further and further and everything grew hazy and so bright, the world and people seemed to go by in slow motion. My senses and conscious mind held little as I put one foot in front of the other and my eyes drooped and begged to remain. I could not think, but walk I did. We continued on like this until I knew if I didn't say something, I'd surely collapse. So, I spoke.

"Will you tell me about your ship, Elysia?" My voice finally broke with heavy exhalation.

She turned and her damp hair swung by her shoulder. "Put your arm around me, Tristan", she said. "Let me bear your weight".

I did as she asked before I fell to my knees. We struggled on among the undying crowds and beneath an unforgiving sun until we reached a clearing with masses of bulrushes. These incredibly tall and suspiciously located bulrushes probably would have drawn more note from I, had it not been for the fact they were towering over a small, bare-chested man crushing an accordion to song.

"Forgive me, but over there... is that a dwarf playing the accordion?" I tugged on Elysia's shoulder. "I need to stop. Forgive me, but I am seeing things... it's disturbing. I can hear his music".

Elysia chortled and placed two fingers to her lips, releasing a short, shrill whistle. The man looked up and the music ceased.

"Cap'n", he cried. His eyes lit up like silver coins reflecting in the sun and he scarpered across on his stocky legs. "Bloody 'ell, where 'ave you been 'iding this past day an' night". He grasped Elysia's outstretched arm with a huge smile on his scrunched face. "We've the lot of 'em out lookin' fer ya".

"Delron. How is the ship? Is she well and about?" Elysia queried, looking beyond the little man, seemingly in a preoccupation for her vessel.

"Aye, Cap'n, she's safe an' sound beyond 'em rushes. Dare say she's been awaitin' yer return. Besides, she 'ad Delron guardin' her, dint she?" he said proudly.

"That she did, Delron, there's no better keeper".

"Cept yerself, o'course... Cap'n", Delron said blushing.

213

Elysia stood up and put her arm around me again while I watched this strange exchange unfold. I looked at Elysia and then at Delron. "You mean to say he's real?" Wiping the teeming perspiration from my face. Delron switched his attention from Elysia and studied me, one eye wide and beady, the other squinting.

"Who be he then?" Delron asked, never releasing me from his beady, one-eyed stare.

Elysia looked at me and smiled. "This be, Tristan".

"An' what business do we 'av wiv Tristan?" he asked, before his face straightened out and his beady stare relinquished itself. "If yer don't mind me askin', Cap", he almost cowered, and switched a doting look towards Elysia.

"Tristan needs our help". Elysia's face took on a wonderfully frank pose, "are there any objections to this, Delron?"

"Aye, Captain, they be none from Delron", he replied and looked at me again. "Tristan, it be good to meet yerself t'day". The little man offered his hand out. I took his grasp and he shook mine fervently. "I be Delron".

"Oh, Delron is it? I'd never have guessed", I jested, taking a chance on humor, as he'd referred to himself in the third person more than once.

His mouth opened to speak, but he paused and his eyes rolled onto me, "Argh, yer better watch yerself, lad", he chuckled, looking up at me like a tough child. "Tell me Tristan, d'ya like the Accordion, yerself?"

As it happens, Delron: I love the accordion. There was once a time me and my gran would watch accordion bands in the park... a long, long time ago", I said, trailing into memory.

"Oi'll play yer somethin' now and take yer back there, hey?"

I looked at Elysia and she smiled and nodded. I turned back to Delron and watched his gaping anticipation to begin. "Play away".

"Lead on Delron", Elysia. We stepped along together behind Delron in the wake of some fine, tuneful accordion notes that seemed to part the bulrushes with their carnival spirit, and they brushed our faces like crowds of well-wishers bidding farewell as we boarded a famous vessel. A clunking met our feet instead

214

of the dry soil... 'twas wood, a gang plank beckoned before us on a slight tilt, with rails and chains guiding us on both sides. I ghosted through, following Elysia, who took steps she had clearly tread many times before. She glanced over her shoulder and returned my stare while ushering rushes from our faces, gradually revealing the way. The accordion continued blustering away to the merry boarding of this hidden beauty whose name I had not yet learned.

Delron vanished into the green and a mound of emerald stems wavered behind him like a sealed door of nature, an impenetrable wall standing before the deck and the mast. My imagination ran wild. I could hear the accordion—but it was in another place, not faint but lonesome somehow.

Elysia stopped and we released each other. "After you, Tristan", she offered her open palm towards the final frontier, or at least the latest one.

I emerged on the other side, fighting the last of the clinging rushes. To my astonishment, the expanse of a ship's deck spread out before me, wide and long and bearing a glossy shine. Barrels and baskets dotted the far side, stacked heavily around a chest bearing a rugged lock. Three great poles ran parallel to one another in the center of the deck, running high up into the air and swamped and groped by nets, ropes and wires. At the very top of the middle one, there was a large cup-shaped basket containing a man: he was holding a telescope to his eye, at a point of interest ashore. Looking around, I could scarcely believe the intricate enormity and detail of the ship. A hand on my shoulder startled me for a moment. Twas Elysia, she smiled and then she, too, took a look around the ship for herself.

"Ah, there she blows". She breathed in contently. "Can you smell that, Tristan? Everything smells better aboard the Lantana".

I could indeed smell the things she spoke of, but could not describe them so easily, for they were more of an atmosphere, tangible and exotic. She wandered beyond me and placed her arms on her hips and looked high up the masts. Elysia turned, still holding her shapely hips. "What do you think of her, Tristan?"

"She's wonderful, magnificent, truly", I answered, feeling as though I was talking about her. "Thank you for what you're doing.

Whatever your reasons for helping me, I am grateful". Stepping towards her, "If it were not for you, I daren't imagine where I might be now".

"Don't go trusting me too much, Tristan". She dropped her hands and approached me until our faces were joined. "That thing inside you is dangerous, 'tis a danger to me, my ship and my crew... so you just be careful while you are aboard". Our eyes searched one another's within an imposing pause. "Do you understand me, Tristan?"

"Completely", I said, losing myself slightly in an attempt to translate her eyes. "I understand completely. I am a danger to the crew and the ship... and to you", though never really believing that last part.

"Good", she stared deeper still. I could hear the accordion playing something slower, more mellow. "As long as you know this to be true", her breath tumbling the words against my lips. She kissed me on the cheek so quickly, it seemed, I almost missed it. "Now..." she spun around, skipping over to a wooden stairwell that was covered with carvings and artistic golden inlays, "...would you like to know what a yardarm is and why it can sometimes be useful for hanging folk from?" She turned to face and smiled fiendishly from ear to ear.

"Sure", I said.

I lay in a hot, steaming bath within Elysia's decorative quarters, scented with extravagant fumes different to the wood and rigging of the decks outside, though no less otherworldly, it must be said. My bath was a huge, brass-bolted wooden boat that stood in the middle of the room like some giant ornament. Beside it was a fireplace with a mantle that wore gold candle holders with tall ivory candles stemming up to a grand-looking golden-framed mirror. A mahogany clock, with three hands, all standing still, stood beside the candles, and a large four-posted bed with veils and draping canopies commanded the room to my right. The bed frame looked like oak and was crawling with strange carvings and emblems. The quarters were situated at the rear of the ship and the entire back wall was a wooden grill filled with panes of glass, allowing me to see the river and city beyond. The room felt like a time capsule, oozing antiquity everyplace the eye did lay.

I splashed my toes against the wall of the bath and saw water droplets leap out onto the boards beneath. Laying my head back, I closed my eyes and pretended to be back home in my own bath, picturing the same familiar décor and the sound of birds singing outside. Mother and father chattering from the garden below, sipping cold drinks beneath the umbrella. Sometimes you could be anywhere in the world, or indeed, in time, just by closing your eyes... just imagine is all you have to do.

Boom, boom, the explosive noise filled the ship. The water in my bath trembled and splashed and a wisp of white smoke drifted past the great wall of windows. The door to the quarters creaked slightly.

"Tristan, do not be afraid, those are just the dummy cannons summoning back the rest of my crew". I didn't answer immediately, though after a short pause she spoke again. "Tristan, are you with me?"

Squirming and swivelling to view the door. "Oh, I see".

"Are you okay, Tristan?"

"Yes, I am fine, thank you... a little sore perhaps", I said, actually meaning incredibly sore. So sore the hot water at first had tortured me. "Forgive me, but won't somebody notice you firing cannons?"

"Yes, Tristan, my crew, so we can sail away from here. Remember, we need to get you to another place, or have you forgotten so soon?"

"No, I meant the police or the army..." I rolled my eyes at my words, "...or someone?"

"Nobody will come", Elysia's voice answered, startlingly closer. She was in the room somewhere behind me. I scrambled to cover myself and managed to look behind me, with an upsidedown view of her standing halfway between the door and the bathtub.

"Elysia, you do know I have no clothes on".

"Of course I do. You're in a bath, aren't you, silly? Clothes wouldn't be much use in a bath now, would they?" she chuckled. "Do not worry, I have my eyes closed. Look if you don't believe

217

me". I carefully negotiated myself around inside the tub and saw the girl standing there in her night dress and bedraggled hair, eyelids firmly shut. "I must take a look at your wounds before they do fester".

"Okay, what should I do?" Looking about the room for a stitch of clothing besides my own heap of dirty, ragged garments. "Stay right where you are, I'm going to retrieve some things from the cupboard across the way". Elysia placed a hand to her eyes and walked across the room beyond the foot of the bath. She stooped down and opened two cupboard doors outwards and took out some towels and linen, and a tray with some unidentified liquids and assorted oddities. She stood with the tray and remained facing the wall. "Closing my eyes again. I shall turn around now. Are you ready?" she asked, with a fluid trickle of amusement in her voice.

I couldn't help but smile and replied, "Of course".

Elysia turned and the tray shook slightly as she began taking steps towards me—an amusing vision, a peculiar one, but a welcome one most of all. I had only encountered threats, vulgarity and assurances of future peril so far. This was a pleasantry to accompany the bitter pill lodged in my throat, of which I couldn't swallow, no matter how hard I tried. She made me feel like I wasn't alone, and there was no greater feeling after my most recent misfortunes.

"Am I near to you yet, Tristan?", she asked, daintily stepping ahead of herself while trying to feel for the bath. Her toe almost grazed the edge. "I must be, Tristan. I make that nine paces. It cannot be more".

"You are here, Elysia. You've reached the foot of the bath".

She bent her knees and crouched down with the tray, placing it on the floor. She stood again, holding the towel and linen. "Catch, Tristan". Elysia offered out the towel before her. I stood and watched the water spill over the sides and drip from my soaking body, and looking out through the windows, I realised I was naked in front of the great Nile—and, quite possibly, some of the more eagle-eyed patrons of the city. I looked back at Elysia in time to watch her sling the towel towards me. I wrapped it around my waist tightly. "Are you decent?" she asked after a few moments.

"I am".

"Then I shall open my eyes". She did so.

"Now what?"

"Sit down in the water".

I lowered myself back in with a creaking stiffness that defied my age, attempting to stifle any embarrassing gasps but failing in such folly, wheezing my way back down with a shameless gripe. Elysia fetched a chair that stood beside a grand looking-telescope. She placed the chair down and sat beside the edge of the bath and embraced my head in her hands, as if looking for a country on a revolving globe. I let out a gasp and closed my eyes, for my head felt like a spent piñata and stung with incredible might; Elysia sighed and cradled my jawline in her hand while gently inspecting my battered skull.

"You must have a head like a rock". She tightened her grip on my chin slightly. "But even rocks can crack". I sensed her close inspection and felt a breath across my wet hair. "I will have to stitch this one, Tristan".

Stitches. Just what I didn't want her to say—stitches meant a needle and thread into my scalp, beneath my skin. More blood, more pain. I sighed and scooped some water up in my hand and let it run over my face, for there was to be nothing gained by complaining.

"Can you do it when I am asleep?"

She drew her cheek against mine, holding my face close to hers. "Unfortunately not Tristan, though I must clean them first". She placed her hand in the water and let the drips from her fingertips drop onto my face, "okay?"

"Okay".

Elysia applied a towel in dabs to the wound for a while and rubbed gently until my head was dry and the towel was bloodied. I felt my eyes tighten and ease with each touch until she began using the creams and fluids from the tray, they seemed to numb things, sooth the ache that bleated at my temple.

"Keep very still for me now Tristan".

I had almost fallen asleep, such was her tenderness and the proximate concoctions that lay on my wounds. I said nothing as I felt the faintest of pricks to the skin on the back of my head. The piercing sensation bit down hard and I could only picture the half-moon-shaped needle being threaded beneath my skin. My arms rallied with goosebumps and the water felt as though it had suddenly dropped a few degrees with my squeamishness.

"Tell me, Tristan, how did you come to be here?"

"It's a long story..."

"We have a long time".

"In truth, Elysia, my memory is enormously troubling... sometimes I don't know what is real and what is not... I feel ashamed to say such things out loud, but nothing is what it seems—or is everything exactly as it seems but makes no sense to me anymore? I know deep down why I was in Jerusalem, but somewhere along the way, the purpose of my being there escaped me... and it never returned".

"Jerusalem?"

"Yes".

"How did you come to be in Cairo?"

"My plane crashed".

"You must have nine lives, Tristan".

"I think I may be on the last of them".

"And you have no memory of why you were in Jerusalem?"

"No".

"Why do you think that is Tristan?"

"For my life, I do not know... but something remains in the haze. There's this bright light and the smashing of glass and pounding of metal. If I try to remember anything before this... well, I simply cannot".

"But you remember your home. Your memories before you came here remain?"

"Yes, I remember my home and my life before".

Elysia wrapped her arm around my neck and I felt her hair drape onto my shoulders. The softness of her breath became apparent and I felt as though her jawline would rest on my shoulder, but it didn't quite.

I thought back to the time my eyes opened in the chapel to see the winding tips of Eleanor's hair hanging above my face, the sweet smell dwindling from my senses as she retreated away. "I lost my friend..." the words escaped me lethargically and I wanted to tip my head back to meet her face, to touch her.

"Your friend?" she replied, gently massaging my head.

"Eleanor", I said her name out loud. And with this spoken word came a crash upon the wooden floor beside us. I turned sharply and my fingers ran against her wet forearm, "Elysia, are you okay?"

She turned my head away to face forward again. "Yes, Tristan. My hand slipped, that's all". A silence wove between us for moments, though I couldn't say it was a comfortable one. "You lost her?" Elysia asked.

She saved me from the things that come for me in the darkness, but I could not return the favour".

"What happened to her?"

"A creeping laughter followed us, two girls with wandering locks and pale faces, their eyes blackened and cruel. They..." I shook my head. "There was nothing I could do, I didn't know".

"Their names, Tristan, what were their names?" Elysia asked hurriedly. She seemed spooked.

"Their names, I never learned. But I think they were her sisters. Eleanor made me close the door before they entered, and soon after they left us alone... the strangest thing is that we had met before, Eleanor and I, long ago, when we were children. She must have been the reason I was in Jerusalem... don't you think?"

"Your wounds are stitched and clean". She patted me on the head gently, "don't get them wet for a while". Elysia stood with the silver tray and carried it back to the cupboard she had fetched it from. "I have something to protect them", she said, returning with a piece of red material. Elysia wrapped the soft thread around my head and tied it off at the back. "There you are". She retreated to a large oak wardrobe and opened the doors with a creaking that was right at home with this vessel. "Here, try these on". Elysia threw a bundle of garments upon the bed.

Clearly the conversation had spooked her and it appeared she had consumed all she was willing to on the subject. Elysia

221

advanced from the somberness and took me with her, at the whisper of a smile and the flick of her locks.

"Tristan, I am showing my back to you now. You might like to change into your dry clothes". She peeked over her shoulder with that smile, her eyes just visible through a veil of dark tresses. She stole her gaze away in a heartbeat, and, turning back towards the wardrobe, she continued to scout among the clothing that hung throughout. I removed my towel and placed on the black trousers, drawing the waist together by drawstrings. The white tunic wore baggy sleeves with ruffles on the cuffs and a chest with bootlace eyelets running down the front. I dragged the garments on with a groan and the sprawling of arms in quite dramatic waves of frustration.

"For your feet", throwing a pair of distressed boots with turned-down cuffs.

I looked at them and sighed. "Elysia, I'd much rather wear my own shoes".

Elysia stopped digging and turned about. "When you invite me aboard your ship, you may wear your own shoes. But as this is my ship and I am the captain, you shall wear what I tell you to wear".

I yielded and dragged on the boots. Admittedly, they were not all that uncomfortable and I felt, dare I say, more formidable wearing these monstrous things.

"There, how handsome you look", she said, spinning around smiling. "Now, Tristan, I shall need to bathe and ready myself for cast-off. Would you go above deck and look out for my crew? If you wouldn't mind, of course?"

"Aye, Captain".

"Oh, Tristan", she called as I was leaving. "You don't have to address me as captain when we are alone". Her expression told no tales. I waited for a conclusion, to which she spent a moment staring at me. And then she smiled.

"Of course," I nodded.

I climbed a small set of steps onto the deck and felt the warm Egyptian air rekindle in my nostrils. The side of the ship I'd boarded was completely shrouded in high-reaching bulrushes, the like of which I had never seen before, heard of, or imagined.

222

They wavered in the air and tiptoed among the furthest reaches of the masts. The creaking sounds of the wood spooked around me and a light splashing could be heard in the rippling airwaves that jostled through the rolled sails of this great galleon. I walked to the side of the ship and leaned over the edge to see a bullish-looking rowing boat harnessed about halfway down, the ropes locked convincingly to the stocky wooden rail that ran along the edge of the ship. More ropes ran high to the masts with a tautness that made them as true as steel rods. I watched the currents of the Nile carry feluccas and small ships up and down the channels past me and beyond, until they became dots on the horizon.

Something cold tapered itself beneath my jaw, frightening me with its sudden proximity, and a hand grabbed my shoulder with a firm grip. Twas a blade, a sharp blade, held just below my Adam's apple, and it pressed harshly into my skin, causing more than a tingle. I placed my hands in the air slowly, yet the blade remained. I would certainly choke if I tried to speak, so I didn't.

"Who might you be then, boy?" a gruff voice whispered into my ear.

An explosion rang out from on board behind me, fizzing like a rocket.

"Mr. Armstrong", Elysia cried. "Take your hands off Tristan and put that knife down". She took several steps forward and I felt the boards creak and clunk with a swift assurance. "Or the next shot will go through your skull".

The knife and the hand moved away and I turned to find Elysia. But what I saw wasn't the princess from the dungeon. Not even close.

She was different.

Elysia wore leather boots with great brass buckles, and black slender trousers tucked raggedly into furred turn-downs. A long red sash ran down her leg and along her waist, infested with black beads dangling like rosaries, and a white shirt gleamed beneath two brown leather belts that crossed each other like lock and key. She placed her pistol away inside a flowing, regal-looking velvet coat that sported gold buttons glinting in the rays of the sun. Her face bore darker eyes but paler skin, quenched slightly by a shadow hanging over her features, cast by the front end of a black tri-cornered hat. Her hair cascaded out from all sides, adding further veil to her snowy complexion. She took another step forward and her boots clunked down against the deck.

"Mr. Armstrong, move away from Tristan and prepare to weigh anchor", she demanded.

A hulking Mr. Armstrong glanced at me and strode away. "Aye, Captain", he grumbled.

First Mate

Elysia spun to another group of figures dotted about the deck. A tall, slim boy stood with arms behind his back. "Jude, can we account for all able crewman?" Elysia asked him.

Jude turned and ushered two more figures from the gangplank, dragging behind them, besides the bulrushes, a wooden chest. He turned back to Elysia. "All able hands aboard, Captain".

"Splendid, we leave now. Drop sails, have the capstan turning double time, Mr. Armstrong". She shouted at a rabble that stood beside the mast. "Jude, take the boot down to the hold". Elysia approached me. "Are you okay?" she asked discreetly.

I nodded and answered, "Yes".

"Anchor coming home", a voice boomed from the back of the ship. Elysia looked towards the rear and approached the mast. "Anchor", she called out and headed swiftly for the opposite side of the ship. "Raise the gangplank and draw cables and lines, release her". She neared the edge and stroked the bulrushes with her gloved hand, muttering something before letting them slip through her fingers.

"Anchor home. Lines drawn and secured, Cap'n", a voice called out.

Elysia turned again and approached a set of stairs, climbing them rapidly and thudding the fresh wood while bodies aplenty rushed around the deck like buzzards in flight.

"Tristan, will you join me on the quarterdeck?" she called from behind the wheel.

I did as she asked and climbed the steps to meet her on the quarterdeck. She was swinging the wheel away from the edge of the land, and a countless stream of bangles jangled around her wrists, as little charms and chains hung from them and clinked against the brass of the wheel. The sails clapped loudly as they were unleashed and lowered, and figures scurried around the furls and the masts, going about their duty while tugging on ropes and climbing nets.

"Raise fenders, lines are let go and underway", Elysia called out.

The entire crew gave a chorus of, 'Aye'.

Elysia looked across at me. "Into the Nile", she said before looking out to the river again. The ship spirited out from the bulrushes slowly, and with a mighty groaning that sang on the breeze. "Afterguard report", Elysia called above her.

"Aft clear, Cap'n. Sails furled and bustling. Downhauls secure and tight", Mr. Armstrong replied.

"Mainsail", she called out over the helm.

Jude slid down the mast and cupped his hands around his mouth. "Mainsail out and blowing through. Main sheets secure, Cap'n".

"Ship about and into the Nile", Elysia cried, spinning the wheel vigorously with both hands.

"Aye", the crew sang again.

Elysia nodded nonchalantly. I felt like a bit of a spare part standing here, but watching her was mesmeric. Was she really the same girl from the cage? Large bangle earrings wrestled among her majestic locks and woven plats and intricate braids ran throughout them with tiny ribbon tie-offs. How had she transformed so quickly?

We moved into the currents of the Nile and commanded the river beside the feluccas and sailboats, bobbing frantically in the aftermath of our passing like some nautical juggernaut.

"Elysia". I looked at her. She took her eyes from our course and laid them against me. I recognized them as the ones from the cage. "Who are you?"

A smile threatened her lips. "I am Elysia, who are you?"

"You know who I am, there is no mystery there".

"No, Tristan, I know your name. I know where you have come from. But I don't know who you are".

"I think you know what I mean… Captain".

She let that smile creep out for a moment. "I do… First mate".

"First mate?" My eye caught sight of Mr. Armstrong whispering between three men, who all wore ragged clothes and stockings over misshapen, bruising heads. "I wouldn't know the first thing about boats or ships. I don't even know what a first mate does".

Mr. Armstrong glared at me like a bully on the school playground, he most definitely did not favour my presence aboard. A shiver ran down my spine.

"Mr. Armstrong". Elysia turned and ushered the bulky man over. "Gather the crew on the main deck".

"Captain, who is this boy?" Mr. Armstrong asked, accentuating the word '*boy*', with no small venom.

Elysia's face froze and she turned back to Mr. Armstrong. He jostled himself backwards but glared at me still. Elysia leered forward. "Mr. Armstrong, muster the crew..."

"But Captain..." he cut in.

Elysia pulled a pistol from her belt and aimed truly upon his nose-tip. "Don't ever interrupt me when I'm speaking", she cocked the gun, "do you understand?"

"Aye, Cap'n"."

"You'd better. Now muster the crew on deck. That is an order I will not repeat again".

He grimaced and then spied me again with a raised eyebrow and gritted teeth. Nevertheless, he backed down and led six men down the steps to the base of the first mast, turned and called out to the front of the ship. A swarm of bodies sprang and skipped to his position, bringing with them a wave of chatter. Their eyes, one by one, locking to the helm of the ship, locking to Elysia and to me.

The captain advanced to the balcony and planted her hands upon the rail. She turned and tilted her head for me to follow. I stepped beside her, looking upon the crew, feeling as though I was teetering on the edge of a shark tank.

"Maximus Thrax", she called over the rabble.

A gargantuan figure appeared and began walking towards us from behind the crowd. The colossus wore a golden helmet nestled above a blonde, curling beard that covered his face. The crew members he pushed aside seemed to bounce off, as mice might, a gold breast plate running across his massive torso. Black shin plates were strapped around the large columns that carried him and woven sandals sprawled out to cover his wide feet. The deck strained with every stride of this toga wearing giant as he climbed the steps and turned to face the crew at the top. Maximus Thrax, as Elysia had called him, stationed himself like a statue and watched over the men, some of whom seemed to scorn his presence.

"Artemidorus", Elysia called out.

A hatch opened up at the other end of the ship, and a figure emerged, ducking through the doorway to stand upright. He was tall—taller than any man aboard, by a clear two feet, and his golden helmet gleamed in the sun like a mercurial beacon. He approached the helm, but the crew had already created a path for him, hastily clambering over one another. A glistening white toga flowed out beneath the base of his breast plate and fell short of black sandals that weaved and climbed to his knees like slithering snakes. Artemidorus stationed himself upon the steps on the opposite side of the helm, stopping to face the crew just as Maximus Thrax had.

"Men of the Lantana, we have a new crew member. His name is Tristan and he is my friend. You will treat him as yours. All of you will accept him aboard this ship, *all* of you shall do so if you wish to remain part of this voyage". She looked across the medley of faces. "Each one of you has a duty to the Lantana, each a responsibility aboard her. She has carried you this far. Through the tides of Blackrock, the falls of Oceanus and the Nile delta. The perils you have weathered and beaten along the way are testament to yourselves... but you have not seen the last of them".

Elysia's eyes held an another-worldliness glow as she pointed before her. "We must return to Blackrock, the place of the Oracles. I am your captain, your leader, and you will follow me or none of us will find that which we seek".

"Who is Tristan? Why has he come aboard?" the questions escaped the crowd.

Maximus Thrax unfolded his arms and looked across to Elysia. She rose a hand and shook her head gently.

"Tristan seeks something we are all seeking. I have made a promise to help him find that which he seeks. He is of no obstacle or hindrance to each of your own personal interests, nor is he to the voyage". Elysia looked at me and then back over the crew.

"To the contrary, Tristan is a sign you are close to fulfilling your service aboard the Lantana, for his being here draws you all closer to your destiny". The captain leaned over the rail. "Tristan became part of this crew when he stepped aboard... he stays", she said with a finality.

"What is this Tristan lookin' fer?" another voice boomed.

"Tristan seeks illumination, as do we all".

"Tristan's an evil omen, is what he is", Mr. Armstrong said, stepping forward and pointing with a chunky, crooked finger. "We be never makin' Blackrock with 'im aboard. The Sun Lotus cannot be found whiles we carryin' death among us lads", he cried with a true malice lacing his breath.

I felt the heat of his anger, his breath whistled past me in a foul gust, casting a great unease in my chest... and with this feeling, something erupted inside. I began to splutter, violently, and crimson streams trickled from my lips, dousing the boards below. The thing within emerged and took over with a seamlessness unlike before. I was back in the oily pools of despair again, watching myself converge over the rail, spitting putrid threats.

"The Sun Lotus is mine. You will languish in Hades, your eyes burnt out and bleeding from your insides, before you see Blackrock", the alien voice cackled from my lungs. Elysia grappled herself around my shoulders in restraint, as blood ran across her arms from my gaping jaws. My face strained and contused and my eyes burned like bunsen flames.

"Maximus, Artemidorus", Elysia bellowed.

Mr. Armstrong's face fell to horror and he wobbled back. "Oi knew it", he crowed, "lad's possessed".

The crowd collapsed in on itself and a sea of writhing, fearful, cursing bodies ran against each other. Maximus Thrax leapt from the steps and attempted to seize order, while Artemidorus did likewise, swinging a silver shield from behind his shoulder blades. I could see all that was happening, but from behind my bleeding eyes, cell windows to my powerless soul. My bodily functions were not my own and an incredible pain sizzled away in the back of my skull. I could feel my heart beating so fast, faster and faster, it sped to become one continuous, mechanical drone. Elysia struggled to keep me restrained as the monster writhed from within, spewing further awful words:

"You will all burn in the fires of the underworld from whence I came. I'll take you there when I'm finished with Tristan, you'll be cut to pieces while you beg for mercy, but there is no mercy for the children of men. You will all burn". The evil words ran through the crew like molten lava down the slopes of an angry volcano.

A man appeared on the steps with his arms raised above his head. The club wielding figure swung with might and effort. I could only watch from the hellish penitentiary my mind had become. My face would be irreparable from such a strike. I tried to close my eyes, but alas, could not. Something intercepted the weapon with superior speed, snapping it in two. Another flash of steel and the man was sent through the air, over the helm and crashing into the panic below.

Maximus Thrax, 'twas he who'd saved me. There he stood, spear in hand, one that shone like a bolt of lightning and bearing a tip as sharp as any ray of sunlight. Another man shrieked obscenity with great rage and ran up behind us as we spun around. He lunged towards us, holding aloft a cutlass.

Artemidorus sprang through the air and landed beside him. Dropping to one knee, he swung his shield around the nape of his neck and crashed it into the marauder's ribs. The man doubled over with a quite horrendous look of anguish on his face, though he had precious little time to feel anything as Artemidorus grappled his leg and swung him over the rails. The scant, gangly body lashed against the sails high up and crashed to the deck in a helpless heap. Maximus dispatched three more in a blinding show of might and skill, lumbering from one target to the next with great strides. Artemidorus had already stopped two certain death strikes upon us both, but another figure had breached the helm and was darting for the captain and I.

Twas Mr. Armstrong this time. He held a sword in one hand and quickly retrieved a dagger from his waist. The brute lunged headfirst and swung his sword over the top... a searing gasp made everyone stop, look and listen.

Frozen were the crew.

The blow would surely have removed my head, but, instead, the blade had lodged itself beneath Elysia's forearm. Her cries of pain ran across me, into my ears and through my mind, tunneling all the way to my heart. The screams grew greater still and echoed thunderously, and light sprayed from the wound like those first rays in the morning. Blood followed the light, trickling to the boards below our feet. Her face dug into my chest and she bit down hard. I knew I had control of my body again when I felt the sting of her teeth on my skin, yet I embraced her bite without sound, absorbing the pain over her yelping. I wanted to share any pain I could that resonated between us both in this moment, for my heart fell heavy as an anvil for her suffering.

Elysia's arm remained wrapped around my skull with the cutlass buried deep within. Mr. Armstrong was frozen like a statue and a look of fear, of stark realization crept across his face like a sunrise. His sweaty fingers slowly released the sword handle.

"Forgive me, Cap'n, 'twas meant for the boy. Please Cap'n'", he cowered.

Elysia released her bite and her heavy breath scorched my chest. She raised her head. The crew, to a man, had frozen on deck when they witnessed what had taken place. Each stunned into silence. Artemidorus approached with huge strides and seized Mr. Armstrong, with a shoulder grip that invoked a painful, pitiful submission.

"Wait", Elysia said quickly.

Artemidorus shot a glance at the order. His face told me he was preparing to crush the man he had clenched in his large hand. "Yes, my liege".

"Put them in the hanging cages and hoist them up. They are not to be harmed". She spoke forcefully, with the slightest of stutter. Artemidorus nodded without expression, as did Maximus. Elysia turned to me. "Will you accompany me to my quarters?" she asked. I could see an unsettling pain in her eyes and her lips had turned palest blue.

"I'm sorry, Elysia. I…"

"Just", she fell short of breath, "just say you will, Tristan".

"Of course".

She turned to Maximus, who neared us like a hulking rhino. "Set a course for Blackrock. Jude will take the helm, stay beside him".

"It is done", the giant man said.

"Artemidorus, you will guard my quarters". We made for the stairs with a limp and descended them, meeting with a path—an opening between a gulf of eye whites—some tired, others wide, though most shimmering brightly with trepidation. We walked side by side, shoulder to shoulder, arm in arm, among the sea of stares and entered into the quarters where I had bathed and she had mended me. Elysia turned once more and looked upon everyone. "Tristan became part of this crew when he stepped aboard... he stays", she said in parting shot. No man murmured.

The voice of Maximus Thrax began to boom orders behind us as   I   slammed   the   door   shut.

"Tristan, would you be so kind as to remove this blade from my arm?"

I sat her down on the bed and steadied her shoulder. "Hold still, Elysia", wrapping some material around the blade. "Ready?" She nodded, staring over my shoulder, never blinking. I tugged with both hands quickly and the bloodied blade slipped out and sent me crashing into a backwards roll. Her cries bounced around the room and tailed into a heartened sob. I jumped to my feet and knelt at the edge of the bed. "Are you okay? Elysia, are you with me?" She lay on her back, holding her arm in silence. I touched upon her leg. "Are you okay?" I repeated quietly.

"I'm okay", she whispered, and then rose from the bed, pushing past me, stopping at the doors to a wardrobe.

"Elysia, you need a doctor. Can I see?" I motioned towards her. She didn't answer immediately but glanced quickly to the side, seemingly to gauge my proximity. "Elysia". I took another step and she spoke.

"I said I'm okay Tristan. Don't come any closer", she snapped. Her regal coat dropped from around her shoulders and crumpled to the ground with a thud. The sleeve of her shirt was, of course, bloodstained and torn. The shimmering red caught my eye against the white cloth. Blood was becoming all too common a sight for me.

"But you could bleed to death, and your arm, it could be broken…" I said, spurred by the droplets of blood cascading near her feet.

"It's not broken, Tristan. And, trust me, I won't bleed to death". She removed something from a drawer inside the wardrobe. "Of that I'm sure".

"But still, it needs to be looked at. You must be in shock, surely you…" I persevered, advancing forward.

"Tristan, I warned you not to come any closer". Elysia twirled around, holding forth a long blade ending just short of my nose, her wounded arm tucked behind her back. I froze just before it went up my nostril and my eyes focused on the incredibly sharp tip quivering before me.

"But…"

"But nothing", she replied quickly. "You are neither here to look after me nor attend my ills".

"Fine". Turning around and walking towards the windows. "I don't understand you".

"Neither are you here to understand me, Tristan".

"Really?" I fired back, turning again to see her strapping a leather guard across her forearm. "So if I'm not here to look after you nor attend your ills, as you so eloquently put it, and I'm not here to understand you, then maybe you can tell me what I am here for?" I waged boldly, and with an attitude no sea captain would favor.

"Oh Tristan", she sighed.

"You are all seeking the Sun Lotus, just like Blackband. You heard Mr. Armstrong", verging on a creeping anger. "How can you find the Sun Lotus with death", I prodded my own chest, "with death in your ranks". I could taste blood in my mouth again. Damned curse was irritating me.

Elysia pressed the arm guard over the wound, as though it had never happened and removed her tri-cornered hat, seeing to it that long, winding locks fell around her face in curls and ringlets. "Are you forgetting that I saved your life? That you would still be locked up in that cage in Blackband's cellar, or worse", she sniped, hands on hips.

"Oh, I see. So, I did nothing?" I noticed my hands were perched on my hips, too, so I snatched them down to my sides. There was barely a moment of silence as we stared at one another. Then she broke into laughter. My blood simmered with her jovial lead and I cracked under a smile. "What are we laughing for?"

Her smile conceded to a light curl of the lips and her eyes softened. "I suppose you did help get us out of there".

I nodded. "Maybe, but I couldn't have gotten up those steps on my own. I think we both know that". I turned and looked out over the mighty Nile waters. "Elysia, am I in danger aboard the Lantana? Have I made a mistake coming here?" I put my hands behind my back and cracked my knuckles, "am I ever going to see the Sun Lotus? Could I ever find it?" Below me, a lone felucca sailed by, carrying and old man with crossed legs. The wind ran through his grey beard and he was smiling. "I am no match for pirates like Mr. Armstrong or those giants you have protecting you. How do I stand a chance of bringing the Sun Lotus back to Blackband? If you could just tell me the truth, tell me I have a chance". I sighed and watched the felucca go out of sight. "If I can't even believe in myself, why should anybody else?"

I felt a hand run down my neck slowly and come to rest on my shoulder, her breath against my skin lightly danced.

"I promise Tristan, you will hold the Sun Lotus in your hands. You will have the chance to save your soul... believe in yourself and you will find her, just believe. The Lantana will take you where you need to go. You'll see".

I turned to face her.

"You still need rest... your eyes are not your own". She touched on them lightly, "they have darkened. The thing inside grows stronger all the time".

"Can I sleep?"

"Yes, you must".

"But where?"

"You will sleep here, take my bed".

"Never slept on such a grand-looking bed before".

234

"This journey will hold many firsts, Tristan. Sleep now and regain your strength". She walked over to the bed and turned down the clothing. "We have things to do this evening that will require it".

I sat on the edge of the bed and removed my boots, every bruise and ache intensified as I relaxed my body. Groans abounded my frame as I sank my head into the pillow and closed my eyes. Elysia whispered, '*Sleep*', into my ear and kissed me gently on the cheek. Everything went black and into slumber I did fall.

Soul Smuggler's Alley

I opened my eyes and the world was midnight blue. I sat up and rested my back against the headboard. My breath escaped me in momentary billows of vapor. Twas so very cold and the air nibbled my protruding toes, so I drew them in and wrapped the blankets around my shoulders.

There, in the great beyond, fought little dots of firelight and shining stars along the Nile and its banks. The ghostly creaking of the ship resonated in the silence as though it was the only sound that existed in Egypt, gently grinding to and fro like many rough hands wringing out the wood of the stern. Then, a sound I'd heard before pandered to the deathly creaking. The bell, ringing slowly and dopily like a drunkard swaying his lazy tongue.

My eyes widened.

The bell chime and the creaking were resurrected from my dream—had I forgotten the vision I'd had that night at Dr. Rambo's home? This ship had to be the one from my dream, the dream that felt so real. Was this also a dream? A longer one, perhaps? Far more elaborate, yes, but nonetheless a fallacy. I touched the bedclothes and felt around, grasping everything I could for the earthly proof I was really here.

A low gust of female laughter rode in, and a mirth of maidens guffawed over the tolling of the lazy bell, before dying out to leave the creaking alone once more. I looked around this haunted cabin and watched as the atmosphere took on a spectral nuance, while phantom shades travelled before my sleepy eyes. I drew the blankets further in around me so they met my jaw. The tall plant in the corner of the room with the black leaves began to dance, and within the mirror, dark figures began passing each other. Pale faces stopped to look through from the other side, wherever that may be, their dark eyes fixating to me as though I was intruding upon their hauntings.

The chest against the wall began to judder and shake like someone was trying to force the lock. I watched these happenings, quite frozen with fear, until they all at once ceased. The creaking had stopped, so had the bell. Dead silence remained throughout and it felt like nothing existed or ever had. Just a midnight void, expansive and lifeless. The chuckling returned with a childlike levity, but there was no one there. One of the candles on the mantle lit up and then another, either side of the clock that did not work, and as if a trigger, the flames sent the three hands of the broken clock spinning around and around. I sprung up straight like a frightened feline and pulled the covers to my chin hairs.

There was someone here, someone... or something. The laughter turned somewhat more mockingly charged, interceded with vague whispers that made the candle flames flicker wildly. "Who's there? Show yourself", I called out with a shudder.

The laughter spiked at my timid request, and my breath was whisked away by the gusts of wind that now blew through the room. The veils hanging from the bed frame quivered and the trembling of fingers and hands breezed behind them. Imprints of figures fashioned themselves with hollow, gaping faces. One of the faces pushed against the veil from the outside, drawing into me closely, and yet another did likewise on the opposite side of the bed. The ghostly apparitions loomed over me with sunken eye sockets and open mouths, almost touching my temple. Closing my eyes tightly, "you're not really there". I took my hands from beneath the bedclothes and quickly waved away the veils. "Show yourself", I said with a frantically induced muster of courage.

A bawl of laughter cavorted through the candles as they twittered against the mirror. Two distinctly female voices spoke into my ears as though they were right beside me. "Soon Tristan, the fearful, soon", they whispered.

I sprang forward and cried, "Who's there?" The room was empty and the laughter died out. The flames extinguished themselves and the clock stopped. 11:11, the hands read. I wished away the darkness, to no avail...

The redolence of wood smoke lay in the air as the illusory trails danced away from the tips of the candlesticks. Just when I thought my circumstances couldn't get any stranger—my life, any more atypical, bizarre, call-it-what-you-will... it always would. 'Soon', they had said. I could expect a return visit? *Maybe it will be the ghost of Christmas past next time?* I thought cheekily. I grinned to myself and wondered where this Tristan had been hiding. *This is no joke,* a voice hissed inside. Drawing back the bedclothes, I reached down and put my boots on, found my satchel and placed it over my head and across my chest. *Calm down, you old scaredy cat,* another voice said in my head. I smiled again. A smile of madness.

Through the peephole, there wasn't a soul. I fully expected to see someone guarding the door, but there was no one there. I turned the handle and stepped out. The sound of distant chatter reverberated through the decking. The boards let out little squeaks as I slowly tiptoed and climbed the stairs to the bow of the ship. There before me was the dark sky and moon from my dream, the bow from my vision, and the figurehead... the beautiful carved woman reaching out to the heavens. I sat down on the hardwood step and held the cross rope in my hand, looking out to the unending dunes that climbed over one another for mile upon mile. I knew what came next.

"What do you see, Tristan?" the voice behind me said. Twas the voice from my dream. Twas Elysia's voice.

I turned to see her standing at the top of the steps, arms festooned over the rails and her left foot slightly protruding her assured stance. Turning back again, I looked at the moon. "I have seen this night before".

She sat down beside me and traced my gaze with her own.

"Your quarters, I think they are haunted".

"Haunted? Nah". She looked at me. "It's not the quarters that are haunted, Tristan".

"No", I murmured quietly, "that would be me".

She nudged her shoulder against mine. "There is a stretch of Nile just ahead, they say teems with fish that bear the souls of dead priests".

"Dead priests? What sort of dead priests?"

"In the days of the great Pharaohs, this part of the Nile was a lush and green land known as the garden of Osiris. The waters that ran over her banks near this garden had strange properties. people said. Stories told of a tear in the river bed where a mysterious gas would escape into the current, giving the waters a strange glow at night".

"Who were these priests?"

"Evil priests who had broken the laws of the gods and attempted to overthrow the pharaohs... murderers", she looked up to the moon, "liars, wicked men of questionable morality. The people would drag them down to the banks of the Nile and drown them in the river, holding them under until their struggles were no more. But every now and again the people would tell of the waters reaching into the body and removing the spirit, taking away the souls of the most wretched and cruel. When this happened, the legends say, they would live on as fish for all time, waiting to snatch the souls of unsuspecting fishermen, travelers... anyone who would get close enough". She looked me in the eye, "even the crocodiles were not safe, they would say".

"Did this really happen?"

Elysia stood up and looked over the edge of the ship. "At least a thousand high priests were said to have gone this way". Her eyes searched the black ripples. "Would you like to see some of them?"

I stood beside her and looked over the side to see the waters splashing darkly against us. A flash beneath, like distant lightening, then another that lit the entire surface as though a single sheet of purple ice.

A cry shot out from the main deck. "Soul smugglers stretch, ahoy, Captain", the voice boomed.

"What is going on, Elysia?"

Elysia grabbed my arm and I spun around to her. "They want the wicked spirit that resides inside you, this is what *they* do".

"This is what *who* do?" I asked, burning a stare into the waters.

"You know who, Tristan".

"The fish?" growing ever more agitated.

Another flurry of shouting ripped the silent night and tore up the fluttering of the mainsails. "All 'ands on deck. Nets'a'ready you men", the heavy clunking of ropes bashed the deck, "souls are fer the takin' now lads. Whatever yer do, don't let 'em 'ave 'em, or it be the locker for yer".

"What do I do?" I asked, beginning to sense a distinct tremble from my loins, as though my constitution was hardwired to capitulate in the event of even a sniff of danger.

"Follow me, Tristan". I did so down to the main deck.

The place was crawling again, with the shadowy crew, and the rusty grinding of the cages lurching and swinging above our heads tapered on the breeze. I looked up and there was Mr. Armstrong sitting crumpled in a hanging bird cage. The burly man wore a grimace that pierced me like a thousand tacks.

"Cap'n, I beg of yer to lemme down from 'ere. Them there fish'll 'ave me soul right outta me up 'ere", Armstrong pleaded, as a child might.

"Artemidorus, Maximus Thrax, hands to", Elysia bellowed.

"Cap'n, please", the prisoner crowed with curdling gravity.

"Elysia", I said finally. She looked at me over the mayhem that straddled the space between us. "Mr. Armstrong?"

"He tried to kill you".

"I know he did, but…"

"But what?" She moved towards me.

"Elysia…" I turned and looked up to the hanging cage. "Mr. Armstrong, if we let you down, do you promise you won't try to kill me again?"

"Tristan…" his eyes lit up, "boy, oi'll not only promise yer that, but oi'll stand for yer too. Yer'll not get 'nother peep from ol' Armstrong", he said, practically dribbling with desperation. "Don't let the river take me soul".

I looked to Elysia for a response.

"As you wish, but you're making a mistake".

Mr. Armstrong cried out heartily and almost spat his tonsils forth with delight. "Yer'll not be sorry, lad. Yer done a great service to this ol' dog t'day. I owes yer me innards", he crowed, beginning to swing the cage like an ape in the zoo.

"Artemidorus, release Mr. Armstrong", Elysia commanded.

Artemidorus emerged and severed a rope with the swoosh of his sword. The cage crashed to the ground and out-tumbled the jovial Mr. Armstrong.

240

"Quiet, everyone", Elysia cried out. Everybody froze and listened, and the whites of the eyes of the crew gleamed against the darkness and shot beadily about as the baited breath of all billowed into the air. The deck was electrified by the heartbeat of each man.

Maximus Thrax stood hunched, with his great spear, fingers and knuckles cracking around it's shaft as he positioned the tip before him straight and true. Artemidorus, in kind, stationed himself in a combat stance with his majestic shield and sword poised.

Elysia walked slowly to the edge and looked over the waters; the sound of ropes ground and each creak of the Lantana widened further the eyes of the crew. I didn't know what was coming, but something told me it wouldn't be pretty. The waters looked like the sky during a storm, electrical combustions rippling beneath a surface of cloudy violence.

A large fish shot from the water like an arrow and landed on the deck, flipping about in convulsion and causing the men to gasp and distance themselves, as if presented with the Nemean lion. I watched the fish flap about helplessly and looked at Elysia. The captain was watching the water and paid no attention to the floundering fish, who's wriggling slowed to an intermittent jolt until becoming very still. Dead still.

A man stepped forward and seized the fish with both hands. He motioned to throw it overboard. Mr. Armstrong cried out a moment too late, "Don't touch it".

The man froze but soon began to shake uncontrollably, and his eyes started to bleed and his fingers turned horribly crooked. Another of the crew attempted to seize him, but Mr. Armstrong grappled that man away.

"Don't be a fool boy, do yer wants to die 'orribly?" he growled into his ear, before pushing him into a cluster of terrified crewmen. The man who'd picked up the fish turned and, foaming at the mouth and retching, violently, tossed himself overboard with maddened screams; every man scrambled to the side of the ship and watched his body disappear beneath the ship.

"Draw swords men, it be fish for supper if they try anything silly", Elysia cried as a wave of fish careered over us in a scaly black cloud. Those drawn swords waved around in the air like fly-swatters and men fell over one another in furious panic. Elysia appeared beside me and held my face to hers. "Let me see your eyes", she grabbed my jaw and stared into them. "Stay beside me, they are going to try and take that thing out of you", she said. "Remember, it's the curse, they want the curse".

I could hear splashes all around as men threw themselves overboard with crazed howls. Most of the crew had retreated to the quarterdeck to form a quivering, mock phalanx, each cowering with raised swords, watching the fish on the deck, flipping and flapping about. One by one, each fish struggled in its final death throes and became still. Maximus Thrax and Artemidorus were standing guard the stairs to the quarterdeck, and behind them the peeping faces of the crew peered over like frightened school children.

"Is it over?" I whispered.

Silence ruled once more and everyone watched the dead fish with complete stillness. One of the fish began to expand, spreading out across the deck in a fluid, floundering, morphing with groans and slurping sounds that parodied the horrific forms now taking shape before us. Shuddering and blackened, a barely humanoid figure wept and slithered itself into a fetal position, much like a giant slug.

"Elysia", I stammered.

"Stay where you are, Tristan".

I watched with a morbid fascination as the other fish began to do likewise, and before long all of them had morphed into slithering wraiths. Each began to struggle upwards with great difficulty, creeping, cracking, blood curdling moans spewing from the unnatural and crude orificium abounding their quite disgusting bodies.

"Captain", somebody called from the huddles on the quarterdeck. One and all looked on as, one by one, the monsters began to stand, each shrouded in dank, slime-ridden cloaks, their hooded heads bowed and dripping with sludge. A foul stench steamed the air as their drooling quenched any last unsullied parts of the deck.

"Give us your souls", they hissed.

242

"Elysia…"

"You", the creature croaked, raising a wretchedly slimy arm burgeoned by a long finger that served as an elongated stabbing device. Twas pointed directly at me. "It is you", the creature said. "You belong with us... down in the depths".

Elysia stepped forward and approached them without fear. "Do you know what grows inside of him?"

"We do", the figure rasped. "Another soul grows inside him, one stronger than his own. It is this darkness we wish to take".

"Priest, you will leave well alone the soul he was born of, this one you will let be. If you try to take it, I will end your existence in this river and send you to a place far worse than any of you damned creatures can imagine". Elysia thrust her sword tip towards him. "Do you understand my words?"

The figure bowed and hissed. Elysia returned to me.

"Elysia, what are they going to do to me?" I asked her. "Are you sure you can trust them? They are evil, after all... didn't you say they were the most heinous of people?"

"The most wretched, I think I said".

"Heinous, wretched, they are liars and killers, you told me".

"Everything is going to be okay, Tristan".

"Famous last words if ever I heard them".

"We have to try to take this thing out of you while we have a chance", she said, taking my hands in hers. "I won't let them take you Tristan. If they try, I will be right beside you. I promise".

"Captain", a voice called. Mr. Armstrong emerged from the crowd and attempted to take the stairs. Maximus Thrax stood fast, but Elysia waved him aside. Mr. Armstrong stepped onto the deck and joined us. "Captain, I don't trust 'em. Scavengers'll take 'im, curse an' all", he growled.

His protestations on my behalf came as a little more than a surprise.

Elysia looked at the dark, swaying figures and spoke, "We must try, Mr. Armstrong. Ready the men for my signal. Cut them down on my command".

Mr. Armstrong looked at me and raised a bushy eyebrow, "Good luck, lad".

"Thank you, Mr. Armstrong".

He turned to walk away, but Elysia grabbed his arm. "On my command only, is that clear?" She prompted him further by the lower joint of his collar. "Anything more and you die with them". "Aye, Cap'n", he answered cordially and awaited Elysia to release him.

Elysia turned back to the unholy rabble and said, "Okay, take what you have come to take and thereafter leave my ship".

The figures all at once pointed at me with pale fingers, their shrouds dripping murky waters upon the deck, washing along in streams between our feet. They began to converge upon us.

I found myself standing beside Elysia, but encircled by the creatures, the crew hovering just outside this circle, swords drawn and teeth gritted. I had never been so afraid in the company of so many allies. The figure seemed to float towards me with one hand raised and primed for my forehead, and another to my chest. My heart beat quickened with their approach, strumming now like a colonial drum.

Elysia, staring coldly at the priest, raised her pistol and cocked it. The other priests slithered and hissed at the sentiment, like snakes encircling a helpless prey. I didn't know what was going to happen, but if they spirited me away, then at least I knew the one breathing his awful breath into my face would get a face full of gunpowder.

A sly smile almost curled from my lips with the thought. Tristan was still around up there somewhere, after all, rolling my eyes as if trying to catch some spiritual glimpse of the voice in my head. My mind, however, was cut immediately by a quite horrendous pain in my temple. A flame had ignited inside my brain and the chanting of these moronic fish-men pierced my ears like needles. My legs buckled, but my body stayed upright as though suspended in stocks. A roar came from the crew and a commotion threatened to veer into us, but I was drawn to a light high up in the sky that seemed to be beaming directly into my heart.

I was chasing the light through a wood, its brightness growing and growing until the wood had been completely engulfed by the light, swallowed by its brilliance, and yet I continued through this white light. The light soon went out and everything faded to black. I was on my knees in the dark, a pure darkness—all except for two dots that shone in the twilight—like distant nebulae they called for me. A warm voice told me to get up, run to the light and you will be home, home and safe. So I ran, sprinting so fast, every facet of my being pulsated, and yet I gained speed. The dots got bigger and bigger, until they became chasmal, weeping fissures like the mouths of the Earth. I flung myself headfirst through the cavernous holes and into the light that shone as the heavens might.

Pain and horror met my body and mind, an electric shock akin to many flickering bulbs exploding along an avenue of no end. And as everything slowed down, a great pressure squeezed my organs like a vice. I found myself flying, arms outstretched before me and out from the caves of light. Elysia's face appeared on the other side, crippled by a terrified expression, her mouth wide, screaming, but silent was she and her motion was slowed many times over. The chanting fish-men and the grasping palm of their leader with his sharp, stinking nails reached out to me like doom personified.

I was leaving my body through my eyes... I couldn't stop myself. I could see my feet and my legs standing limply as I left, and slowly but surely time began to resume to a normal pace and the sounds of screams and shouting began to grow exponentially. With a crash, I felt the cold wood of the deck smash against my face. My earthly body remained standing upright and that foul creature had me in its grasp, claws burrowing into my chest skin. The ghoul was trying to tear the heart from my very chest.

That curse, I dread so, would have my body all to itself now. What would become of me? I looked at my arms and saw that my skin was grey and wet, oily, scaly like theirs, my clothes stripped and torn, beginning to burn and disintegrate to leave withered rags clinging to my limbs.

Bang... the sound of gunpowder startled me, the thunderous roar of Elysia's pistol as the hammer snapped down. Orange and yellow flashing lit up the panhandle and the pale night. The shot exploded upon the demon's face, blowing his head into a thousand shards of oily scum and fishtails. I could see the crew of the Lantana converge behind my body like a swarm of locusts upon the circle of lecherous creatures. Two of the hoods escaped their fury and dragged my soul with them, across the boards to the edge of the ship. I clawed at the wood, causing it to run up my finger nails and plow deep into my skin, but drag they did with an incredible muster. Over the side, the two hooded devils jumped, taking me with them. I managed to grasp the spindles that ran along the sides of the ship, but my fingers would surely break and tear off after long.

"Elysia", I cried.

"Tristan", she cried back.

Twas too late. I had let go.

An eternity seemed to pass, a timeless void. And then I hit the water. Overwhelming coldness enveloped me and crushed my spirit as I squirmed for the surface, but those creatures would not let me go, dragging me down to my watery fate. A dull crash resonated from the surface and the water turned white and violent, eating the last of the bubbles escaping my lungs. Through the clouds of aquatic fury and out from a puff of angry white bubbles, Elysia's face appeared once more. Her legs kicked back with great force, hair standing wildly like the train of a peacock. She gained on me with the pace of a mermaid.

I tried frantically to kick my legs, but the ghouls kept an ever-tightening grip, their claws digging into my ankles mercilessly. We descended so deep, so quickly, and it was so dark down here. I didn't want to live down here with them... I didn't want to be a fish. Elysia's eyes widened as she saw she was losing me... we were losing each other. She wouldn't give up; I knew she wouldn't. The look on her face had me convinced, and with each kick and reach, she instilling me with hope beyond such despair. My anger fought my terror, a patent duel of which terror normally won out without injury, but just this once, anger rolled my body, somehow dragging my legs, kicking and cursing, into such a rage one of them broke free.

Twas enough to slow us down and Elysia caught my fingertips and entwined them between hers. She tightened and locked them together. The descent halted.

But now, the claws on my ankle squeezed and slashed away at both my legs so furiously I thought I'd lose them. Elysia grappled her arm around mine near the elbow, and, linking them together, she reached down to her ankle. Her hand returned, holding a dagger, one she swiftly jammed between her teeth. She swam down my body, never letting go, and there, astonishingly, I saw she had tied a rope to her ankle. I took hold, almost choking on my own fortune, looking back to see Elysia sever the hand of the ghoul, filling the water with murky scum.

As the fish-man's blood clouded my sight, I glimpsed her cutting the throat of the other as he struggled in a futile attempt to shake this angry mermaid from his back. I pulled on the rope and Elysia appeared through the cloud of blood. Deadly and ruthless, she tore us both away with an arm around my shoulder, kicking like crazy... but my breath was lost and a lungful of water entered my soul. I felt my eyeballs roll towards my temple and my lungs stung and burst. A great pressure forced my eyes to a close.

Thump, thump, thump... Thump! I opened my eyes to see my chest being pounded upon. An up rush of water and bile projected from within and I gasped for breath. The crew cheered and a multitude of heads leered in. Elysia was knelt over me with her eyes closed, her hair dripping across me as she heaved out heavy breaths.

"I'm dead, aren't I?" My words spluttered.

Elysia opened her eyes and fixed them to mine for a moment. I expected her to smile, but she didn't. Instead, she looked behind her, where a group of men shuffled aside. And there I was, my body tied to a barrel. Me. Tristan. I was looking at myself, slumped against a barrel, with ropes bound to my chest.

"We gots a live one 'ere, Cap'n", Mr. Armstrong crowed, dragging a shrouded figure along the deck by a skinny appendage. Its jagged nails, protruding gruesomely from a gown that was torn to ribbons, scraped along the wood of the deck. I stood and pushed my way past the faces of the crew. Elysia followed, wrapping a blanket around me.

"That's me". I turned to Elysia, "my satchel, my clothes, my face. That's me, isn't it?"

"Yes", she nodded, rubbing my back gently.

"Then... who am I?"

"You are still you, Tristan, the physical apparition of your soul, your spirit".

I nodded dopily and looked at my body lying there. "This isn't how it was supposed to go..."

"Cap'n", Mr. Armstrong said again. He was holding the ghoul by the scruff of the neck. Without hesitation, I lunged at the creature with a swift rage that took everyone unawares, kicking and punching the creature repeatedly.

"You took the wrong soul, you took the wrong one", I cried. "That's my body, I was born in that body, it's mine".

Elysia and several crewmen attempted to restrain me, but I fought through their grasp and began attacking the creature again. Mr. Armstrong did nothing to remove the monster from my grasp. Elysia screamed for me to stop, until the crew grappled me away from the furor like a rabid dog.

"Cut his throat, Mr. Armstrong", I cried as they dragged me away from the vile demon. "I got you out of that birdcage, Armstrong. Now you will return the favour". Armstrong nodded and smiled. "You must kill him. You must".

Mr. Armstrong fetched his blade from his waist and brandished it closely to the creature's face.

"Mr. Armstrong", Elysia cried. "Relinquish that weapon. I am your captain and that is a direct order".

The burly pirate looked up from the ghoul and groaned, but not before striking the creature against the chest with the back of his hand, sending him crashing against the oak...

Armstrong had spared the creature.

"You're letting that thing live, Elysia?" I asked her angrily, "after what they have done? They lied to us and took my soul". Elysia stood me square in my face. "I will kill him myself", I vowed—not the breadth of a hair from her very lips and nose tip.

"Tristan". She spoke and the scent from her tongue extinguished the brunt of my rage. "Tristan, calm yourself", seamlessly cooling any further pockets of resistance that may have still lingered in my chest.

I bore no cuts or scars and when I touched myself, there was no feeling. I was a ghost, a ghost of my former self. *The ghost of my former self.* I wallowed over to my body and looked upon my face, my eyes were open and faint trickles of blood ran down my cheeks. I knelt down and ran my hands over my eyes, closing them and wiping away the blood with my thumbs. One thing struck me as strange, however.

"Why have you tied my body down?" I asked, turning to Elysia. Her eyes widened and a look of shock took her face. I looked back at my body and my face rose to meet my own. Those terrible eyes, the one's from the mirror, opened wide into blood-red ovals of swirling hatred.

"Hello Tristan, your skin belongs to me now", the voice said. "Your bones, too", it cackled.

I stumbled backwards and watched myself come to life. The captain placed her hand on my shoulder and squeezed, but I could only manage a word, "Elysia".

"I'm so sorry, Tristan".

I retreated back through the crowd, crashing into Elysia's quarters and slammed the door shut. Sliding down to the floor, I curled my knees to my chest and wrapped the blanket around me so that it covered my face. *You can't live without your body. What would I say to mother and father? They would surely notice my skin is blue, sometimes grey and I see scales beginning to appear...*

...Who said you're even going home, dummy? The voices in my head squabbled.

"Tristan… Tristan", Elysia's voice called through the sliding latch.

I poked my head from under the blanket. "Yes, I'm here".

"Let me in".

I stood and opened the door. She entered, still dripping wet and we stood opposite one another for a moment. Wringing out her hair, she walked directly to the wardrobe and took out a pair of trousers and a shirt, throwing them upon the bed.

"Put those on, maybe that thing out there can tell us how to get you back into you". She turned to me, "understand?"

"Yes, I think so, but that thing outside is evil and wants me at the bottom of the Nile with the rest of them. Besides, the curse will never let me back in. How would I ever get back in?"

"I will find a way, Tristan. We will not stop until we find a way".

"We never should have trusted them. Never".

"You're right, Tristan. I'm sorry... I just thought..." she rolled her eyes to the heavens, and a look of precious sorrow glinted by her eye for no longer than a distant star might in the night sky. My heart sank, knowing she only wanted to help me. Elysia bowed her head and then made for the chamber door.

"Elysia, wait", I called out. "This isn't your fault, you were trying to help me, you've been helping me since the moment we met". I neared her. "If this doesn't work, I want you to know I don't blame you for any of this, not even a little bit". She bowed her head. "Okay?"

She raised her eyes to meet mine. "Okay".

We walked out onto the deck side by side and stood over the figure. The creature was sprawled against a large chest, spreadeagled like a drunken sailor.

"Mr. Armstrong, remove it's hood", Elysia commanded. He did so to reveal a quite disgusting face. The creature's ears resembled gills and had beady shark-like eyeballs either side of a pointed nose surrounded by protruding, circular bones. The skin appeared green to this degree of light and shone translucently by the moonbeams. Elysia knelt down at the foot of the creature and removed a knife from her belt. Green plasma-like gunk still clung to the blade from the earlier dismembering. Twas a potent incentive to cooperate, I thought as she brandished the tip close.

"Listen to me very carefully, wraith. We came here to offer you the evil inside my friend, and we would gladly have given you the wretched spirit that clings to him so". Elysia pointed the tip of the knife towards my possessed body. "Even now it resides inside him, yet his own soul does not because of you and your priests". She brandished the blade very close to its face. "You are going to tell us why you took his soul… and then you're going to show us exactly what we must do to return Tristan to his rightful body". Elysia looked back at me and then glanced around her crew. "If you don't… well, you don't want know what we'll do".

Her words gave me a chill. She commanded a presence among the others that was undeniably sharp, and yet she was but a girl with all the good graces and charms usually expected of one. Elysia held a proverbial elegance, a rawness that transcended anyone I'd ever met. I was growing increasingly certain she was not of this world. But what other worlds could there be?

The creature hissed and belted a shrill cry from an unpleasant hole where we humans have a mouth. Serrated, piranha-like teeth lined the top and bottom of this crevice, and they were tipped by a foul-smelling slime that dripped upon its black shawls like sewage. "He has two souls", the priest hissed. "The soul that stands among you now. The one you call *Tristan* has left his rightful body to come with us". The creature seized forward but quickly slumped back in submission. "The soul that remains is strong, violent and full of rage. It does not leave so easily. We took the only soul we could".

"Two souls", Elysia mused. "Then he is not cursed, but possessed? Who could do this? Who possesses him?"

"One who seeks the Great Sun Lotus", the creature replied.

"Who?" Elysia pressed the knife against his throat and began to gouge.

"It matters not for the boy. He belongs with us now".

Elysia sighed, dragged him up from the boards and turned him around. "Do not let it trouble you, wraith, for there is no place you belong anymore". She leaned into its ear and whispered, "because you're dead". Elysia plunged the knife into the creature's back and tore upwards with ferocity, splicing its body apart as though stripping peel from a banana. She let go, leaving the blade buried up to the hilt. The deafening sounds coming from the creature were akin to a butchered pig's last squeals on this earth, as blood sprayed upon us all like mushy pea juice. "He's all yours, Mr. Armstrong", she said, wiping a glob of green blood from her cheek.

Mr. Armstrong's eyes lit up, much like a dog's at feeding time. "Aye, Cap'n", he said with extra zeal. He then proceeded to smash the creatures face against the side of the ship several times. The burly brute wasn't done, not even close, as he began stamping upon its head over and over again until jet streams of blood sullied our feet and boots. It took several crewmen, their damnedest, to muscle Armstrong away from his brutal onslaught, while another two of them endeavoured to spirit the corpse over the side. The savage splash from the ghoul sent foamy water cascading against the timber cladding of the ship. The vehement Mr. Armstrong grunted and chuckled, dusting off his hands. "Knew we couldn't trust 'em... never trust 'afella with green blood lads".

"What does this mean Elysia? What was that thing talking about, two souls?"

"You are possessed by a spirit, maybe human, or something that was once human. It must be using you to go after the Sun Lotus", Elysia replied.

"Blackband was lying?"

"No, Tristan, 'tis a curse to be possessed. We need to get you back into your body before it's too late". Elysia turned away. "Jude, take the helm and straighten us up. Pull up the mainsail, half-mast, Mr. Armstrong".

I followed closely behind her. "Shouldn't we have tried a little harder to find out who?"

"That thing would not have told us, Tristan". She turned again to face me. "You must repossess your body, take it back".

"How do we do that?"

"We kill you".

"Sorry?"

"I have an idea. Do you still have the potions the doctor gave you?"

"The blue potion, of course".

"If we can stop your heart long enough, you could re-enter— the spirit inside would be powerless to stop you".

252

"But Elysia, how is that even possible? I mean, how on earth can I get this body back into that one?"

"This is not a body, Tristan", she said, touching my forehead. "It's your soul, a spirit, the physical realization of who you are beyond flesh, it's simply an apparition. Just because I can touch you means nothing. The soul does not live by the same laws as your flesh".

I looked up to the sky and saw a sparkling constellation and remembered Dr. Rambo. "How did Eleanor know, she..."

"Cap'n", a cry came from where my body was slumped. Delron was clinging to my arm, attempting to wrestle my satchel away from me. That thing inside my body was trying to toss the bag overboard.

"The potions", Elysia and I cried simultaneously. We both turned and lunged for the bag, just as my possessed body swung them high. I flew through the air and snatched them from the jaws of the river, tumbling across the deck and into a mound of heavy rope.

I looked up and there was Mr. Armstrong offering down an outstretched arm. I reached out and he heaved me up. "Nice catch, lad".

The face of my possessed body contorted and wept blood. "Come any closer and I'll chew off his tongue, bash his head against this barrel until his brains pour out". The thing inside used my own arm to point at me. "Do you understand, boy? You'd better listen to yourself", the spirit chuckled.

Elysia approached my body stealthily, watching the soul pour its evil through my eyes. She seized a length of rope and grappled the rigging into my gaping mouth, and all at once the taste of burnt rope hastened me, hastened too, the surreal scene upon us and upon the dark soul. My body wriggled like a snake to free itself, but she was equal in strength and guile.

"Tie his shoulders tight and steady his legs, Maximus, Mr. Armstrong, hold him down". Elysia tied off the rope. "Delron, fetch me the jasmine vessels", she called out. "Tristan, the blue vial. Give it to me".

I dug into the satchel, took out the wooden box containing the vials and set them on the deck. There was a little of the potion missing from whence it had tumbled the cage floor. "Here", passing the vial to Elysia.

She took it from me, carefully removed the lid and held it up to the moon. The liquid glistened, illuminating her hand and face like some wonder from yonder the abyss. She turned to my restricted body and put her finger to her lips and stooped down to meet an evil glare. My body, the vessel of this wretched soul, began to judder and struggle, but it was no good, 'twas held down tightly. Though, quite disturbingly, my bloodshot eyes appeared to boil over like ponds of acid.

The crew drew closer with lanterns abounding their fingers and gasps riding their tongues. I advanced with them and came face to face with the devil inside and felt a vacillating shudder run through my detached spirit. Elysia put her hand gently on my face and ran her palm down my cheek. "You will sleep now", she whispered. "Mr. Armstrong, remove the rope when I tell you".

"Aye, Captain", he whispered back. Crouching closer. Breath heavy.

A few silent moments went by as I watched the orange glow of the lanterns on my own face.

"Now, Mr. Armstrong".

Mr. Armstrong wrenched the rope free and Elysia immediately thrust her hand into the biting jaws, and as they snatched viciously down, a heavy ripple of consternation ran over the crew. Elysia reviled in pain. Such did not hinder her for a time long enough, as she immediately applied the top of the vial into a small gap between her fingers. The liquid flowed in until empty. She threw down the vial and grasped the bridge of my nose. My possessed, and all-too-mortal frame went into acute convulsion, fighting, one might imagine, from deep within an estuary of seething wickedness.

"Elysia", I gasped, quite literally, alluding to the fear of the irreparable damage my body may sustain while vacant of I, its rightful heir and soul. My existential and panic ridden meandering sent a volt to my mind and a voice told me to be silent with such foolishness.

Elysia wrestled against me and forced my very constitution to accept the potion, cackling and retching like a rabid animal as it ran down my throat until seizure-like jolts were all that fought back. Then, complete limpness. Stillness... dead stillness. She removed her bloodied hand from my mouth, and set my head gently against the chest like a child would her most precious doll.

A peace ran over my face like a cool northern wind and my skin drew pale and snowy. Trickles of crystallized blood ran down my lips, like that of a slumbering vampire. Elysia felt for the pulse in my neck. She neared closer still and placed her cheek beside my lips, her eyes closed, but only for a moment. Elysia turned to me with a graveness. "You're gone".

And with ghostly grimaces the crew watched my possessed body as mournful sighs billowed up through sorrowful stares on the faces of youngsters, the fairer flesh but adorned too, the brutish, sea-beaten features and skulking, pale, pumpkin-headed deck hands. One and all took off their hats, ribbons, stockings and beat them to their chests.

Elysia removed a glove from her pocket and covered her bloody hand. "Now, Tristan, you must return". She looked at my *corpse* and then back at me. "We can bring you back, but you must hurry while there's still time".

"How do I return?"

Delron fought his way through the crowd with short, plodding strides and emerged holding a basket. "Yer things, Cap'n".

Elysia took the basket from him. "Thank you, Delron". She looked at me again and reached out. "Sit down, Tristan", pressing against my shoulder.

I lowered myself and sat on the deck, watching the boots and clogs of the crew surround me like a procession—an unkempt shoe store for pirates. Elysia took a place opposite and crossed her legs. Her gloved hand reached into the basket and took out a bottle of blue liquid and set it down on the deck. Elysia then unfurled a dark material and spread it out across the boards, placing a golden dish upon the material that bore signs of heat, erosion, and ash. She removed three decorated clay jugs and stood them beside one another. A man with a spear attacking a boar-like animal was painted on each at different stages of the attempted slaying, for in the third the man lay dead with the spear pointing to a star in the sky. The Bore victorious.

"Place your lamp in the center and do not touch it again", Elysia said.

"Okay". I stood my lamp before me and looked at the faces of the crew, riveted and ashen. I gulped and took my hands away from the lamp. She took out four bamboo stems, or maybe they were incense sticks, and placed one into each jug, but the fourth she offered to me.

"Hold this and point it directly skyward, halfway between your chest and the lamp and do not move it for any reason".

I nodded.

Elysia reached again into the basket and took out the detached head of a flower—a jasmine flower. From this, she gently plucked three petals and dropped one into each jug. Then she retrieved a small golden box from her person and pinched a handful of black dust from inside. Elysia ground the dust into her hands before throwing it into the air.

"Winds", she whispered as the dust swirled across every man and thing like a small, twisting tornado. The crew muttered and shuffled about as a breeze passed over my face with the dust, eyes flickering as it speckled my cheeks and forehead.

"Clasbeema un senkatuka, virbalis an ullundessa", she chanted, speaking an unknown tongue. A blue flame appeared in the dish. "Lamshi I neulisa setumnocki evictuse", meandered the words as the flame grew taller and glowed red like the sky in autumn. "Delron, bring me a strand of Tristan's hair".

Delron scampered to my slumped frame and plucked more than a few hairs from my scalp. My head jolted forward against my chest and sprang back again with a clunk. "Sorry, Tristan", chuckling as he delivering them to Elysia.

"Didn't feel a thing, Delron".

"Silence", Elysia whispered. She cast the strands before her, turning the flames green for a moment. They soon roared back and danced in crimson like devils at a carnival. My incense stick ignited with a flicker and a spark, and all at once the others combusted at the tips and burned into the air a ghostly white smoke. Elysia plucked the incense stick from the center jug and held it just above the rim. The bottom end of the stem burned and blue smoke was ghosting from the mouth of the vessel. She let go and it remained suspended, alone on the air. I felt my eyes widen as she did the same with the two remaining jugs, slowly and methodically, her eyes alive with flames and wonder. The silence from the crew was deafening and pierced the smoke and the creaking of the ship.

"Tristan, take your hand away". Her words seemed to saunter within the very realms of the smoke streams.

I removed my hand and the stick remained still and independent on the very air I was breathing. The sensation was indescribable. Awe possibly, though disbelief couldn't pertain. Elysia picked up the bottle and sipped the liquid, her lips tinged blue as she sprayed the remnants out through pouted lips across the flames and onto the pyre. A great and mighty reaction soared up into the sky, like lightening and the flames escaped themselves, ensconced in fiery pods reaching up to the heavens and leaving hot trails of fading violet.

The crew roared backwards and cast their attention to the sky, where the fire meandered among the stars. By various degrees they regained their collective composure and redressed their wide eyes upon the source of the wonder. They had seen this before, I wagered silently.

Elysia drew her hand across to her left and doused a stream of the bottles content across me, and did so again from her right side. "Alambu mishma condenseera, visku septumerus alemera", she spoke the words, closing her eyes as she did so. With those last words, the scene came to life as a trail of smoke materialized, running across the tips of the incense sticks like a tangible electrical current, feeding and flowing into the fire and turning the flames emerald green. Elysia held up a hand with all five fingers pointed apart, "kalanteeba threstisum". She moved her hand over the jugs and squeezed her fingers into a fist. "Zeetush cleptimun", she cried out.

A trail of white smoke zipped up to join my hovering incense stick, so they were all connected through the emerald pyre flames. And as a breeze picked up, stronger ones came, whooshing in, beating wildly the sails above.

Chatter mouths became the crew, and they pointed and stared at me in ripening animation. I looked at my hand. Something strange was happening. I held both my hands up before my eyes and I could see Elysia. Not between them, not beyond them, but through them. I could see the faces of the crew within the palms of my hands. I soon realised that my entirety, my whole body, was becoming transparent.

"Elysia". Little more than an utterance emerged from my lips, staring at that which could not be. "Elysia, what is happening to me?" Watching my fingers begin to break up and dissolve like ash, mere particles breaking apart and fluttering away in the breeze like embers from a smoking pipe in the mist. My own face, my sight and awareness all danced along into thousands of sparkling atoms as my mind was carried away, descending into whirling revolutions which cajoled my being into the streams of the lamp. My spirit was disbanding to become a flow of glistening droplets bound for my lamp, whereupon, my consciousness, now a dizziness of sorts, faded to dreamlike spinning. Finally succumbing to the darkness once more.

I opened my eyes slowly, and a light of sorts crept in like an annoying thief stealing away my peaceful abyss. Stolen by a reel of illuminated mugs, some prettier than others. Though I did find myself to be slouched against a barrel, hands bound, and a gritty taste of burnt rope and an equally potent one of blood in my mouth. I didn't fear for either. Those beautiful elements were the most welcoming, unpleasant, bitter-sweet sensations my palate would ever encounter, for one could not taste or feel such in the realms of the dead. I had repossessed my body. I had taken back what was mine.

My eyes jutted themselves a little northward and were met by a calm and twinkling constellation that was very beautiful: the stars danced around each other and sparkled in the face of a huge full moon. I moved my fingers and rid them of their stiffness. I wiggled my toes and blinked several times and felt my own smile broaden my features. I knew that thing was still inside, but it was a fair fight again. As even a playing field as I was going to get. I was back to stay and would not be leaving so hastily again.

"Tristan". Elysia touched my face. "Is it you, Tristan?"

My eyes met hers, "It's me".

She bowed her head, doing her damnedest to conceal a smile. She looked around at the crew. They each bore shadowy grins, and from among them, Delron pottered forth.

"Nice to 'ave yer back, Tristan. We was reckonin' we might 'ave to throw yer over board fer a while", he said with a grin.

"Let's hope not, Delron. I don't think I'd do too well down there", I replied, shuffling upright against the barrel. "I think it's safe to untie me now, don't you?"

"Mr. Armstrong, cut him loose", Elysia commanded. "Delron, take my things back to my quarters".

Mr. Armstrong hacked the restraints free from my wrists and removed the rope from around my neck. Elysia stood and offered me her hand. I took it and sprung up with stiff legs and a head like a spinning top.

"Back to your posts, men. We have a course and I intend to keep it". The crew dispersed to every nook of the ship, some climbed the masts and others disappeared down hatches. "Jude", she called towards the helm.

"Aye, Captain", a voice came back from the quarterdeck.

"Are we clear of the strait?"

"Leaving now, Cap'n. No one follows".

"Keep her steady in the black water, stay tight to the channels, close hatches and portholes. Keep a keen eye on the portside".

"Aye, Aye, Cap'n. Portside watch. Tight and straight", Jude called back.

Elysia looked at me. "Tristan, we are not alone. Somewhere out there, he's watching". She looked out to the dark dunes. "He rides beside us... even now".

I watched the dark embers of night. "He follows me always".

TO BE CONTINUED...

Printed in Great Britain
by Amazon